Between Men

BETWEEN MEN

a novel

Fiona Lewis

THE ATLANTIC MONTHLY PRESS
NEW YORK

Published simultaneously in Canada
Printed in the United States of America

FIRST EDITION

Library of Congress Cataloging-in-Publication Data

Lewis, Fiona.
Between men: a novel / Fiona Lewis.—1st ed.
ISBN 0-87113-586-8
I. Title.
PS3562.E9398B47 1995 813'.54—dc20 94-12907

DESIGN BY LAURA HAMMOND HOUGH

The Atlantic Monthly Press
841 Broadway
New York, NY 10003

10 9 8 7 6 5 4 3 2 1

FOR ART

1

Alice's mind, barely this side of stupefaction, felt ready to explode. In desperation, she rolled down the car window. The noise from the freeway surged up with an ear-splitting roar. The air was dense, sultry; steamy ripples rose from the asphalt, and what little breeze there was smelled of tar and burning rubber. This was nothing new. The blistering summer, now well into August, had caused the whole city to reek. Carbon monoxide, deadly pesticides, God knows what. By noon everything was blazing like an incinerator, and the rush-hour traffic was an all-day affair. Continuous. Now a colossal sea of cars, choked in fumes, crawled down the hill to Burbank. In the next lane, a man in shirtsleeves was bent forward in his tan Sirocco. His limp jacket swung behind him on a hook. Mouth open, hands gripping the steering wheel, he was screaming silently. Maddened curses at the world. And who could blame him? Alice was ready to scream herself. Already fifteen minutes late for her appointment, her frustration and the torturous heat made it virtually impossible to think. *Keep it brief,* she reminded herself. *Don't let their eyes glaze over. Succinct enough to be repeated to an executive further up the ladder . . .*

In nervous anticipation, she had spent over an hour selecting her wardrobe that morning, finally settling on loose pants, a linen shirt, and a light wool jacket with leather on the elbows. The jacket was now an obvious mistake, but she had been aiming for a particular look: the controlled bohemian, possibly the servile but bookish lesbian. As a novice to the profession, she had recently learned that there were men in Hollywood who considered an attractive woman in skirt and panty hose a stranger to the subtle workings of a first-class screenplay. And as it was, Alice felt somewhat of an imposter. In fact, she had recently been having a hard time putting her life in perspective. Alice the lover, would-be adventurer; ace journalist, would-be screenwriter—potential *novelist.* On a shelf in her office was an old box file containing a thick wad of yellowing paper. Four or five different typewriters in evidence here, and on every page indecipherable scribblings filled the margins. The labors of eight years or more. In some odd way, however, the unfinished manuscript represented hope, self-knowledge, spiritual awakening. Not what she was, but what she *might* be.

Every few minutes the traffic lurched forward. An erratic burst followed by a delayed screech of brakes down the line. Old plastic bags—aqua blue, tangy orange—these indestructible puffs of color dotted the embankment. Higher up sprinklers hissed, feebly trying to dampen the dry bushes, and beyond that a line of parched eucalyptus slanted dangerously against the fiery sun. A wasteland soon, thought Alice, forcing her eyes upwards where the muddy haze dissolved into blue. If she could just concentrate. After all, these things could be murder.

. . . A *politician's wife takes on a series of lovers. She uses sex to discover herself, to escape the boredom of her bourgeois existence; yes, very European, risqué, but certainly not pornographic. Sensual. Perhaps a nod to Buñuel here, but definitely not a throwback to the witless, demoralized seventies. Not* Last Tango in Paris. *No. Regard it as a subtle comment on the times: That in matters of loving and loathing, because of our desperate need for attention, nothing has changed! We offer ourselves as willing victims. Call it, if you will, a kind of love story within a cry for help. Then the second act, the progression. Inevitably, the woman falls for one of her young lovers . . .*

Of course, there was always the danger that an executive would presume the story echoed Alice's own less-than-perfect life. And it was important to appear serious, not frothy or shallow-witted. Alice glanced at herself in the rearview mirror. Flushed cheeks, small Irish nose, square-set jaw. Was she losing her looks? At thirty-five things begin to happen. A rather unappealing tightening round the mouth, a slackening round the eyes. Right now, the face of a person determined to keep up a good front. A woman occasionally confused but not desperate. Not yet. There had been a time, barely six months ago, however, toward the end of her marriage, when she had felt as though she were being propelled down a one-way tunnel. Things hurtling toward her and she unable to get out of their way. DO NOT IMAGINE THE WORST IS BEHIND YOU was a note that had surprised her one morning. Giant capitals scrawled on wax paper, pinned to the refrigerator door. She had no memory of writing it, but there it was in her own distinctive hand.

Half an hour late, exhausted, slightly feverish, and unsure of her ability to speak clearly, Alice sat waiting in a cramped cubicle, somebody's outer office in Producer's Building number 2. On her arrival, a secretary had informed her that, instead of the male executive Alice had been expecting to see—Joe Lovett, a Yale wunderkind famous for his facility with the corporate giants upstairs—she would meet a female junior vice president.

It was close to the lunch hour. Through the doorway of the adjoining office, Alice could see a slim redhead bent flat over her desk, her dress unbuttoned at the back. Directly behind her, a beefy young man in a white warm-up suit was busy kneading her shoulders like a pastry chef. Incredibly, it appeared the junior vice president was having a massage.

"Hi, you might as well come in," she called out. Her mouth was mashed into the blotter, and the words came in short sharp gasps. "You don't mind, do you? It's only for ten minutes. I'm having a hell of a job bending my neck. Joe had an early lunch across town and couldn't get to you in time," she managed to say, but clearly the exertion had winded her. Panting, she clung to the sides of her desk as though the muscle man might push her body clean through the woodwork.

For maximum comfort, the blinds of the junior vice president's sanctuary were half drawn so that the light, a murky yellow glow, slanted soothingly across the carpet. It had been important for some studio executives, eager to portray artistry at a base level, to decorate their offices with a theme. This tasteful gray cube was minimalist, with a dash of fifties. The desk was molded plywood with chrome legs; the bookshelves, metal and opaque glass, supported a stack of scripts and a fluorescent lava lamp. As Alice sat gingerly on the edge of the industrial-grade sofa, listening to the air conditioner purr softly and the sound of flesh pummeling flesh, she had the strange feeling of being cloistered in some antiseptic cell of a post–World War II asylum.

"Nice shoes," murmured the redhead, lifting her flushed face an inch. "Why don't you go right ahead. I may not look like I'm listening, but I am." Once again the big bruiser's hands sank into her shoulder blades. The executive's head dropped, her eyes turned moist. There was a sharp intake of breath and she gave a low moan, seemingly in the throes of some near-sexual upheaval.

Precisely this vision made Alice think for a moment that the redhead might be receptive to a story of a woman's passions bubbling beneath a reservoir of calm, until the junior executive added, "We're looking for something light. Comedy. Broad but tasteful—something for the youth arena." It was said with all the veiled hostility of a twenty-eight-year-old whose virulent ambition was the driving force of her existence. No, thought Alice, she would never buy this idea. There would be questions about disease, about safe sex, about audience response in middle America. Market potential in *Kansas*. And what kind of message was this anyway for the eighteen- to twenty-five-year-olds: a woman prostituting herself to alleviate the boredom of marriage?

Inexperienced as Alice was in the deceptions of the trade, she had learned that a seasoned screenwriter usually had something else in store, a tamer second serve more likely to clear the net. She remembered an old story, something she had trotted out previously in over a half-dozen executive offices.

The redhead's watery gaze wandered over to the sofa. Alice detected a flutter of impatience as the young woman flicked away a hank of dense hair—impatience, no doubt, because the writer opposite her was having trouble speaking.

In point of fact, Alice was experiencing a terrible tightness in her chest. Her temples hummed; the desire to please this woman seemed all at once compelling and yet loathsome. Typically, Alice discovered that her mind had switched off, that quite alarmingly the floor was sinking rapidly beneath her. She tried to imagine herself as a child in her parents' living room joking and cavorting for the relatives or cleverly reciting one of her dreamy poems to the delight of her mother's woozy upper-crust cocktail guests. Like the sporty front-liner she used to be, she forced herself to step into the void.

"Let me start by saying that this is a fairy tale. It's romantic, it's witty—early Hepburn and Tracy. First we have our hero, the son of a wealthy publisher who, on a bet, goes and works at a rival newspaper under an assumed name. He starts at the bottom. An upper-class layabout who's never done a lick of work in his life. Say, Tom Cruise. Of course he falls in love. And of course it's with this beautiful, radical journalist with a conscience—imagine a young Jane Fonda. So it's oil and water. She represents labor, he management, everything we know she detests. But at first *she* doesn't realize this; she thinks he's a genuine *working stiff* . . ."

It was terrible. Awful. And yet this was something she had practiced countless times in front of her bathroom mirror. At home she managed to hit the high notes with ease. She could pause skillfully as the drama unfolded and still keep the arm-waving to a minimum. Here, watched by the near-slumbering princess and the beefy sportsman, she heard herself roar on, hands flying. As small moans emanated from the tousled head on the desk, Alice was conscious of her voice picking up alarming speed until it became one resounding echo in her head. " . . . So here's our heroine, irate because she thinks the workers never get a fair stake in capitalism. Then she uncovers a story, a scandal involving his family—our *hero's* family—which, incidentally, we find out is trying to put *this* paper out of business. *Then* she discovers who *he* is and thinks that he never really loved her because . . ."

"Let me stop you right there," interrupted the redhead. Flexing her thin shoulders, she bounced the big man's hands off her back. She was up now, breathing heavily, taking in a good supply of the office air. "This is a class thing—am I right?"

"Yes, but only as a kind of backdrop for . . ."

"A sort of double fish-out-of-water thing?" she went on, forcing a thin smile. Then, as though captivated by her native cleverness, she leaned back and gazed dreamily at the ceiling.

The reverie was interrupted only to blow a farewell kiss to the muscle man heading out the door.

Alice continued feebly, encumbered not only by the now leaden jacket but also by her mounting embarrassment. "Well, it's more of a traditional love story. In the second act the hero gets caught up with the morals of what a reporter should or *should not* be held responsible for. The *ethics* of journalism become the determining factor in their relationship," she explained—not altogether sure what she meant.

"Look. I'll be honest with you. We've got four 'class' movies in development and two 'fish-out-of-waters' already. I'm sorry." The junior vice president was distracted again; she was wiping her neck with a Kleenex, head bent low, making big sweeping strokes with her white hands and bloodred nails. "But, you know, there's a book I was reading that you might be right for, an adaptation." The neck was finished. She delved into her cleavage.

Depressed, swimming in the murky depths, Alice surfaced like a porpoise, arched and playful once more. "A book?" she inquired lightly, crossing her legs and displaying her manly suede loafers.

"Yes, I was listening to it in my car, and I think it has great potential storywise."

"You listened to it?" asked Alice pleasantly.

"Yes. On tape. I got through the whole thing in a major rush-hour fuck-up. I mean, who has time to read?"

Alice felt the desperate need to laugh. Relief or anger? Whatever it was, she swallowed it, then leaned forward, embracing the moment. Bent from the waist for the powers that be. Who has time indeed? The redhead was probably Joe's secretary last week, she thought. Miss Knee Pads of the Christmas party. After two glasses of cheap champagne, she'd be handing out photocopies of her pale naked ass.

"Fabulous. So what's the book?"

"The Stranger," said the junior vice president, lowering her head and assuming a more confidential tone. "By Camus. Have you read it? Of course the end has to go. Too downbeat. And there needs to be more of the woman. Her angle on the whole thing." Engrossed in this concept, she went to write something on a yellow pad. "Listen," she continued, pen poised, "if you don't mind me asking, where did you get those shoes?"

It was not that the rejection was so ground-shaking but that the feeling of disappointment was becoming so familiar. Perhaps Alice was simply not cut out for this line of work; perhaps she did not have the appropriate bravado, the commercial instinct, the slick one-line idea that catapulted a novice ahead of the pulsing crowd. Besides, didn't she have a perfectly good job already? A position her father had arranged for her with a great deal of "finagling"—so he said. "I had to pull strings, impress upon the man your seriousness, your *dedication,*" he had informed Alice, his booming Celtic voice, as ever, full of doom and despair.

At the age of eight, Alice's dream was to become an ice skater; at ten, a nurse just like the shapely Miss Sommers in her father's employ. At fifteen, her secret and curiously shameful desire was to be a writer. "A *writer?*" Her father's forehead, normally furrowed like a plowed field, had shot up in amazement, his mouth cracking into a reflective grin. "Christ, I'm not sure you can even spell your own *name* correctly!" As if his adorable little cream puff had announced she wanted to be a test pilot or conquer Mount Everest.

Despite the bristle-cut hair that rose military fashion from his domed forehead, the strong wide nose, and the square, masculine jaw exemplifying his American straightforwardness—and (he liked to boast) his striking resemblance to Sterling Hayden—Charles Wilder was, in fact, a gentle and humorous man. Though in the past he had felled many of Alice's friends with his confrontational stare, he could switch from introspection to gay cavalier in a twinkle. Virtuous, strong-willed, he represented everything that in the fifties had made gods of ordinary hardworking men and that, three decades later, was considered irrefutably square. A man of habit, aloof but elegant, he never allowed anything but a plain white shirt to touch his back before sailing forth each morning. Without too much exertion, he had managed to ignore life's skirmishes, choosing instead to immerse himself in the more weighty pursuit of his medical career. That and his photography.

It was this unwavering loyalty to his patients, as well as the lengthy afternoons holed up in his "darkroom" that caused a certain amount of resentment and jealousy at home. In contrast to the doctor's calm rationale, Mrs. Wilder, of noble Russian descent, was a woman immersed in melodrama. Her life was spent reeling from life's many deceits and hoaxes, horrors that were acted out daily in the battle zone of their West Sixty-seventh Street living room. Here, in heated tempo, she would attempt to push her husband beyond the boundaries of his relentlessly sane "discussions." Stoic, cool, Dr. Wilder would talk but not argue. He would pace back and forth across his wife's prized Aubusson carpet (reputedly saved in the nick of time during the German occupation of Paris); then, at some critical point, he would simply disappear into the small box room next to his study, his haven in the storm, where domestic turbulence evaporated. Even as a child, Alice suspected that her father's obsession with his Hasselblad C500, his Alpa, his assorted Nikons, not to mention his prized collection of Cartier-Bresson and Man Ray photographs, was nothing more than an escape from the dark uncontrollable passions of his life.

"California? Are you crazy?" the great man had exclaimed in the autumn of '81. One of the doctor's beefy hands was clamped across his heart, a favorite gesture in recent years, since he had been diagnosed with a mild heart condition. And despite his appearance—a mighty bulwark in winter tweeds—for maximum effect, he then slumped back against the red vinyl. He and Alice were in the Russian Tea Room. A booth near the door was their reward for being associated with the hat-check girl, one of Alice's mother's distant relatives, newly arrived from old Kiev. "Are you *crazy?*" he repeated. "And what are you planning to do out there in lu-lu land? Write that great *novel?*"

And Alice had laughed as she always did. Because to admit to her own frustrations and doubts might mean subjecting her father to a scrutiny of his own not-so-brilliant life, with its disappointments and vanished dreams.

Nevertheless, through an old patient of her father's who was an editor at *Newsweek,* the doctor had managed to secure for his only daughter a coveted position at the *Los Angeles Recorder.*

The building was a mammoth Hearst slab from the thirties. Though outside it resembled a Spanish-Moroccan palace, inside was something else altogether. The editorial floor was a badly ventilated, low-ceilinged room, a yawning cavern of bureaucratic squalor with peeling columns and vintage metal desks. Occasionally the maintenance department tried to paint over the six layers of hospital green on the walls, which cracked every year around November when the heating vents exploded into the room. But as Seamus McCorkindale, the city editor, commented dryly, the neglect was "a reflection on the state of the paper; like putting Band-Aids on a leper." The Weekend section, where Alice worked, was housed in the dankest corner, up against the ornate balustrade of the original staircase.

Leonard Lativsky, the Weekend editor and friend of the man at *Newsweek*, had officially given Alice her job. He was unbearably thin with a raging thatch of gray hair, big enough to swab the editorial floor. "Oh, you're the one Freddy Newcome told me to hire," he said jokingly in front of a disgruntled Monday morning lineup, a remark received with raised eyebrows and a ripple of indiscreet muttering. Reeling from this embarrassing initiation, Alice was led to the offices of Henry Worth, the managing editor, for what she would later learn was called "the Worth once-over."

Henry Worth was a pigeon-chested man who had once worshiped great talent. Behind his desk were photographs of himself in the fifties, arm slung around Hemingway, or John Huston and Bogart, in some seedy watering hole—souvenirs of the good old days when real men were on board. Now in his late sixties, he had shifted his allegiance to the staid company of his fellow art collectors and golfing partners, namely, the reigning Hollywood agents and studio heads. The only nod to his former dashing days lay in the colorful cashmere sweaters and matching socks he wore under his chalk-stripe suits. He was an inveterate smoker, and in endearing contrast to his outdated chic, a light sprinkling of ash peppered his lapels.

Henry instructed the new arrivals—Alice and two terrified, sallow-faced boys joining the city desk—about the grim determination necessary to achieve greatness. "Do you know how we justify our treacherous lives as journalists?" he asked. A question to which he received no reply. "For every person we betray, we say, 'It's the public's *right* to know.' " Then in case this had nurtured any fancy ideas, he went on swiftly, "Look, this business has changed since I was slugging it out in Chicago. You think this is an art? It's a job. It's a craft at best." He cracked his knuckles, rocking back on the heels of his glossy-toed Chelsea boots. "You get reporters who are a major pain in the ass who *do* deliver and reporters who are a major pain in the ass who *don't* deliver—why? Because newspaper people now are hopelessly immature. In the old days we used to spend all night out there busting our asses for a good story. Now everyone wants to go home to their kids or their lover, *and* they want to elevate themselves. They want to write *fiction*—no, worse, *fucking screenplays.*"

This was, of course, precisely the secret desire festering in the minds of a great portion of the staff. However, any writer who openly tried to succeed in the movie business was scorned as a base opportunist and a low-life deserter. The Weekend department, in particular, was a cauldron of bubbling petty jealousies. Cameron Fischer, the elitist and somewhat foppish movie critic, was disliked but pandered to, thanks to his occasional distribution of screening passes and his inside gossip about actors' sexual derring-do. Movies reviewed by him were openly re-reviewed the same morning by the staff of experts, each of them lit up with sarcasm and razor-sharp wit. And when Alice arrived, because her position had so obviously been arranged, she was treated with as much distrust as a pampered heiress from Park Avenue. Though she knew her studied air of nonchalance made her seem like a person to whom things came easily, she was not yet confident enough to convince her fellow workers otherwise.

Their disdain evaporated sometime during her first year when she was assigned to cover Beverly Hills matrons at their leisure. Here she distinguished herself (mildly) by writing clever and superficial banter about their fashion shows, jewels, and rich husbands. (What had happened, she wondered, to that high-minded dream to write about the poor and downtrodden, the plight of the working man, and global hunger—not to mention that other fantasy: the novel?)

And then, out of the blue, she was given her own column. Something she felt she didn't deserve, and, frankly, neither did the rest of the staff toiling behind their hefty pre–World War II desks.

It was to be a breezy Friday piece, featuring lighthearted chats with actors and directors, which would occasionally proffer an inside view of the hierarchy that made the whole town tick. How could she have landed this coveted position? What kind of chicanery had prompted management's oversight of the other worthy hacks, notably Cameron, who for some time had been angling for a column of his own? There could be only one answer: She must be sleeping with Leonard Lativsky.

The rumor had started thus: One day Leonard had taken Alice to lunch, ostensibly to discuss the animosity so apparent between herself and Cameron. More likely, Alice had thought, to rid her editor of his guilt for the lascivious fantasies he had harbored about her for the past two years.

"Cameron has a problem with women like you," remarked Leonard, casually moving aside the basket of dinner rolls and slipping a sickly looking, ice-cold hand over hers. "The trouble is you're too pretty and too smart."

Exactly. The woman's curse, thought Alice. A lethal combination that had previously slayed more noble a man than Leonard. "Thank God, then, I have an amazing sense of humor about it," she said pithily. But by that time, Frank Davies, the literary editor, was bending over their table, eyes popping. He was staring at the hands lying together as if he were actually witnessing the debauchery of two writhing bodies.

So her fate was sealed. And Leonard never wasted an opportunity, be it by a wink or a nod in her direction, to imply that the rumor was true. Nor did he look in the slightest bit surprised when Alice complained of overhearing some cunning Weekenders suggest that Leonard occasionally wrote her column for her.

As it happened, Alice's knowledge of movies was more extensive than the staff of experts imagined. Grandfather Alexis, her mother's father, had often taken her as a young teenager to the Thalia Theater on the Upper West Side to instruct her in what he called *la vraie mise-en-scène.* "Style in movies is not just an embellishment; it is the method by which meaning is *expressed,*" he had proclaimed, referring to the "auteur" theory, a quote that she later discovered he had lifted from *Cahiers du Cinéma.* On rainy afternoons she sat through Godard's *À Bout de Souffle*, Louis Malle's *Zazie dans le Métro* (a character Alice thoroughly identified with), *Les 400 Coups*, *Lola*, and *Tirez sur le Pianiste.* Then, moving forward, or rather backward, in a more nostalgic vein for old Alexis, who claimed several "fine drinking friends" in Hollywood, they went to see Hitchcock and all the Preston Sturges movies.

Mesmerized by the tortured romance in *Notorious*, she dreamed of a future that would include passion, suspense, duplicity, and some smooth savior like Cary Grant. From then on, movies became an extension of her secret life, an inexhaustible reservoir of make-believe, an escape from her mother's interminable harangues, and the beginning of a lifetime's dedication to *romance.* Ah, yes. An independent woman involved in spectacular liaisons. The power of love. The *idea* of love, the very anticipation of that great passion that allowed a girl to sail through the worst.

≈

After her lunchtime encounter with the redhead at Warner Brothers, Alice drove to the Los Feliz area. She had a two o'clock interview with the actress Niki Palmer. Springer Avenue was an old street, mysterious, faintly magical. The houses were huge: gaudy twenties and thirties, badly neglected mansions with leaking swimming pools, their gardens strangled by matted blankets of ivy. Silent monuments to long-gone mighty men.

She parked her '69 Mercedes behind the line of movie trucks. Sitting on the back end of one of the big vans were two union boys. Shirts off, stomachs hanging over their belts, they were greased up, playing cards in the sun. Alice asked where she could find Miss Palmer, and one of them pointed to a rambling mock Tudor house down the street. On the second floor, through thc giant banana leaves lapping against the windows, Alice could see the greenish white glow of the arc lamps inside.

Downstairs, the house was in a frenzy close to pandemonium. Electricians, grips, and general workmen squeezed in and out of rooms, some stripped to the waist, some in partial combat gear, the more seasoned hurling lusty one-liners at each other as proof of their rugged individuality. Every corner was a maze of metal light stands or deep boxes filled with cellulose filters, flags, and reflectors. Thick gray bands of camera tape snaked up the walls, securing the cables for the twenty or so lights balanced over doors, wedged behind kitchen cabinets, or clamped to the stair railing. This rather prosaic and yet still exotic vision of moviemaking never ceased to excite Alice. Naturally, it was part of what had attracted her to Hollywood from the start. Fantasyland. A place for those who wish to leave their past behind, a haven where all is permissible.

"I hope you're not part of the modern narcissistic elite

who think they have to pick up and fly somewhere every five minutes just to prove they're *going places,*" her mother had remarked when Alice announced her plans to move to the West Coast. The tiny woman's voice had barely camouflaged her distress as the tears formed in the corner of her beautiful gray eyes. "Not running *away*, are you?"

"No," Alice had replied. But of course she was.

Niki Palmer was upstairs. Outfitted in a turquoise one-piece, plunge-back bathing suit, flesh-colored tights, and high heels, she was busy arguing with her makeup lady. As the woman winged a moist sponge in and out, nervously trying to smear beige number 4 Pan-Cake deep into the folds of the actress's young and magnificent breasts, Niki fidgeted like a two-year-old, whining that the thing was too damn cold.

Alice waited politely. This was obviously a child's bedroom. Baby bears and lambs romped across the wallpaper. A suitable setting for such a nubile creature, thought Alice. Eventually the makeup woman left and Niki threw herself down opposite Alice on one of the twin beds. The film's publicist had described the movie to Alice as "a one-woman story about beauty pageants." Lost illusions out there in the hinterland where hard work and heartbreak quickly replaced the initial glamour. Deferentially, Alice inquired about Niki's acting technique. How was it working in a low-budget picture with a talented director? Did she consider this a meaty role? What careful preparation was needed to play a voluptuous, ambitious girl from a small town? (If any, thought Alice.) For ten minutes Niki answered in monosyllabic grunts as she methodically picked a hole in her tights and chain-smoked Marlboro Lights, flicking the burnt matches from the top of her kneecap into a wastebasket across the room. Surprisingly, she was an excellent shot.

“You know, most people are only interested in the directors I’ve slept with,” she said suddenly.

Alice politely inclined her head as Niki blew a perfect smoke ring, then poked her tongue through the middle.

“Of course I slept with them all,” she went on. “Who wouldn’t? Directors are powerful. I was getting the goods while most actresses out there were sleeping with below-the-line stuff. The cute ADs or the electricians—or *other actors*. Can you imagine?” said the dewy creature. Her eyebrows flew up. She made a disgusted guttural noise in her throat; then, totally exhausted, she rolled over.

“Smart girls go for talent,” Alice remarked congenially, but Niki’s head had disappeared over the side of the bed. Alice could hear sounds of rustling paper, then swearing, then a metal top being unscrewed. Niki’s floating legs had a bronzed, airbrushed look—appearing unnaturally flawless in the spandex tights, until Alice noticed a large yellowing bruise on the inner left thigh and a darker one at her ankle. When Niki swung back, her face was flushed, her full mouth wet and glistening.

“I mean, let’s face it, Hollywood is suburbia. Provincial as hell. Every studio executive should be made to spend a month in Europe to learn how to treat women. How to treat women who actually *like* sex. Because out here, in this town, it’s still all Peter Pan collars and who has class. Serious actresses, *stars*, are supposed to be at home tortured by their interpretations of life. No time for *sport* fucking.”

Alice was beginning to like her. At twenty-four, Niki still had that blond prepubescent glow, if slightly tarnished and a little bluish around the gills. Due to several years of drinking and drugs, Niki’s career happened to be at a low ebb. Despite this, Alice thought she had a certain lithe wantonness on screen, a nymphlike quality that transcended her acting skills. And though her voice sounded too girlish—a sort of sensuous, breathy whine—she was intelligent. A smart girl who looked stupid on the screen: a curious Hollywood reversal.

The hole in the actress's glossy tights was now the size of a grapefruit. Chuckling to herself, Niki leaned forward on the bed and lit another Marlboro, then exhaled loudly, nimbly flicking the dead match with her thumbnail. This time, instead of hitting the wastebasket, it bounced off the door just as someone came in. It was the director, Oscar Lombardi.

Alice had first seen Oscar the summer before at the Writer's Guild when he was a guest speaker at a screenwriting seminar. Tall and lanky with rumpled clothes, he had stood awkwardly on stage, his rather beautiful hands floating through the air as he spoke. His voice was resonant, teasing. His eyes, lit with what appeared to be an insane glitter, darted back and forth, a dark mass of unruly hair falling over his grave face. The nose, though oversized, was distinguished and rather romantic. And despite the fact that he looked more like a disheveled medical student than a prominent movie director, Alice had been immediately attracted to him. "Writing a screenplay is not like assembling a picnic table. Beyond structure there is magic, wonder, laughter, fear, motion, and *passion*," he had said, rather nobly. "And remember, Godard said a movie should have a beginning, a middle, and an end—but not necessarily *in that order*."

Now, standing in the doorway of the bedroom, wearing chino pants, a T-shirt, and a crumpled gray linen jacket, he looked harried, slightly crazed. Anything but the captivating director. The lankiness was still there, but the prominent nose appeared rather beaky, the eyes colorless and weary. Perhaps a family disaster had occurred, or possibly this rather forlorn appearance was simply evidence of the strain undergone during the grueling twelve-week schedule.

"Ah," he said, eyes widening, fatigue suddenly replaced by keen animal concentration. "I need to talk to you for a minute, Niki." Then, as if he had just noticed the stranger on the bed, he barked, "And who the hell are you?"

"Alice Wilder. From the *Recorder*. Weekend section," she replied, the words flying out of her. She forced a laugh to inform him that she was merely doing her job, then added, "We were almost finished."

"Well, God save us all from the press!" he shot back. "And you can leave my name out of your second-rate rag. I can do without the publicity, thank you. In my opinion journalists should be burned on a great pile of their own endless scribblings."

Was there some nuance here she was missing? Or was it just plain rudeness? Why was he so angry? At her? No. But then it didn't look like he was particularly angry at Niki either.

"We've got a tricky scene coming up," he said, drawing in a deep breath to underline just *how* tricky. He was smiling in a sly, ominous way now, as if quite pleased with the bad impression he was giving. "You two can catch up with each other later," he added dismissively. Then he hooked an arm around Niki's waist and, as though maneuvering a sickly child, hoisted her off the bed.

Alone in the room, Alice realized why Oscar had become so embittered toward the press. For his first movie he had been heralded with acclamations of near genius. Not since the early days of Louis Malle, or Bogdanovich, or was it Truffaut? had a filmmaker been so interested in exploring his country's identity; never had a man's imagery and imagination been so at one with his characters' real-life urban experience. Having been dubbed a high priest, Oscar was doomed to fail when, for his third movie, he'd insisted on pushing the boundaries of simple storytelling by dwelling on man's preoccupation with death. He had betrayed his devotees—the press—and for this he had been greeted with scorn. Nevertheless, he still maintained a loyal cult following who considered him a prodigy manqué. Actresses loved him. He nailed them where it counted. He praised them, slapped them around, destroyed them, rebuilt them, and taught them who they were.

No wonder Alice was attracted to him.

He was also the opposite of her father and everything her imperious mother would have despised.

Dr. Charles Wilder claimed he had fallen in love with his wife the moment he'd set eyes on her. As she sat in his overheated waiting room, barely visible beneath the brown sheared beaver coat and matching hat, unable to speak because of an acute strep throat, he was, in his own words, "smitten right off the bat." The patient was accompanied by her father, Count Alexis Plemianakoff, who like other Russian émigrés arriving in Manhattan after the war had been forced to take temporary employment. He was currently serving as night doorman at the Plaza Hotel. His story (recounted that day to the doctor) was that in 1917 he'd left Russia and the family fortune for Paris where, with his new wife, he'd moved into a small apartment on Rue de Navarin. Having no known skills, aristocrat that he was, his commercial ventures of mushroom farming, book binding, and dry cleaning had failed miserably. And in '47, his wife dead of tuberculosis, and further impoverished by the indignities of war, he had sold off the last of the family jewels and sent his two teenage daughters, Natasha and Olga (both renowned for their astonishing beauty), to New York to marry into money—there being none left in Paris. However, after serving two years as chauffeur to the French minister of foreign affairs, the count had been caught in a compromising position with the minister's wife and was forced to follow his daughters to the great American city. Then, shortly after his arrival, the catastrophe had occurred: Natasha's whirlwind romance and subsequent engagement to the meat-packing heir Colson Towers Jr. was destroyed on the eve of the wedding by her sister, Olga, who had done the unthinkable. She had run away with the groom. Natasha's shock, the high fever, and subsequent loss of voice were the reasons for their visit to Dr. Wilder's office.

Alice's father admitted that he had won his wife on the rebound, that he had stolen her. A sentiment echoed frequently by Alice's mother in response to her husband's lighthearted jokes about the "ruined Russians": Natasha Plemianakoff had married beneath her.

Whereas Alice's father could forgive a multitude of sins if the sinner were a person of ethical, honest, upstanding character, her mother's bereavement for her lost ancestry sent her worshiping indiscriminately at the feet of New York *society*. In her European confusion and desire to be "totally American," she interpreted this as anyone remotely associated with money. For her, the rich were always "glorious beings from another planet."

At age seven, Alice was sent to St. Teresa's Convent. Mrs. Mackintyre, one of her mother's illustrious society friends, assured her that the food was superior and that the sisters concentrated on turning out "young ladies." Religion was of secondary consideration. Under the civilized tutelage of these heavenly creatures, Alice began her education. While Gentle Jesus watched over the young girls' wayward souls, Sister Mary Magdalene posted herself as guard in the locker-room doorway every afternoon in case the half-naked girls might have any untoward interest in each other's stringy bodies. Alice dutifully learnt her Catechism and the Stations of the Cross. On saints' days she sat in chapel next to Mrs. Mackintyre's spoiled towheaded daughter, Jennifer, both little girls dressed identically in white satin. Repeating parrot fashion *in Spiritu Sanctu, Dominus vobiscum,* Alice crossed her chest with holy water and imagined herself levitating miraculously out of the knee-breaking pew, just as she knew Jesus had done on the third day.

Occasionally, in warmer weather, her mother came to collect her. "*Mon petit lapin rose!*" she would shout, striding along in her tailored linen dress, silk scarves flying, jade bracelets clinking, as she whisked Alice off to meet her society girlfriends for tea at the Plaza. A slave to etiquette, Mrs. Wilder sat at the table pole-straight, knees together, shoulders back, her head slightly cocked as though constantly on the alert for a ringing telephone. Perched on her right was Alice. Under a blue haze of cigarette smoke and the powerful odor of tuberose toilet water, the child listened to this majestic woman boast coquettishly of the French baron, the Russian prince, and the countless others who had been mesmerized by her charm. Apparently all members of the opposite sex were at her mother's beck and call. If only she had retained the family fortune as well as the title . . . "A woman without money," she sadly informed Alice, eyes fluttering, "is forced to rely on the generosity of men." For all the years spent learning to speak the English language, in her diligence Mrs. Wilder had adopted the arched vowel sounds usually associated with the drawing room comedies of 1940s Hollywood movies. This, as her husband frequently reminded her, was due to the fact that she watched so many on TV. Her voice ranged from a low martini whisper to a birdlike, breathless hysteria. "My talent with men," she would say, her voice in full crescendo, "is that I listen. *J'écoute* with tremendous patience and *énergie.*"

Alice adored her. How could she ever match up? In her girlish daydreams, she too would *make* men love her. "Prepare yourself for life's great adventure," the divine creature with the ivory skin and soft brown curls would murmur as she crouched on the bedroom carpet folding lavender sachets into her sumptuous satin underwear. While making contrition and praying for her place among the angels, little seven-year-old Alice also asked God if she might have a "talent with men," whatever *that* might be.

But by the time Alice was eleven it was apparent that she was not turning out to be what either of them had hoped. She had her mother's beauty, the penetrating eyes and delicate oval face, but she was not as pert, not as button cute. And for all the deportment and ballet lessons she was paralyzingly awkward. She walked with a lunging gait, knees knocking together. She was already too tall and, unlike her mother, overly sensitive to false attention. When Mrs. Elkin from the apartment next door threw a hand to her cheek in order to express amazement at seeing two such fresh beauties pass by on their way to Elizabeth Arden (her mother actually *swept* past—chin raised, she *dared* people to stop and speak to her), Alice cringed sullenly, hands clenched in her raincoat pockets. She had not the faintest desire to draw attention to herself, to "stand out in a crowd": a requirement in her mother's eyes for any young lady worth her salt. "Don't slouch" was the battle cry as they hit the streets. "First impressions are essential. How you carry yourself determines how *interesting* you are." But for all her mother's insistence about manners, her idée fixe about deportment and charm, Alice knew that compared to this enchantress she was hopelessly ordinary.

Attempts were made to impress her mother. Distorted clay ashtrays, embroidered napkins, and a schoolgirl rendition of van Gogh's *Sunflowers* were brought home from Alice's class workshop as offerings. But they were of little interest to the distracted Mrs. Wilder. She put them away for safekeeping. From whom, wondered Alice, the Germans? The Bolsheviks? From her wicked aunt Olga who had stolen the meat-packing heir? Stored just like her mother's ocelot coat each summer, except that Alice's little gems never made it out again in the fall. Still, Alice tried to please her. Arduously she scribbled her thank-you notes. Humbly she followed her mother into the bedroom and asked to be shown once more how to put chamomile tea bags on her eyes, or how to correctly blend in Elizabeth Arden night cream with her fingertips ("tiny dancing motions, *chérie*"). Never mind being able to answer *all* the questions on the TV quiz shows or being happy to sit quietly in a corner with her world atlas and her precious books for hours on end. No, forget that. What this eleven-year-old should be cramming for was life's big upcoming test on how to be a *sophisticated woman!*

Around three o'clock Alice was downstairs in the Tudor house taking notes—a colorful overview. She had managed to extract a few printable quotes from Niki, enough for the short piece, when she ran across the actress bent over the coffee and snack table. Niki had been laboriously scraping mayonnaise from the insides of a packaged ham sandwich. No matter what she did, she informed Alice, she did *not* eat oils. Now Alice was on the living-room set where Niki and her movie mother would argue whether or not the beauty queen had the talent to become Miss Illinois. The mother sat silently in an armchair. A blousy, red-haired woman, her chest exploding from a wardrobe-issue bathrobe, she had the vacant, startled expression of a person who has spent most of her life waiting to "go on." Diligently, Alice noted the general atmosphere: chintz armchairs, oak dining table with pressback chairs, plaster ducks flying east across the wall toward the French doors. From where she stood she could see Niki in the backyard, head bowed, a bewildered expression on her face, as Oscar whispered minute and specific instructions in her delicate ear. No sign now of the sneering cynic in the bedroom. Oscar appeared perfectly pleasant, magnanimous, ingratiating. And for some inexplicable reason Alice felt left out. Could she be jealous? Of what? Of the loose-limbed, wanton Niki, owner of those impressive leg muscles now relaxing in the flat Capezio pumps? Or jealous perhaps of the majestic swell of her famous (if not globally, then surely, *nationally*) stunning breasts? Alice was debating this when, suddenly, she heard loud shouting from the street.

She went outside and joined the small crowd that had gathered to watch six irate women circling in front of the house. They held placards that read JUDGE MEAT NOT WOMEN, I AM NOT A BARBIE DOLL, and WE WILL NOT BE SLAVES TO THE PERVERSITY OF MEN. To illustrate her contempt, one of them had draped her naked body with thinly sliced cuts of raw beef. In further protest, she had painted her mouth with a messy swirl of lipstick, the result so appalling that the bottom half of her face resembled a gaping wound.

Two unit security guards were trying to hustle the women down the street when out of nowhere a strapping brunette, wearing sackcloth and tennis shoes, threw a plastic bag of blood. It exploded against one of the trailers with a noisy pop, then splashed into the street. At this shocking display of barbarism, the small crowd (the local residents who had emerged meekly for the sideshow) gasped and scuttled back to the sanctity of their tomblike mansions.

"Look, for Christ's sake, we're not applauding beauty pageants here, we're *denouncing* them!" Oscar shouted as he stepped off the curb, avoiding the stream of blood gurgling in the gutter. "This is a *movie*. It's not real. These are just actresses *portraying* the parts of the contestants." Having to explain this made him more frustrated, and when the brunette with the rippling shoulders lumbered toward him he leaped forward. Grabbing her arm, he screamed, "It's an exposé! Get it? We're on the girls' side. So back the fuck off, sister!" The woman howled as though a wild animal had taken a bite out of her ear. Then she lunged at Oscar with a nail-bitten clenched fist, nicking him smartly on the chin. He was stung for a moment; then, as though suddenly fascinated by this peculiar little mise-en-scène, he opened his arms in surrender. For a moment he studied her. Imbued with his superior, more reasonable, masculine power, he sauntered forward as the confused woman recoiled. Almost trotting, she danced backward until she reached the safety of her group hovering slyly at the curb.

Alice was dazzled. He had that easy showmanship she was often attracted to in men. Style over substance, dementia over depth. Just then she realized Oscar was staring at her from across the street. He smiled. It seemed like a perfectly pleasant smile, without a hint of sarcasm. Barely did she have time to acknowledge the gesture before it was gone. But he had indicated something. Friendship? Desire? Whatever it was, it surprised Alice and left her feeling oddly exposed.

It took five minutes and the skirmish was all over. In a flurry of activity, three or four teamsters moved in, and after sharp words and raised fists, all six women piled in the back of their van and sped rapidly away.

In order to remove herself from the temptation of taking one more look at Oscar or entertaining any whimsical thoughts (totally misplaced, she reminded herself), Alice headed down the street toward her car.

But he caught up with her seconds later. He was hurrying, bent forward, a man pressed urgently against a ferocious wind. "Wait a minute," he shouted breathlessly. Then overtaking her, he stretched himself across the door of her car, like a man who owned it and anything that might come with it.

"Mr. Lombardi," said Alice. She was alarmed that her voice sounded so girlish and coy, everything she hated about herself.

"I'm going to take my life in my hands and tell you the absolute truth," he began, running his fingers rather agonizingly through his thick mop of hair. "Is it possible for a journalist to keep a secret?"

"You mean when she only tells her friends and doesn't write about it?" replied Alice quickly. She turned away from the harsh afternoon sun and, not uncoincidentally, from Oscar's penetrating gaze.

"I'm way over budget. I'm behind schedule. The studio is screaming bloody murder. My esteemed producer is worried about the comic tone of the movie. So if the women-and-meat thing gets in the paper, frankly, I'm dead." She was impressed with his somber husky voice, the seriousness of his tone. But then she imagined she was supposed to be. "I guess you have to decide whose side you're on," he went on. "Commerce or women's rights."

Moving closer, one of his rather beautiful hands squeezed her forearm. It was a moment of startling intimacy. She felt her face flush. His whole being seemed to penetrate her skin, pulsing right up to her hair, which she imagined might have suddenly caught fire. It occurred to her that there had been no attempt at an apology for his tirade in the bedroom, but by that time she heard herself say, "I'm not sure how much women's rights go for on the open market these days. I'll stick with commerce." Master of the quick quip, a traitor to her gender.

"Funny, good-looking, and smart," he replied easily. "Where have you been hiding?"

"In a nine-to-five job. Regular obscurity."

The cynical smile was back. He was beginning to look a little crazy again. "So what's it like working for a newspaper?"

"Interesting. Not lucrative."

"I'm surprised."

"There's a saying around the office. Are you on welfare or do you work for the *Recorder*?" Then, fearing he had heard the faint note of exasperation in her voice, she added, "Actually, I've been writing a screenplay."

"Really? So is *that* what you want to do?" he asked. The smile disappeared. He proceeded to nod silently. Of course, she thought, he was nodding because hadn't everyone, including the person who had sold him his creased linen jacket, written a screenplay? And never one to leave a silence unfilled, she felt the urge to inform him further. Breezily, she described her life at the paper—the hard work, the backbiting, every writer's burning desire to get into movies—all couched in sarcasm and wit. Her life as vaudeville. She even told him that she thought the critics were unkind about his previous movie, *The Last Weekend.* She had interpreted the slow pace ("languid," she said flatteringly) as a reflection of the hero's frustration with his tedious life. With mounting self-consciousness, eyes scanning the dusty horizon, she was about to add that she had separated from her husband some months ago and this was one hell of a town to meet anyone decent in, but when she turned back she saw he hadn't been paying attention. He had moved away from the car.

"Tell me," he said in a cool, salubrious voice now, as though the scenery had suppressed some inner demon. "What do you do on weekends?"

"Sleep," she said. Eager for escape, she opened the car door and climbed in. It was a furnace; the heat took her breath away.

"Do you ever get up for meals?" he asked, bending down.

"Well, the thing is . . . I'm seeing someone," she said apologetically. After a lifetime's tuition at Natasha Wilder's school for correct manners, she hated disappointing people. Anyone. A friend, a pet. And, of course, men in general.

"Well, as it happens, I'm seeing someone too." The smile reappeared. Though full of charm, it still boasted a hint of insanity. "To tell the truth, I was only thinking about *lunch.*"

She knew, of course, that he was married, although it was possible that the fact had slipped her mind during the last ten minutes. And the provocative way he had referred to his wife as someone he was "seeing" did not seem so cavalier as it might coming from another man. While she was seriously considering the question of lunch, something else occurred to her: It was never the plain decisions in life that were dangerous but rather those you slid into foolishly that eventually trapped you.

"I don't really think I can," she said quickly. "But thanks." She started the car, eyes trained on the steering wheel. Then, as if narrowly escaping from an armed robber, she pulled away at top speed.

Of course, nothing had happened. But as she drove home, a touch lightheaded, she was convinced that somehow it had.

If Alice was confused about her initial response to a man's attention, she was convinced the blame lay with her mother. During her first encounter with the opposite sex at age fourteen, Alice was astonished to find she had thoroughly disgraced herself. Alice and Tommy Rizzo had shared an early bond: Both had suffered the wrath of Mr. Herrera, the demonic piano teacher, who reserved the right to hammer their knuckles with a weighted baton if allegro was not achieved with a precise and subtle touch. The oafish, thick-necked Tommy was the first boy to worship Alice's practically nonexistent breasts (they would never come close to her mother's magnificent orbs) and sent her notes of flowery prose that, even with her limited experience, Alice knew reeked of cheap sentiment.

One afternoon after class, on the pretext of needing to use the bathroom, the fifteen-year-old Tommy asked Alice if he might come into her apartment. Once inside, however, he hurled his lumpy body at her like a cannibal, forcing her onto the sofa, where he frantically rubbed his clothed body against her school uniform. As his beefy hand snaked between her legs, she was aware of the wet patch spreading on her serge skirt (this she later realized to be her first contact with semen) and just then she looked up and saw her mother standing in the hallway. She froze and slid a pillow over Tommy's head, hoping he would disappear. Curiously, this shocking tableau produced little indignation from her mother, merely a steely silence. The dramatics came later.

In the kitchen that evening, one hand pressed against her forehead, the other wielding a knife over a blanquette of veal, her mother exploded. Didn't Alice *know* sex was a woman's only weapon against men's tyranny? How could she be so weak and stupid? Once a woman relinquished that jewel, she lost her *power*. "What power?" the polite but incredulous convent girl wanted to know.

"Over *men*, of course."

Not only was this loutish boy so *not* what Mrs. Wilder had in mind for the launching of her daughter into the *haut bourgeois*, but, as far as she was concerned, sex was merely a dangerous diversion in the relentless quest for that Holiest of Grails—Position and Wealth. Contrary to the raging current of permissiveness out there in the late sixties, her mother's idea of feminine advancement was to hold out forever or at least until you had a man right where you wanted him. Where was that gay abandon, her mother's wicked Parisian *vie sexuelle* that had playboys and barons weeping at her feet? Like a convert of the worst kind, she had embraced American clean living of the fifties and never moved on. "You must understand, *chérie*, men are businessmen," she said, pinching Alice's white cheeks to force back a little color. "The only thing they understand is the *deal*."

Had Alice been the obedient seven-year-old, she would have dropped to her knees and begged forgiveness. But somewhere between the child she had left behind and the woman her mother aspired her to be, Alice had lost confidence in God Almighty and her ability to match up to this divine creature.

With the doctor her relationship was more straightforward. She could make him laugh. Though engrossed in his photography and his patients, he was also a fanatical fan of TV comedy shows. From an early age she would visit him in his office and make him shake with laughter at her impersonations: Bob Hope, Jerry Lewis, and then, as a showstopper, *both* parts in *My Fair Lady*. "Did you get a load of that? The perfect English accent? She ought to be on *The Ed Sullivan Show*," her father would say proudly, nudging a wheezing patient who, moments before, had been scolded for neglecting to have his nose passages drained per the doctor's strict instructions.

And though at fourteen she had become a far different child (burdened by other people's expectations, she had instinctively withdrawn to a quieter place), she still performed these tricks for her father. Because if love came from this man under the guise of applause, she would break her neck to get it. After all, in the winter of 1966, he had cured (almost single-handedly, so he claimed) hundreds of New Yorkers from the Asian flu, and she worshiped him, albeit too often from afar.

"Come on, baby, show Mr. Grossman the doctor thing," he pleaded one wintry afternoon. And perky, doe-eyed Alice, the frolicking Pollyanna, now a blossoming teenager, two tongue depressors in her mouth and a stethoscope in her ears, did a turn impersonating Lucille Ball examining an ailing Desi. Her father howled while Mr. Grossman, a thin waxlike man with huge transparent ears, looked on confused. He was a celebrated music publisher presently set back by a throat infection who, though a personal friend of the great Toscanini himself, was completely unfamiliar with the shenanigans of the classic American TV series. She might have been barking like a seal, balancing a ball on her nose, for all the humiliation she felt, but the show went on.

Partway through this exhausting charade, her mother arrived to pick her up. "Isn't she just *something,* honey!" her father shouted, one scrubbed red hand still slapping his knees with amusement. But the petite flushed-faced woman in the doorway, swathed in fox fur, was clearly appalled. She lowered her eyes and looked away. And all Alice could think was *Oh, God, here it comes.* After all, manners and self-control were her mother's tools for chic survival. But there was nothing. Silence. Only a look of . . . what? Loathing? Despair? It was a look that stayed with Alice well into her twenties. It was—and this seemed an incredible thought, almost blasphemous to the teenager—a look of *jealousy.* Except that who could blame her? If her mother was disappointed in life, she had reason to be. Most of the time, the good doctor was off somewhere. If he wasn't making house calls ("Last of a dying breed," he would announce proudly), he was driving his black Buick out to Coney Island, his chest bandoliered with cameras and lenses, to capture what he called "a slice of real life." Real life taking place out there when it was *supposed* to be happening in Natasha Wilder's living room. Now her husband was carrying on like some ringmaster in his swivel chair while her usually disenchanted and glowering daughter made demented noises in front of, God forbid, a distinguished *man* (lo, the emblem of Alice's bright future!).

Like most children, Alice was more perceptive than her parents realized. And though she was horribly aware of her mother's hidden distress, she knew she was not *meant* to know (was in fact mortified that she knew) and so kept quiet. From that moment on she decided that it was easier, safer, to keep all her terrifying emotions to herself. When she found herself tongue-tied in front of relatives or friends, her inclination was to make them laugh, if only to camouflage her own discomfort. In this way, she retreated to the safety of observing others. And by the time Alice reached fifteen, she frankly hadn't a clue who she was supposed to be. Except that the humor came as a blessing; it allowed her, thank God, never to have to reveal her true tormented self.

Fortunately, the savior of her teenage years was her grandfather. For Count Alexis Plemianakoff life was simple. Men were swine unless they were artists; women were either beasts or jewels depending on whether or not they loaned him money. He was a tall, handsome man with a rakish smile. A poet and a dreamer who ate his evening meal early, stocking up at embassy cocktail parties. He always wore one of the two sharply tailored suits that had been made in Paris before the war. One in cream linen, the other a gray bird's-eye tweed. He smoked Cuban cigars (sent from a store on Curzon Street in London in a plain brown wrapper) and drank daily what he called "a necessary amount of alcohol to ward off life's constant disappointments." He was broke, but he was a fanatical schemer and had inventions up his sleeve that would revolutionize everyday life and make him a millionaire. On summer afternoons he took Alice for walks through Central Park, where the heady perfume from the rose gardens somehow reminded him of "young women's bare legs in summer dresses" and compelled him to launch into stories of his decadent life.

There were the drunken evenings in Montmartre, arm in arm with Henry Miller, lounging around with the other rummies in cheap prix fixe restaurants or causing a rumpus in dance halls with fleshy foreign girls. Yes, he, too, of course, had tried to write. "But if your opening paragraph can't match up to *Crime and Punishment*," he scoffed, "why in hell bother?" The count had discussed Marxist philosophy with Sartre and Beauvoir, whom he referred to as the "Desi and Lucy of the Latin set." He had sipped cocktails with Winston Churchill in Marrakech on the terrace of the Mamounia Hotel, the rosy dusk of the desert and the Atlas Mountains yawning before them. The great statesman had explained the medicinal benefits of mint tea along with the secret to understanding the French. "We should not be offended that they hate us," Churchill had told the count. "The truth is, dear boy, they hate *each other* far more."

At the Metropolitan Museum, the count instructed Alice on the subtle differences between the cornflower and periwinkle blues of the Fauve painters, then escorted her to tea at the Carlyle. Having briefly served time in this establishment as a headwaiter in '49, he now ordered smoked salmon sandwiches and Dry Sack sherry with great revelry. Naturally Alice's mother objected to this liaison. Fortunately by this late date, the spring of 1968, Mrs. Wilder was temporarily consumed by a sweeping though platonic passion for her tango instructor.

Stroking his faded mustache, one of his yellow eyes

swiveling like a watchful condor, Grandfather, a little tight, regaled Alice with salacious tales of women, forgetting no doubt that she was of the same gender. Recently he had met a charming if slightly faded "jewel" in her fifties. Their affair had been steamy and satisfying until he had met her daughter, a topless dancer in a bar frequented by aging leches such as himself. Realizing her magnificent breasts "wouldn't last two years in a job like that," the count rescued her, after which the grateful girl thanked him in the only way she knew.

After six months of sleeping with both mother and daughter, he was suddenly "inexplicably repulsed" by his behavior. Feeling that his soul, if not his blood pressure, was in grim danger, he broke off with both. "Even though men are incapable of sexual fidelity, you must search for love at all costs," he told Alice. And then, as if to counter this absurdity, he added, "Disregard my last remark if you plan to live *here.* This is a country that kills its young, its own *presidents,* for God's sake. You know what love is, in this garbage pail of a city, this sewer? Love is a *poodle's chance in hell of obtaining happiness!* As soon as you are old enough to leave your poor, disappointed mother, we'll move back to Paris. With me you'll see life in the raw, kid!"

Like a girl taking a summer course from the Marquis de Sade, Alice listened with total devotion at his elbow. When she was sick in bed, he brought her library books (stolen some decades previously according to the date on the flap): Flaubert, Brontë, Faulkner, Céline. "You are never too young to learn about women's insatiable and irresistible desire for their own destruction," he said, ordering her to study these classics thoroughly. "A gentleman realizes this and makes it his mission in life to save them."

A gentleman savior. How could she not be swayed by such romantic possibilities? But what did this have to do with her mother's search for Position and Wealth and the men who only understood *the deal?*

"You'll go blind, reading in that light," her father would shout from the corridor on his way to bed. Alone in the sanctity of her tiny yellow-walled bedroom, her heart racing with Emma Bovary, Alice dared imagine her own metamorphosis. Under the guidance of her grandfather, she saw herself emerging spectacularly like a snake out of its skin, bound for greater destinies than her shortsighted parents could ever imagine. Then came the tragedy.

In the autumn of 1968, Count Alexis Plemianakoff was arrested in Macy's handbag department for shoplifting. A gift for a lady friend, he offered as a defense. Even though he was released on bail, the humiliation and stress of being temporarily incarcerated (he fought two cellmates bare-knuckled until restrained) caused him to suffer a heart attack the next day. Clutching his chest on Madison Avenue, he managed to hail a cab for the hospital, where he died several hours later.

The blow was unimaginably severe. Alice, convinced her world had collapsed, wept in her room while her father comforted her mother. But how dare her mother cry; it was *she,* Alice, who had loved him the most. Night after night, she moaned in her sleep but no one heard. (Or perhaps she imagined this, perhaps she only moaned in the daytime.) "It's your fault he's dead," the distraught child hurled at her mother. "You abandoned him. You never liked him. You refused to let him come and live with us." So awash was she in her ruinous loss that if someone had lain a protective hand on her, she would have bitten it off at the wrist.

"Don't take any notice of her!" shouted her father as his wife ran weeping to the bedroom in search of aspirin. "Our little girl is just upset."

"Well done, you noticed," said Alice, scowling like a

six-year-old. "Do you *know* why mother never liked him? Because he was broke. He didn't care about *money*. He was a dreamer, a free spirit . . ."

"What? Why are you behaving that way?" her astonished father wanted to know. "Don't joke, baby, at a time like this."

"I'm not *joking*. And don't call me baby. I'm not a baby *anymore!*"

More tears. Howling. Doors slamming. "I hate you all. I hate you. I'm going to *kill myself*," said the spiteful child bent on her own destruction.

Two weeks after Grandfather's death, she was still putting her parents through the wringer. Her mother either wandered round the house like a zombie or was bent over a tisane in the kitchen, staring morosely at the wall. Alice did likewise. And when her father came home, what had become a daily routine of skirmishes started up again.

"Look, would you please stop moping. I think you're doing this to torture your mother."

"Why can't I be in mourning too?"

"Don't be dramatic. He was eighty-nine years old. He lived a great life, although, let's face it, the man was more or less a criminal." Without having raised his voice, he collapsed into his leather chair to watch a game on TV. A great lover of sports, he boasted he had voted for Nixon mainly because of this mutual passion. Alice, overly tall in her hip-hugging pinstripe pants, stared down at him, trying to bore a hole through his forehead. "And could you please make yourself presentable?" the doctor said, eyes never leaving the set. "Put something *decent* on, for God's sake."

These were the days before parents worried about a child's self-esteem, self-worth, and precious individuality; days of throbbing music and terrible clothes, the sixties horror of wearing everything *and* the kitchen sink. Alice, more conservatively but to equally annoying effect, dressed as much like a boy as was possible (not any boy, but James Dean—likewise misunderstood and her hero). Pain, isolation, loathing, and persecution were the order of the day.

"You've upset your mother again. What are those? *Men's shoes*? Take them off."

"I like them."

"They're ridiculous, you happen to be a girl."

"*Woman*," Alice replied indignantly. "And in case you didn't know, schoolboys in Sweden now study needlework and homemaking and girls take courses in car repair. Everything's *changing*."

"I don't care. Take them off."

"It's not *fair*."

"No, life is *not* fair. You might as well get *that* straight right off the bat."

But this was not what brought her parents to a state of exasperation. That incident came a few months later.

"It was a Monday afternoon, the streets lashed with rain . . . ," Alice wrote in her journal in an effort to bare her soul. Sheltered from the downpour, she had been standing in the fiction corner of the Unicorn Bookstore, leafing through a hardback of *Of Time and the River*. She was wondering if she, too, had "the hunger and urge of the Creative Artist"—the description of the book's hero on the flyleaf—when a man brushed against her. He was tall with thinning corkscrew hair and a morbid look on his sunken face. About as cuddly as a vulture.

"Grossly overwritten if I might say," he murmured with a terrifying calmness. Then he ran his hand over her fringed Lone Ranger jacket, purchased at a nearby thrift shop, as if he were selecting a bolt of Harris tweed for a new sports jacket.

"Oh yeah, and who the hell are *you* to say?" Alice shot back with her brash teenage audacity, bred of recent desperation.

He told her. Robert Tarkington, a professor of modern literature at Columbia. His hobbies included windsurfing, cooking, traditional mime, and Shakespearean myth analysis. Currently, he believed that Elizabeth I was responsible for at least two of the Bard's plays. For some reason Alice was impressed. He had a hallucinating if somewhat repellent quality that not only fit right into her desire to squash the memory of her grandfather but might also, she hoped, terrify her parents. "Come with me," the professor said, and led her like a tame spaniel to the paperback section. Here he pulled out an assortment of Henry Miller, then, a few paces down, *Lolita* and *Story of O.*

Nothing happened. "*Nothing happened!*" Alice screamed at her mother, who waved the incriminating piece of paper. Mrs. Wilder had come across the billet-doux slipped between the pages of *Tropic of Cancer*, the book lying hidden under Alice's dresser. "You came across it?" Alice demanded to know. "How? On your hands and knees?" The note, written on Columbia University stationery, laid out a few lines of Lord Byron's *Don Juan* followed by a saucy postscript from the professor's own imagination. In an effort to keep up with the tyrannical demands of current fashion, her mother, silk jabots and trailing scarves, was looking more and more like a music-hall coquette. Pale-faced, she announced she was "frankly, at the end of her tether" and demanded the lurid details, otherwise she was going to call Dr. Tarkington himself.

Alice hesitated between the urge to deceive and the need for confession. Finally, rather cockily, she ran through an abbreviated list of their secret rendezvous: a civil rights rally in Central Park, a poetry reading in SoHo by Rod McKuen—"who's brilliant, in case you didn't know"—and a matinee of

Performance at Cinema 5. She left out the Saturday afternoon at Dr. Tarkington's Greenwich Village cubbyhole. Here, imperious and commanding, he had sat in a gilt chair and read passages aloud from *The Alexandria Quartet*, while Alice, spellbound, crouched close by on a tiny deerskin stool and furiously smoked Gitanes. She was in awe until he led her into the kitchen and, bending her over the sink, crushed his red brocade waistcoat against her rib cage and frantically tried to remove her underpants, whispering, "Beauty calls and Glory leads!" At this point she had run downstairs and escaped into the street.

And not because the idea of sex terrified her, nor because her attraction to the forty-year-old professor was zero. No. She escaped because she had suddenly become a participant in the *game*. It was a revelation. The hold a girl had over a man when he liked her, loved her, *wanted* her. Could her mother possibly be right? Was this what she had meant by *power?* Whatever it was, this grown-up attention gave Alice a sense of euphoria she had heretofore never possessed.

Her mother called the dean of Columbia immediately and informed him that one of his professors, "a subversive, a child molester, and most likely a Communist," had tried to seduce her fifteen-year-old convent-educated daughter. The professor was suspended. And because of Alice's scandalous behavior, she was slated immediately for Dr. Arnold Fleishman's therapy couch. It was a practice her grandfather had rigorously scorned as licensed buffoonery, handed down from that snake charmer and drug addict Dr. *Fraud* (whom he had met, thank you), a man the count said encouraged people to wander around in packs, groaning like oxen about phallic symbolism, and a theory that Alice in her loyalty echoed triumphantly at the dinner table—but to no avail. Her mother washed her hands of her. Apparently, when it came to men, Alice was doomed.

That night, perched on the sill of her bedroom window, Alice decided to end it all. Grandfather gone, Dr. Tarkington gone, and all sense of her budding identity gone with it. She would embrace the vast all-encompassing nothingness. Lately she had barely been able to stand on a subway platform without her back pressed to the wall for fear she might throw herself in front of an oncoming train. Death would now be welcome. Sound the trumpets. Aschenbach dying against the stone fountain in a squalid back street of Venice. Alice (not quite so poetically) soon to be sprawled on Mr. Bradshaw's flagstone terrace three floors below, where all summer the arch conversation of his intellectual outdoor dinner parties had wafted up and bored her late into the night. Of course, she would write about this. But how? How could she if she were dead? And now that she thought about it, wasn't suicide a mortal sin, a blasphemy against Gentle Jesus? Hell and damnation awaited her. Instead of death, why not *real* freedom? Escape. Simply walk out. Suddenly her desire to run away was overwhelming. To get rid of the child she had been, to leave *herself* behind.

But in reality, her escape came three years later when she enrolled at Sarah Lawrence. Here she distinguished herself not so much in Modern Literature 101—Melville to Pynchon—as in the student protest marches and stolen afternoons in the forest smoking marijuana. After that, she moved into her own two-room apartment downtown on Tenth Street. But for some reason she was still not happy. Wasn't living fifty-seven blocks from her parents distance enough? (And yet living there had never seemed *close* enough!) How far did a person have to go? Did Neil Armstrong, spinning around the globe in *Apollo 11*, feel he had finally *gotten away from it all?*

≈

Three days after their initial encounter, Oscar called Alice at the paper. She was at her desk.

"Hello, is that you?"

Alice recognized his brash, boisterous tone immediately.

"Yes, hello, it's you."

"About lunch," he said.

"Oh, yes," she replied casually, as if this were something that had slipped her mind. Then, in case the entire editorial floor sensed her discomfort, she shifted her chair toward the window. Down on Spring Street, four floors below, a bum, his head a mass of matted cornrows, sat on the sidewalk and fried in the midday sun.

"Well, the problem is," Oscar continued, sounding a bit regal, "I'm shooting."

"Yes, I know."

"I'm exhausted," he went on, then with an exaggerated groan, "Christ, do you know what it's like having to talk to actors all day?"

"Somewhat," replied Alice. Out of the corner of her eye, she could see Cameron Fischer watching her as he sucked on the end of his Mont Blanc pen. Purposely, she crossed her legs and gave him some thigh. But he turned away, as she knew he would.

"Shall we risk it?" she heard Oscar say.

"What?"

"Eating together. Lunch?"

For a moment she didn't reply. In the background, on Oscar's end, she could hear high-pitched Hispanic voices and the rattle and whir of a Pac-Man game. For this call the director was using the safety of a 7-Eleven phone. "Listen," she said finally, "perhaps when you've finished the movie we can, . . . I mean . . . under the circumstances, well, it might be better . . ."

She floundered on, all the while thinking that she couldn't wait to hang up. Then somehow she must have done *just that*, because the instrument was no longer in her hand. Instead, she was staring down at Spring Street. The bum was there, sitting contentedly; it was Alice who felt so inexplicably out of joint.

What was it about Oscar, she wondered, that was so unnerving? A man she had known for only a few minutes. Was she, in some wave of adolescent insecurity, drawn to him simply because he liked her? No, *appeared* to like her. And why pursue this, anyway? Didn't she have enough on her plate as it was?

Because, when she had left her husband six months before, swearing allegiance to celibacy—if necessary a lifetime as a recluse, a Carmelite nun—she had almost *immediately* found another man to help shoulder the blame for her misery. Though careful all these years to suppress her own emotions, she nevertheless required a constant return of love. To be loved. Selfishly. Of course, it was possible this need was actually a mawkish quest for the same old thing. Romance!

In her early twenties, before she'd left New York, Alice had briefly turned herself over to an Englishman, Kevin Humphries, an impeccably mannered man almost twenty years her senior. Not only did he represent the intellectual superiority of the mature man—those gods, those arbiters of taste like her grandfather, and, to a lesser degree, Dr. Tarkington—but he also claimed an even loftier ledge as a *writer*, if only for television. With his velvet jackets, flowing hair, and a worldliness unfamiliar to the tiresome acid-headed boys of her age, Kevin provided her with an idyllic romantic figure as well as a platform to air her spontaneous wit. The affair blossomed on airplanes: to London for the Henley Regatta; to Siena for the Palio in August; then back to New York, where he was scripting an epic about Florence Nightingale and the atrocities of the Crimean War. (Kevin claimed to be one of the creators of the great Movie of the Week phenomenon.) The liaison lasted a year and a half, then one day the romance died. There was no surliness from Alice, no display of emotion or bad manners; she simply left, seemingly unscathed, neither grief-ridden nor elated. And even though it was he who had thrown her out, it was *she,* in fact, who had rejected him. Why? Because even this aged cavalier had insisted, *finally,* on scratching beneath that brittle and amusing surface, the one Alice (and her mother) had worked so hard to create. It was his interest in her hidden soul that had finally terrified her.

Since then the idea of a man penetrating her tricky inner self was something she feared, yet desperately desired. Occasionally, buoyed by the doctrine of the times, she convinced herself that she could manage her own redemption. How was a woman to progress if not by her own strength? However, so far she had lacked moral fiber. Too busy just trying to get through, she told herself. But she was always looking for that exceptional and dedicated somebody *else* to pry loose the secrets of her heart.

Oscar called her several more times at the office. She instructed the switchboard to take messages and ignored his pleas to call him at the studio. Though the idea of seeing him gave her a curious feeling of optimism, she fought it. Her mind was full of him, however, and when at night the image of his oddly fascinating face finally receded, she was alarmed to find herself trying to imagine his wife. The unknown woman rose like Aphrodite, growing tall and beautiful with thin thighs, thick lustrous hair, and perfectly manicured unused hands. His lifelong confidante, his mate under fire. And then, with a perverse leap, she visualized Oscar screwing Niki

Palmer in the upstairs bedroom of the house in Los Feliz, his hands massaging her yellowing violet bruises, his mouth whispering placating words in her ear to drown out the girlish screams. Alice's ex-husband, Walter, had often accused her (among other treacherous things) of belaboring the writer's supremely annoying habit: exaggeration. Not only was Alice anxious to wrap up the third act, but apparently she couldn't help inventing a glorious first and second to go with it.

In rebellion against her better judgment, she decided to call Oscar. After all, she reasoned, if she couldn't trust herself with a perfectly decent man now, in her glorious though marginally desperate prime at thirty-five, when *could* she? This was not Daniel being dragged blindfolded into the lion's den, for God's sake, this was simply lunch.

After a considerable wait, an assistant director brought Oscar to the phone. The young man had told her he was "getting Mr. Lombardi from his trailer," an image that, due to a lifelong reverence for the "artist," immediately served to humble the caller.

"Listen, I had a thought," she said quickly, as soon as Oscar picked up. "I know you're up to here with work, but how about next Saturday? An actress friend of mine, Jessica Bing, is away doing a picture in Yugoslavia. Her summer rental in Malibu is empty. I've never seen it, but it has to be relatively near water. Cool, refreshing. You could relax a little."

She had made the breezy speech without drawing breath. She heard her words vibrate over the wires and beyond that an impatient but respectful somebody shout Mr. Lombardi's name.

"OK," he agreed finally. "I'll bring lunch."

Surprisingly, the apartment building, built in the early sixties, was little more than a slab of unfriendly concrete on the wrong end of Malibu Road. The top half of this large gray box was cantilevered over the sand, while the lower half, supported by metal posts, served as an open garage for tenants' cars. On the upper story, in a faint effort to enliven the dreary façade, a jaunty fish motif and a sunburst of mosaic chips spelled out EL CHOLO VILLAS.

This unexpected ugliness, however, did not dampen the sense of euphoria Alice had begun to feel on the drive down. The shimmering ocean, the wide blanket of sheer blue sky, and the sweet smell of salt wafting through the car filled her with a sensation of weightlessness, a giddy freedom. Only when she let herself into Jessica's apartment did she realize her glaring error. While busy contemplating Love Burning Bright she had been driving fast and furiously toward Sex in the Afternoon. And nothing in the one-room apartment even remotely suggested the presence of her sophisticated friend, Jessica. The walls had been painted what could only be described as earthen—a sickly terra-cotta—while the furniture brought to mind fiery chemicals. A sulphurous green kitchen divider with matching stools was offset by a sectional sofa in phosphorous orange. Over against the salt-gummed sliding doors lay the futon bed. Once a heady tropical print of toucans and jungle foliage, its cover was now faded chalky white from overexposure to the sun—no doubt worn-out, thought Alice; a tireless slave to afternoon love matches. Except for the view, she might have been standing in a room at the Holiday Inn in Phoenix. But the green of the Pacific Ocean was deep and magnificent, like salvation at the end of a tunnel.

She found an old half-empty bottle of vodka in the freezer. She poured herself a glass and the liquid, ice cold and shocking, helped calm the inner turmoil. After all, a grown woman could surely stave off the sexual advances of a married man if she so chose.

Jessica, domineering and protective and a connoisseur

when it came to affairs of the heart, had a theory about Alice. That she begged for men to fall in love with her to bolster her flagging self-esteem so that, finally satiated with attention, bored but gloriously uncommitted, she could *move on*. And Alice would have been inclined to believe her, except that when it came to the subtle maneuverings of men and women, her friend had many theories. Soon after puberty, Jessica liked to say, men learned to dislike women. It wasn't the men's fault. Whereas European men were judged by how well they got along with *women*, poor American boys were judged by their relationships with *men*. So Jessica deemed it her mission in life to release them. A free spirit, she was dismayed at the eighties breed, the scorned females who ran in packs screaming of men's brutality. She was a true believer in the unrestrained sixties attitude toward sex. *Vidi, vici, veni—I saw, I conquered, I came*—was still her battle cry. This old-fashioned bravado struck Alice as daring, dangerous, and in its simplicity blazingly female. In a not so secret way, she aspired to be like Jessica.

She had left the outer door to the street open so that Oscar could find his way. Pouring her third vodka, she heard the crunch of wheels on gravel and posed herself as alluringly as possible against the arm of the shocking orange sofa. A minute later Oscar swept through the door. He was positively glowing with confidence, a bottle of Dom Pérignon tucked under one arm, a small paper bag in his hand.

"Christ, it's bright in here," he said, beaming boyishly and giving the room a cursory glance. Then he swooped into the kitchenette and took a tin of Sevruga caviar out of the paper bag. With a flourish he removed a box of crackers and two small napkins from his trouser pocket. "Hello there," he announced, arranging his booty on the Formica.

She noticed the small embroidered *Ls* in the corner of

the napkins. She wondered if he always kept a selection of linens (ironed at home every week by the Guatemalan maid) in the trunk of his car for afternoons like this.

"It's a furnace out there," he went on, busy opening the champagne. "On the radio they were talking about a brushfire in Topanga Canyon."

Such energy and ease. He was behaving as though they had known each other since childhood while Alice virtually held her breath to keep things on an even keel. "Oh" was all she could say. Then, aware of how peculiar she sounded, added, "Oh, well . . . champagne and caviar."

His cotton shirt had a small worn patch by the neck. There was a grass stain on the knee of his khakis. Nothing special here, she thought.

"I almost didn't come," he said cheerfully, opening cabinet doors in search of glasses. "These sorts of things usually end badly."

"What things?" she asked. By this time, they were both squeezed into the kitchenette. Alice opened the refrigerator in search of ice. Beating back waves of uncertainty, she allowed her face to bask for a moment in the cool air.

"Lunch with the improper stranger." He held two glasses at an angle and poured until the frothy liquid reached the top. He waited for Alice to empty the ice into a bowl for the caviar, then handed her a glass. "But I said to myself, 'Well, you've been married for twelve years. You never stop working. And you haven't had time to be friends with anyone . . .' "

Alice was about to speak, but the champagne had gone down too fast; bubbles were exploding inside her nose.

"You know," he said, clinking her glass, "I'm not usually very relaxed with women."

"Really?" she managed with a slight smile. They were

both leaning over the Formica counter. Despite the circles under his eyes, the messed-up good looks, the cynical, well-worn air, there was something decidedly youthful about him. Lackadaisical. In an attempt to match his nonchalance, Alice tucked the starched napkin into the top of her silk blouse and spooned caviar into her mouth as if she'd been doing it for years.

"Are you one of those men who likes to play pool with the guys and introduces your woman as the little lady?" she asked.

"No. But I spend all weekend in front of the TV watching sports in my underwear. What does that make me?"

"Familiar," replied Alice. They both laughed. For a second, their voices broke the stillness in the room. Then it was quiet again, and hot; a fly buzzed against a window.

"Your face is flushed. You look wonderful," he said, pouring more champagne.

"Terror brings a certain glow to a girl's cheeks."

"I mean you look beautiful."

And he might just as well have told her she was too tall or thin or stupid, for all the embarrassment she felt.

"I read the Niki Palmer piece. Thanks for all the support," he said. "I thought it was very well written."

"Really?"

"Yes. More champagne?"

Without waiting for a reply, Oscar took the bottle and both glasses to the coffee table. He sat on the floor, his back to the sofa, and waved at her to join him. Alice had already drunk far too much. As she let go of the counter, a wave of alcohol surged up from her stomach, and by the time she made it to the sofa, only with a stupendous effort was she able to lower her body with any kind of dignity.

"Are you trying to get me drunk?" she asked weakly.

"No, I'm trying to get me drunk, and I'm tired of doing it alone." Without warning, he pulled her down onto the carpet. Taken by surprise, she slid next to him like a freshly caught tuna, her face ending up an inch away from his. His forehead was sweating; the cynical smile was back.

"You have a nose that most actresses would cut off their right arm for," he said quietly. Then he kissed her. His wide mouth sucked her in like the tide. Her neck strained back, the muscles tightened in her throat. He pushed her body beneath him, trapping her legs under the coffee table. As his tongue plundered the inside of her mouth, the waves pounded on the beach—a thunderous roar that swept through her. Suddenly, abruptly, he broke away.

"Well, now we can relax."

Alice was lost at sea. Her mind blissfully adrift, her body not far behind. She was paralyzed by desire—or possibly by the wonder of being desired. Eventually, noises seeped back. The fly buzzing, the crackle of a twin-engine plane above the water. She wanted to say, *Look, we simply can't do this,* but instead asked, "How was it for you?" relieved that her voice sounded somewhat controlled.

"Unusual," he said, laughing.

"Unusually good or unusually bad?"

"Unusually worrying because I don't fool around. And I very badly want to see you naked." High above her, he was polished and witty while Alice, sprawled awkwardly on the carpet, was parched and exhausted, lost in a hot African wind.

"Well, that being out of the question," she said, rallying, "I'll light a cigarette, and we can get down to some serious conversation." She felt like she was in the sixth round of the one-liner finals.

"Were you ever married?" he asked. He was leaning back now in order to get a better view, framing this new vision of her against the blood orange sofa.

"Yes."

"Really?" He sounded surprised. "What happened?"

"Miscommunication."

By saying the word, she realized how calmly she had come to view her marriage. Could she be that drunk? Well, he had asked, so she might as well tell him. "We weren't honest. We never discussed anything. We lived in a permanent state of competition and hostility, carefully couched in wit and perfect manners. So that when I let the toothpaste run out or he left the toilet seat up for three days in a row, we attacked each other like animals."

For a moment Oscar stared at her. He looked mildly panicked, like a man who has just remembered an important business meeting somewhere else. He got up and walked to the window. The sun was low, burning orange in the already stifling orange and green room. Distant voices echoed from the beach below. Children were shrieking. Minute red sparks and cinders drifted across the sky. Someone was having a barbecue.

"So, he was funny like you?" Soothed by the view, he was smiling again.

"Not exactly. But let's say we outsmarted each other right to the finish."

"Did you leave?"

She was about to burden him with details: the letter, the silences, the betrayal. Because Oscar had that captivating quality—or was it cunning, perhaps—that made her want to tell him everything. But she held back. "Yes. I'm afraid to say, I did."

"What about the guilt?"

"I had enough for a whole army. Maybe deep down I'm Jewish."

"You don't look very Jewish. But then you don't look much like a writer either."

"Thank you," she replied, not exactly sure if she should be pleased.

She stood up and went over to him. Hands in his pockets, staring out to sea, he reminded her for a moment of her ex-husband. Walter was shorter, stockier, with sandy hair and a ruddy Irish face, but he had the same distracted sulkiness while gazing out of windows.

"I'm Jewish and Italian," he said finally, "so I suffer from guilt and shame."

He was looking at her benevolently. "I like to tell this to women so they'll think back and forgive me later on."

"Which women?" Alice asked. "Niki Palmer?"

Oscar was silent. He had a look on his face usually reserved for backing out of motel rooms. Alice hoped she was smiling, but she couldn't tell. Somehow, seconds before, she had slid down onto the futon, still alert, still casual, but obviously dead drunk.

"Is it my imagination, or is it hot in here?" he inquired.

"Roasting," she replied, relieved to move on.

"Do you really think it's possible to stay friends when you split up with someone?" he asked. And as though suddenly wearied by the thought, he sat down on the futon close to her feet.

"When I left my husband, he asked if we could be friends. I said, My friend quota is full, so unless one dies or slips into a coma, I couldn't possibly take on any more."

"That's very amusing," Oscar remarked coolly.

"Yes," said Alice. She was watching him watch her. His left eye, slightly bloodshot, flickered.

"Do you always make a joke of everything?"

"No."

"Because if you don't take yourself seriously, no one

else will. And I like you just as much when you're not funny."

Alice felt the color rise in her already-boiling neck. Could this be true? Was Oscar, as they say, the Sir Galahad of her egocentric dreams? The knight-errant who would forgive her, wipe the slate clean, and reinvent her? A soul-stirring thought, which washed over her for a good fever-pitched minute, until the muted sound of his voice (How long had he been talking?) filtered through.

"You must have been an interesting combination of exotic woman and best friend to some men. Headstrong, winsome, and then these very beautiful, childish legs," he was saying from what seemed like a distance of several miles. By this time her shoes were off and one of his hands was sliding leisurely up the back of her thigh.

She was about to get up, to explain in no uncertain terms that she had to leave. But the alcohol had settled behind her ears like a swamp. Drowning, glassy-eyed, her mouth gurgling open, she imagined she might be hyperventilating. With her head thrown back across the edge of the futon, her right leg now floating in air, the humiliating thought occurred to her that Oscar could easily have picked her up by the heels, waved her outside the sliding doors, then dropped her from a great height, and she would never have seen it coming.

What did in fact happen next, *no one*, not even Alice with her terrifying imagination, could have predicted.

She remembered Oscar pulling her legs toward him, unbuttoning her pants quickly, expertly, while he covered her mouth in a slow kiss. As one hand worked across her back, the other slid under her ass and lifted her easily, as if she were just so much baggage that *had* to be shifted. She remembered trying to breathe in the hot, cloying, sultry air, her throat making small puppylike noises. And when the idea of *not* giving in to him crossed her mind, she heard Jessica's convincing words:

Look, there's no point holding back because, if the guy's bad news, you might as well find out right up front and not waste any time.

There was a smell in the room . . . What was it? Sex? Something organic, scorching, like burning rubber; even the walls appeared luminous, as if radiating their own steaminess. Alice sucked in her stomach, grateful finally that his shadow fell over her thighs. No woman minded being naked in front of a strange man—a whole room full of crazed, demented men—she thought, if her thighs were thin. Perhaps Niki Palmer's thighs were better? Perhaps not. Oscar's mouth slid over her breast, and she heard herself gasp. If it's going to be brief, if it's going to end badly, she told herself, so did a lot of affairs, and it's simply too late now to back out. . . . Above her, Oscar was panting like a giant terrier, not completely undressed yet, not as naked as Alice. And she thought: Is it better or worse than he imagined? Are my breasts too small? Then later, *afterwards*, when she would be trotting off to the bathroom (on tiptoe, to make her legs more gazellelike), would he glance up at the white span of her ass, turn away, and decide *once was enough*? His hand felt up inside her now, and with her head arched, neck taut, mouth dry, and the air as thick as soup, her breath came wheezing in short sharp gasps. The condemned woman ate ravenously, she thought; the tinkling pebbles of lust had turned into the almighty avalanche of wanton surrender. His face tangled in her damp hair, his chest burned hot against hers while their sweating thighs, knees, elbows, paws, gyrated—everything moving toward the actual but not yet completed *penetration*—when, suddenly, there was a loud banging noise, a furious pounding. Alice saw large black flakes, or was it small black *birds*, flying past the window. Then a voice whispered in her ear, "Stop . . . I can't do this. I just can't do this." She hoped, mercifully, it was her own sane cry for help until she realized it was Oscar's, pained and plaintive, like an agonized child. And something else was wrong. The sky was red, sparked crimson and black, and there was swirling gray ash now *inside* the room as someone hammered again, then shouted, "Anyone in there? *Is anyone in there?*"

Oscar leaped to his feet. There was the sharp, cracking noise of someone striking the front door with an axe. Now Alice jumped up. On the roof, water gushed above their heads, gurgling in fat streams down the window seams. Voices outside were screeching, panicked. Finally, the door gave way and like a tornado two firemen blew into the flaming orange room. Streaked with dirt, their slickers dripping, they stopped abruptly, staring in astonishment at the naked silhouettes standing by the window.

"The fire jumped the highway. Right down the canyon," one of them yelled.

The two lovers stood there cringing, silent and dazed.

"Jesus, didn't you know?" shouted the other fireman. "The whole building's *going up!*"

"I'm glad we didn't die in the fire," he said as they sat in his car. He turned on the windshield wipers and the paper-like cinders stuck to the blades.

"Yes, me too," said Alice, laughing a little too loudly.

"Imagine how bad it would be," Oscar continued, his voice full of wonder and remorse, "my wife reading the papers tomorrow and finding out I was with *you!*"

Alice was silent in her astonishment. Wallowing in a kind of Jewish morbidity, Oscar had just revealed something too absurd and too alarming to comment on: guilt from *beyond the grave!*

Even though they were now somehow bound by the

peculiar circumstances of their rendezvous, Alice was relieved they had been prevented from consummating their Lunch at the Beach. Unsullied, their intimacy (and the inevitable grief that would come with it) could be postponed. Perhaps indefinitely.

2

The first thing Alice thought when she saw Walter McKinley was that he seemed like a man making a monumental effort to conceal his boredom. It was in the summer of '83. He was standing on the terrace of the Beverly Hills Racquet Club, all English tweed and leather, his cheeks scrubbed, his stiff reddish blond hair watered down and parted to one side. He was strong and square-bodied, just like his father, the movie star George McKinley; but by some fortunate accident he had been spared the famous man's thin-lipped sneer. Instead, hovering just above the squared-off chin was a sensitive mouth now forced into a smile—suggestive, that warm evening, of the dutiful child who decades previously (at no doubt grander events) had waited out the grown-ups in order to sneak a quick smoke behind the garage. Though Walter was at least twenty-five years younger than the other guests—those on the downward slope, with surgically altered jawlines and bad hairpieces—he was present that night to celebrate the eightieth birthday of the veteran actor Raymond Gibson.

Because at that time Alice had made few friends in Los Angeles, she looked forward to covering what were deemed by other reporters as the lowly B parties. She wore her black satin cocktail dress with the spaghetti straps that a publicist friend at Fox had once remarked made her look like Ava Gardner. Consequently, she brought it out for every occasion. While waiting for someone to repeat the compliment, she would affect Ava's slit-eyed smile or throw back vodka gimlets with what she imagined to be a salacious laugh.

However, it being early in the evening, she stood gingerly by the buffet of iced prawns and crab claws. Fascinated, she was watching the relatively young Walter when into his halo of light stepped Raymond Gibson. He was tall, deeply bronzed, with a pencil mustache, and as wrinkled as a prune. While at a distance his white double-knit pants and navy reefer jacket gave the impression of a matinee idol in his fifties, on closer examination, the open Vegas shirt collar winging gaily over his lapels revealed the deep ridges in his livid brown neck and his bony, concave chest.

But he seemed in remarkable health. He played two sets of tennis every day, and the rumors of his legendary orgies with Errol Flynn still caused some of the middle-aged women to flutter at his side, only to reel back from the wave of Aqua Velva and cheroot smoke. Now, already a little drunk, he nimbly slung one arm around Walter, the other around tennis immortal Hector Chavez, who just then had emerged from the shadows. All this without disturbing the drink he clutched in a purple-veined hand—one of his famous Chihuahua Floats. In the old days, legend had it, Raymond laced the harmless-looking fruit drinks with cocaine and paraffin oil and slipped them to young girls fresh off the Greyhound bus. Later, while these nubile creatures drifted on their backs, drunk and naked in his Olympic-size pool, he would turn to the guys and say, "Look, Chihuahua floats."

Alice was thinking of introducing herself when Raymond waved, then beckoned. Rather self-consciously, she drifted toward him, one hand at her throat, the hint of a troubled heroine smile on her lips.

"Oh, hello, hello." It was Walter who spoke first. "May I introduce you to Raymond Gibson and Hector Chavez. And I'm Walter McKinley," he added, noisily clearing his throat.

"Very nice to meet you," said Alice. Hector softly repeated her name, his lips fluttering over her hand. Then Raymond angled in like a crane, teeth bared, treating her to one of his dazzlers.

"Hector and I go back a while," remarked Walter, in order to explain the unlikely friendship. "He used to give me tennis lessons in Malibu when I was a kid."

"I used to teach the boy a hell of a lot more than that," Hector said, laughing. With a tanned, powerful right arm, he crushed Walter around the shoulders. He gave Raymond a showy wink, then the two old jocks leaned back and cackled—the alcohol, cigar smoke, and saliva catching in their throats, their thin lips exposing acres of brownish gum.

Taking advantage of this jocular interlude, Walter grasped Alice's elbow and graciously steered her away, leading her down to a grassy bank by the clay courts. There, with old-world courtesy, he laid out his jacket for her to sit on. Walter had brought an open bottle of white wine from the bar and two plastic glasses. Except for the tinny wail of a Tijuana Brass number wafting down from the clubhouse, they drank in silence.

When Walter finally spoke, his voice was low and formal, with a precise lilt. "You know, you remind me of my mother," he said. He was staring at the nets or perhaps beyond that at the huge shadowy eucalyptus trees. "She died in a swimming accident when I was five."

"Oh, I'm sorry."

"My father died four years ago." In place of sadness, the memory produced a flicker of aggravation, which Walter made no effort to hide. "George McKinley, the actor. Did you ever see him?"

"God, yes, in lots of things. *River Run*, *London Skies* . . . and what was that great part with Maureen O'Hara, the thing in India?"

"It was Malaysia, actually."

George McKinley was famous for his suave gentleman roles, his impeccable screen manners, his diction, and his drunkenness. It was well known that he had almost strangled a young actress to death one night in his Jaguar XK 150 when she refused to perform oral sex at a hundred miles an hour on Mulholland Drive.

Alice lay back. Her satin dress slid halfway up her thighs and she decided to leave it there. Walter told her that he didn't have many friends his own age. He and his younger brother, Grant (one of the best assistant directors in town, he said proudly), had grown up with his parents' contemporaries, old drinking pals of his father.

In accordance with his heritage, he wore a gold watch chain looped across his vest and handmade English shoes. He told her that at the age of eleven he had been sent to Bishops Stortford, a British boarding school, a second-rate establishment where he got chronic bronchitis from the obligatory cold morning showers and the coatless five-mile winter runs across the Essex moors. Everything was said in the same soft voice, the words meted out slowly, as if he were explaining significant landmarks in his life to a foreigner. "When I got there, I refused to be a 'fag.' I didn't realize that 'fagging' was what they called new boys who were duty-bound to slave for the sixth form. Julian Farnsworth, a friend of mine, was made to sit on a prefect's toilet seat every morning to warm it up for him. Then he had to press out the creases in that morning's *Times* with a hot iron."

He was laughing. His big lower jaw was thrust forward while his shoulders rocked back and forth. He was athletic and outdoorsy—the magic of manliness, she thought. She imagined him smiling through family dinners, engaging in light banter about weather conditions, then politely guiding her mother by the elbow as she stepped into the hallway after the last fatal martini. Swift to open car doors, retrieve dropped napkins, or bend an ear to the schoolboy humor of her father and his medical jokes, all the while promising to take care of his daughter. It was everything she was afraid of and yet hopelessly drawn to.

They were married three weeks later under the arched trellis in the two-acre garden of his father's Beverly Hills house. The Tudor mansion had once belonged to Clark Gable and Carole Lombard, or Betty and Bogey, depending on whom you talked to. During the weeks leading up to the wedding she had serious doubts. She had not meant to marry, never meant to or even *wanted* to. But she thought it might be good for her: ennobling, decent, and more important, sane. Instead of perpetuating her role as the tyrannical child, for once she would do something *right.* Not only would marrying Walter—this beacon of social excellence—allow her to become the dutiful daughter, but, in a curious way, it might also provide her with a kind of longed-for independence. Independence without danger. Such were the wild delusions of a woman who had known her husband-to-be for precisely twenty-one days. Coolheaded, restrained Walter had told her practically nothing about his adult life except that, a year before, he had loved ("mildly," he admitted) a woman named Eleanor, who after a bad car accident had suddenly married someone else.

The wedding was small. Alice's parents came from New York, her mother decked out in a yellow silk Galanos number, bought on sale at Bergdorf's, with matching shoes, gloves, handbag, and a floating hat of immense proportions. At first, she had stood speechless, trembling at the thrill of Walter's celebrity heritage and Alice's glorious destiny. Soon, however, due to her roaring curiosity and a steady stream of champagne, the shyness melted. "Lovely, lovely," Alice heard her exclaim to Walter's brother, Grant, her thin voice rising skyward. Grant, the best man, had his brother's shiny apple cheeks and smelled of scotch and marijuana. He was bigger than Walter but just as tweedy and despite the fine weather wore a moss-colored vest under his gray suit. "Simply a perfect day," her mother cried, as she had done at least five times already, hands aflutter owing to the proximity of such famous guests. Not only Raymond but Alexis Smith, Rhonda Fleming, and Mel Ferrer with his slender wife were there, as well as many more of Walter's father's old friends.

And it *was* a perfect day. The sky was clear, the sun not too hot, and the ceremony mercifully short. Music washed over the terrace steps; a slight breeze licked across the swimming pool and gently lifted the women's skirts. Flattery, frivolous chatter, the exchange of kisses and handshakes as heels sunk into the mossy lawn, rolled for the occasion as flat as a polo pitch, and stretching like a lush carpet as far as the banana palms.

Alice's mother regaled a small band of unfortunates with tales of her daughter's own noble lineage and carefully structured childhood while her father, drunk too early and with watery eyes, put in a word for her inherited humor. Each claimed this magnificent advancement in Alice's life as a reflection of *that* parent's own influence and sparkling qualities. For once, Alice bathed in the glory, happy to reward her parents for their life of struggle but even happier to be owned, finally, by someone else.

Upstairs that morning, Alice's mother had presented her with a pearl necklace, three graded strands, each with a faint purplish hue, the pearl near the clasp no bigger than the head of a pin. The priceless piece had belonged to her grandmother, Tamara Yasnilovna (and, supposedly, before that to Catherine the Great). They were in the late Mrs. McKinley's room, the rose chintz bedroom overlooking the cactus garden. It had been left exactly as it was the day the poor woman died, her handmade clothes in the closet, six monogrammed silver hairbrushes lined up on the dressing table. Alice stood behind her mother. Sitting sideways on a mahogany stool, with pursed lips, the older woman applied another coat of Schiaparelli pink in a sweep of hand and wrist movement perfected over the years. Impetuously, Alice had cut her hair short for the occasion—a kind of late tribute to Jean Seberg—and expected the usual admonishments from her tricky mother. But no. On this blessed day, with words that clearly did not come easily, her mother said, "*Chérie,* you look angelic and *so beautiful.*" Alice hugged the tiny woman, who that morning felt more like a frail child herself. In return, her mother kissed her. "You're very lucky to have him. Try not to ruin it," she whispered. "And remember, don't talk too much. Rich men don't need smart girls."

Groceries arrived miraculously; cleaning was returned promptly; the pool man, the fence man, the Japanese gardener drifted in and out; and a professional in dazzling white overalls came once a week to "detail" the cars. Father's cars: a 1971 Bentley and 1962 Buick station wagon. Consuela, the housekeeper, ran the entire show. She had known Walter when he was in short pants and remembered the late Mr. George as the great stylish man he had once been. The master bedroom was a shrine to old George's seemingly inexhaustible appetite for clothes. There were fifty Hawes and Curtis suits, a double line of Lobb shoes, trilby hats from Herbert Johnson, Carroll and Company cashmeres, and several natty pairs of monogrammed silk pajamas made to order in Hong Kong. Every day, Walter wore a selection of these, even though he was not gainfully employed and had nowhere to go except downstairs.

Arriving from an uneventful afternoon at the *Recorder,*

Alice was constantly amazed to be standing not in a plain and simple home but in what appeared an elaborate movie set for *Rebecca,* so incredibly serene and magnificent was the living room: the antlers over the massive stone fireplace, the Steinway, the matching portraits of the regal Clare and George.

With the shades drawn to prevent the afternoon sun from burning up the Persian rugs, Walter would be sitting, pitched forward in his wing chair, notebook in hand, glossies of his father fanned out at his feet. Each photograph was more dashing, more fantastic: George's airbrushed profile in top hat, in rakish fedora, in pinstriped suit or doublet and hose. Here lay Walter's heredity. Nonchalance on parade.

"Did you have a good day, darling? Bit busy right now," he would murmur, meaning he had made some headway in his five-year struggle to write his father's biography. Rarely was he without a drink in his hand, his face aglow with the broad smile that since childhood had saved him from revealing any unnecessary emotions.

Just when Alice thought that the comfort of holy wedlock would safely enable her to reveal herself, it appeared that insofar as honest feelings were concerned, Walter was even more closed off than she. In fact, he might have been on another planet. What she had taken to be his adorable shy boyishness was actually the honest manifestation of an emotional *recluse,* a man who worried that any overt emotion might be misconstrued as soggy or weak-kneed. And by unconsciously mirroring Walter's civility, or blindly misconstruing it, Alice found that after only a few months her own humor had completely disappeared. She justified this, however, as a needed maturation. Marriage was a serious enough challenge, she told herself, without the wisecracks.

"Are you really *happy?*" she would inquire, interrupting one of his dinnertime reveries. To complete the fantasy of their fairy-tale life, they sat at opposite ends of a polished mahogany table, a smooth lake of uncertainty stretching between them.

"Of course, darling. This fish soup is incredible. Will you tell Consuela please *not* to move anything on my desk. Oh, and Charlie has a box at Del Mar this Saturday for the Derby, I thought that might be fun." A burst of fire across the divide; Walter smiling gaily, a hopeful look on his face, as the fourth scotch rose to his cheeks with a hearty flush.

What stopped them, at first, from discussing these silences, this life of majestic monotony, was their blazing social life. Walter hadn't lied when he said that his only friends were those of his parents. There was a gaggle of them: ex-actors, ex-wives of famous actors or dead directors, tired socialites, show-biz luminaries of yesteryear, all well over sixty-five and so jaded by their long uneventful days that when they were let out for an evening bash they frolicked like puppies.

•

"Come over here, dear, and let's get a look at you," said an excited Lottie Kasnar the first time she met Alice at Elsie Mayo's house, a ruined mausoleum with frayed tapestry-covered furniture and marble pillars in the hall. Lottie, a frizzy-haired former call girl and actress, now bejeweled and dazed, tapped her red nails against her highball glass marking time as Alice obligingly walked toward her. This attractive display caused Marshall Rawlinson to glide over, slipping a little on the parquet flooring. "I hear you're a writer," he remarked, disbelieving but in high spirits. An imposing man with milky eyes and a few strands of weedlike hair drawn across his large bald head, he was well known for his promotion of elaborate African safaris but more famous as a purveyor of young nubile boys. "You know, I've been thinking about doing a bit of writing myself, just never seem to have the time," he went on, puffing self-consciously on a Camel. "Leeds, old man," he shouted to his ex-lover, "here's some competition for you!" Leeds Arlington, the screenwriter, tight-lipped and with a permanent air of fatigue, waved but remained collapsed in an armchair by the bar.

With mouselike steps, a maid arrived at Alice's elbow offering nondescript things on toast, then the women—Lottie, Elsie Mayo, and Barbara de Cicco—closed in. They eyed Alice possessively, checking her expression for signs of gullibility.

"Oh yes, charming. Look at those cheekbones! George would have loved her," said Barbara, as she put on her famous diamonds (a gift from her husband, director Harvey de Cicco, now deceased). Though she traveled by limousine, she was terrified of armed robbers and kept the gems hidden in pockets her maid sewed into the lining of her dresses.

"Red or green?" she whispered, a hand disappearing into the folds of her dress.

"Red," decided Alice, mystified but anxious to join in. Whereupon Barbara extracted an almond-sized ruby from somewhere. She allowed Alice to admire it for a brief ten seconds, then whisked it away. She was a festive creature, however, who liked to amuse the crowd with stories of her Yorkshire terrier, Geoffrey, whom she had taught to pee standing on the toilet seat.

Finally Raymond Gibson arrived. To make up for his tardiness, he did a complicated buck-and-wing routine down the marble steps into the living room. Applause was in order, and Elsie Mayo, well in her cups, clapped the loudest.

"Have you *met* her?" Elsie shouted over to Raymond who had scuttled off to the bar to make something lethal. "Isn't she simply divine?" Then she whispered to Alice in her throaty voice, "Perhaps a little more lipstick, dear, and show some cleavage."

In an unconvincing display of youth, Elsie wore garish makeup and short skirts and drank like a sailor. She had a forty-two-year-old Spanish lover, Franco, who had spent countless years producing bad oil paintings of his mistress in various states of undress. Only those from her friskier days, however, were permitted to adorn the living room walls. Later in the evening, stewed to the eyeballs, Elsie would glance at her tanned boyfriend, raise a withered hand to her mouth, and groan for all to hear, "Thank God the only words he knows in English are 'OK, baby.' "

A black bartender carrying a silver tray of refills, ice clinking, was now silently gliding toward the group. Close on his heels was Walter, who had been discussing with Leeds a horse running the next day. As he approached, he was greeted by a chorus of "Our darling boy!" from the overexcited women.

Before Alice married Walter, he had been everyone's darling boy. As a single man, he was hungrily snatched up by ladies for opening nights and other galas. They loved him; they nuzzled him; they ran their birdlike hands across his tweedy back, barely restraining themselves from ruffling his hair. He complained mildly, but he loved it. At Elsie's, he leaned against the mantelpiece, one leg lazily crossed over the other, wearing his father's houndstooth-check jacket, his Mark Cross tie pin, the emerald cufflinks from Harry Cohn (recently discovered to be fake)—all this, without fear of ridicule from his contemporaries. He had no contemporaries. Marvelously comfortable here, he could pose in one of old George's roles: a leader of men, a hero in the trenches, John Wayne after sunset.

In the beginning, the women fawned on Alice greedily. Regarding her as a satellite to their star, they showered her with a litany of bons mots, all wet eyes and suggestive eyebrows. And in return, like an awestruck Emma Bovary at the ball, she smiled shyly, enthralled by their time-honored celebrity. But as these raucous evenings became commonplace (at least once or twice a week during the first flush of marriage), Alice found herself slumped back on the velour dining chairs, her interest piqued occasionally only by the flow of the Château Beycheville or Léoville Barton, which she drank in vast quantities in order to stifle her boredom. She imagined their vintage years might have provided some witty conversation, unique drolleries from a bygone era. Not so. With alarming bravado, they hung on to the remnants of their hazy youth by unloading their ghastly secrets. Soused to the gills, they unleashed it all.

"I fucked Walter's father, you know," Lottie whispered to Alice one night, leaning sideways across her sodden husband. There was lipstick on her teeth as well as a delicate sprinkling of cigarette ash floating on her vichyssoise. "He couldn't get it up unless there were a couple of colored girls in the closet, but he had the *nicest* manners in town."

"You see this scar? Open heart surgery." It was Barbara's gravelly voice, eyes gleaming savagely as her chalky fingers gripped Alice's arm. "I was the first woman to have her heart replaced by a pig. The doctor said my body was magnificent—like a twenty-year-old." With her glass tipped at a dangerous angle, she casually unbuttoned her dress to show Alice the vicious scar that ran down to her waist.

"A pig?" inquired Leeds, surfacing for air. He was listening to the end of some sporting event while he ate, a tiny transistor earphone screwed into his ear.

"My husband was a brilliant man. A great director. A genius consumed by his work."

"Don't you mean a pig's *valve*, dear?"

"He couldn't resist women. He liked to be blown under his desk at the studio while he had story meetings. It meant nothing, of course. He had a voracious appetite, like Picasso. A genius. Make sure the house is in your name, dear. Did you know that Marshall is buying up all of Rarotonga to make a theme park? Where the hell *is* Rarotonga, anyway, Marshall?"

"For Christ's sake, get me a whiskey. Whiskee, *por favor.*"

"OK, baby."

"More wine, Alice dear?"

"*Please.*"

It was horrible. Stupendously grotesque. And though Alice sensed a kind of dread permanence to it all, it was obvious that her husband, smiling across the table at her, was thoroughly enjoying himself. A man, she realized, she barely knew. In fact their life at home was conducted with the utmost courtesy. Like boarders in a small hotel, house rules of conduct were strictly observed. For fear of mutual inconvenience, they slithered around each other in the bathroom, then did the same in the long dark corridors, often a genteel fight ensuing as to who would let the other pass. In the evenings each graciously agreed to watch the better half's dreary TV shows, all in the name of something called good manners and *civility.* The house literally hummed with forced bonhomie. And if either thought of confronting the partner about this ludicrous and mutually exhausting behavior—days when they were practically splitting at the seams from tension—restraint was applied. They were both too desperate to *please.* With growing unease, something else occurred to Alice. Could it be that both she and Walter harbored similar longings? To meet a stranger, a liberator, who, instead of forced elegancies, would *demand* honesty, anger, intimacy—the real, raw, heartbreaking stuff? And perhaps this secret desire they shared was the *very thing* that had made them choose the safety of conventional marriage in the first place. A mutual fear of real life had landed them in this unnaturally even-tempered hell.

Did she love him? Unlike her father, who required only a ten-second glimpse of her mother's pale, suffering face to know "right off the bat" what love was, Alice could be sure of only one thing: She hadn't a clue. Down the road there were small glimpses of love. Stolen moments. Brilliant flashes they both clung to. But what really stopped Alice from leaving was the sacred institution of marriage. Although the ceremony had not been officially blessed by the church, in Alice's eyes (good Catholic that she was) "for richer or poorer" had always meant *eternity*, with the threat of damnation not far behind. And so with a kind of martyrlike relish, she decided to save the marriage. She would make it work, not only to create a better person of Walter but also, she imagined, to make a more worthy woman of herself.

In this spirit, she threw herself into domesticity. She fired the Japanese gardener and planted her own vegetable garden. She hoed straight lines for radishes and lettuce and tied snap beans to tripods of bamboo sticks. Consuela, formally a distant force in the dark area beyond the kitchen, became her new friend. They baked seven-grain bread and made beef Wellington. Consuela and Alice, the Flying Hernandos. They ordered new slipcovers, rehung paintings, and put fresh flowers in every room. Alice could do it all: career woman, cook, hostess. For a few months she wallowed in her perfect wifey-ness, until she realized that emotionally she was only a half step ahead of her mother, still anxious to serve, still desperate to be wanted by a man. "Now tell me what you did today, sweetheart," she would plead, like a parent inquiring of a sullen seven-year-old. "I will dear—later," came the muffled reply from her husband. The elder statesman, traveling alone (and going nowhere) in his wing chair, listening as he now did every evening to Wagner's *Ride of the Valkyries*—one more joyless blast across the same gigantic silence. Alice was suffocating. In the noiseless house, every room a rainbow of glinting glass cabinets, faded porcelains, and polished woods, she may have been living in Beverly Hills splendor, but she was dying in fin de siècle Vienna.

They went into therapy together. And here, suddenly liberated from his cool self, Walter rose to the challenge. He baited the therapist, Dr. Kellerman, then accused him of indulging in Freudian platitudes. Alice watched, close to awe, as Walter wove elaborate stories of horror, degradation, and cruelty about his father or grew mournful at memories of his mother in satin evening gowns, bending down to kiss him good-night. What a show! And this served only to whet the doctor's appetite. Like many members of the Beverly Hills psychiatric establishment, he was addicted to the plight of the celebrity family; he reveled in their mad inconsistencies. When, in front of Dr. Kellerman, Alice asked Walter why he seemed so reluctant to talk to *her* about this, Kellerman—the worthy professor in his old corduroys and knitted tie—was only too anxious to reply for him: "He's always been afraid, Alice, of getting too close to people in case they leave."

What the doctor did suggest was that they try to liven up their sex lives. By introducing a little more dash and daring, they might break loose those bonds by which they had so successfully curbed all displays of untoward emotion. "Open the floodgates," Kellerman had ordered, unable to suppress a smarmy self-satisfied smile, "and let a little vulgarity in." Frankly, Alice welcomed the chance. Like everything else of late, sex had dwindled to almost nothing.

However, in order to bring it back to a normal level, let alone raise it to the heights of something lewd or libidinous, Alice suspected it would require nothing short of a miracle.

One Friday night they polished off the last four bottles

of his father's 1966 Château Beycheville, and Alice, blind drunk, dared Walter to fuck her while she wore one of his mother's dresses. Not waiting for permission, she ran upstairs, slipped into a Lanvin ball gown circa 1953 (eau de Nil off-the-shoulder satin with rhinestones) and took him on the floor of the living room directly beneath the imperious portrait of the former Mrs. McKinley. Miraculously freed, the next evening, again drunk, and armed with two of old George's silk Sulka ties, Alice bound Walter's hands to the posts of the mahogany bed and commanded him to eat her while she sat facing south and smeared Vaseline on his genitals. "How much do you love me?" she howled. Wildness had overtaken her. She was the wicked teenager who had taunted Dr. Tarkington and who now made Walter scream as she lowered her mouth, packed with ice cubes, onto his penis. "More than you love me," he groaned. Still no straight answers. But he was enjoying himself.

He encouraged her (and she so willing) to crawl doggie fashion across the bearskin rug while with one of his father's riding crops (Asprey) he beat her until she begged him to stop. As they squealed and yelped around the room, old George—apparently a dab hand at this kind of thing himself—gazed at them from a framed eight-by-ten on the night table, one eye in shadow, one hand posed under the Brahmin chin.

Scampering like a squirrel at his feet, Alice cried, "I want you to be my lord and master," meaning, of course, that she wanted him to rise from the ashes and save her. Then, sprawled naked on the bathroom floor, she wanted Walter to be her slave and commanded him to paint her toenails fiery orange, but she changed her mind and blew him instead.

In the morning, still exhilarated, Alice tried to relive the drama or at least discuss it. "Weren't we awful and didn't you love it?" she murmured, head still deliciously buried in a pillow. "Hmm, interesting," Walter replied, nodding as though reviewing a slightly shocking piece of gossip about somebody else. Only from the safety of the bathroom was he able to confess that he had accepted these indignities merely to please her. Alice, crestfallen, and now a little guilty, suggested it might be better to do these things to please *oneself*. And when this remark was met with complete silence, she announced—actually, screamed above the roar of tap water—"Obviously, I'm the only one who has the guts to admit there was *plenty* of good healthy selfishness involved on *both* sides. Or should we just carry on being bedfellows in deception?" Finally Walter appeared in the doorway, robed, regal, the lower half of his face masked by a ripple of Dunhill shaving cream. "If you really want to know," he said gravely, "I did it because I *need* you and can't live without you. Not because I ever *wanted* to."

A cryptic admission. He had hated every moment.

So, on the theory that you can't have everything, Alice concentrated on her career, and their erotic excursion was put behind them. It was a few months later that Alice was promoted at the *Recorder* and given her own column. At first, Walter reacted with silent but bristling resentment. Clearly it was a tart reminder of his own failings. Then as the weeks went by and she worked less and less frequently at home, he began to criticize her about the day-to-day running of the house. It was with a prissiness and an unconvincing display of calmness that he informed her she was spending too much money on little things, on fashion magazines, makeup, vitamins, what he called "sundry items." How many boxes of Kleenex did she use in a week? he wanted to know. "*Four?*" He was aghast. She might have said forty. "Darling, how could anyone get through that many? Do you know what that adds up to in a year? For a grown woman, you have no concept of money." All of this spoken calmly through the bottom of a full glass of scotch.

But soon after that, he was lying in wait. As her car pulled into the driveway, she would first hear his authoritative voice, then see him standing red-faced at the front door. And as though he had spent his idle hours upstairs counting, he would blurt out, "*Shoes*, Alice! Who could possibly need so many pairs of shoes?" His lower jaw clenched tight, he reminded her of the small blond boy she had seen scowling into the camera on several pages of the McKinley family album.

"I can't believe this. People don't buy things because they *need* them," she yelled back. "And all women have a thing about shoes, in case you didn't know," implying, of course, that he knew nothing whatsoever about women and *less* about their habits.

She could do nothing right. Gone was Walter the elder statesman. Suddenly Alice, the disobedient child, was once again confronting her aggrieved mother. She had forgotten to call the exterminator, and a battalion of ants had invaded the kitchen and crawled into his jar of Dundee orange marmalade. "You may not mind, but I simply cannot live in this *squalor!*" The piano tuner had arrived for his biannual visit and no one was home. The tree trimmer, unsupervised, had cut "almost to the ground" the forty-five-year-old privet hedge planted by Clare on her darling son's first birthday. The walls were crumbling and it was her fault! "To be honest," Alice said—and she *was* being honest, the table manners now gone—"I've been too busy *working*. That's what I do every day, I go to work to earn money so that I can waste it any damn way I please. So that I don't have to dip into *your* precious capital!" she screamed.

But beyond his accusations, she was accusing herself

and wondering just why she was letting everything "go to seed," as he so quaintly put it. How could she save this marriage and why couldn't she make it better? She had tried every trick, every weapon—cajoling, manipulating, reasoning—and now she wanted to strangle him. She wanted to knock his head off, squeeze that ceremonious reserve out of him. Or late at night came the more romantic vision: a car wreck, an air crash, a terminal disease, and then perhaps—yes, finally, for good measure—she could hurl *herself* out of the window.

Because she felt Dr. Kellerman was unsympathetic toward her as a working woman ("No, this reflects your *own* feelings of unworthiness," he smugly corrected her), in desperation she went to a psychic. It was a hard ticket. He was courted by the movie industry, having predicted Oscar nominations, TV miniseries for out-of-work actors, and third and fourth husbands for grateful socialites. Mr. Salamba lived in a rented house on Electra Drive in the old Mount Olympus area of Los Angeles. That afternoon he was dressed in blue serge pants, a green iridescent Nehru shirt, shower thongs, and a soiled turban. "You have been living with your brother because you needed a brother, and you have walked through the forest of darkness together," he said in a furry Indian accent as his bulging eyes fluttered heavenwards. "Now you have emerged from the forest, and you want to travel into the sun, while your brother wants to go back into the shade." His voice gurgled salubriously, his tongue glistening a pale purple as it flashed across lips of the same color. They sat on cushions in the living room, empty save for the wall-to-wall shag carpet and a small shrine in the fireplace. Arranged on the altar were two grapefruits, a vase of tall, withered gladioli, and four beeswax candles. On the mantelpiece above, among several photographs of celebrities, Alice recognized an old shot of Burt

Reynolds, bearing the inscription *Heavenly, all the best, Burt*, although somehow the signature looked fake.

"So, my dear, you have to decide," he said. His accent had grown stronger and there now seemed a touch of Peter Lorre in his eye-rolling. "If you throw a bright rock in a pool, some people will say, 'How can you throw this brilliant thing away?' Others will wisely remark, 'See what beautiful ripples the rock makes on the water.' "

But Alice was incapable of throwing anything away, bright or otherwise. One Saturday afternoon she was in Walter's wood-paneled dressing room, a place she rarely ventured, looking for a tie he had mislaid in order to prove she had not foolishly left it at the dry cleaner's. And there, in the top drawer of his Biedermeier dresser, underneath a pile of initialed linen handkerchiefs and boxes of mother-of-pearl dress studs, she found a packet of letters and a photograph of Eleanor Gunn, the girl he had loved only "mildly." In sharp contrast to her horsey no-nonsense face, the letter Alice read (dated two weeks previously) was full of sweeping adolescent passion. After the salutation, "My dearest darling Walter," scrawled in elaborate green-inked loops, it went on to lament her failing marriage—less of a traumatic burden now, however, since her "glorious afternoon conversations" with Walter. Eleanor felt that she and her "most precious one" were actually the same person, with the same beating heart and identical longings. Queen Eleanor had dared herself, apparently while sitting alone in Pasadena listening to Wagner (yes, *Wagner!*), to dream the impossible: ". . . that you will never forsake me, darling, in the dark and terrifying night of my soul." Scott Fitzgerald in his cups couldn't have penned it better. Alice, dazed by the concept of her husband and Mrs. Gunn's mutual reveries, stood there for a full fifteen minutes. She was vaguely aware that outside Walter and Grant were playing tennis. The echoing *whop, whop* of the ball and the muffled shouts wafted up from the cracked court below. Alice had been avoiding Grant since he had remarked sourly that she drank too much. "No woman drinks that way for pleasure," he had said, more astutely than he realized; and naturally, in defiance, she had drunk more. The two brothers were hugely competitive in sports as in everything else. Alice went to the window and watched them. After a series of Walter's vicious backhands, Grant—as emotionally guarded as his brother—challenged his opponent in the only way he knew how. Within seconds, he peeled off his shirt. Quickly Walter did the same. Then, beefy shoulders thrown back, legs positioned in perfect Queensberry boxing stance, both stepped forward and took an almighty whack at each other. No worry here about the tricky boy-girl thing, the inconstancy of love, or the inability to conquer mountains. No, they were simply two healthy American boys standing up to be counted.

Alice realized she was no match. She left the letter on the bed, then, leaning out into the hazy afternoon sun, shouted the words she had been practicing for months: "I'm leaving you, Walter! *I'm leaving you* . . ." Not that Eleanor's note meant that Walter was sleeping with her; he probably wasn't. And the fact that this woman had climbed to the lofty height of confidante was perhaps a small thing, a minor defection for Walter; but for Alice, as a reflection of everything else, it was the last crushing blow.

3

In stark contrast to the twelve-room mansion, Alice moved into the Paradiso Hotel. A dilapidated place. Many a rock star had tried to kill himself here and some had succeeded, immortalizing the hotel, securing its place in the annals of rock history. Alone in her small room, her sense of jubilation seemed, even to her, quite astonishing. She took long dreamy baths. In the tiny kitchenette, she made tantalizing meals, tuna or sardine sandwiches for one, and ate them sprawled across the hard bed—her own bed! After midnight, she drove silently on the empty freeways, the dramatic shadows of tall palm trees flashing overhead. (Walter had automatically commandeered the wheel of the Bentley at night—arms high, racing gloves snapped on—while she sat beside him like a dreamy twelve-year-old.) Finally, she was free.

And all of this lasted precisely seventy-two hours. Suddenly the flush of exuberance was gone; guilt and depression overwhelmed her. She was convinced that by abandoning Walter she had missed her last chance at happiness and now, at thirty-five, she was *alone,* right back where she'd started. During her convulsive nights, transfixed by vintage Hollywood comedies on TV, her heart sank, the characters reminding her of Walter's smoothness, his old-world charm. Then it dawned on her. Secretly, she had loved him—no, completely *adored* him. The lost and abandoned boy. And because she was convinced that she had failed him *and* herself, one night, close to dawn, she picked up the phone to call him, to tell him . . . well, she wasn't quite sure what. After the first froggy hello, he was silent. Then realizing who it was, he shouted—*finally* he shouted, "Damn you, damn you, Alice, I don't want to discuss *anything!*" And she was reduced to tears again because the truth of it was that he had never called her. Not once in three weeks had her stoic husband ever made the faintest effort to contact her or to get her back. And who could blame him?

In her bleakest hour she dreamed of escaping to some idyllic place, a poetic haven. Except that after five years of marriage, she wasn't sure she had the strength to haul herself to an airport check-in gate without a *man* to carry her luggage. She stopped eating and increased her drinking, but as a pacifier the vodka no longer worked. At the paper her coworkers, particularly Cameron Fischer, remarked that she "looked terrible." And Leonard Lativsky, though sympathetic and cloyingly concerned during her unhappily married years, now faced with her sudden freedom, was fearful of some obligation on his behalf, and kept his distance.

One morning after another wretched night, she went to the Burbank Studios to do a piece on Truman Capote. He had a cameo in a thriller-comedy in which he played a wealthy recluse with an icy wit. She met the small pink-skinned man in his trailer. Not yet in costume, his own clothes had all the ebullience of a man whose optimism (or rather, irreverence) prevailed to the last. He wore a checkerboard green and pink sweater, and on his feet, one pink and one green shoe. He sipped something that he called his "tea" from a small thermos and smiled cherubically until she took out her tape recorder—whereupon he howled. He reminded her that a good journalist needed nothing more than a pad and a pencil. "I never used those damn machines, honey; it was all stored up here," he said, tapping his wispy-haired head. But a few minutes later, when she asked him how his latest book was coming, he announced that he didn't feel like talking anymore and wanted to get a drink. Frankly, she was too weak to argue and wanted one herself. So, strolling like two buddies, they went off the lot to a rib joint called Smokey Joe's. Here, at three in the afternoon, they ordered double margaritas. Capote spoke of love, friendship, disenchantment, and betrayal. Then suddenly sensing her malaise, he took her hand in his small chubby fingers, squeezed it, and said: "I realized years ago, honey, that once you love someone and make them show you all their secrets, their imperfections, their horrid little scars, they begin to hate you. True love lasts for about six weeks, then it's a slow death, dear. It's all scrambling around being nostalgic, trying to remember what the fuck happened those first few nights." Quickly he had gone from being sad to resigned. Now he was giggling like a schoolboy, noisily slapping the table for more margaritas.

The encounter, though in essence magical, only served to depress Alice more. She knew she would go mad if she didn't do something positive. Something for *herself.* So she sat in her dank bathroom at night—cooler here, farther from the pounding music in the next room—and tried to finish a screenplay she had started some six months before. The story, not uncoincidentally, was a lurid tale of a career woman's desperate search for romance. Absorbed by this task, it occurred to her that her longing for Walter was perhaps only pity for herself, and this might well be what people often mistook for "love." But none of this sobering insight stopped her from wanting to scream at the tile walls, "I am completely *alone* . . . ," because the reality of it seemed so daunting. It was hardly surprising, therefore, that the first man she ran across who could boast a thin coating of charm got her full attention.

≈

She was on her way back from the ice machine—a nightly hangout for the more distressed and disoriented rejects of Hollywood, to whom Alice could now add herself. Because this great institution was about to be torn down, the inhabitants wandered the halls till all hours exchanging sorrowful tales of nostalgia and woe. Deciding to go the long way back to her room in order to savor a quiet moment among the sago palms and the overgrown jasmine, she went down the gravel path leading behind the main building to the hotel bungalows. It was as she passed the side door of bungalow number 3 that a shock of icy water hit her bare legs. She let out a scream. Seconds later a young man's head appeared in the doorway.

"Oh, no! Christ, I got you."

Cradling an empty plastic ice bucket, the man pulled her quickly inside the bungalow into a yellowing kitchenette. It was not dissimilar to her own, seams of grime around the sink and a smoggy glaze up the walls. He held her arm to steady her, and wiped her legs with a towel. Silently he scrubbed at her thighs, up around her shorts, all in a matter-of-fact way, as if performing a brisk rubdown on a nine-year-old after a chilly swim. "Hold still," he commanded. And Alice, surprised and temporarily immobile, did just that, captivated by his thick tanned neck and the muscles working across his broad back.

"That part's dry," he said, slightly out of breath. "Can't believe I didn't see you. A bull's-eye."

Alice could hear people talking in the next room. She made out three young men in their early twenties. Two of them were slouched across a threadbare sofa, shoeless, feet slung over the arms, drinking beer, while a third—a thin, angular boy—stood flattened against the wall, his face ghoulishly lit by a tilted table lamp. He had a flaming thatch of ginger hair that began about two inches above his eyebrows, and his collarbone showed through his T-shirt. Dead-eyed, panicked, he drew in a breath, then blurted out: "Excuse me, ladies and gentlemen, if I could *please* just have a moment of your time . . ."

The young man in the kitchenette asked Alice to take off her moccasins. Fascinated, she obliged. He wiped carefully in between her toes, then placed her shoes inside the oven on the top rack. It was an old Coronet model, the burners rusted through.

"I think they'll dry with just the pilot light. God, I feel like a major jerk. How can I make it up to you? I'm Mike Pearce."

"Alice Wilder. You do a nice job of mopping up."

He was tall and shockingly handsome in that way that terribly beautiful women were: smooth pink cheeks, a delicate mouth, and lustrous wavy hair. So young, it appeared, there was not a mark on him. Only his eyes showed a slight steeliness from exposure to a less than perfect world. He seemed completely aware of his looks, almost bored by the effect they had on people, so that when he smiled—as he did at Alice, revealing, not surprisingly, a dazzling array of teeth—he quickly tossed back his head and shrugged off the whole thing.

Taking Alice by the hand, he led her into the living room. It was an airless recess, decorated in gloomy shades of brown. From the worn furniture rose the pungent smell of damp wool and yesterday's fried onions.

"This is Chris Summers and Ryland Willet, and the guy against the wall gasping for air is Josh Peterman," he announced.

"You'll see, my best is yet to come," shouted Josh.

"OK, guys. This fabulous creature has agreed to come in and rate your miserable performances even after I gave her a full frontal hose-down. An amazing sport. Gentlemen—the gorgeous Alice Wilder," announced Mike. He spoke the words with relish, as if each moment of his young life were a constant and delightful surprise to him.

The boys clapped. Josh groaned and Chris flopped forward in an exaggerated pose of surrender. Alice smiled back, only mildly embarrassed by the hearty introduction. Ryland, a sinewy boy with brooding eyes, looked Alice over. He was flirtatious for a moment; then, with a kind of invisible nod, he ceded her to Mike, the team captain.

"We're comedians," said Mike.

"Actually, we're all lawyers."

"Now that's funny," murmured Josh.

"Lawyers, not yet allowed to practice. We take the bar in February."

"We study, we cram. We have no lives," groaned Chris, his pink marzipan face bobbing over the back of the sofa.

"The only recourse to lighten our load is comedy. We're taking an extension course in stand-up. Tonight we're practicing monologues for the end-of-quarter exams," said Mike dramatically. And with a flourish, he placed a dripping beer bottle in Alice's hand.

"Hey, if you don't mind," interrupted Josh, "I'm losing the moment."

"Josh is ex–Wall Street, a casualty of the decade. Notice the two-hundred-dollar haircut and the deep shame in his eyes," Mike said, laughing. He sat on the arm of a chair and pulled Alice into the seat beside him. Then, as if she still needed steadying, he rested one of his square hands on her shoulder. The other he stuck lazily in the pocket of his chinos. Though bristling with exuberance, he was astoundingly calm. A man created for heroism and early death, thought Alice. Then speculating further, she guessed he must be at least eleven years her junior.

"So, I used to work at a Wall Street law firm," Josh said,

breathing hard, trying to pump up his voice. "I left because it stifled my creativity . . ."

"Insider trading!" shouted Ryland.

"Thank you. Actually, I had the Marie Antoinette approach to the market. When things got bad, I lost my head." Groans from the boys on the sofa. "Thank you," Josh remarked caustically. "So, now I'm destitute. I can't even afford to have lunch anymore. It's been dreadful. I haven't said, 'I'll start with a mimosa,' in over six months. All I'm asking is that you find it in your hearts to transfer some of your money market funds to my account. I'd be most grateful. Here, take this leaflet. It's called 'I Provided the Laughs in the Eighties.' It's for all you middle-income people I used to make feel good in the mornings. When you picked up the Business section and saw another one of us going to jail, then said—'Fuck 'em, they deserve it . . .' "

Alice was laughing, then was embarrassed to find she was the only one. Josh's front-row competitors, Chris and Ryland, were curled over their beers, stoically studying his every move, while Mike stared coolly at her. Then he straightened up. He tilted back his head, and like a sword swallower proceeded to drain his beer in one breathless gulp. The showy move was possibly to divert attention from his right hand, which—as though not connected to him—was sliding up Alice's bare leg.

"Cold?" he whispered, wiping a smudge of foam from his lip.

"No, not really."

But he pulled the old gray UCLA sweatshirt off his back and wrapped it round her knees anyway.

"You are so gorgeous, I'd like to eat you with a spoon."

And though it was clear he was somebody's polite and devoted son, the words were spoken crudely, almost indecently, his big thigh brushing against her arm. She noticed his pants were wrinkled and his socks were unraveling around the top. So unlike Walter, she thought, big and gangly as if he had grown in giant spurts. Josh was still rambling through his monologue as Mike's hand slipped down and cupped her left breast. It would have been easy to push it away. Obviously, he was merely giving it the sporting try. Instead, she gave him a look, an inquiring squint, to imply that she demanded good manners and at the very least an honest sense of enthusiasm. She was hoping that this ruse of sophistication might cover her boiling excitement.

". . . Maybe you didn't hit your wife that morning, you felt so good," Josh continued, red-faced and on a roll. "The dog ate your shoes, but you gave him a break. You stopped going to the shrink. You used *us* as an outlet for your anxieties. Don't you think we deserve something back? A thousand dollars? OK, say five hundred so I can at least take a girl to lunch at Le Cirque . . ."

Under the sweatshirt, Mike's other hand was already beneath her shorts, roaming the nether regions of her underpants.

Because her moccasins were still wet, Mike carried her to her room and laid her gently on the bed. Here, in a startling move, he whisked off her shorts and underpants in one go. Like a magician swiftly removing a tablecloth and leaving the dinner service intact. Then, before Alice had time to object, he buried his head between her legs. Stunned, she sucked in gulps of air, furiously trying to rearrange her breathing. It had been almost nine months since she and Walter had romped through one of their drunken brawls, and now here was Mike, the antidote to her gloomy life. Or perhaps, she thought, still making excuses for her behavior, her subjugation was an act of vengeance to prove to Walter (and herself) that at least *one* man still noticed her. Whatever it was, she felt giddy, almost virginal. It was a strange sensation, this unknown man's head pressed between her thighs, he so relaxed, she quivery but trying to breathe some mature serenity into the room. Presumably, he would not judge her as an older man might. No naked truths need be revealed. And though Walter's face swam in front of her eyes, she forced the image away, until the young gladiator, finally exhausted, fell back onto the bed.

"God, you're fabulous," he said, and kissed the tip of her nose to prove it.

She smiled dreamily, hoping he wouldn't notice the electric shock in her eyes. She was about to speak but again he became the magician—Houdini. In one swooping movement, he escaped from his pants, then sent the rest of his clothes spinning across the room. Proud of his sportsmanship and his thoroughbred legs, he straddled her, holding his erection for both of them to see. She closed her eyes and he lowered his body onto her chest; he was rock hard and slippery, hairless from waist to eyebrow. And when he kissed her, she felt as though she were kissing her own mouth. She felt smothered, yet soothed; her intrepid Don Juan had put her out of harm's way.

"Comfortable?" he whispered.

She nodded.

"Am I too heavy?"

She shook her head like a deaf-mute. His sudden gentleness was relaxing but seemed a touch impersonal, as though he felt obliged to nurse her through her frenzied submission.

Afterwards, they lay silently; he held her hand and smoothed her hair. A mosquito buzzed above their heads. He batted it away protectively.

"Been a long time?"

"What?"

"A long time since you've made love?"

She felt herself turn scarlet in the darkness.

"I think you needed it."

Alice was stung. Had it been that obvious? Had she, in some kind of sexual delirium, screamed like a banshee or even worse *thanked him?* But his smile, she realized, was not one of triumph. No, genuinely concerned, he was happy to have met her need.

Without being invited, he stayed the night. In the morning he brought her coffee and orange juice from Harry's café downstairs. With care, he tucked a paper napkin under her chin and arranged a pillow behind her head. Earlier that morning, she had stared at him in the white eerie light. Arms flung recklessly above his head, his face in repose, the skin tanned rosily like a baby's, he had looked even more angelic than he had the night before. Then at 7:15, the chiming Casio watch on his wrist sounded, giving him thirty minutes to dress and get to class.

Alice stayed under the sheets, which she draped seductively over her cleavage. She drank coffee and watched him, entranced. Gracefully and with incredible agility, he bounded back and forth from the bathroom to the bedroom, picking up clothing, flexing, showing off, removing the wisps of his beard with her throwaway razor, romping through his own wonderfulness.

"Look at you," he said, his shoulders filling the doorway. "You pale hunk beached over there. Of all the girls in all the cheap gin joints—who'da thought I'da run into you, you big babe."

"Bogart?" she inquired.

She was smiling, despite an odd feeling of embarrassment. Was it for him or for herself? Or was her discomfort due simply to a lack of familiarity with these plucky boys in their twenties?

"You guessed," he shot back, beaming. "I also do a great Ronald Reagan." Whereupon he lapsed into an rambling parody of the old cowboy himself. His self-confidence was dazzling. In fact, his unflagging youthfulness made Alice feel desperately used up, soaked with too much experience. Unlike her, Mike was too young to have experienced failure anywhere. He was all playfulness and hope. When she squeezed past him in the bathroom, he trapped her sportily against the sink. "Hey, c'mere . . . ," he said, hands grabbing her waist. He was casually staring at her bare ass, the look neither approving nor disapproving but almost clinically *interested.*

"So I take it you don't live in the hotel bungalow?" she said, reaching for a towel and quickly checking the mirror for crow's-feet.

"Josh lives here. I live in a swamplike hole off Olympic, with sock balls on the floor."

"And you really want to do stand-up?"

By this time, he was bent over, scrubbing away at his teeth with her toothbrush. With a noisy gurgling sound, he swished the water around his perfect mouth.

"Maybe I have the need to humiliate myself," came the watery reply. "No, seriously, folks, *seriously,*" and for this he raised his torso to its full height. "I *do* think the lawyer-comedy material complements each other. There are certain principles of timing, the right pause, the lilt of your voice, that are as critical in comedy as when you give a summation. You're trying to persuade a jury, or you're trying to make them laugh—to get them on your side. And of course, comedy is a great training ground for *tenacity.*"

A mustache of white foam rode his upper lip. "I think tenacity is the key to show business, maybe to life, don't you?"

He was serious. The look on his face was one of banal expectancy, like a dog with a new ball. The assumption that if you worked hard, life flew by without anxiety.

Wrapping the towel across her midsection, she went back and collapsed on the bed. He followed her, then sat down, his back to her, in order to pull on his thick tubular socks. "OK, here's a joke," he said, lifting each muscular leg easily. "A young guy with an older woman, not that you're old, but you know what I mean."

"I know what you mean."

"So the joke is: The woman asks the young guy, 'Where were you when Kennedy died?' And the young guy says, 'Oh no, you mean—*Ted Kennedy is dead?*' "

He collapsed with laughter and fell back onto the bed. His head landed above her right breast; his exquisite face was positioned directly below her nostrils. Saddled from childhood with puffy eyes that left her blind till lunch, and dazzled by the harsh morning sunlight that now cast a sickly pall on her skin, Alice suddenly felt like Vivien Leigh in *The Roman Spring of Mrs. Stone.*

She turned her head and threw a leg seductively over his pants. "Well, you're very funny," she said.

"Thanks. But do you know what I'd like to do right now?" he murmured soothingly, once more the insatiable lover. "I'd like to hang you by your ankles and eat you one bite at a time." And choosing to ignore her blank expression, he crawled up under the towel and proceeded to lick the inside of her thighs. After a moment his head reappeared and he said, quite seriously, "You know, you have remarkably little cellulite for a woman of your age."

"Really," she replied, straight-faced.

But he was already bent over putting on his shoes. "Got to run," he groaned. "I've got Corporation Law. Third-party bennies." And with that, he jumped up and bounded out the door, limber legs flying.

She considered this interlude in her otherwise solitary life a one-night—at most, perhaps a two-night—stand. A delightful diversion that would temporarily prevent her from moping. So she was surprised when their wild nighttime thrashings continued, and soon Mike was coming over once or twice a week, whenever he could get away from his bar review course. Though often passionate, Alice happily assumed the basis for their relationship was one of mutual camaraderie and sexual convenience. Even so, she experienced flashes of loneliness, a hollow sense of dread that rose up as he dozed contentedly at her elbow. Like all innocents, he had a knack for passing out the moment his head hit the pillow, even though he insisted he needed the television on all night to ensure sleep. He had grown accustomed to the sound, he said, using it to drown out the roar of traffic in his cramped one-room apartment on Pico Boulevard.

He was happy to do the dishes piling up in the sink, load the washing machine, run out for Chinese food, and then slavishly rub her shoulders until she whimpered like a puppy. Beer in hand, he liked to sit on the end of the tub while she soaked.

"My father's much older," he explained, as if striking a comparison. "He was with the OSS in World War Two. He liberated the famous restaurant La Pyramide just outside Vienne. He was privileged to eat the first liberation entrée—tournedos with béarnaise sauce and *pommes dauphinoises,* I think. Followed by a perfect crème brûlée."

So the love child knew a thing about food. He had his

standards; he was soigné to a point. More justification, she thought, for their charming affair.

"Your accent is very good. My mother would like you. Her eyes get moist when anyone talks about French food."

"Mothers do like me."

"I bet," she said.

"Are you going to get a divorce?"

"Eventually."

"Good. I'll be your lawyer."

Then during one of these charming tête-à-têtes, he would suddenly leap to his feet. "The new Elvis Costello? Have you *heard* it? It's incredible, it's so *cool.*" Bursting with excitement, arms out, feet sliding across the linoleum floor, he would belt out a chorus, lost in his fantastic and innocent world.

If being with Mike was like spending a few weeks with a foreigner, it was to her advantage not to labor on the nuances of the language or the peculiar mannerisms. With growing fascination, she watched what was for her a new breed of man: terrifyingly domesticated, respectful of women's rights, and so *positive* about life. Although sometimes she felt that his high spirits had little to do with her, that possibly she was just the kind of mirror image he required in order to play his dashing part. But so what? Wasn't she benefiting too? "Beautiful . . . skin like a teenage girl," he would murmur (something she imagined he knew a thing or two about) as he vigorously rubbed moisturizing cream into her arms. She was appropriately flattered and soothed. Because, having lived for so long in voluntary exile and influenced more than she liked to think by her mother's all-pervading dogma, she was still under the illusion that, without a man, a woman didn't actually *exist.*

≈

After four months at the Paradiso, she rented a house in West Hollywood. A small bungalow, it was classically Californian in the Spanish tradition—dark and boxlike, with the requisite stucco arch over the front door. Julio, her new landlord, was an odd-looking specimen. His pudding face, almost comically wide, was colorless, with oversized eyes and a button nose belonging to a boy twenty years his junior. Though broad-shouldered and muscular (some of it, admittedly, running to fat), he walked with a deliberate old man's shuffle. Later, however, as Mike and Alice carried her two suitcases and thirty-four boxes (mainly books) into the house, Julio's dragging gait was gone. In fact, he appeared almost magically, popping up a touch breathless in their path. "That shelf is broken," he warned, barring Mike from unloading Alice's stack of first editions. Then, minutes later, springing from a closet, he announced, "Plenty of space in here, though." Finally, he planted himself at the entrance to the living room, arms outstretched. "Careful with matches here," he yelled, grinning wildly. "Possible gas leak in the heater. But we'll be fixing that *pronto*."

He wore a loose tie-dyed shirt, frayed jeans, tooled leather boots with spurs, and a battered cowboy hat—which he informed them had belonged to James Dean. "The one he wore in *Giant*." Though presenting himself as an old hippie, complete with stringy ponytail, his odd demeanor suggested something more interesting. As though he had never consciously succumbed to any such vintage trendiness, let alone considered moving *beyond* it.

He owned three bungalows on the wide, weed-strewn lot. Built in the twenties, they each had two tiny bedrooms and a screened-in verandah, which Julio rather wistfully referred to as the "lanai." The larger bungalow, the one directly across the yard from Alice, was inhabited by himself.

As the unloading continued, Julio busied himself in the garden. Wielding an old hose, he watered a greenish mass inside a ten-by-fifteen-foot construction of bamboo poles, strung with shade netting across the top. From the peculiar way his eyes scanned the sky, presumably for helicopters, Alice suspected the structure housed his marijuana plants.

During the rest of the afternoon, Julio seemed completely absorbed by his garden activities. However, when Mike and Alice finally threw themselves on the bed, their backs breaking from their four-hour struggle, he suddenly appeared at the window, hose in hand. Under pretext of dousing a few rusty geraniums growing outside her bedroom, he flushed a shattering cascade of water across the pane—the noise so startling to Mike and Alice that they sprang off the bed, shrieking like nine-year-olds.

When Mike finally roared off in his 1969 Pontiac GTO, Julio came over and stood beside Alice in the driveway. "Decent car, needs work," he said, looking curiously smug. With childlike deliberation, he presented her with a Zacky's butterball turkey, a twenty-pound bird similar to those Alice had seen on special across the road at Food King. "I have a recipe for great stuffing," he added, without a touch of irony, then shyly lurched back toward the garden.

In the weeks that followed, Alice found Julio's increasing interest in her somewhat unnerving. Although most of his days were spent sliding in and out from under the 1955 Buick Roadmaster he was rebuilding, occasionally, with a leery smile, he would roll across the pathway on his mechanic's trolley and, braking dramatically at her feet, stop her just as she was leaving the house. Holding his beefy, grease-smeared hands in the air, his bulbous eyes squinting into the sun, he would ask if she wanted to go somewhere with him—to the beach or to a studio screening. The inquiry was made at top speed, more anxious than flirtatious, his gaze hovering somewhere over the palm trees, as though a friend had dared him to or, more likely, he had dared himself. Politely she explained that she was extremely busy. She mentioned the newspaper and deadlines. And though she knew he was aware of Mike being in the picture, Alice chose not to mention him, so neither did Julio.

But he made a habit of dropping by the house. One day, when he was fixing the pilot light on the heater, he gave her his family history. Down on his hands and knees, his head pushed inside the vent, his hipster bell-bottom jeans working their way over the brow of his ass, he said his mother had been in the wardrobe department at MGM—"in its heyday," he remarked proudly. His father, a prop man, had been killed when a teamster backed a truck into him during a rehearsal of *Ride the High Country*. "Dad was right there, bending over, readying a pack of Luckies. Silver foil torn open, one cigarette tapped up, so's the actor could grab a smoke during the scene. And then—*boom!* this back fender crushes his head against a generator." He spoke matter-of-factly, no apparent interruption in his work. "Of course, the studio paid for the burial. That Christmas they sent Mom a bottle of Korbel champagne with those fancy, fluted glasses and an autographed eight-by-ten of Joel McCrea. I was only six," he said solemnly, "but I was fascinated by those glasses."

His mother died soon after, he told her, and all three bungalows had been left to him. Often, late at night, Alice could see him across the yard, slouched on an old leather sofa. Transfixed, cowboy boots stretched on the driftwood coffee table, one fist frozen round a Bud, he would be staring vacantly at the white fuzzy light of a vintage movie. He knew them all. He could quote liberally from *My Man Godfrey* or

Citizen Kane and in the same breath bring you up to date on which female extra Mr. Welles had (as Julio so charmingly put it) been "planking" during the shooting of the Rosebud scene. Though he was absorbed by these fantasies, it appeared that where his own life was concerned he was totally ungrounded, drifting in a kind of starry-eyed limbo.

4

Without question, she felt lost. And if someone had asked her who she was waiting for, she would have been unable to reply with much dignity. It had been two weeks and many phone calls since her dramatic escapade at the beach with Oscar. Like most dabblers in adultery, they had had serious discussions about keeping the relationship at a low boil. Lunch was still the order of the day. This time they would simply talk, presumably in a more civilized fashion, in the safer environment of the Beverly Hills Hotel Polo Lounge. Sobered by the passing of time, Alice was not at all sure what lunacy, sexual or otherwise, had actually taken place at the beach. In fact, driving to the hotel, she had decided she would flirt outrageously throughout the meal, then inform Oscar that she just could not see him again. The finality of it appealed to her. She imagined them, months later, running into each other in some fashionable restaurant where, eyes locked across the tops of menus, they would mouth their silent hellos.

But on arrival, as she walked through the lush, tropical gardens of the hotel, all resolve evaporated. Overpowered by the sweet, pungent odor of jasmine and orange blossoms, a smell curiously suggestive of Eastern bazaars, intrigue, and sex—which, she imagined, lurked with erotic fervor within the famous hotel walls—it occurred to her that the last thing she wanted was to talk or, in fact, *think* at all. She was swamped by some disgraceful desire, some terrible, reckless urge to let it all go.

Now, on her third—or was it fourth?—tour of the cool pink and green lobby, she received a small nod from the mustachioed desk clerk. No doubt an animal reflex from one who sees all and, by the esteemed courtesy of this polished establishment, divulges nothing. She told herself to relax. She was, she feared, a blazing advertisement to passing guests that she was up to no good. On the other hand at least one thing seemed clear: Though not desperate enough to settle for a relationship with a younger man with whom she was not in love, she was clearly not yet sane enough to refuse a man she felt irresistibly drawn to, despite the fact that he happened to be married. In a curious way she felt strengthened by her last three months with Mike, what she considered her "vacation from difficult men." So renewed with confidence, in fact, that she was ready to face life again with all its humiliation and torture.

And though not entirely swayed by this logic, as soon as she caught sight of Oscar racing up the red-carpeted walkway toward her, leonine head bent low, green eyes darting nervously left and right, the exhilaration rose up inside her. As much as she tried to force herself to be calm, in that instant the sexual attraction was back. Her cheeks burned; her head swam.

Clutching a bulging briefcase, he rushed over. "God, you look beautiful," he whispered, grasping her arm.

She laughed stupidly, at a loss for words.

"I thought we'd get a room," he said. And seeing the look of bewilderment on her face, quickly added, "Sorry, I meant to phrase that better. Should we get a room? Order lunch and . . ."

"Yes" was her unimaginative reply.

He turned and headed for reception but within seconds was back, squeezing the briefcase to his chest. "I think they're going to ask about luggage." Apparently, the mere idea of this floored him, and for a moment they stood staring at each other.

"In this hotel? I don't think so," she said, forcing a smile.

"You've done this before?" Oscar asked, a note of disappointment in his voice.

"No."

"Neither have I," he said. Then in order to hide his anxiety, he added, "I mean, I live here, in L.A. I have my home, my office, my car."

"Your car?" asked Alice.

Oscar sighed. "No. I didn't mean . . ."

He was about to head off for reception once again when suddenly someone grabbed his arm. It was an expansive move, as if the person were saving Oscar from falling over a precipice. The young man, tall and oozing charm, wore a fifteen-hundred-dollar gray Italian suit that hung in easy folds and a yellow dotted tie that suggested wit and a certain irreverence.

"Hey," he shouted, thumping Oscar on the back. "Why aren't you *shooting* for Christ's sake?"

A bright red flush crept up Oscar's neck. "I am. Nights," he managed to say, then, laughing, jolted his body forward, shifting his weight in order to conceal Alice.

"Look, I'm afraid it didn't work out with Harvey Keitel for the cameo." Eyes cast downwards, the man was anxious that his own disappointment be felt. "He liked the script, but he just doesn't seem to *know* you that well as a director."

"I see," murmured Oscar.

"So you're a little cold right now," the man offered more cheerfully. "Wait till this next one comes out."

Oscar's eyes darted back to Alice, who had moved away a few paces. Assuming the detached expression of someone's secretary, she was waiting obediently for commands. But the tall man had seen her. He leaned across Oscar, hand outstretched, his buffed nails shining like oyster shells.

"Hi. I'm Tom Emery, Oscar's agent," he said, his face cracking into an electric smile.

"Oh—yes, Alice Wilder. The *Recorder.*"

He vigorously pumped her hand, his eyes gauging her importance in an instant. Then, almost indiscernibly, his glance skimmed over her head, sweeping the lobby for action, before turning back to Oscar. He was shockingly smooth.

"Having lunch?" The question was tactfully directed at the ceiling.

"Oh, no," said Oscar, by this time mildly hysterical. "*No,*" he repeated forcefully, then caught himself and laughed. "So, I'm cold."

"Hey, Mike Nichols was cold once."

"When? When he was ten?"

At this Emery gave him a bear hug, an athletic college grip, his fresh face lit up like the *Queen Mary*. Princeton crew? Ivy League? wondered Alice. An agent of the eighties. A twenty-five-year-old sportsman who had not yet had the full, shattering experience of Hollywood that would someday make him guarded.

"Look, I'll call you. There's a book Columbia just bought. You're perfect for it."

"Have you read it?"

"Sure, coverage to coverage," Emery replied cheekily. Hands in his pockets, he was now walking backward, his feet performing an easy two-step.

When he was finally out of sight, Oscar turned toward her with an exhausted smile. "Have you noticed that agents are better looking than movie stars these days?" he said, gently taking her hand.

"God, he's so . . . poised."

"Believe me," said Oscar, "he'd stab *himself* in the back for the right deal."

They lay in the inky silence, listening to the sound of air-conditioning wafting over their naked bodies. A thin strip of light seeped across the top of the heavy silk drapes, and watery ripples played on the ceiling, reflecting the bougainvillea outside. Selfish and greedy, they had devoured each other. The room had been plundered. Sheets and blankets were strewn across the carpet, clothes were in messy balls. The luxury of absolute surrender. And somewhere during this engaging stupor, murmurings of extreme emotion had been exchanged.

Now Oscar leaned over and kissed her. It was an effortless kiss. They were eye to eye, daring each other to glance away. Alice thought this was a good sign. She had recollections of lovers who, after a stunning bout of intercourse, had a hard time looking directly into her face. Often a man might be trying to recall a phone number for a taxi or, without moving, attempting to reach under the bed for his pants.

"You're not behaving like a married man," she remarked.

His head sunk once again into the pillow. "I'm not?" he said, miles away.

"You haven't looked at your watch once since we got here."

She rubbed the side of his cheek and he closed his eyes. He smelled of leather and old leaves.

"How do you feel?"

"Not bad."

"Is that good?" she asked.

"Yes," he replied slowly. "But I'm feeling guilty for not feeling bad."

"Of course. It's a religious thing." Though she said the words casually, she was suddenly conscious of her every move: the tone of her voice, her foot resting on his, and, essentially, the effect he was having on her. "A friend of mine says that sex is the great leveler."

Oscar opened one eye and rolled off the pillow. "A woman I know says it beats doing the dishes."

They basked in this mutual conspiracy for a moment, aware of who *that* woman was. But even in her exquisite pleasure, as Oscar slid down to kiss her rib cage, just then Alice couldn't get the idea of his wife out of her mind.

"You know, it's odd. I feel like I'm with one of the guys," Oscar said, looking up at her. "Most men only feel a need to talk to an unfamiliar woman *before* they sleep with her. A lead-in to seducing her. After that, they can be silent until they want to sleep with her again. You see, men know that women love talking."

"After centuries of screwing around, this is what men have discovered? A cocktail party must send you all into a pre-orgy dilemma."

"So mock me. I feel comfortable with you, as if I'm with a guy. With you there's no agenda."

"Like a guy with breasts?"

"Yes."

"But who hates sports."

"Ah . . ."

The phone rang. It shrieked. Oscar, disoriented, sat up like a man rising from a tomb.

"What? Oh . . . Judy. Yes." He rolled away from Alice. All-business now, he snapped on the lamp. In the yellowish glow, Alice could see the signs of worry, the hard creases around his eyes. "OK. I'll call her back. Anything else? What time is it . . . ?"

Alice slid out of bed and headed for the bathroom. She

heard Oscar say a few more words, then hang up. "By the way, what's your wife's name?" she asked, aware that her voice sounded altogether too earnest.

"Ruth," he replied. Of course, Alice knew his wife's name but wanted to hear Oscar say it.

"Thank God," she said.

"That was Judy, my secretary." One foot out of bed, he looked distracted, on the verge of going somewhere.

"You gave this number to your secretary?"

"We're shooting. Things come up."

"I'm sneaking around the lobby in dark glasses, and the whole studio has this number?" Using the bathroom door handle for support, she crossed one leg seductively over the other. In her nakedness, the gesture required a smile, something alluring at least.

Oscar went on staring at the carpet. "I have to call someone," he said apologetically, reaching for the phone.

Alice closed the bathroom door quickly. The glare was fantastic. Brilliant white light bounced off the antiseptic glaze of white tile. As she feared, something had already slipped away inside her. Was it jealousy? Or the familiar feeling of postcoital self-doubt? Burdened with too high an opinion of one's lover and too low an opinion of oneself, was it impossible *not* to experience a terrible sinking fear that the balance of power had shifted? According to her friend Jessica, seduction was the thing you started *after* sex, the very second your satiated body lifted from the bed. As you smiled, offering him tenderness and serenity—*that* was the moment you had to start being clever.

She was considering this when Oscar walked in, his dark bulkiness surprising her. He stood behind her and slid his hands around her breasts. She relaxed under the weight of him, his body tan and warm against her skin. Resting his chin on her head, he said, "I think I love you." The words hung awkwardly in the air.

Alice felt her face flush. In the mirror she saw her eyes were mere slits against the iridescent whiteness of the room, her dry mouth fixed in an awkward smile. "There's an old saying in journalism: If your mother says she loves you, check it out." Spots of color spread on her cheeks. Her ears were humming.

"So funny. And you're blushing again," he said.

"Am I? Usually I only get this kind of reaction with shellfish," she replied. God, she thought, could she ever, just once, say *nothing?*

Shyly they looked at their reflections. It seemed unnaturally comic. The thrill and shyness of every slight movement—raw skin, open pores, matted hair. Two naked strangers pulsating in the Mojave Desert. Frankly, this was not the image she had prepared for him to adore.

"Look, you don't love me," she said, closing her eyes in an attempt to hide her thoughts.

"You think it's too soon?" he said. "Maybe I'm simply in a weakened condition."

"Why? Because you didn't get Harvey for the movie?"

He squeezed against her, pushing her stomach into the edge of the sink. She inclined her head, finally silent.

"Here's how it works: I'm making a movie, but it's not the one the studio wants me to make. The word is that I'm out of control. I am not out of control. In this business, I know that the only way to win is to do good work, *quality* work, as they say. If you fail with a bad movie, you might as well slit your wrists. If you fail with a *decent* movie, one that at least gets good reviews, they still come back. They hate your guts, but they have to hire you because Hollywood needs to make a hundred pictures a year and the list of directors is woefully short. This is what I tell myself. So, no, I'm *not depressed.* But I am married and *this* feels serious to me."

He bent over and kissed the hollow in her neck, a gesture that temporarily caused her knees to give way. "I promise not to be serious," she murmured, sinking under mountains of tenderness and fear.

"You look so young and beautiful."

"I'm thirty-five."

"Heavens." He rubbed her shoulders gently.

Outside, in the gardens, she heard the Spanish maids' high voices. Through the window she could just see the tops of their glossy blue-black heads and their pink uniforms.

"Not long ago men used to call me 'babe.' Now, at gas stations, guys call me 'ma'am.' "

"You're finally getting what every woman wants. Respect."

"After that it's sympathy, then loathing, then death."

"Did you ever consider doing stand-up?"

"Sorry. It's a nervous thing."

"I know, I know," he said. "You think I don't *know that!*" Then laughing, he added, "Henny Youngman."

"Take my wife, please," said Alice, laughing right along with him. "Or in this case, take *your* wife."

Oscar shook his head in wonder. There was the noise of a lunch cart in the corridor, wheels clacking. The doorbell rang.

He had ordered Caesar salad, champagne, slices of fresh mango, and a mountain of French fries wrapped in the complicated folds of a pink napkin. Sitting on the end of the bed, he divided the salad, then opened the champagne with a flourish. A man intent on preserving the moment. Both wore the giant, thirsty robes provided by the hotel. In the pocket Alice found a printed card, a cunning reminder to guests that these articles could be purchased at the patio shop. It was hoped that the crass idea of stealing could be diplomatically strangled at birth.

Alice picked up the strewn clothing. She loved the uncomplicated hugeness of his clothes, big square shirts and boxlike shoes. Were all women domestic at heart? she wondered. Whatever was expected of a woman, in anticipation of love and life everlasting, Alice voluntarily had given more. Curb that impulse, she thought, scooping up his undershorts. Fight submissiveness or die.

Oscar turned on the TV, then opened the complimentary copy of *The New York Times* lying on the cart. What a picture! Almost suburban in its tranquility: food, TV, newspaper, the little woman scurrying in the background. Alice, feeling giddy, and all rationale aside, imagined herself married to this man—cocktails at six, dinner in the oven—forgetting not only his situation, but that this was precisely the horror from which she had recently escaped.

"Did you know that in Washington, twenty-two percent of politicians sleep with their wives? Another twenty are doing it with their secretaries, and the remaining fifty-eight percent say they don't know who they're screwing. Imagine. Right here in *The New York Times.*" Alice laughed in disbelief. "Come and see," he said. "Here—come and look."

She went over and leaned against him. He eyed the bundle of clothes with some amusement, then removed them from her arms and hurled them over his shoulder. "I was lying. A cheap trick," he whispered, then pulled her down on her knees so that her eyes were level with the serving cart. "How do you feel about mango?"

"I live for mango."

With one hand he fed her a thin, glistening slice, while with the other he busily clicked through the TV channels. Being a director, she imagined, his desire for continuous action was an impulse he couldn't control.

Eventually he found an old movie playing on cable. Alice remembered it: *Twice in a Lifetime.* Gene Hackman, a blue-collar worker, passively discontented with his humdrum life. Married to Ellen Burstyn, with grown kids, he is having an affair with Ann-Margret. She, the lusty barmaid of a working man's delirious dreams, was now on screen, wearing a tight red pantsuit, lounging in her sunny pinewood apartment. All curves and breasts like torpedoes.

"I know a lot of men who were in love with her," Alice said. Oscar was feeding her French fries, dipping the ends in ketchup. "Perhaps it's that vulnerable Swedish thing."

"And the breasts," said Oscar.

"Men and breasts."

"This fascinates you?"

"When I was in college, there was a girl named Deborah Moore who was extremely well endowed. Every time she came into the room, the guys would start groaning like animals. The girls would object and then the guys would say, 'Look, it's *just a breast thing.*' As if it were mountain climbing or drinking. You know, a man's world. Not real life."

"And you've never forgiven us?"

"I think it's why some women confuse lust with affection."

"But not you."

"No. I'm older. I'm grateful. And you seem like a very mature man."

"I'm a sensitive Jew who loves women more than he loves movies. In this town, that makes me almost extinct." He wiped a smudge of ketchup from her cheek, then offered his red-smeared finger. She licked it obediently. Down on her knees, she was reminded of the former (but clearly ever-present) devotions of the naïve convent girl.

Oscar opened her robe. He was about to kiss her breasts when, as if on cue, there was an agonized scream from the TV set. Dressed in her shabby apron, the picture of monumental poverty and sadness, Ellen Burstyn was accusing husband Gene—now face down on the bed after a hard night in the steel mills—of having an *affair*. The scene, shocking in its grimness, caused a chill of reality to sweep through the satin-draped room. Alice's sudden vision—and she feared, Oscar's as well—was of the two of them trying to live in some equally squalid apartment while his distraught wife wept on their doorstep.

Oscar's hands slid away. The smile lingered, but the light was gone from his eyes. "I don't think you can love someone without having to own them, do you?" he said, airing a lengthy sigh.

His sleeve trailed in the butter dish. Crumbs were caught in the hair on his chest. Where the robe sagged open Alice saw the definite beginnings of a paunch. Already she felt a distinct womanliness in forgiving him his imperfections. Do they enslave us, she thought, or do we seek to enslave ourselves?

"I don't know. Perhaps for a while," she replied.

"Well, do you think a man can love two women at the same time?"

"Yes. As long as one of the women doesn't know about it," she said wittily. Humor, she reminded herself, created precisely to cope with awkward moments such as these.

"Be serious," he said.

"I am," she replied, still unable to sound normal.

"No, *be serious*," he repeated, his jaw tightening. "I've never felt exactly *like this* before."

And the impatient look he gave her betrayed him. Alice felt the distance between them grow.

"You exaggerate," she murmured.

"Yes, sometimes," he said. "To make a point."

He pushed his salad to one side and, leaning over the lunch cart, immersed himself in the TV. Without thinking, she asked him what she had promised herself she would never ask: "By the way, do you still sleep with your wife?"

He didn't reply. She was relieved. Perhaps he hadn't heard, mesmerized as he was by the other drama taking place in the room. On screen was a close-up of Gene Hackman's face. Eyes pinned to the floor, guilty, remorseful—an expression not dissimilar to Oscar's at that moment—suggesting to Alice two very different men anticipating the sober reality of their lives.

After a minute, Oscar stood up. Then, by wrapping his robe tightly around his body, he managed to remove what was left of his intimate self.

Quickly, he put on his pants. He was shaking his head, silently scolding himself. When he bent over to search for a missing sock, he swore under his breath, aggravated now by the mess of underwear and sheets. As the music swelled from the TV, as Gene told Ellen Burstyn that he had to leave—that he needed his freedom—neither Oscar nor Alice could bring themselves to look at the TV screen.

"The melodrama of the midlife crisis," mumbled Oscar. Eyes trained on the carpet, he was fighting to get an arm in his shirtsleeve.

"Statistics show that men never end up with their mistresses, you know," Alice informed him. "Too much spilled blood. Too many ghastly insults and broken promises. Eventually the man does leave his wife, waits three months, then marries a twenty-three-year-old cocktail waitress who hasn't heard any of his jokes." She realized she was making things worse, but her only thought was to *get out* of there. She was furious with herself. Furious that she had been swayed by her own romantic notions and furious for having had such notions in the first place.

Oscar flung back the curtains. Sunlight flooded into the room. It was like coming out of a movie in the afternoon. The intimacy of sex evaporated with the shadows.

Then, in a moment of confusion, Oscar fell back across the bed. He had been absentmindedly buffing his shoes on the sheets when somehow he lost his balance. Lying there, he appeared so confused, so worn out, that on impulse Alice sat down beside him. But when she leaned over to smooth back his hair, he flinched and rolled away.

"I have to call the office," he said, checking his watch. "I'm shooting at five."

"OK," she replied simply. Then, in order to gain a little strength for her next remark, she stood up. "Look, I think it would be better for both of us if we didn't do this again." She had no idea why she said it. Perhaps to say something, *anything*, to match his coolness. She found her dark glasses and put them on, not sure what her eyes might be doing. "Easier, I think."

Oscar was surprised but calm. "Seriously? You think so?"

"Yes," said Alice, wondering how they had slipped so rapidly into this polite discussion. Two strangers, now more awkward with each other dressed than they had been a hour ago, mouths pressed voraciously to each other's genitalia.

"Well, I'm sorry you feel like that."

"I do."

He nodded. He was about to say something but instead picked up the phone and started to dial. "By the way," he added truthfully, "I *do* sleep with my wife, on occasion. I mean, it's not as if I *dislike* her."

Driving out of Beverly Hills and into West Hollywood (at a terrific clip), she remembered something Jessica had told her, a line attributed to Madame de Tencin, Montesquieu's mistress: "From the way he treats us, it is easy to see that God is a man."

5

She had met the actress Jessica Bing at a large dinner party given by Tado Dandini. Tado was an art dealer Alice had known briefly in New York who, for the purpose of promoting several aspiring West Coast artists, had rented a house in Santa Monica Canyon, an architectural gem that boasted a ballroom and a Diego Rivera mural over the fireplace. The guests were a mixed bag: a few famous, a few rich, some dedicated art fans, plus the obligatory long-suffering fleshy party girls. But it was Jessica who drew the attention of the mob feigning boredom at the bar. With Capraesque gaiety, as though in anticipation of great things, she entered the room laughing. It was a laugh that welled up from the depths like a volcano. Brazen, with a sort of crackling charm, she could melt the crowd at fifty feet. She appeared almost a foot taller than any of the women there and wore a short white dress, army combat jacket, hiking boots, and a green felt beret crowning a bob of white blond hair. Though her appearance was daunting, especially with her wide, almost military shoulders, she had the serene, unmuddied face of an angel.

Because at that time it had been only two weeks since Alice had left Walter and because she was feeling temporarily demoralized as a brand-new single girl, her initial reaction to this extraordinary-looking woman was jealousy mixed with fear, not to mention a tinge of dislike. For Jessica, life was obviously nothing more than one great rollicking expedition. Alice told herself it was among the other women guests that she would find camaraderie and understanding.

At dinner she was seated next to a woman in her late forties, a producer named Peggy Shuster who had made a career chasing down sob stories for the glory of television. The first to contact Mrs. Klinghoffer after the *Achille Lauro* disaster, she had tracked her down in temple and slipped a form contract across her knees, barely interrupting the poor woman's prayers. This season, boasted the entrepreneur, she was producing a miniseries about Mother Teresa.

Alice, wistful after her third glass of chardonnay and mistaking Peggy for some kind of sturdy mother figure, confided to her the lack of sexual gratification in her marriage. Peggy eyed her for a good twenty seconds, then without bothering to lower her voice, remarked, "You look like you've been fucked enough to last a lifetime, dear," and turned back to the young actor on her left. What Peggy meant, of course, was that good looks belie unhappiness or at least eliminate the need to *complain*. Alice had firmly been put in her place.

And after that, much to her dismay, the topic of her separation—or as some interpreted it, her desertion of her husband—was passed back and forth across the table like a tantalizing side dish to the *frisée* salad and the poached salmon. Some of the women chided her for being ungrateful, for expecting too much from life. "A lot of people have marriages like yours. Have you never heard of *compromise?*" one elderly patron of the arts inquired, followed by a rather drunken actress, laughing across the top of her glass: "And what the hell do you think is out there anyway?"

Even in the bar before dinner, a married woman, well fed and well lied to, smelling danger, had steered her roguish husband away from Alice just as a mother might restrain a child from reaching out to pet a runaway dog. By the end of dinner even the men, spurred on by the uproar, had turned hostile. "Walter came from such a tragic family," said the stylish Tado in his unplaceable European accent. Reed thin, he had for some years been determined single-handedly to bring back the Nehru jacket. "He must be devastated, my dear. You should crawl back on your hands and knees."

Then Morgan Greco, the Italian director, leaned across the table, nostrils flaring, eager to join in. "You have to realize, Alice, that being an attractive, intelligent woman, you'll probably spend the rest of your life *alone*." That got a good laugh. At which point Jessica surfaced. She was sitting a few places down from Alice. Although it was clear Jessica held her booze as well as any man twice her size, Alice noticed that her initial burst of vitality had dimmed slightly since the first few drinks at the bar. She was still regal, the image of splendor and strength, but now, one hand gripping a full glass of vodka, she appeared slightly threatening. Like Grace Kelly holding a hand grenade. Stoically Jessica observed Morgan from the shadows. It was as though she were trying to place him, trying to match his face to some young freak who had briefly amused her. After his remark, she exploded with laughter. And when Morgan beamed back at her, Jessica bellowed out another gut-wrenching howl, which finally received the attention of the entire table. "Well, I can't remember how long it's been since I've had *this* much fun," she announced, leaning back in her chair. Then, eyeing the guests, she picked up her napkin to delicately wipe the corners of her mouth. Except that along with the napkin, she had also gathered up the hem of her skirt. A stunned silence followed. She was stark naked to the waist. In full view were her bikini mark and bright reddish brown pubic hair, trimmed into an arched triangle. It was an alluring beacon, a rusty glow against her pale skin. Confused for a moment, people started to chuckle, then the laughter trailed off in embarrassed silence. Jessica pulled the skirt back over her knees. "I have to go," she said. But as she squeezed past the back of Alice's chair, she bent down and whispered, "I do it to amuse myself, to stop the crushing boredom. These sourpusses and dick-wavers will kill you. Call me."

They became friends immediately. It was an odd thing. While Alice was still cautiously crawling through life, Jessica, like a race-car driver, needed a constant threat of death or burnout around the corner to validate her as a living being. She existed in a kind of semidelirium, advising, scolding, proselytizing, then moving on . . . ever forward, ever hopeful of life's rosy pleasures, the past dead and buried behind her. Smart and surprisingly well read, Jessica foisted her opinions on people everywhere—in restaurants, in the street—striking out with a clever quip that left her victims either dazzled or outraged. From the beginning, Alice felt a mysterious loyalty to her, borne not only out of gratitude for Jessica's rescuing her at dinner but also out of admiration for her originality. Gratefully, Alice adopted her as the elder sister she had never had. (Although Jessica admitted to thirty-eight, Alice guessed it was more like forty.) Because of this affection and because of her friend's apparent keen knowledge of men, she trusted Jessica's judgment more than her own.

However, when Alice called to tell her about Oscar, breathlessly running through the sequence of events (now complete with dramatic distortions from the near death at the beach to the final humiliating words at the hotel), her confession was met with a stunning silence. Finally Alice heard the sound of a cigarette being lit, followed by a lengthy exhale. "Can't talk now," came Jessica's syrupy voice. "Come to my AA meeting tomorrow. Nine o'clock at Cedars."

≈

Despite the early hour, the Simon Weisenthal building was boiling. There was no air-conditioning and the atmosphere was heady, electric, and somewhat sweaty. This particular Sunday morning meeting catered to a cross-section of Hollywood. Like a cocktail party, groups were crushed into corners, while others prowled back and forth between the rows of folding chairs, shouting and waving, the elite rubbing shoulders with the also-rans. Studio executives moved discreetly, while young, newly dried-out agents, bolstered by the sense of camaraderie, hopped lithely from group to group to discuss that weekend's movies. They rattled off the grosses, the winners, the potential flops, eyes bright as they roamed the crowd for a good business contact or a famous face. Young actors dressed in customary blue denim stood idly with a line of giggling actresses, some barefoot, their mouths moist, desperate to be discovered now that they had been saved. It was quite a parade. By comparison, there were the older women. These were the lonely survivors, the decades of struggle distinctly visible on their ruined faces. And though they quickly laid claim to the front seats, then buried themselves in the Sunday newspapers, the importance of this social event was all too apparent.

Jessica arrived breathless, hair like a wild shrub, dressed in a tiny leather skirt, fishnet stockings, and a voluminous white shirt. As usual, she followed no particular fashion, and however outrageous her outfit, she wore it with a cool nonchalance. Like a masted schooner she drifted back and forth, teeth blazing. Eventually she saw Alice and came over. She led her to the back row, where without hesitation she shifted a man's leather jacket to a seat farther down so that the two of them could sit together. If Jessica had been moody on the phone, she was now her usual hearty self, equipped with all the answers.

"So Oscar Lombardi actually *told* you he still sleeps with his wife?"

"Yes," replied Alice. Though it was already sweltering in the room, she felt a quick flush spread across her cheeks. "Well, I asked. And he told me."

"God save us—the *honest* kind." Jessica was shaking her head, bent over now, pouring watery herbal tea from a thermos into two enamel cups. Caffeine was also something she had given up. "I hope you're not serious about this."

"No," said Alice. She was trying to remember if she had implied otherwise on the phone.

"Because he's got two strikes against him. He's Jewish and he's married—no, *three strikes*, he's a director!" she exclaimed. And as though a necessary medicine, she handed Alice some of the lemon-scented tea. "An ego from here to hell and back. Champagne at the beach, champagne at the hotel. Phone calls from his office. The familiar setup. The whole thing *reeks* of tired old adultery."

"Yes. You're probably right."

Never had Alice heard the liberal Jessica criticize so vehemently any sexual dalliance with a man, married or otherwise. And even though Alice agreed with her, she was not up to the task of condemning Oscar and decided to change the subject.

"How was Yugoslavia?"

"I played my usual in the movie. The tight-lipped woman spy with a serious knowledge of weapons. No accent this time, but I did a nude scene." And as if to illustrate the point, she crossed her wondrously long legs so that the small, balding man next to her—owner of the leather jacket, it turned out—was for a moment fixated on her noble expanse of thigh.

"I'm sure it was tasteful and integral to the plot," remarked Alice, smiling.

Jessica let out a throaty howl. "Here's the depressing thing about getting older: They clear the set before I undress, and not one of those Yugo boys even *tried* to sneak back to get a look. And the director was a prick. He wanted me to go deeper, to *feel more.* I said to him, 'Look, this is a B picture at best. We'll be lucky if it gets to the Cineplex in Pomona. I like to read on the set. You shout "Action!" I hike up my skirt and go stick a gun in someone's ear. Then I go back to my book. Don't tell me how to act, how to *sweat—I come in wet, OK?* And I don't go home with my part. I'd rather go home with a guy.' "

Jessica laughed again. The balding man, neck flushed scarlet, unable to tear his eyes away during her speech, now turned with obvious relief toward the podium where a man in a blue sweatsuit was bent over the mike. "Good morning, my name is Jake and I'm an alcoholic," he said cheerily, and the noise died to a schoolroom hush.

With an enthusiasm worthy of the Academy Awards, he went on to announce the week's "birthdays," the celebration of those members who had abstained for one or two or more years from alcohol or narcotic substances. Lurking behind Jake was his helper, a woman in a flowered shift who with considerable dexterity was stabbing candles into a tray of muffins.

"Happy Birthday" was sung to those members as they came to the podium. As each spoke, Jessica supplied Alice with a running commentary. "A famous valet parking attendant," she explained as Mario, a soft-spoken Ricky Ricardo, thanked the crowd. "He used to leave a packet of cocaine under the floor mat of your car. You'd tip him a hundred when he handed over the keys. Quite a racket."

Although smoking was not permitted in the room, under the seat a cigarette burned slowly in Jessica's fingers.

An elderly woman named Doris blew out her candle.

In a dainty voice, an amused smile on her lips, she calmly recounted the day when her father had tried to kill her with a carving knife. There was a young actress who, career in ruins but sober for two years, was working her way back at Sea World. And then Lionel March, the old character actor—his weathered face bearing all the intricacies of a clenched fist—stood up to thank his dear friend Jimmy Cagney for putting him in the program twenty years ago.

"Married six times," said Jessica, taking another surreptitious drag. "The fifth wife—the richest—insisted on being buried wearing her canary diamond. Two weeks later his new fiancée, an Indian princess, had the diamond hanging round her neck. Lionel actually *dug up the body* . . ."

Even when Jessica whispered, it produced an echo. A low rumble from somewhere beneath her rib cage. Two women sitting in front of them turned repeatedly to scowl at her. Both had moonlike, magnolia white faces and crucifix studs in their ears. The larger one, in a black voile dress and orange hair, held the hand of the thinner woman, who wore white gloves and had shaved her head. Alice wondered if it was an artistic interpretation or a question of hygiene.

"Remember, AA is nothing more that a million dollars' worth of information shoved up your ass one nickel at a time," Jessica said pointedly to Alice, then casually blew a thin stream of smoke over the women's heads. If Alice hadn't known that Jessica came religiously to these meetings three times a week, she might have thought her friend despised the whole business. But since Jessica had quit drinking (as committed now as she had been to *not* giving it up three months ago), she told Alice she'd been reborn into a state of bucolic grace. Where once there had been excess and pain, now resided dignity and strength. To Alice, however, she seemed unchanged, her charm as ever triumphing over any unorthodox behavior.

"Now, let's discuss *Mike,*" said Jessica, her voice taking on a gravelly depth. "He's funny, great-looking, and *young.*"

"Perhaps too young," murmured Alice.

"Listen to you. There is no *too* young. What do you want, an old guy with a heart condition?"

"I know, Mike's perfect. He's considerate. He worries if I don't wear warm clothing. If I eat enough. And he's so happy to see me all the time."

"Now *I'm* jealous."

"But I have this weird feeling Mike's just as happy to see the woman at the cleaner's."

"You're scared that he'll love you."

"Probably. Because he makes me feel grateful for so much. Suffocation disguised as shelter. And every time we eat out, I pay."

"Just because a man has a penis, it doesn't mean he has to pick up the check," said Jessica. Her voice carried three or more rows down, causing not only the pale beauties but half a dozen other people to turn. "And my guess is it's enormous. Big enough to tow a car with," she added, exhaling another fine stream of cigarette smoke. By now, several people were complaining. Even her former admirer, the balding man, coughed and waved his arms in order to bring attention to this terrible infraction of the rules. Fortunately, just then Jake announced the fifteen-minute break.

Like desperadoes the crowd surged toward the coffee urns at the back of the hall. Alice caught sight of someone she recognized but couldn't place. The man was wearing Ray-Bans and crisp pants and shirt in subtle tones of beige—a sort of fashionable white-hunter look. Standing in line for the bagels and cream cheese, he stood abnormally straight, his soft round face turned upwards.

Though the air outside was just as stale and heavy, people hurried for the exit, paper cups in hand. Fanning herself, Jessica arched her body dramatically against the glass doors and lit another Winston. As though simply picking up the conversation, she said, "Let me explain to you about *Jewish* men." And at the mention of the word her eyes rolled to the ceiling. "My ex-husband was Jewish. His mother took his temperature, rectally, until he was twenty-three years old."

"Stop it," said Alice.

"OK, maybe fifteen," she said with a wry smile.

"You were married?" asked Alice, surprised.

"Briefly."

"You never mentioned it." In fact, it was the first Alice had heard of it, and she wasn't entirely convinced it was true.

"His mother refused to acknowledge me. When she called the house she said, 'Is Mitchell there?' Never a hello. No '*How are you*, Jessica?' Nothing. Mitch never told his father he'd married a shikse; the man was on his deathbed, so he wanted him to die happy. When I wanted a child, Mitch said, 'First we'll get a dog. If you get along with that, we'll consider a baby.' *He* was the child. They're all children. Mitch still calls me when he's sick. You have to realize that with a Jewish guy there is another Jewish guy inside who remains attached not only to his mother but also to the *first* woman he was married to. If Oscar leaves his wife, which he won't . . ."

"I don't want him to," said Alice, quickly. "In fact, I told him I didn't want to see him again."

"But you will."

"I swear I won't. Who needs the responsibility?"

"This is not a matter of logic. You get that soggy look every time I mention his name. Are you in love?"

"With Oscar?" Saying his name suddenly gave her a little trouble.

"Yes, with *Os-car.*"

"Check my eyes," Alice said coolly. "No glassy film. I

am not happy beyond my wildest dreams. I have not lost eight pounds."

Her feeling of unease, she decided, came only from confusion. Her childishness at not being able to handle, gracefully, one perfectly good afternoon of sex with a married man.

"Anyway," Jessica went on, "if he leaves, you'll have to live with the guilt. Centuries of guilt going back to the first Jewish husband who looked up a handmaiden's skirt." She paused for a moment of serious inhaling and exhaling, then asked, "Is he good in bed?"

"An animal," said Alice, feeling the need at least to defend *that* part of their short relationship.

"When they're good, they're fabulous. The old magic wand. I was addicted to Mitch. I mean, I didn't even *like* him. But when my mind kept saying no, my body said, Who the hell asked you? Does Oscar talk about his penis?"

Alice laughed. "He barely talks about his *wife*."

"He'll discuss both interminably. You'll become his mistress, then his doctor. He *and* his penis will get mysterious illnesses unknown by the Western medical profession."

"Maybe you're biased."

"Possibly," Jessica said, grinning.

"Anyway, I'm not sure, but I think he may be only a little Jewish and mostly Italian," Alice remarked innocently.

A pretty thirty-year-old wearing a *Woman on the Verge of a Nervous Breakdown* T-shirt and black jeans came over to greet Jessica. "Hello, Susan," said Jessica. "This is Alice. We were talking about men in bed." Then, glancing at Alice, she added, "*Italian* men."

"Please!" said Susan, and with one hand she waved away the entire race. "Such egomaniacs, they scream out their *own* name in climax." She took a quick drag from Jessica's cigarette, savored it dreamily, and wandered away.

≈

The break was over; people drifted back to their seats. Due to the overwhelming heat and the lack of decent ventilation, a weariness had swept across the room. And when Jake announced that morning's main speakers, there was only a faint ripple of applause.

"Of course, it's obvious what you're doing," Jessica continued. She brandished an enormous yellow bandana and proceeded to wipe her forehead.

"Trying to bolster my damaged ego with the affection of two men," replied Alice, and for the first time realized this was probably true. "I'm a failure as a modern woman."

"There is no modern woman. We're all the *old* woman, and frankly we're getting nowhere." Head down, Jessica snapped open her Zippo and lit up again. Without turning, the thin woman with the shaved head put her hand over her mouth and made exaggerated choking noises.

"Do you know why you want Oscar?"

"He's the father I never had?" suggested Alice, trying to introduce a little humor. Somehow the conversation was beginning to depress her.

A woman named Helen, tall, imperious, with flowing gray-streaked hair, apparently a one-time singer, was speaking softly. She cradled the mike with both hands, as though protecting a small bird. Juiced up for fifteen years, she had been to County General and back with several side trips to jail. At thirteen she began with half a diet pill and by twenty-two she was shooting heroin and cocaine and dropping acid twice a week. Eventually, weighing ninety-seven pounds, she found herself screwing bums in telephone booths on Crenshaw Boulevard. Her mother told her she was worthless and she believed her. But she drank and took drugs to make sure no one else would find out. Such was the nature of her calm revelations. And by the time she finished, profusely thanking the organization for saving her lost soul, a few people had started to sob. Even Jessica, now silent, sank back in her seat. Then Helen tacked on a message that seemed perfectly rational: "If you wait for others to give you love, like a drug, it will never be enough . . ." An eerie hush descended over the room, the effect of which was not lost on Alice. Was she also desperate to be loved? she wondered. If so, what did this mean? That she possessed needs that ultimately *no one* could fulfill? She felt gloomy and more than a little stupid. On top of that, the meeting itself was beginning to be unbearable. The flat cream walls, the airless room, the sea of boiling faces, the rapt attentiveness—the whole thing reminded her of the chapel at St. Teresa's. Confessions and prayers and more confession. Demons to be faced, humility and penance and *mortal sin!* And such a numbing claustrophobia swept over her that she couldn't wait to get out.

But there was one more speaker. Jessica was fixated on this person. In fact she was wearing an expression of intense concentration, plus a smile that usually denoted some scheme afoot. It was the man in the safari outfit. He removed his Ray-Bans and Alice recognized him. Adam Logan, a senior executive at Universal who several weeks previously had called her in for a meeting. He had read her one script, *Going for Broke*, and liked it—barring the fact that it was "much too talky"—and was considering her for a possible writing job. The man was a smoothie. An ex-trader from Wall Street, he had scored heavily in hand-to-hand combat, the natural progression leading to Hollywood, where his stamina and grit would serve to gain a higher profile. Even though Alice had been excited at the prospect of being hired, she had been unable to dredge up the correct enthusiasm for his idea to remake *Lost in Alaska*, an old Abbott and Costello movie. Coolly and not without aggravation, he had warned her that it was a mistake to intellectualize the process of moviemaking. He reminded her that "character-driven concepts with meaningful relationships have all but played themselves out."

She watched him now. He talked with the same effortless air of superiority, his unnaturally large brown eyes sweeping the room, his pudgy hands chopping the air. Grandly, he was describing the "nature of the beast" in Hollywood. By fighting his enemies—rejection, insecurity, and ultimately that irresistible tool for success, cocaine—he had risen to the pinnacle. He explained to the captive audience that he owed his meteoric rise, post drugs, to his ability to "suffer along with the artist" and to his discovery of the subtle difference between "error" and "mistake." "I'm driving a big bus," he said, referring presumably to his lofty position of power. "I have to make lefts and rights, and occasionally I make a wrong turn. But at least these days I know where *I'm going.*"

"He's cute," said Jessica.

"Really? He's not your type."

"You know him?"

"We met briefly about a job."

"I've never been out with a studio executive." Jessica spoke as though she were thinking of taking up cooking or origami classes.

"Aren't you seeing someone?" asked Alice, remembering the background murmurings during the previous night's phone call.

Jessica laughed, waving whoever it was away. "Not really."

"You like the look of this guy?"

Usually Jessica preferred simple, well-built guys whose energy radiated from the groin; Adam couldn't have been more different.

"He has a certain smoothness."

"A possible Mr. Right?" asked Alice, somewhat baffled.

"No. But a definite Mr. Right Now!"

≈

The meeting was over. Close to a hundred chairs scraped against the floor. Once again saved, it was time to get on with the process of living. Alice and Jessica waited near the main doors; when Adam came out, Jessica introduced herself.

Jessica's motto was that a woman was never given what she wanted in life, so she had to take it. Completely comfortable in the role of consumer, she treated all suitors equally, like small boys. Consequently, just as children obey parents, eager to please, men curled up willingly in her lap.

"I'm a *great* fan," Adam managed to say, after his initial surprise, pools of red spreading across his round cheeks. "I thought you were fabulous in *Above Suspicion.*"

"Thanks," Jessica replied, flashing a tantalizing smile. She had the ability to be fatuous, bored, exhausted, and amused all at the same time. "Nice speech. In fact I think we should discuss it further."

Alice could see her sizing him up, leaning forward with her silky body like a big white wave waiting to break.

"Do you know my friend, Alice Wilder?" she asked, her angelic face dissolving into the familiar grin.

But he didn't remember and, smiling politely, turned back to the stately goddess. Alice noticed his fingers nervously working the crease in his two-hundred-dollar chinos as words poured out of his mouth. It was a lava flow of admiration, a desperate and unwise attempt to impress upon Jessica his worth.

It was while she was driving home that the image of Adam, unctuous, buttery, and so obliging, refused to leave her. In a pitiful way, it reminded Alice of her own behavior with Oscar. The same unguarded eagerness of a person intoxicated with the possibility of passion, intrigue . . . and then what? Deliverance? Thinking back to that fated afternoon at the hotel, she tried to remember exactly what had happened. For the past few days all she could think of was her sullen, accusatory "Good-bye" as she swept out of the hotel room. But was Oscar really to blame? She had asked him if he still slept with his wife and he had answered truthfully. So what had he done wrong? Nothing, except affect her far more than she had dared imagine. Now the thought of him obsessed her (obsessed her because driving endlessly through the streets of Los Angeles, the sun beating down, eventually dementia set in). So that when she arrived home and found a message from him on her machine, she felt something close to childlike elation.

It was a rambling emotional plea: First, how could she have walked out so coldly? How could she have wanted it to be over when they had only just begun? Didn't she believe what he had said in the bathroom? Did she think he was complimenting her simply because he'd just got laid? Well, believe it or not, outside of having lunch with an agent, getting laid was just about the *easiest* thing to achieve in this town. Second, if she had been demoralized by his mood, she had to forgive him because that's just the way he was sometimes. He had a movie to direct. And third, would it be so bad, without the what ifs and the what might bes, to indulge in each other a little more for what it *was*? Could they handle that? Would it damage their lives so terribly?

And Alice might have thought this victory enough, as women do when a man is willing to simply *acknowledge* his wild desires, had Oscar not called her again the next day.

Being mature adults, they discussed the futility of the relationship, the moral consequences, and the distinct ordinariness of their situation, and for a good ten minutes they were resolved. Until Oscar introduced a new element that made the idea of an affair sound irresistible, almost rational if not foolproof. He told Alice that in exactly a month he would be leaving for Chicago, accompanied by his wife, to shoot location sequences for the movie. Would this not be a perfect amount of time to liberate themselves from what was clearly nothing more than a sexual obsession? Four glorious weeks, he suggested. Surely time enough for even the fiercest passion to fade.

6

And so, in this state of grace, they sallied forth, protected by their magnificent lie. They searched Los Angeles for new hideaways, each one a little gem to be remembered when it was over, each providing a setting for a new bout of passion. Sometimes Oscar could get away from the set for only a short period of time, so they would meet briefly on park benches, in gloomy saloons, or at beachfront trattorias, no bar or café too sordid or low-class. They would start out respectfully enough, clinking glasses, murmuring in each other's ear; then the slightest body movement, a leg entwined under the table, a hand resting on a thigh, caused them to lunge at each other over the Pouilly-Fuissé.

One of their favorite places was Tia Juana, a place downtown on Olympic Boulevard, close to the Palace Ballroom where a considerable amount of *Body and Soul* was being shot. It was a fetid pit with greasy oilskin tablecloths, suitably base and irresistibly clandestine. Here Hispanic workmen, cement splashings on their shoes and overalls, stood at the bar and ate pork burritos in newspaper wraps. Alice liked to sit at a back table near the shrine to the Virgin of Guadalupe—a bright blue plaster statue set into the wall, votive candles flickering on a ledge beneath her. Under her watchful eye, how could Alice not be saved?

For Oscar everything was exotic and memorable. Either he was genuinely unjaded by life or he was experiencing this kind of pleasure for the first time. Or, possibly, it occurred to Alice, he was a director simply creating a romance.

As they ordered another round of tequilas (drinking was the only thing that helped drown the roaring adrenaline), his cool hand would slip inside her sweater to fondle the curve of her breast. "Do you know you're the first drinking partner I've ever had?" he would say, gliding a kiss across her neck. "My first true woman friend—*and* my first introduction to true illicit romance." Eloquent words for her pleasure and also perhaps for the boys at the bar, whose eyes swiveled back and forth in wonder. While they necked furiously, dreamy and oblivious, the clientele would goad them on, murmuring excitedly in Spanish. Eventually, however, the workmen's enthusiasm was reduced to the shuffling of feet and an embarrassed silence. In fact, wherever they went, their impassioned fervor inevitably served to depress or infuriate somebody. So much torrid passion in the middle of the afternoon was apparently just too sickening to watch.

Then they would retire to the parking lot. The twenty-yard walk to their respective cars would be punctuated by bouts of feverish lust, both of them grabbing wildly at each other, their bodies arched over a car hood or a back fender.

"We're behaving like animals," Alice would say, slipping a hand down the front of his pants.

"You love it. You love to be loved."

"Yes."

"Of course it's not love," he would reply, burying his face in her breasts. "It's just *sex.*"

"Exactly."

One afternoon they were pressed against the garbage cans behind a 7-Eleven market, Oscar's right hand voraciously exploring the inside of Alice's blouse while his left clutched a bottle of recently purchased Veuve Clicquot champagne. A man driving a Ford station wagon drew up beside them. "Hey, why don't you get a room? Take it *down the block*," he shouted, outraged by their audacity. "Children are trying to *live* in this neighborhood." Then he sped off, red-faced, hands gripping the steering wheel, the top of a baby's car seat just visible in the back. They grinned foolishly, undaunted in their ardor. The very idea that they were doomed infused them with untold bravado.

"What we really are is best friends."

"Best friends in love with love."

"Too bad it has to end."

"If I weren't married, this wouldn't last five minutes."

"So at least we have *something* to be grateful for."

At the Huntington Museum, famous for its magnificent azalea garden, not yet blooming in October and so completely deserted, they played the thrilling game of Professor and Student (reminding Alice briefly of the swinish Dr. Tarkington). Lying on the grass, book in hand, she was surprised to discover a hand fervidly traveling up her skirt (an innocent floral number chosen specifically for the occasion). Then, suddenly, arms and legs flying, the two of them were laughing and tumbling across the spongy lawn. Oh, the exhilaration, the greed, as they worked themselves up into a lustful lather! And all this panting and throbbing was merely a saucy prelude to their blissful afternoons in a hotel.

Because Alice couldn't, of course, take Oscar home. She convinced him that movie-mad Julio might leak the scandal to the *Hollywood Reporter.* So far she saw no need to mention the possibility that Mike might drop by.

"This affair gives me a sense of insecurity I've never had before. It's fascinating," Oscar said, lying across a bed one Saturday afternoon, eyes fastened on the ceiling.

They were at the old Georgian Hotel in Santa Monica, a damp place with gurgling toilets and frayed towels. The French doors were open wide and they could smell the salt from the sea and the sweet dusty resin from the pine trees outside.

At one point, during a lascivious bout of sex, Alice had insisted her lover take her bent back across the ornate iron balcony. "Have you no pride?" he had said, devouring her. "That's a luxury a mistress can't afford," she'd whispered back. Below, under the giant palms, on the strip of park that bordered the cliffs, old men had been stationed at rickety card tables since breakfast. Sprawled on blankets a few feet away, their wives quietly discussed lunch, family disasters, and recent operations, oblivious to their husbands' exalted cries and fiery accusations of cheating. "God, I love fucking you. . . . Isn't fucking incredible, just *incredible* . . . ," Oscar shouted, their two naked bodies hanging precariously over the street. "I don't think the people down there got that," shrieked Alice, laughing. And in fact, not once, to the lovers' dismay, did one of the Saturday picnickers raise an eye upwards to catch the stunning performance above their heads.

Afterwards they doused the flames in the shower, soaping each other up, hands everywhere in the frothy madness, still ravenous but also with the innocence of two people exploring the possibility of the perfect *affair.* What splendor! To be able to love someone without conditions and then let go. To move forward, drifting in carnal stupor as though tomorrow they might die.

Now, as the fiery sun slipped into the ocean, they lay naked and immobile on the bed, listening to *La Traviata* on Oscar's CD player. It had become *their* opera—an appropriate choice for an afternoon of frenzied passion and hysteria. So that Alice would feel like a true mistress, Oscar brought her a little something every time they met to make love: perfume, silk stockings, marzipan chocolates, and once a lemon-colored canary in a cage. Today he had given her a Polaroid camera, an opportunity to drop the affair to a more salacious level.

"You realize that we've packed in more sex than some couples do in a lifetime. Without the drudgery," said Oscar.

"You'll never have to tell me you hate my cooking."

"Or *not* tell you and hate you anyway."

Was Oscar a sexual enslaver, or liberator, wondered Alice? Was this what she meant by freedom? *Sexual* freedom? Of course, there had been other strictly erotic liaisons, mostly brief—a week or two of familiarity being enough to put out the fire. And though at first she had considered the affair with Oscar as purely promiscuous, now she regarded it as a kind of terrific dare. If pushed to the limit, might she not abandon her old self and experience a fabulous release of spirit?

As Mike had been the opposite of Walter—cool comfort as opposed to stifling domesticity—then perhaps Oscar was the next step in her search for deliverance. Either that or he was the man to finish her off for good.

The sun had cast orange shadows on the wall. Alice rolled closer to him, his odalisque, his warm slave. "Normally, a relationship is a balancing act between freedom and intimacy," she whispered. "Fortunately, we only have to concentrate on the intimacy. We're lucky."

"You're talking again," Oscar whispered back, his eyes closed.

"You see, that's it. We can talk because we're best friends. If we were really together, you'd be lecturing me by now. Men love to lecture women, to victimize them with knowledge."

"Ah, the terrible plight of women," he sighed. "Men are never victims? Don't you know that men have this hopeless dependence on women? We play games to keep our heads above water. We *pretend* to be in charge. We know you're smarter. We're just terrified you'll get the upper hand."

"Your fragile egos. Your maleness. Your erotic identity."

"Thank you."

"Forced to be little John Waynes when what you really want is to weep at our sides."

"Do you write about this?"

"I'm too shallow. I write about show business. Do you think men are constantly striving for emotionally free sex?"

"I can't imagine what you mean."

"*Twenty-two*-year-olds."

"Dull, dull, dull. I don't like younger women."

"My God," said Alice. "I love you for that." And she did. She rested her head on his shoulder. As if they had been dozing peacefully this way for years, Oscar affectionately ran his hand up the back of her bare legs. Even though Alice had made serious attempts to shut off her consciousness, suddenly the thought of him stroking the back of his *wife*'s legs in the same way dismayed her. So she forced herself to concentrate on other things: the surge of Pavarotti's sublime voice, the smack of the boys' skateboards as they leaped the curb below.

"Do you know," she murmured as he stirred next to her, "sometimes I believe that love for a woman is a series of sacrifices. In that way she can actually *dominate* her lover." And for a moment, she thought this might possibly be true.

"This appeals to me."

"Of course, a woman pleases her lover in order to please herself. But if she gives the man the *power* to love her, she remains in control. Simone de Beauvoir might have invented feminism, but she spent a lot of time giving Sartre neck rubs and removing his coffee cups from under the sofa."

"And he was unfaithful to her all the time."

"You see, we're lucky. We'll never have that problem."
"Too bad it has to end."
"Yes, too bad. Too bad . . ."

Alice reveled in her courtesan role, aware that she might have lost all sense of herself. When Oscar told her he disliked her manly suits, she bought narrow little skirts, wearing them shorter and shorter until finally she complained that she resembled a game-show hostess. "You look ravishing," he said, then noticing her face flush a spectrum of rosy hues, he added, "Yes, I give you permission to be smart *and* beautiful."

And it was true. For the first time in her life she didn't feel that one of her God-given attributes could flourish only at the expense of another. Contrary to her mother's dire warning ("Men can only appreciate objects of beauty in a *quiet* room, dear"), she felt gloriously released.

As she walked down the street radiating what she imagined was a salacious glow, she wondered if this were a woman's strongest or weakest moment? Wide open, wanton, existing solely for pleasure. But whose? His or her own? Did Alice now live and breathe only through her sexual appeal? An embarrassing thought. Jessica, the stern voice of reason, suggested that she was a "victim of her own bad taste." For Alice, however, it was the very transience of the affair that was so thrilling. For as long as the spell lasted she would be invincible.

Heavily doused with alcohol and hysteria, they had an enormous capacity for self-deception. The more their emotions sucked them under, the greater pains they took to deny it. Nonetheless, Oscar's jealousy about Alice's past kept surfacing.

"Look, did you sleep with a lot of people?"

"What?"

"I mean before you were married."

"Oh, you mean in the late seventies."

"Yes."

"Actually it was exhausting and lonely pretending to have such a good time. While you were happily making documentaries at UCLA about the underprivileged, we single girls were forced to spend entire weekends with people we barely knew."

"So there *were* a lot of men?"

"In terms of our arrangement, you have no right to ask."

They were sitting at a table by the window at Le Dôme, a restaurant frequented by people in the movie business. Sometimes they met openly here, pretending to conduct a meeting, not really to fool other people but to fool themselves. Emotionally they were torn between the realities of yes, it had to end, and thank God, it *will end* before it kills us both.

At lunch the place was bursting with agents and studio executives, the superachievers, the kids from Ivy League colleges earnestly bent forward over their mineral water. Because each had accepted the fact that he or she must be more conniving than the last, the voices were constantly raised, cryptic words of wisdom and scandal echoing loudly off the walls. These were the people who got Oscar fired up, whom he accused of never rising above the development deal, whose only talent lay in their "vulgar aspirations to greatness." Just being in the place made him crazy.

"Have you noticed Hollywood is a business of short frustrated men? It's a one-company town. A cottage industry closed off from civilization. People here can't imagine their lives outside movies. And this is a place where executives earning less than a million a year consider themselves *underpaid!*"

Hair flopping over his forehead, face red, eyes swiveling, he sounded off while he knocked back several glasses of new Beaujolais. The first time they had had lunch there, the esteemed clientele had made sidelong glances at the table, presumably, thought Alice, to find out who the woman with this controversial director was. Now they stared openly. To go with the barking voice, an odd wave of lunacy radiated from Oscar (the same wave that had no doubt intrigued Alice from the beginning), which drew the attention of the entire restaurant.

"So how could executives possibly understand about being *creative*," he shouted, making no attempt to hide his outrage. "God forbid they should put themselves out there to be criticized. Like *I* have to. Like anybody who *does* something has to do. They don't know what it's like."

"Is this the familiar cry that the artist is never appreciated in his time?" Alice asked, adopting the role of smiling conspirator.

"No, no, no!" he shouted, his voice reaching as far back as the kitchen. "You see, the studios don't know what talent does, but they earn bigger money than we do, so they *feel* they must be more talented. Money equals prestige and, of course, *power* . . ."

By now waiters were making a wide berth. The bad boy, the untamed director, clearly no worshiper at the altar of manners and respectability but a free spirit. He was out to prove to the pious corporate boys that a true artist pays homage to no man.

"And don't think you can *embarrass* these people!" Oscar barked loudly, as he leaned back in his chair to receive the appalled stares of two studio executives. "You *can't*. No wilting flowers in this game. By the time they get to the top they're impervious, *uninsultable*."

Laughing, he slammed a hand on the table, his high

forehead pink with a three-glass flush. He was thoroughly enjoying himself. In fact she wondered if he hadn't chosen the restaurant in order to demonstrate his irreverence, to sound off to a full audience. "Christ," he yelled, once again blessing the room with one of his drunken smiles, "what a town!"

Yes, indeed. And as much as Alice knew this might be an accurate picture of the hell into which no sane man or woman would consider entering, she still wanted some part of it.

"What exactly have you got against me writing screenplays?" she asked, not for the first time.

As usual, Oscar tried to dissuade her. "If you have something to say, write a book. Contrary to what people believe, rarely is film a writer's medium."

"You spent three years rewriting your first draft of *Deception*. You told me."

"Oh dear," he groaned loudly, "you mean when I thought everything was more interesting in *film* than in life." Then in a voice tinged with what was close to theatrical despair (the business of movies either made him wildly exhilarated or despondent), he added, "Look, you shed blood for a hundred and twenty pages, and then they get three girls from *Wellesley* to decide if your script is any fucking good."

"Are you saying nobody important reads?"

"Yes. No one reads. *Thalberg* didn't read. It doesn't matter. Hollywood is a *whore*. She'll bend over backwards for an original idea, however stupid it is!"

The subject was closed. The wine was finished. He looked steely-eyed and pensive. Perhaps he was worried that he had laid it on a bit thick. But no; Alice realized he was busy staring at someone.

"And who the hell *is* that? Some guy keeps waving at you," he said.

There was no need to look. Alice knew the person who for the last five minutes had been signaling at her from across the restaurant.

"He's an actor. I was kind about a movie he did."

"I bet."

"You're jealous."

"I'm not jealous, I'm resigned." The alcohol had finally deflated him. He was worn out. "Let's face it. Life with you would be hell."

Because of his jealousy, it was irresistible not to push things beyond their set boundaries, even flirt with disaster. During one of their steamy, sybaritic afternoons at the Georgian Hotel, Oscar pressed her again for details of past lovers. And at the end of a wisely abbreviated list, that included Dr. Tarkington, an English viscount, Kevin the TV writer, and a suicidal composer, Alice happened to throw in Mike.

"Mike?"

Oscar made the name sound blunt and banal. It resonated across the hotel's flat cream walls.

"Yes. Mike Pearce."

"Are we speaking of the present?"

"In a way—yes."

He tried to appear casually fascinated, but the wind had been knocked out of him.

"He's a lawyer. Studying to take the bar. I see him sometimes."

Oscar looked stupefied as the full implication of this astounding information sunk in. Had it never occurred to him that she might not be completely his for the taking?

"So he's a lawyer. Is he young?"

They had dressed in silence and were descending in the hotel elevator. It was an old creaking box, the pink neon light causing Oscar's face to look more haggard than usual.

"He's a lawyer *and* a comedian."

"Wouldn't you know. Everyone's a hyphenate." Then as if to cushion the blow, he asked offhandedly, "Is he better than me in bed?"

"God, no," she replied quite truthfully. And, minutes later, the moment seemed to have passed. As they went through the lobby and out into the bright sunlight, he cackled wildly. Alice realized he presumed the whole thing had been a cunning ploy to make him jealous.

On the other hand, Alice couldn't bring herself to tell Mike about Oscar. Fortunately their paths never crossed. Mike was busy with his bar review course. Why burden him needlessly with something that was about to end? After all, she had been content with the adoring student until she met Oscar. In her more lucid moments, she saw her obsession with Oscar as a kind of temporary chemical realignment, a vague distortion of the *whole.* Late at night, when she and Mike sat watching old movies—one of his hands lazily stroking her hair, the other resting on his volume of *Torts* (with great patience he had tried to explain to her the doctrine of estoppel)—she would think: This is sane; this is where I will lay down and rest when the madness is over; the bliss of tranquility will come soon, but not quite yet. She looked forward to the day when the mad intoxication would subside, when dubious longings would be fulfilled and she could slip into the serenity of Mike's devotion.

Oscar had often invited her to come to the set. However, no longer a journalist on location but an apprehensive lover, she purposely stayed away for fear that their pulsing intimacy would leak out and light them up like a beacon. More than that, there was the question of her work at the paper. Cameron Fischer was constantly taking swipes at Alice. "Late *again,*" he would say in front of Leonard (always an eye on

Leonard), marveling snidely at her aptitude for *consistently* missing a deadline. Or as Alice slipped out dressed in something revealing to meet Oscar, he would snarl: "I see we have overcome the career woman's plight. We *can* have it all."

Feeling guilty, she persuaded Leonard to let her do a longer piece for the Sunday edition on Peter Tobin, a young director with one low-budget hit to his name. *Dead Lucky* was a slick send-up of a horror movie, the opening shot lifted from *Un Chien Andalou,* in which a woman slices open her eyeball with a razor blade. In his wisdom, Cameron Fischer had panned it: "A screwball addition to the overworked fright-flick genre . . . of no interest to the thinking man." But it had gone on to do stupendous summer business, winning some horror award, and the studios were now clamoring for the director's attention. Peter was a sickly looking boy with albino skin and a deviate's smile. Proudly he declared himself part of the Venice street hoodlums and invited Alice to meet him in a tattoo parlor on Rose Avenue.

The interview did not go well. In a dazed yet excited state, the young director had to calm himself with several tumblers of Wild Turkey. Unable to concentrate on more than one thing at a time, he ignored most of Alice's questions and fixated on the tattoo artist. Between his groggy murmurings of "*Fan*-tastic" and "Whaddya think, Georgia O'Keeffe, huh?" in reference to the cow skull being drilled on his shoulder, Alice managed to get only one printable quote before he slipped back into a liquor-induced reverie: "The size of my imagination is always more important than the size of my budget."

Alice was forced to follow him around for two days in seedy pinball arcades, up to her ankles in candy bar and hot dog wrappers, and on endless gloomy walks on Venice beach. Once again she wondered at her ability to pull off this kind of thing with any originality. Every piece she wrote somehow turned into a valentine to the *artiste,* lauding his gifts, his expertise, his vision. The originality of his throbbing youth. Just as good manners often prevented her from divulging terrible truths, she also found it impossible to write about people in a way that wasn't *nice.* She would, of course, tone down Peter's retching in doorways and his drunken pass at her while she bent over to retrieve a fallen notebook. ("I guess that's a 'no,' babe." "You guessed right.") His antics, infantile yet so charming, invoked by her magnificent phraseology, would simply radiate the boy's creative talent.

Late one afternoon, having spent a long day witnessing Tobin mercilessly pummel a young Hispanic boy in Gold's Gym (the director shrieking as if Sugar Ray himself lay winded on the mat), Alice came home to find a message from Oscar on her machine. He sounded desperate. It was not what he said—he simply asked her to come—but the brittle tone of his voice that told her something terrible had happened.

7

Wearing a plastic raincoat cinched tightly at her waist, Niki Palmer stepped out of the black Camaro, a newspaper held above her head against the pelting rain. Light from some unidentified source, a mossy greenish glow, swam around her. Walking with stiff mechanical steps, heels clicking, she was making her way across the parking lot when suddenly, out of nowhere, a young man appeared and grabbed her by the arm. She screamed, wrestling wildly, her feet jumping up and down on the Tarmac. Though the rather tame manhandling seemed barely sufficient for so much noise or for the exaggerated footwork, Niki's howling continued, shifting into a low moan when the man lunged forward in an attempt to kiss her on the mouth.

"No, no, no, no, no. For Christ's *sake*, Charlie!" Oscar's voice boomed. He appeared ghostlike out of the gloom, pushing the hood of his yellow, tentlike slicker from his head. There was a clunk, then the light faded along with the whirring noise; the rain stopped and the grips manning the water trucks climbed down. The rest of the crew, huddled under umbrellas at the far end of the parking lot, resumed their lounging positions against the front windows of Du Pars coffee shop and took up conversations left off before the take.

Charlie Reese was in his mid-twenties, a bratty boy, all sexed up, with doleful matinee eyes and a thick mouth. Despite two moderately successful movies that had sent young girls into spasms of lustful adoration, his insecurity was all too apparent. Defiantly he stood his ground, face turned away from Oscar. "Look, I know I'm *supposed* to be angry. I can feel angry. But it's here, *inside*," explained the actor, tapping his chest, anticipating the director's frustration. "But I don't feel my character would realistically lash out at her. I can't justify it. I see him as more cerebral."

Niki, both feet turned sideways, was smiling smugly down at her shoes. Like a murderously spoiled child in a playground, she idly jerked her body back and forth.

Oscar sighed wearily. He bent forward as though to address the stubborn objections of a five-year-old. "Let's delve into the character's dark psyche," he told Charlie. "Maybe something happened to you as a child. Maybe Niki reminds you of your mother, or maybe a crazy *sister* you hate. When she was bad, somehow you, Charlie, always got the blame—always, Charlie—until one day, *tonight*, right now, you can't take it anymore."

As though on cue, Niki moved forward, mouth open, bug-eyed, waggling her tongue from side to side, imitating what she imagined to be a supremely annoying sister. But the actor was oblivious, immersed in his own thoughts. "I'm sorry," he announced flatly, "I don't feel that's an *intelligent* reason."

"Christ Almighty," moaned Niki, lighting up a cigarette.

"Let me *give* you an intelligent reason," said Oscar, moving closer to Charlie's damp peachy cheek. "It's after ten, we've done fifteen takes, we're six days behind, and because I SAY SO. On this set, I AM GOD. Do you understand?"

Charlie must have been getting the idea because he went to move away. But Oscar held on to him and started to shake him as rigorously as Charlie was supposed to have shaken Niki. The actor's head bobbed back and forth. Rainwater ran from his hair and down the side of his face, his lips flapped foolishly; only when tears began to form in the corner of his eyes did Oscar let go.

"I thought your job was to inspire and motivate," Charlie said breathlessly, his voice breaking.

"My job," Oscar said quietly, "is to scare the living shit out of you." He stepped back, composed, even refreshed by the little set-to. "Look, the rhythm of this character is very important. The way he carries himself, the rapidity of his body movements. His anger is always *out there* because he is incapable of going below the surface." Charlie, out of fear or stupidity, looked at him stony-eyed. "OK," Oscar went on. "You're not buying that, but your resistance is what will give it an edge. *Use it.* Because, believe it or not, people are often doing one thing and *thinking* another."

Finished, Oscar turned to a distracted Niki, who was busy coiling a strand of damp hair around her forefinger. He lifted the cigarette from between her pouty lips, cupped his hands round her face, and jerked her toward him. For a moment their mouths touched. "And that's how you kiss her, Charlie," he said, "only longer."

Then he stuck Niki's cigarette in his own mouth and walked briskly away across the wet Tarmac as an assistant director announced the dinner break.

For the last hour Alice had been watching Oscar from a distance. With his hands in his pockets—the languorous slouch offset by the sharp dimensions of the yellow slicker—he resembled the unwilling hero of a boy's adventure story. One minute he was joking with the crew, the next he was wandering back and forth, jaw set, as if he were about to defuse a bomb. Occasionally Alice had managed to catch his eye, but he had merely glanced at her, in passing, as if some weeks back he had invited a distant cousin to the set and now that person had actually turned up. What could have happened?

Then, only a minute ago, when the Madonna-faced actress smiled, mouth obediently tilted upwards for Oscar's kiss, Alice, the spectator, had experienced a terrible feeling. Dread, as it were. And what was that secretive look between them as he walked away? Something implying Oscar held the key to this woman's perpetual desires? Or was Alice imagining this? She was beginning to wonder about her own feelings; this passionate attachment that had come out of nowhere. The so-called perfect affair. Not that Oscar had been anywhere close to perfect lately. Sometimes after an afternoon of giddy sex, his mood would change abruptly. Like a man straining against sentimentality, he would try to humiliate her. A slight stab to see if she was holding up. He would ridicule her bony, boyish figure or brag about his wife's fabulous cooking: "I'm on my way home to one of her sumptuous roasts, three kinds of vegetables . . ." Showing her that he had everything—a good wife *and* a mistress—engorging himself with his divine life. Alice's mother used to say that men couldn't resist that kind of behavior, "They're all peacocks, all feathery show, with those tiny brains . . ." But so far Alice had refused to cower under his torturous jabs. Because they had no future, she had graciously let him defend his own fears at her expense.

All this ran through her mind as she watched him, shifting her position every minute or so, stepping aside for the comings and goings of the crew. She reminded herself that, no matter what, they had only one week left; that passion fades; that good sex was certainly not love—every imaginable excuse to guard against the possibility that Oscar was sleeping with his leading lady.

≈

Oscar walked across the parking lot, head down, mouth pulling on a cigarette. He looked up at Alice and was about to speak but was immediately distracted by someone calling his name.

A large man with a florid complexion and a balding fuzzy hairline was trotting toward them. Due to the absence of a neck or perhaps the dire effort of pulling along his cumbersome body, his shoulders appeared perpetually hunched over, distorting the shape of his jacket, an expensive number that had the flowing lines of a short kimono. As he broke into a lumbering run, one of his chubby arms jerked upwards; he was pitched forward waving something: a long tube of rolled paper.

"Oscar, there you are! We need to talk," he shouted excitedly. What remained of a southern drawl gave a slight twang to his voice.

Oscar glanced at Alice. "Look, I'm really sorry," he said, with unexpected solemnity. "But I . . ."

"It's fine. You're busy," said Alice, already wishing she were somewhere else.

"No, no," he said. "It's just that . . ." But before he had time to go on, the red-faced man was panting beside them. With an exaggerated groan, he lifted each leg to shake the water from his ostrich-skin loafers.

"Do you know how much these fucking machines cost, Oscar?" he demanded, ignoring Alice.

"Hello, Marvin. Yes, I do."

"Why is it still raining?"

"Because it was raining in the last shot. It's a match."

"Maybe it stopped raining while they were driving in. They're in the car, right? Then the girl says, 'Oh look, it's stopped raining.' And I could save about twenty *fucking thousand dollars*," Marvin boomed, his head nodding furiously to underline this fact.

In the gloomy light, the circles under Oscar's eyes seemed deeper, giving him a forlorn, rather desperate air. "Can you wait a few minutes?" he asked Alice, raising an eyebrow in Marvin's direction.

Like many overweight people, Marvin was surprisingly nimble. Though he huffed and puffed, his feet could turn on a dime. He swung round to take a close look at Alice. The slight grimace suggested that, though she was not uninteresting to him, he couldn't place her as part of his entourage, his big plan.

"Let's eat," he said, grabbing Oscar's sleeve.

"I'll see you in fifteen minutes?" Oscar said to Alice, as Marvin dragged him away. He managed a smile, but the effort seemed exhausting, more than he could manage right then. "Why don't you get some dinner, too?" he shouted back at her.

"Take a look," Alice heard Marvin say, as they headed for the coffee shop. "Tell me what you think." With a flourish, he unfurled the paper tube. Alice could see that it was some kind of mock-up of the poster for the movie. *Body and Soul* was splashed in red across the top of the page. Niki, arched backward, breasts oozing from her bathing suit, was couched in the arms of a taller, more buoyant Charlie Reese.

"Honestly, Marvin?"

"Yes."

"It's shit," Oscar said casually, stubbing out the cigarette under his foot.

Most people were familiar with Marvin's story. A hustler from the South, an ex-salesman in bathroom fixtures, he had married a dancer in Vegas, then progressed to antique-car sales, a venture that somehow had been his entrée to show business. Oscar had told Alice that it was never a question of Hollywood giving Marvin money, it was simply a matter of *how much.* Full of himself, he was convinced he had won some kind of victory over the rest of the town because, so far, he had experienced only success. His two movies, *Death Run* and *Death Run II*, had each grossed over two hundred million dollars worldwide. On hearing the original story idea, delivered by some unknown writer, Marvin had excitedly leaped to his feet. As millions of dollars flashed before his eyes, with his coatflaps lifted, his ass bent toward the novice, he had delivered the cunning words, "Fuck me here, I want it so much!"

Holding a cup of coffee and an apple, Alice found herself standing in the center of Du Pars coffee shop. The awkwardness she had been feeling during the last hour was now magnified by the air of insane chumminess that had swept over the crew. An extra offered to carry Alice's cup. Then two grips whistled at her to join them. The larger one—belly exposed where his T-shirt failed to meet his work pants—opened his arms in a sweaty surrender while his associates cheered him on. So long was she frozen in place, eyes glassily fixed on some unknown horizon, that the only seat remaining was in Oscar and Marvin's booth. She was debating this move when Niki skipped past her, cigarette in one hand, a salad in the other. Behind her trotted her hairdresser, a horsey woman skewering pin clips into the actress's wet hair. In passing, Niki gave Alice a molten, furtive little smile. This Alice interpreted to mean that not only was she aware of Alice's affair with Oscar, but that, more than likely, the two of them discussed it daily—no doubt with much hilarity—as they rolled around between takes in the director's trailer. Plagued by the thought, Alice felt compelled to sit down immediately.

All previous humiliation paled, however, compared to what she felt standing at the end of Oscar's booth. He made no move to let her in; in fact, he looked up at her astonished. Then when it was clear she wasn't going anywhere, he pulled her into the booth with such force that her silverware spun onto the floor. Marvin noticed nothing. Paper napkin tucked into the neck of his cashmere polo sweater, rosy forehead bent, he was too preoccupied with his food: a plate heaped with meat, potatoes, and corn, all swimming messily in gravy. And when he began talking again, though he looked startled to see Alice, he was clearly too agitated to acknowledge her.

"Look, have I breathed down your neck so far?" he moaned at Oscar, fork in midair. "The rain is a tiny thing. It's after eleven and you've only done one setup tonight. We can't work like this." And as one hand hit the Formica, the other continued to shovel food into his mouth. "And who *is this?*" he managed finally, the fork now pointed at Alice.

"A friend. It's fine," said Oscar, giving nothing away.

Marvin hesitated, but he was bursting, swept up by his own indignation. "You don't understand, Oscar. Harvey and the mental midgets upstairs are all over me like a swamp. I'm the schmuck who has to tell them what the fuck is going on."

"You handle them well, Marvin," Oscar said dryly.

Alice had tried to touch Oscar's leg—an innocent, reassuring squeeze—but he had eased himself away. Head bowed, he was now busy trying to slide tomato wedges into a cheeseburger.

"Of course I do. That's what I get the big bucks for. You're an extremely talented director. *My* genius is that I *recognize* talent. I revere talent. I'm a maverick in my field, and I'm only here to help. After all, what are heroes without shoulders to ride on, eh?" Marvin chuckled, delighted by his own wit. "Listen, I know what it's like. I've been in the trenches. Did you know I directed second unit on *Death Run II?*"

Oscar brought the cheeseburger to his lips, then set it down. "Really? No, I didn't know that," he remarked with only a hint of sarcasm.

Being there, Alice realized, was a colossal mistake. She was about to speak but Marvin was banging the table again.

"You think I don't get it. But I do. Artistry is expensive and you can't rush it. You see, I got the micro point of view about making a film and the macro point of view about what the studio *wants*. But Oscar, Oscar! Help me out here. Where are all those sharp angles you promised me? Where's the fucking get-up-and-go? Where's the plot, Oscar?"

"This was never a movie about plot."

"Of course it wasn't," Marvin groaned, throwing up his hands as though insulted. "What do you take me for?"

"You said you wanted to do art, but you can't resist schmaltzing it up," said Oscar. He turned to Alice, but it was only to reach across her for the salt. "These are subtle characters," Oscar went on. "Maybe a little too eccentric for you."

"Eccentric. Hey, I know eccentric. Eccentric has a core audience. I've made hundreds of millions out of *eccentricity*," insisted Marvin, mopping a spot of gravy from his chin. "I created a new genre. People said to me, 'What's the difference between eccentric and bad taste?' And you know what I said to them?"

Oscar inclined his head, feigning interest.

"I said, '*Money! Ask the English!*' " Marvin was laughing now, food particles flying. He pummeled the Formica, incredibly pleased with himself. "They quoted me in *Time* magazine. So don't tell me I don't *know*." He had winded himself. Gasping, he eased himself back, running a hand over his extended stomach. "Look, I can sell anything, kiddo. Just tell me what the fuck this movie is turning into."

Because of the rumpus, Marvin's barking voice, and his hand endlessly and rhythmically slapping the tabletop, all heads were turned in their direction. Across the room Niki was squeezed into a booth with three burly, leather-clad stuntmen.

She was signaling to Oscar, pale arms aloft, so that Oscar was obliged to wave back. Encouraged, Niki leaned her head on one of the enormous shoulders next to her, then collapsed into giggles. Humbert Humbert's own dream-child, thought Alice. The grin, the startling white teeth, the sun-flecked complexion. Smug. Well, a little of that went a long way.

"Oscar, I have to go," she said, touching Oscar's sleeve. But she was immediately drowned out.

"*Talk* to me, Oscar," Marvin bawled. "For Christ's sake, *talk to me!*"

"If you can explain it, why make it?" Oscar said, his voice a cool breeze against the storm. "Of course, I'm paraphrasing Francis Bacon."

"Berkon over at Fox? That dick-head doesn't have an opinion unless someone gives it to him."

Oscar was checking his watch, presumably to inform Marvin that as far as he was concerned the conversation was over. "Look, I do the best I can. I'm sorry if I'm not Martin Scorsese."

"Thank God. His pictures never make any money," snapped Marvin. Distracted for a moment, eyes closed, he was attempting to remove a food particle from his teeth with his tongue. Oscar stood up. Relieved, Alice stood with him. They were halfway out of the booth when Marvin exploded. He lunged across the table and grabbed the director's arm, almost removing Alice's eye in the process. "Hey—I backed you when no one else would!" he yelled at Oscar, hanging on. "After your last fiasco, frankly, you couldn't wipe the shit off your shoes on a studio doorstep. If this fails, I take the heat. You go and do a nice sensitive piece for cable about deaf children."

"No, Marvin. *I take the heat.* You'll be forgiven. You took a chance with a failed director. You want to fire me?"

Oscar was shouting now. "Then fire me and *cancel the fucking picture!*"

It was a death threat. Marvin went white and let go of Oscar. "Cancel the *picture?*" he screamed.

"Look, Oscar, I really have to *go.*" In some horrible piece of mistiming, Alice had spoken a split second after the producer, puncturing the void after his final, excruciating wail. She heard her words reverberate, her voice too loud, too shrill. The silence was stupendous. Oscar stared at her. In what seemed blank astonishment, he murmured, "Alice, could you wait a minute, please?"

"Yeah, could you wait *just a minute,*" echoed Marvin, furiously waving her away. Alice felt herself turning beet red and sank down into the booth.

Breathing like a wrestler, fists jumping on the tabletop, Marvin pushed his face across the table. "Hey, who am I?" he howled. "I'm nothing. I'm a product man. A *schlep. I* don't have to like everything. I'm not making pictures for *me.* But let's face it, Oscar, broad-based audience appeal has eluded you. I'm here to save your ass. I *know* what they like in Kansas. I want Niki to be more out there. More *fun.* She's playing it like she has six days to live. If she's drinking again, I'll sue her dumb ass. You know what Hitchcock said about actors—*cattle.* Well, cattle get slaughtered. And let's put back the scene where Miss Dallas tries to kill her with the tire iron, *shall we?*"

Out of steam, he slumped down. He pulled the paper napkin from his neck with a flourish, a finishing bow. Then, satisfied, he smiled broadly at Oscar—a gesture from the reigning don that it was all over. "OK, killer," he added breezily, "now go get 'em."

But it was Alice who was pushing her way out of the booth. "I'm leaving now," she said quietly to Oscar.

"Do I *know* you?" Marvin's voice rose in a crescendo again.

"No," she replied. "I'm Alice Wilder."

Marvin looked at Oscar and then back at Alice. He shrugged his shoulders as if to say "*So . . . ?*" Alice waited for Oscar to introduce her, to cast her in some favorable light. But he said nothing.

"From the *Recorder*," she said, the color rising in her cheeks.

"Alice Wilder!" Marvin's chubby arms were suddenly outstretched. "I've read your stuff. Well, you don't *look* like a writer, does she, Oscar? Not like the schmucks we have to work with." Head bobbing, he eyed Alice's body, then wiggled a suggestive eyebrow at Oscar. "Here, sit down," he said, slapping the brown Naugahyde. "You want to talk to me about the movie. Sit, sit. Oscar's got to go back to work in a minute, anyway."

The fact that Marvin had heard of her was small compensation. But she sat anyway. As she squeezed in next to Marvin, he angled the top half of his body away from her, no doubt so that she could have the full journalistic benefit of his magnificent profile—minus a couple of chins. He slid one chubby arm along the booth's wood divider and then, to Alice's astonishment, with a fleshy hand proceeded to squeeze her shoulder. He smiled. Small teeth with a pink tongue protruding. "Do you take notes?" he asked rather coyly, shifting closer.

Oscar stared in disbelief. For a moment, Alice thought he might lean over and take a crack at Marvin, or both of them. She smiled back at Marvin. A rapturous, wicked smile for Oscar's benefit. Two could play at this game, she thought. For good measure she gave Niki a wave across the way. "No, not necessarily," she replied graciously.

"Clever you," said Marvin. He paused theatrically and tilted himself forward. The huckster now. The unctuous showman. "I admit, I've made hundreds of millions of dollars. Do *I* understand what the public wants? Nobody does. But you know what I say about movies?" Experience told Alice this was not a question. "I say it's like *life*. You gotta be like a sponge, you gotta have the ability to absorb stimuli."

"I *said* fifteen minutes . . ."

"But I'd already been there over an hour. Have you any idea how I feel?"

"Yes, you made it extremely clear at dinner. I'm sure the whole crew knows how you *feel*."

They were standing in the deserted Farmers' Market square behind the coffee shop. During the day it was a favorite tourist spot. Now the fruit stalls and fast-food joints were boarded up. Metal chairs and tables lay scattered where people had left them.

"You asked me to come to the set, something I hate doing. I was horribly embarrassed."

"You didn't seem so embarrassed cuddling up to Marvin in the booth, *did you?*"

"This is crazy. Will you look at me? Stop pacing like that."

Oscar, eyes focused on the ground, was navigating between the metal tables at an amazing clip. "You were actually flirting with him. I now realize this is something you do with *all* men. All those other men like, what's his name—*Mike?*"

"I told you about Mike. We discussed this. I was seeing Mike before I met you." She tried to move closer, but he shot off, knocking over a chair, cursing under his breath.

"Let me ask you," he shouted, now positively seething, "does it ever feel just a little tacky sleeping with two men on the same day? I'm curious."

"That's never happened," she replied. She considered the idea for a moment and wondered how she had managed to avoid it.

"Both Mike and I are extremely grateful."

"*This* is why you're so angry? Because if we're going to point fingers here, let's discuss Niki."

"What about her?" Oscar's hands shot up as if the subject matter was exhausting, a constant burden to him. "She's difficult. She's insecure. I have to be careful how I treat her—what I *say* to her."

"Why don't you tell her that breasts are no longer a substitute for talent?"

"You're wrong. She *is* talented."

"In what way?"

"In an *original* way. I think she has some kind of basic raw abandon."

"In bed or on the set?"

"What?" He looked dumbfounded. "It's not my policy to sleep with my leading ladies. It's unproductive and *unethical.*"

"I didn't realize you were so big on ethics."

He stared at her sideways, surprised and a little hurt.

"Sorry," said Alice, suddenly aware of how angry and jealous she sounded.

He stopped pacing and slumped down onto one of the metal chairs. "Christ, this is hell," he moaned.

"*What* is? Will you at least look at me?" she pleaded. "Is it the movie? I realize you're having a god-awful time with Marvin."

"Hey, I listen, I say nothing. I do the work."

"Why don't you fight back?"

"Fight back?" He was indignant, ready to boil over again. "This is the movie business. Don't show any sign of a struggle or they move in for the kill."

Oscar was sitting, head down, his limp arms casting long shadows behind him. Where was the passionate man who had caused such an uproar at Le Dôme? The fire was gone, and Alice realized that she was suffering from a mild case of disappointment. As if sensing this, Oscar said, "You have to understand, it's not that easy. I work where I can work. I do the *best* I can. As Coppola says, When you do a movie for personal reasons, shoot as much as you can today, because they might *fire* you tomorrow. So I work hard. I go home. I separate my plastic from my paper garbage, but I don't consider I'm making any real *difference* in the world. In this business there's a mutual agreement to fuck each other. And I'm simply trying *not* to get completely *fucked* by the other side."

He got up. Though the cloud had partially lifted, there was something else eating him up inside.

"Are you telling me you don't care?" Alice asked, her voice echoing across the square. "You used to care. You were passionate about movies. You spent an entire lunch telling me you hated the studio system. Are you saying you've sold out?"

"Sold out? What would you know? Stop being so goddamn clever."

"I'm not."

"You are," he insisted. "The facts, the *facts*. You sound like every journalist I know who fell in love with the director's *early* work. Of course you want me to stay put. Well, I can't. I take chances. Life shrinks or expands in proportion to one's courage and *so on* . . . Everyone needs to move forward."

"With Marvin Shapiro?"

"Look. My movies are about emotion, obsession, neurotic fear, human *failure*—messy stuff. Marvin has to think it's about something else because that's his job. His *business*."

"So you like him?" asked Alice, astonished.

"I respect him—in a way. He's smarter than all of us. He shits in Hollywood but he eats somewhere else."

Alice laughed. For a brief moment Oscar seemed to

relax. In fact he was on the verge of smiling when he uttered a low groaning noise and started pacing again. "Oh, God, Alice."

"*What?*" she asked. "What is it? Look at you, you have veins popping out on your forehead."

"I don't know."

"Tell me. Will you please come over here and tell me what the hell it was that was *so* important? Why you dragged me up here?"

"It's just that—well, we've been getting sucked under by this thing. It was crazy to think that . . ."

"You're walking away again. What are you trying to *say?*"

Oscar shook his head as if he had done everything to spare her the worst. "Ruth found out."

"About us?"

"Yes."

"How? Did someone see us?"

"No."

"How then?"

Oscar looked away. "I told her."

"You *told* her?"

"I had to be honest."

"What kind of *honesty* is that? When you're so guilty, you can't hold it in anymore?"

"Please . . ."

"What you mean is," said Alice, incredulous, "you *unloaded* your guilt?"

"She was unbelievably angry."

"What did you expect? In case you didn't know, there happens to be a fine line between truth and sadism."

"She tried to stab me with a knitting needle."

"Oh, God."

"She's been knitting things for the boat people."

"Ah" was all Alice could manage to say.

"She's part of this group . . . Anyway, she just *came* at me, it was terrible."

Alice had lost him. He was already back home, admiring Ruth's ability to save nations with shawls knitted by the good women of Beverly Hills. His face grim, he came over and leaned against her, unable to speak.

"Well, I guess we knew it had to end," she said. She was behaving as she always did in moments of deep anxiety—rational, calm, stoic—terrified of showing any emotion lest she be deemed weak.

"God, this is awful."

They stood there foolishly. Light casting bright green pools on the slick asphalt made the moment seem surreal. After a minute—perhaps it was five, so spellbound were they by their own peculiar dilemma—Alice was aware of someone else standing with them. It was the second assistant, just visible against the awning of a Mexican food stand. He murmured soft words into a crackling walkie-talkie, then coughed apologetically before he spoke:

"They're ready for you now, Mr. Lombardi."

It was hard to believe that the whole thing had just fizzled out. She had imagined the sensational farewell when he left for Illinois with Ruth, something along the lines of the great classics: oceans of despair, blood and guts on the sidewalk, then last rites as the great monster was put to rest.

Instead, she was overwhelmed with panic, disbelief, and the sensation of having been dispossessed. She had forfeited something unexpectedly, something she had considered at a later date might quite easily be given away. Driving home was like moving slowly underwater. Traffic noises filtered in, car headlights beamed across her face, but in reality she was swimming back there with Oscar. The parting had been anticlimactic to say the least. With the second assistant standing awkwardly in front of them, Oscar had managed nothing more than a brief squeeze of her hand before walking stiffly back to the set.

Alice awoke at six the following morning to find Mike asleep next to her. For a moment, she couldn't imagine how he had got there. She thought perhaps she might have dreamed the episode with Oscar. But as she sat up, the full roar of her stupendous hangover swept over her and with it the bizarre details of the previous night.

She remembered coming home from the location. She had undressed in the darkness. Then, with a tumbler of vodka resting on her knee, she had sat motionless on the end of her bed, waiting for her emotions to subside. Her only movements in the next hour were to search for and successfully find a ten-milligram Valium hidden at the back of her desk drawer—saved for emergencies such as these—then drag a small chair close to the window to watch the wonders of the backyard at one in the morning. The great thing about alcohol was that it put a comfortable distance between the person and the event, an opportunity—she told herself—to address the situation *objectively*. This wisdom, as she watched two sprinkler heads (apparently the only ones working) feebly come to life on the far side of the lawn. With the effect of the Valium swelling up inside her, the sputtering hiss of the water, and the sound of the gentle rustling breeze as it moved through the palm trees, she was relieved to finally have rendered herself oblivious to the pulsing, hostile world. That is until she looked up and saw Julio sitting naked in his living room window, staring across at her. It was at this point that she had called Mike.

≈

On the phone, she dared only admit to a growing fear of her landlord. But when Mike arrived, her body awash with the truth drug, she told him all about Oscar. She left out his name and their stunning bouts of sex, downplaying the whole thing to a palatable level: the tedium and disappointment of adultery, her humiliation, and her own naïve stupidity. Amidst chokes and sobs—all the outward signs of emotions she had been unable to show Oscar—she heaped her sorrow upon Mike. With furrowed brow, he listened for a good ten minutes, then asked, "Is it over?" And when she nodded silently, he removed the half-empty vodka glass from her hand and said, "I suppose you'd like another drink to go with the eight or nine you've already had?"

"Yes," she murmured, blinking stupidly. Having unloaded her grief, she felt temporarily uplifted.

"*No*," he said, his voice soft but chastising. Then wrapping her in a blanket like some half-crazed refugee, he whispered, "Poor little thing."

She felt guilty talking about Oscar. By making him the villain and herself the innocent victim, she had betrayed her former lover and now, by lying about it, was actually betraying Mike. But Mike seemed to be on a different track. There were no recriminations. He was the voice of reason, the confident, authoritative adult. Where had he learned this smooth bedside manner? On the first night they had met, while Alice was busy studying the astonishing alignment of his muscular back, he'd told her that once on a train he had helped a woman to give birth. He, the only sane person among the hysterical travelers, had had the dexterity and wherewithal to pull the infant clear, cut the umbilical cord (with his Swiss army knife), and wrap it in one of his own clean Brooks Brothers shirts. No nonsense, a quick and efficient operation, with one or two sharp commands to quell the crowd.

"You're such an idiot," he said now, clicking his teeth in disapproval.

And she nodded her head. "I know," she managed to croak feebly. She wanted to be an idiot. It felt safe, just the right babying she needed, knowing how cowardly it was to have called him in the first place.

"How could you fall for that old thing? The married man. The lies, the deception, the broken promises. It only ends in disaster," he said, still sounding more the stern father than the jealous lover. "At your age, you should know better."

There it was, the age thing again. And soaked with Valium and self-remorse, Alice's eyes started to water.

"Hey, come on, buck up," he added. "No moping."

"I'm fine, really. Thanks."

"Good. Because I need to get some sleep. I've got a squash game at eight with Ryland, then Constitutional Law."

More tears from Alice—although at that point she hadn't the faintest idea why. The last belt of vodka had hit her and a new, giddy wave of euphoria was washing up to her brain.

"Listen, what's the difference between an Italian and a Jewish mother?"

Through her muddy haze, she realized he was telling a joke. Unsinkable Mike.

"The Italian mother says to her child, 'If you don't eat, I'm gonna kill you.' The Jewish mother says, 'If you don't eat, I'm *gonna kill myself!*' "

He laughed heartily. Alice imagined Oscar's mother bending over him, a little boy in short pants, nose wrinkled as he stared at a full plate of kishka. The thought of him made the blood rush to her cheeks.

"That's better," said Mike. "For a moment you looked like you were passing out on me."

He sat on the bed and took off his shoes.

"Now listen," he whispered, bending his face down next to her. "I like to be lied to as much as the next sap. But this is it. I'm a man of principle. I only make so many concessions." And incorporated in his cockeyed smile were also the words *Bad girl, are you sorry? Have you learnt your lesson?* "So, understand, this is the last *other* boyfriend, married or not, that you're allowed."

A second later, he was naked. Like a weary schoolboy, the layers of clothes had come off in one clean peeling, thudding ceremoniously against the bedroom door. In the dim light she was reminded that his body was indeed a marvel. Yes, she told herself, bolstered by a thick wall of vodka—this is good enough for me. More than good enough.

He lifted up her body, placed it between the cool sheets, then slipped in beside her. "And I kid you not. OK?"

"OK," she bleated softly.

In the middle of the night, Alice had the vague impression of Mike speaking in soft soothing whispers to someone on the phone. Later she realized she must have been dreaming. After waking at six, she dozed off again for an hour to be awakened by Mike's voice, then his face smiling at her round the bedroom door. His hair was wet, slicked back from the shower, and as usual he was alarmingly bright-eyed. "Good-bye, you adorable stringbean," he said. Then with the solemnity and forbearing of her beloved grandfather, who decades before had often left her with the same somber salute: "Remember, you're only a *girl*. And girls need to be taken care of." With that, he was gone.

At 8 A.M. she took more Tylenol for her headache. She got up and lay on the sofa in her small, awkwardly furnished living room in order to soak up the soothing rays of the morning sun. She felt curiously calm—infused with a sudden lighthearted relief. It was over. Without Oscar in her life, her days would now become luxuriously free. No rushing out to meet him at a moment's notice, dropping her work, making feeble excuses at the paper. She was astonished and proud of her powers of recovery. Yes, passion did burn itself out, and how quickly! Besides, there had been that look in Oscar's eye when he had talked about Ruth—a whole universe of human suffering that she felt too young (or was it too old?) to bear. Or could it be, she wondered—her sense of relief now starting to ebb away under the crashing weight of her hangover—that overnight she had become a coldhearted betrayer of her own passion?

Mike had reminded her that she was only a girl. Dr. Julia Hansrud, a therapist Alice had seen a month after she'd left Walter, had informed Alice that this was a large part of her problem. Whereas the esteemed Dr. Kellerman had been concerned only with Alice's repressed anger against her "terrifying and controlling mother" (a conjecture that Alice had systematically denied, mainly to annoy him), Dr. Hansrud waved this aside as redundant: "Old stuff," she announced. She was more interested in the grown woman who, the doctor claimed, was busy posturing as a defenseless little girl. "Men are obliged to see you as a girl," she insisted, "because *you* always refer to yourself as one." She accused Alice of fashioning herself for men and not for herself, allowing herself to be held hostage by men until, in desperation, she ran away. It seemed the beating Alice had taken was no longer the fault of her mother but was a result of the "abnormally strained relationship" she had had with her illusive yet demanding father.

Dr. Hansrud was of German descent and in full recognition of her heritage wore tweeds, sturdy hose, and crepe-soled walking shoes. Despite her twenty-five years in the

States, she spoke with a pronounced German accent that Alice was convinced she exaggerated merely to intimidate her patients. She reveled in her cool foreignness. In fact, her only concession to the sunny California skies was a David Hockney print on the wall and the golden nut brown color of her skin, acquired, she said (in an unusual moment of candor), during weekends with her boyfriend in Palm Desert. Though unflattering, her dress was appropriate for the freezing conditions of her small, overly air-conditioned office, which she jovially referred to as "the meat locker" and which was decorated entirely in what could only be described as vibrant flesh tones. "Womblike," contended Alice, which caused the impatient doctor to roll her eyes in exasperation. In effect, the stern gaze, the regal bearing, and the peculiar outfits (on cooler days Alice had noticed a velvet cape and feathered cap hanging inside her door) reminded Alice of her mother, arousing in her a feeling of insecurity and dread, emotions she typically misinterpreted as respect.

Alice protested, explaining that from a tender age she had been bewildered and more than a little scared by the attention men paid her. When mailmen and delivery boys flaunted their secret desires, their brazenness served only to humiliate her. Was she, out of good manners, obliged to return the compliment? At nine, she told Dr. Hansrud, when she had allowed a Jehovah's Witness to wait in the living room for her mother to return from Christmas shopping, the man had tried to seduce her. Perched on the edge of the sofa, a collection box in his lap, the thin, swarthy-looking gentleman had impressed upon Alice the need to open one's heart and, more important in these troubled times, one's wallet. But it was obvious, explained Alice to Dr. Hansrud, that when the man beckoned for her to come closer, what this middle-aged zealot really wanted was to open up something *else*. (Not a flicker from the cool doctor, but Alice continued.) With a nicotine-stained finger, he had grabbed the hem of her school uniform. Then, as carefully as if he were handling a delicate lace tablecloth, he had lifted her dress and suggested he might touch her "down there," if in turn she would stroke what he referred to proudly as his "Jimjo."

Dr. Hansrud's icy response was to raise her left eyebrow—a gesture that Alice had come to realize signified total disbelief.

"Ah yes," she said, curling her thin upper lip, "a lifetime at the mercy of men. You're a writer, Alice. You're a storyteller, an artist who typically deals in fantasy. When your life is humdrum you simply *invent* things in order to make yourself special and so *creative*. Then not only do you become infatuated with that thing or person but with the *drama* of it, so that finally you can't tell one lie from another. Naturally, to keep the theatrics alive, it becomes necessary to *change* the object of affection—whatever it is, the man, the adventure—when it fails to intoxicate you anymore." Dr. Hansrud was suddenly so revved up, moving uncharacteristically an inch or two in her Eames chair, that Alice was convinced she must have recently written a paper on this very subject. "Eventually," she went on, her large head thrust forward, "you drown under the weight of your imagined life. Unable to create—and you have admitted to me your difficulties in writing anything you consider *worthwhile*—you turn on yourself. Because if you cannot be creative, what do you do?" "What?" quickly inquired Alice, anxious out of politeness (or was it fear?) to play the game. "Destroy," replied Dr. Hansrud, "*destroy* . . ."

When Alice met Mike she stopped visiting Dr. Hansrud's icy lair. Not only was she positive the doctor would regard her much younger lover as another narcissistic and undignified attempt to *destroy* her life, but in all honesty Alice found that spending the $150 fee on a new article of clothing gave her a sensation of well-being far greater than any explanation of Jung's *élan vital* could provide.

Later that morning, still in her robe, Alice went outside to pick up the newspaper. She noticed Julio leaning against his car. Rocking his torso to some imaginary beat, he gave Alice what looked like a pretty good impression of a psychopath's smile. His outfit, too, might have been pulled together by a maniac: cowboy boots, electric yellow shorts, a black string vest topped with a furry bolero, and of course his James Dean hat.

"Feeling better?" he asked, grinning.

The idea that he might imagine some mystical moonlit connection between them from the night before caused her to be momentarily rooted to the spot. Fortunately there was no need to reply; her phone rang and she bolted inside.

"You can't end something until it's over."

It was Oscar.

"We only had a week to go."

"I know, I know." He was speaking softly. Alice guessed that Ruth was around somewhere, perhaps sewing woolly sleeves onto sweaters.

"Did you tell your wife that you wouldn't see me again?"

He hesitated. "Yes."

"Then that's it. It's over."

Another pause. "Christ. I'm not sure *I* can give it up just like that. Remember the beach, those incredible afternoons at the hotel?"

"We were drunk all the time."

"Exactly. And who am I going to drink with now? I *miss you.*"

Alice felt a catch in her throat. There was a predictable voyeurism about the whole thing that was beginning to depress her—that and his breezy attitude implying nothing had changed. In fact, as soon as Oscar had admitted divulging all to Ruth, the romance had started to deflate like an old tire. Now the more Oscar talked, the more Alice distanced herself from him. She was experiencing the strange sensation of leaving her body and drifting through the rest of the house, putting things in order, attending to chores that had been neglected during the recent delirium: laundry, dying plants, lightbulbs to be replaced in the hallway—and of course her work.

"Listen," said Oscar, "who knows what will happen between us down the road?"

"Nothing."

"*No*, nobody knows that. Ruth and I, I mean, we've had our problems . . ."

"Stop it, Oscar."

A sigh. "You're right. Women are smarter about these things."

"Women *need* to be smarter."

"And what do men need?"

"Careers first, I think. Then money."

"Ah . . . so clever," he said. "So I won't see you again?"

"No."

"OK, if that's what you want."

"Yes."

Silence. It was as if they were relying on each other to stand firm.

"OK. Good-bye, then. I'll call you in a few weeks," he said and hung up.

Two minutes later, the phone rang.

"It feels like a few weeks already. Can we have lunch?"

"No. Tomorrow, you'd hate me."

"Good. I'm tired of only hating myself."

"Don't do this. Please, *please*, Oscar."

The force of her last *please* cut him off. Finally beaten, he said wearily, "All right," then hung up.

Alice sat quietly for a moment, vibrating with the sense of her own strength; the power that came from taking control. Her mother, not to mention Dr. Hansrud, would finally have been proud.

The morning Oscar left for Chicago her agent, Carol Gottleib, called. Alice was still lying immobile in bed. The night before, unable to sleep, she had stayed up late watching TV. Due to the fact that it was the eve of her ex-lover's departure, nervously anticipating a resurgence of desire—a vision of romance soon to be *literally* in flight—she had spent hours flipping channels, and coincidentally she had come across Oscar's first movie, *Deception.* It was a grisly tale, lauded by critics who had put him on the map as a definite comer. The genius manqué. It was the story of two brothers who grow up on different sides of the law and who later do unspeakable things to destroy each other's life. Astonishingly, when Alice had first seen it some eight years earlier, she had never noticed the conspicuous absence of the woman's point of view. This passionate man, this self-proclaimed lover of women, had indulged in only one brief scene in which the elder brother's wife hurls the dinner service across the kitchen, then sinks, wrung out and speechless, into a chair, humbly acknowledging her husband's superiority. Everyone in the movie (shot effectively in black-and-white) shuffled around, head bowed, mute and seething until each one exploded in another wave of violence. Among these characters, the Oscar she knew (or thought she knew) was nowhere to be found. All of which confirmed Alice's suspicion that any further liaison with this man—a man who, for *posterity*, had characterized women as unbalanced hysterics—would have been tantamount to self-impalement.

"OK, this is short notice," Carol said, her voice crackling with action. "Billy Hawkins needs a writer. He's got about eight different people working on this script, but he's having no luck on the female angle. Hardly a big surprise."

In a business of individual striving, Carol was no exception: Instinctively she had championed Alice's first screenplay, *Going for Broke*, not, Alice realized, because she considered it particularly good but because so many others had rejected it. She welcomed the challenge. She was a fearless woman, a monument to the Horatio Alger philosophy, a bona fide member of the boys' club, and many had been skewered on the barbs of her sarcasm.

"This is his first time as a director," she went on briskly, "so expect the worst. And let's hope he's taken a shower lately."

Alice sat up in bed.

"Today?"

"Noon. Can you make it?"

"Yes."

"Good. Jody will give you the details."

8

With the prospect of a screenwriting job, life was back to what it was or rather what it should have been. Dressed in her manly (and therefore serious) linen suit, Alice waited at the front door of Billy Hawkins's somber stone house in Bel Air.

Billy was huge, in terms of box office rather than physical stature. Publicity photos showed him as handsome in a traditional brooding way, perfect dark curls tumbling around a strong if slightly pushed-in face, with a Herculean chest. He had once been described, quite accurately, as a cross between a young Tony Curtis and a short gorilla.

Apart from his tempestuous and well-documented six-month marriage to a stunning seventeen-year-old black model, Billy's overriding passion had always been boxing. As a starry-eyed teenager, he had forfeited his education, hanging around the Crotona Gym to watch his idol the fighter Joe Tavalino go the rounds with his Bronx boys. Eventually Joe took Billy on. He sparred with him, helped build up his stringy body, then the training was advanced to encompass the mysterious ways of grown men and serious drinking. In fact, in the early days, Billy's fame came not from his minor roles on TV but from his reputation for bar brawls; in this his talent was unsurpassed. Having taken on the best, he would then unscrew the overhead lightbulbs, which for the pleasure of a cheering audience he would eat down to the wire. The bad-boy reputation stayed with him, facilitating his credibility when he took on the role of the intergalactic space mercenary Panic. After three successful sequels, he had become the ultimate hero to his young worshipers, the hot-tempered warrior who lived by his own terrifying amoral code.

After a few minutes, an imposing man in shorts opened the door. He was enormous. Legs like giant tanned redwoods were anchored into oversized running shoes, and high above that, peering down at Alice, was a large sunny face, wearing the benign but cautious smile of a headwaiter. Billy's trainer, Alice guessed.

"Hi," he said. He managed to make it sound like a question.

"Alice Wilder. I have an appointment at noon," she offered professionally. "I'm a writer."

The cavernous hallway was empty except for an old 1950s jukebox and what looked like a medieval throne, something King Arthur might have used to send off the troops. The trainer, heels springing in his mattressed soles, leaned over a mahogany banister and shouted up into the void. A muffled voice, maybe two voices, answered back, and Alice was directed upwards.

The staircase was of gigantic proportions. An antebellum folly, it was curved and sweeping; the carpet a deep-red pile patterned with mighty swirling gold crests. Dazzled, Alice climbed the fifty or so stairs to the top landing where the splendor literally erupted. Flocked gold-embossed wallpaper, gold and red upholstered rococo chairs, and then to the left, in the bedroom, a mammoth four-poster bed swathed in mossy red velvet and a baronial fireplace big enough to roast a small horse. Everything in the house seemed designed to make ordinary folk feel diminished. Of course, usually Alice could manage this quite nicely on her own.

It was from the direction of the bedroom that she heard a voice call, "In here." The *in here*, it turned out, was the master bathroom—another fantastic area, every surface covered in gilt and green marble. Suspended over the roomy tub was a life-sized stone replica of Michelangelo's *David*. Artistic license had been taken with the arms, which cradled a dolphin restrained in midleap, the shower head just visible inside the creature's mouth.

Billy and a man were bent over in a corner. Alice noticed that the star was indeed shorter than he appeared on screen. In fact his legs looked truncated in comparison to the splendor of his bulging upper torso, which served as a sturdy platform for the square head and satiny hair slicked back from his forehead. He had a West Coast gangster look about him. He wore a black silk robe, the words TOUGH IT OUT, PAL, made famous in his *Panic* movies, embroidered across the back, and in his left hand he held an unlit cigar. It was enormous. Castro would have been proud. The other man was balding and slight. A beanpole next to Billy. He wore a jogging suit, the zipper undone several inches to expose a few knots of springy gray chest hair.

"What do you think?" Billy asked when he saw Alice. He smiled. The famous lopsided grin, from whence emanated his charm. She advanced gingerly. Apparently he had been speaking of the toilet. "I just had this put in," he said, running a hand over the cool surface as if it were a sleek pet. "The stone was quarried some place outside Siena, Italy. Very rare. Do you know how difficult it is to carve a whole toilet out of one solid piece? I designed it myself."

"Incredible," said Alice, genuinely amazed. The balding man pushed down the gold handle and water cascaded into the bowl.

"He's got a great eye for décor," the man said reverently.

"This is Jim Lynch, my manager and producer," said Billy. Jim smiled at Alice, but it was the star who extended a hand. It was immense. His grip, however, turned out to be surprisingly gentle.

"Let's go down by the pool," he said, sweeping past her. His legs moved with a gentle loping gait while his upper body remained as stiff as a ballroom dancer. In no time he was across the bedroom and down the stairs. A man who was accustomed to being followed, thought Alice.

Outside Billy took off the flashy robe, revealing a small pair of weight-lifting trunks, and positioned himself in the roasting sun next to the Olympic-sized pool. Alice took refuge under a striped awning while Jim sat close to Billy, arms folded, wearing a snap-brim hat pulled down over his nose and aviator shades. After Billy ordered iced tea (the order conveyed by Jim via intercom to unseen workers in the kitchen), there was a respectful silence. Though the actor already sported a perfect suntan—so uniform and glossy that it might have been sprayed on—Alice and Jim waited while he rubbed oil across his massive tundra of chest and arms.

A year earlier, fearing his dramatic talents had gone unchallenged, Billy had veered from his celebrated role as Panic to do a serious movie. A heartwarming tale. A neurosurgeon who loses his eyesight. The movie, however, had been a tremendous flop. His fans saw it as a betrayal, and the press descended, thrashing him mercilessly. Wiser now but no less cocky, he was back as Panic, and the studio, grateful for his return, was allowing him to direct. But it was a sore point, and he had been trying to silence the skeptics ever since. On the way down from the bedroom, they had walked past a poster for *Terminal Case*, and presumably to clear up any lingering doubts regarding his talent, Billy had burst into an explosive defense.

"Let me tell you, they were throwing rocks at that movie three months *before* the thing came out," he said, waving a meaty arm. "Typical. The press takes you to the top of the mountain, then they can't wait to throw you off. I try to do something serious, and suddenly it's on the six o'clock news that I failed."

"What *failed?* One lousy movie with no box office?" Jim, in defense of his star, was outraged at the mere suggestion.

"Right. How many movies did De Niro make that didn't make a dime?"

"Too many," said Jim.

The iced tea arrived. Billy took a sip and leaned forward on his padded lounger so that Alice would get the full force of his sincere intentions. "With this new movie, the investment is so enormous, it won't be *allowed* to fail."

Billy's brows grew together over his misshapen nose. Big and flashy, there was, nonetheless, something alluring about him. A man who had taken his licks and survived. Alice was impressed and suddenly scared to death. For the purpose of her newspaper interviews, her own qualifications were never required. However, as a novice screenwriter she had the feeling that, were she to make one false move, the job would be whisked away from her. She smiled and gazed out onto the expanse of tropical garden where more marble statues stood nestled incongruously between the tall trees. She sat up straight in her lounge chair, to imply professionalism, attentiveness—no, better than that, *reliability.* Of course, for a woman, there was always the temptation to flirt. But she considered herself above that. She did not *fawn.* Cool and efficient, her perfect manners on display, she was determined to be judged purely on merit.

"So, here's the key, okay?" Billy was saying. "We make *Panic and the Second Journey* as predictable as possible and toss in a few surprise morsels. My character always has to be the same. The audience likes that—don't get me wrong, I mean, I *respect* this character. But I can be more cynical, deeper, even removed in this new one—the extent of which I'll experiment with. But once you put the camera on me, and then you blow up something big, it's there on the screen, and they believe it. So, *I* believe it. Okay?"

Billy floated behind his own words, a man rarely interrupted, never questioned. And though he spoke in what seemed an incomprehensible stream, Alice was fascinated. Right then she felt like some star-crazed ingénue herself.

He dragged his lounger in from the glaring sun and positioned it at Alice's feet. Jim followed, scraping his chair across the brick so that finally the three of them were huddled together, almost touching.

"But here's the thing," Billy went on. And Alice presumed the clenched jaw was to inform her just how serious he was. "People are hipper now. They want more of the personal issues, the caring stuff. So we've created a woman's part for this one. To bring in the *older* audience."

"Older?" Alice asked. And quickly her gaze fluttered toward the treetops for fear she might have been caught out—caught out because seconds before, when Billy had uncrossed his bare legs, her eyes had automatically wandered down to his tiny trunks. Like a person who tries unsuccessfully not to stare at a twitch or a nose job, she had been momentarily riveted. Was Panic, the intergalactic hero, worshiped by girls everywhere as they squirmed in their seven-dollar seats, carrying—as her friend Jessica would say—a "decent set of luggage"?

"Yes, older. The over-twenty-*fives*," replied Billy. And to Alice's dismay, he grinned and gave her a sleepy-eyed look—an acknowledgment of her sly glance. "So far, no writer has been able to lick this part," he went on, now incredibly pleased with himself. "This woman has to be real, okay? She has to have sharp lines like a guy. A woman like a man, with a sort of hip humor. Maybe she has a child in there somewhere. Also, I'm thinking about . . . What *was* it, Jim?"

"An ecological theme."

"Right. But basically we have the violence, then the romance—big crossover potential there, with the major action coming in as a sort of punctuation."

"A *big* punctuation," said Jim, one hand chopping the air. Then, reaching under his chair, the producer pulled out a leather script binder. He took out fifteen or so pages and handed them to Alice, explaining that there was no need to see the rest, other writers were busy working on those.

The two pairs of eyes watched her closely, Billy's big hands rubbing together in anticipation. Silently Alice read. As she squinted in the harsh sunlight, it occurred to her that the first paragraph could only have been written by a man.

> Panic bursts in. He rips the Ingram model 11 out of the guard's hands. Opens fire. Blows the entire room of people away. They drop like bowling pins. Flesh flies, blood splatters on walls. One guy is left. Panic jumps him. Pushes the man's nose up into his skull, then rips his throat open with his bare hands. The dust settles. Silhouetted, the woman TANIA stands alone at the end of the room. She is tall, dark, great tits—in other words, his equal. His footsteps echoing, he walks toward her. Then he hits her. *Crack.* She tries to stop him, but he's choking her with his other hand. She kicks him twice in the balls, *crunch . . . crunch . . .*

"So he's standing there . . ." The dark mass, suddenly looming over Alice, blocking her sun, was Billy. "His face is twisted with pain, he's doubled up in agony, and she's *laughing* at him . . ." Groaning, one hand clutching his crotch (his tiny shorts now level with Alice's polite smile), the intrepid space warrior was acting out the tussle between himself and the feisty Tania. "He slams her in the neck. She elbows him in the kidneys—ooh, ouch! *Then,* finally he picks her up by her throat and, *wham,* throws her against the wall." Shoulders snapping, a hand flying across Alice's head, Billy tossed an imaginary 130 pounds of female flesh in the direction of the pool. Though his lack of subtlety was engaging, Alice wondered how much directorial talent could possibly exist behind such a stunning physique. "Now," he said, bending down a mere inch from Alice's face, dropping his eyelids to half-mast and flashing her his cockeyed smile. "Now, we have the love scene. No, forget that, the *sex scene.* We're talking hot, hot, hot."

He was adrenalized, steaming. However, crouched in her chair, Alice could manage only a slight nod in return. She was terrified that she might be expected to act out the role of Tania, although for a fleeting moment she actually considered it if it meant securing the job. The fact that her talents were hardly suited to write this epic did not, of course, stop her from wanting it.

"Here's where we need something more than just the tough, cynical woman warrior. And I have a couple of ideas." Billy straightened up and ran his hands across his chest. Then, with a rather theatrical swagger, he began to pace across the patio. Watching him, it occurred to Alice that there was no difference between the star at large and the working actor. A one-man functioning machine, he was his own raw material. "Number one," he said, "she disarms him with fast, clever, witty dialogue. Reads him the riot act, so to speak, about his bad behavior as a person, as a so-called hero. So, let's put *that* idea on one table. Or—number two—she actually beats the shit out of him. In the last scene she's just driven a spike through some guy's head, so we know she's mean. But she seduces Panic by *beating* him at his own game. Then she collapses into a sort of private hell, some horror she's reliving from her childhood. Maybe she's been abused. Anyway, when he comes to, she's crying like a baby. *This,* I have to say, appeals to me. We'll put that idea on another table. What do you think?"

"So—we have *two* tables?" The words spontaneously left Alice's mouth. When no one spoke, she blushed, mortified by her sarcasm.

However, instead of treating it as a bad joke, Billy took it to mean that she hadn't understood him, as if, accustomed to women not grasping his subtle remarks, he took pride in his abundant patience and generosity. With his princely smile, he stared down at her. In the shade, his eyes had turned an extraordinary deep blue. Alice realized that the almighty defender of the universe, bolstered by her apparent girlish confusion, had suddenly become attracted to her. And there lay the confusion. All at once Alice was torn between wanting to be liked and wanting to be respected. The root of all trouble for the working woman.

"What I meant was . . . ," she started to say.

"Look," he said—and there was a touch of the Godfather about him now, his voice barely above a husky whisper—"I've got a good feeling about you."

A coyness crept over her. She actually blushed.

"Do you think you could make her funny and original? Not *too* original, of course, but someone who *grabs* you. Someone larger than life, the thinking man's sex symbol. Someone, frankly, *I'd* like to fuck." He hesitated, no doubt to assess her reaction. Alice, however, was conscious only of having blinked. He had seen her as weak and vapid, and apparently out of good manners she had become exactly that. "I don't know," he continued rather slyly, "this is tough stuff. What do you think? Do you feel you could really write it?"

Any more doubt and Alice would be down on the brick patio, grasping his ankles, pleading to be given the chance. She stood up, then walked the fifteen feet to the edge of the pool. After reflecting a moment, she turned to face him, assuming a pose she had once seen Bette Davis strike in *All About Eve*. Smart, she hoped, strong, and, yes—all professional reserve now gone—*seductive*. "To be honest," she said, "I hate the idea that a man would be attracted to a woman because she's on the floor weeping. What does that say? He wants her only when she's weak? When he feels in *control*? The whole point about making a great love scene work, a great, steaming *sex scene* work is when an audience feels that two complete strangers discover—through humor, mutual intelligence, *and* animal magnetism—that they have something undeniably in common. And yes," she said, "I think I can write the shit out of this."

Billy looked over at Jim. Hat tipped back, arms folded behind his head, he was stretched out in his chair as if to imply neutrality in any decision making from now on.

"Let's do it," said Billy, rubbing his big hands. "And for Christ's sake, sweetheart," he added, "don't let me down."

What power she felt. An honest-to-God screenwriting job. And then, an hour later, the exhilaration all but vanished. She was doubtful of her ability to pull it off. On top of that she couldn't help thinking she had landed the job by default—by flirtation, willful or not. She was so used to the disappointment of rejection that easy victory seemed improper, almost dishonest. Perhaps she didn't deserve it. And that was another problem the imperious Dr. Hansrud had tried to illuminate. Uncomfortable with success, she told Alice, she rationalized failure before it happened. Consequently, she was quite comfortable when she was let down. Because in that way, the good doctor explained, she could avoid confronting any new challenge that, in turn, might become a bigger *opportunity to fail*. Billy's last words had been "Don't let me down." And, inevitably, three hours later, as she lay prone on the sofa, they were the *only* words ringing in her ears. Did she really have no sense of her own merit? And if so, as Dr. Hansrud might say, "From *vence* did this come?"

She called home hoping to talk to her father, from whom, she liked to think, she had inherited a persistent drive and stunning work ethic. Instead, her mother picked up the phone. Might Alice have finally fulfilled one of her mother's airy dreams? After all, this was iced tea by the pool with a movie star. Position and Wealth, her mother's touchstones for success, were in evidence.

"You accepted the job without asking how much money?" her mother exclaimed, choosing to be the stern voice of adult reason.

"That's my agent's job," said Alice, already deflated. "I write. She argues about money. This is a great opportunity to be part of a movie that will definitely get made."

"Well, I hear Billy Hawkins is *not* a very nice person. Apparently he's being sued by two women, both pregnant with his children. The one in Texas is only *thirteen* years old."

Typically, when Alice's mother responded to a question (usually unasked), it was as if a man with a minicam on his shoulder had stopped her on Madison Avenue and demanded comments for the six o'clock news. The stream of formulated opinions continued, and Alice found herself defending Billy Hawkins's honor.

"Look, he's a very nice person. Straightforward. Really quite intelligent."

"I hear his IQ is about the same as his neck measurement."

"Well, I don't think his fans would waste time measuring his *neck*, Mother."

"Whatever happens," she replied, ignoring Alice's dim joke, "promise you won't leave your job at the newspaper."

Alice was lying on the sofa her mother had shipped out to her when she moved from the Paradiso Hotel. It was one of the many items that had been stored in the basement of their New York apartment building, where relics of her mother's wild decorating schemes lay abandoned. Artistry, her mother liked to say, was in her blood. Acquired during her "fifties" fling—*Cecil Beaton and His Inspiration*—the sofa had a curved frame in the Empire style with a gold-leaf wash, blue satin striped Regency upholstery, and matching tasseled bolsters. It looked like something out of the Riverside Drive apartment in *How to Marry a Millionaire*.

"And what good is all that money, anyway, if you're a woman *alone*?"

Ah! There it was. The ever-present cause of this poor woman's sleepless nights. Not that, for some decades now, either of her parents had felt comfortable discussing what they referred to as "Alice's situation." Even when she had called to break the news of her separation from Walter (though lonely, she had been too humiliated to go home), they had hidden their disappointment with cool bravado. "I had a feeling it wouldn't work. The numbers on the street address added up to *thirteen*," her mother had remarked most sagely, drawing on the wisdom of a lifetime's superstition. "Well, why didn't you mention it earlier?" Alice replied, irritated by the lack of compassion. "Because we don't like to interfere," her father explained, as though referring to some unsavory street brawl. "Anyway, all that's water under the bridge now," he added cheerily, as usual looking on the bright side. "You have to *move on.*" And in such a manner they had wrapped up her five years of marriage.

"I'm not alone. I have boyfriends," insisted Alice, sliding further into the sofa cushions, closing her eyes.

"Teenagers have boyfriends. Women have husbands."

Another gem. Pearls of wisdom from the woman who, though outwardly reconciled, had never forgiven Dr. Wilder since he had strayed with his receptionist.

This happened while Alice was in her second year at Sarah Lawrence. The good doctor, unable to resist the permissiveness raging around him, had briefly run off with his thirty-year-old nurse, Kendall Sommers. He moved into her tiny one-bedroom apartment in the Village, furnished with Indian wall hangings and beanbag chairs. Here, close to asphyxiation after his nightly four or five Spanish brandies, plus the heady aroma of Kendall's patchouli body oil (the doctor later confessed to Alice), he had surrendered himself to the delirium of exhibitionist sex and the pounding rhythm of Jimi Hendrix.

Alice canceled her summer vacation. She had planned to go to Connecticut with her classmate Pamela Gore to visit Pamela's mother, Celia (referred to nonchalantly by her daughter as "first-generation lesbian"); instead Alice went home to commiserate with her mother. The place was in an uproar. Slipcovers had been removed from the living room sofas, shelves had been scrubbed, rugs rolled, and when Alice arrived her mother was waxing every inch of parquet floor. Some people turn to drink or indiscriminately distribute large sums of their husband's money in department stores. In moments of deep distress Alice's mother cast off her expensive clothes (her armor against life's sorrow) and with violent determination turned to housework, seeking refuge in something that for years she had abhorred. What energy! It was as if she were washing this man not only out of her hair, but right down the street, across the river, and back to New Jersey where he came from.

And as though to make up for a lifetime of capriciousness, Alice diligently followed her mother around, armed with rubber gloves, apron, and a pail, like a night nurse on duty at Bellevue. But it was as if they—father *and* daughter—had left the forlorn woman. Both deserted their Mother Courage.

"You're not helping," she had complained, on her toes, straining to swab the top of the refrigerator.

"But I am. Look, I am," replied Alice, up to her elbows in dishwashing water.

"No. You're not helping because you don't understand. You *never did*. Because you're not as sensitive as I am. You don't *feel things* like I do."

Which was a reasonable assumption because Alice had been careful not to show one iota of her feelings for at least a decade. And though all kinds of buried emotions came rushing to the surface, the bleak and reproachful look from the unhappy woman stopped Alice in her tracks. It said it all. She realized that her mother was unable to bear the fact that her own life seemed finished while Alice had the whole of hers to look forward to—however mediocre a prospect that might be. Moreover, it was as though her daughter had inherited a weakness: Alice was going to fail; she would make the same mistakes and become everything the poor woman despised about herself.

"I *do* feel things. And I know what you're going through."

"You couldn't possibly."

"Maybe I *could*."

"You *don't* and that's the pure and simple truth."

"Mother, the truth is rarely pure and never simple."

"You with your brainy words and books. Always an answer."

"*Cogito ergo sum*; I think therefore I am" was the arrogant college girl's reply.

And so the rift, which might very well have been mended that summer, once more rose solidly between them.

Often Alice wondered if the friction between herself and her mother had not in fact been manufactured, actually *invented* by herself, that it was Alice who kept the relationship at such a constant angry boil in order to justify her struggle for freedom. "To free oneself is nothing. It's *being* free that is hard," her grandfather used to say, quoting liberally from Gide, with whom he claimed to have got drunk many nights at the Crillon, along with André Malraux. "Dare to be yourself, kiddo." All well and good, thought Alice. But who *was* that?

Despite their alienation, Mrs. Wilder never gave up the fight. On the assumption that no decent man could be attracted to a woman who wore men's trousers, she sent to California copies of her old Chanel and Patou suits. Handmade silk brassieres and camisoles would arrive every few months by Federal Express. Supposedly, on seeing these costly underthings, any man worth his salt would be so entranced, he would immediately propose. These were the items Alice had romped around in (or rather, in and out of) on many a hotel rug with Oscar. Lately, when obliged to present highlights from her dating life, Alice left Oscar's prominent role out of the picture. Mike was the star of the show, although she lied and said he was a respectable forty-year-old, soon to be made a partner in a prominent Century City law firm.

"Lawyers are tricky, they can't recognize the truth because they have to lie for a living," warned her mother, a connoisseur of the trade. "They are all frustrated actors. They are incapable of making interesting conversation and so give vulgar *speeches.* Which means, my dear, you must pretend to agree with them on everything."

"Thanks, Mother," Alice replied. "I'll bear that in mind."

9

For more than two weeks she had been living an untroubled life with Mike, almost suburban in its ordinariness. On the hot, sultry evenings, he would come over after his bar review course and they would lie silently together in bed, the windows open, to listen to the comforting sound of crickets and the gentle melodies of the old dance bands on Alice's favorite radio station. On Saturdays, wearing his team colors, she sat beside him in the stands at UCLA eating hot dogs, cheering his baseball team until, just like the cheerful boys and girls sixteen or eighteen years her junior, she grew tired and hoarse. Being with Mike was like convalescing after an illness; she could thank her lucky stars more damage hadn't been done. Unlike her heady days with Oscar, the impression she was making was never a consideration. She drifted lackadaisically while good-tempered Mike put all his energy into making life sane and grounded, only too eager to take her along.

Complementing this feeling of mutual well-being, there had even been a self-conscious exchange of favorite books. A leatherbound volume of Tennyson's *The Princess* from him and a treasured copy of Céline's *Death on the Installment Plan* from her, heavily underlined, schoolgirl scribblings crammed in the margin. Theirs was a college romance. Nontaxing yet dependable, it allowed her to get on with the task at hand—her *writing.*

Once or twice she accompanied Mike on his late-night visits to the Laundromat (he seemed to go through an amazing pile of wash every two days). With the place deserted, the whitish green light bouncing off the machines, they sat happily in their plastic seats, notepads on their knees. While Alice labored with the tough but winsome Tania, her ever-cheery student devoured his burdensome Civil Procedure. Later, in the fluff-and-fold room, Mike would rip off his Grateful Dead T-shirt, his baggy Dartmouth hockey shorts, his underwear, and dive into the clean clothes as they tumbled out of the dryer—a nondescript heap, most of the things faded with split seams. His poverty appealed to her. As the reigning defender of his blossoming adulthood and with her new wealth (small by Hollywood standards), she bought him silk shirts and a cashmere sweater. Seductively she reminded him that he must allow her to show him some of life's little optimisms.

One afternoon he took her to Venice beach with his law buddies Chris and Josh. It was Sunday, still red-hot despite the fact that it was October, and a great proportion of Los Angeles's weary were laid out on the sand. By noon the huge expanse was packed as far as the shoreline. A hundred radios throbbed and thumped. Couples giggled and massaged warm oil into each other's backs. Muscle men strutted. Elderly fat women positioned umbrellas and heaved themselves into the shade while sun-worshipers lay rigid, moving a precise six inches every half hour to rotate their gleaming bodies westward.

Close to the water's edge, the students had staked out their spot with a semicircle of empty beer cans. In the center lay an ominous pile of textbooks, plus an assortment of sandy, bruised fruit. Chris had brought along another student, a rather sensible girl named Liz. A stern organizer, she made the boys kneel while she applied thick coats of tanning cream to their backs, then tested them tirelessly on their Multistate Bar questions.

Alice lay a few yards away. The heat was tremendous.

And though she had covered her deathly pale skin with sunblock, after ten minutes hostile blotches started to appear on her kneecaps and across her chest area. Already parched, she felt horribly exposed, as though lost on some fiery continent. As it happened, she had come prepared for something quite different. Armed with a wide-brimmed hat, a simple black bathing suit, her toenails painted a deep sinful red (a holdover from her Oscar days), she had dared to imagine herself as a mysterious siren for these young men, the perfect object of their boyish longings. Admittedly they had been friendly, even respectful. When she tried to land *The New York Times* on her stomach and the hot wind had blown it to pieces, they had scrambled to save every page. When her hat followed, Josh had cantered off to fetch it. But, in truth, all their attention was directed at Mike, who was busy entertaining them with front flips on the sand. Olympian leaps performed with measured ease. It was he who mirrored their exuberance, epitomized their youth. And so Alice had assumed the pose of the unseasoned traveler. Moving closer to the beer cooler, which rose soothingly like a temple in the desert, she had wrapped her body in a towel and curled up to concentrate on her Tania notes: love goddess, slave, soon to be Panic's witty companion.

"Isn't this great? Hot, hot and steamy!" shouted Mike, skidding to a halt at Alice's feet. Arms extended, he mercifully blocked the sun for a second. "You look great."

"It's too hot," she said miserably.

"No. All this fresh air is good for you. Puts color in your cheeks." He removed a beer from the ice chest. Then he kneeled down and ceremoniously peeled away her towel. The red burn on her kneecaps had expanded. Her shoulders were crimson, and her face stung from the dry salty air. "Hmmm. A nice tenderloin of beef," he said, and rolled the icy bottle over her scorched thighs. "All you have to do is remember to turn every twenty minutes." He removed the yellow pad from her hands and kissed the tip of her pink nose. "And no more work."

Just then two young California girls bounded over, tossing a Frisbee. Big blond Valkyries. Surefooted things, hair flying, bodies gleaming with oil, breasts exploding from minute bikinis. They bounced back and forth with sporty ease, then joined Mike's audience with hoots and applause as he deftly executed a couple of perfect cartwheels. The more voluptuous of the girls drank thirstily from a bottle of mineral water—gulps big enough to cross a Sahara—while the other, large-boned and doe-eyed, moved her hips in a rhythmic roll as a transistor radio strapped to her waist echoed some thunderous beat.

"Ahhhhh!" Mike shouted, and he was off again, hurling himself down the beach. He ran for the water, hitting it with a blood-curdling scream. The Amazons were mesmerized, necks craned, their hands resting on their firm bronzed thighs.

And the brooding, flushed earth mother in her mossy velour bathing suit reached into the ice chest for a beer, then rolled over on her side. No wonder she felt so dispirited. Had she ever been like these dreamy smooth-skinned girls, breasts rising and falling in anticipation of life's big adventure? Their self-assurance was draining. Or perhaps she was jealous because of their fascination with Mike. Except she wasn't exactly sure *what* she felt about Mike. It had occurred to her that being so relaxed around a man might mean she didn't really care. No, she was flattered. She had snared the handsome boy. "Ah, you great sturdy thing. I love you. There, I've said it," he had whispered one night, pulling off her decidedly unsexy cotton pajamas. Lately her dress had become even more boyish, bordering on sloppy. She wore shorts, old sweatshirts, unconsciously, perhaps, to make herself younger, more in tune with him. "I plan to take care of you," he had told her, laughing. "I am on permanent standby to rub your temples and soothe you with lies." Then, softly, he had added, "You know, I can't wait for this relationship to *solidify*"—as if to imply mysteriously that something might be standing in their way. Secure in her bliss, she had never inquired what that thing might be. Instead she had the luxury of whispering back, "Yes, I love you too," without fear of the usual complications. She realized that she was behaving the way a man does when he first seduces a woman. Saying those words, hoping to perpetuate that exquisite feeling of *being* loved. Yet here was a man who was so substantial, so decent, how could she not eventually be smitten?

The rest of the afternoon slipped by. Mike dashed in and out of the water. Liz peeled fruit and patiently tested Chris on Criminal Law. Josh, swathed protectively in his giant towel, only his carrot-topped head poking out, tried to flirt with the bronzed beauties. Though he was getting nowhere, the ongoing dilemma seemed to make him morbidly happy.

"Look at them. Such *goddesses!*" Moving sideways like a crab, he scuttled over to Alice. "Imagine being me, waking up every morning knowing that I will never be allowed to get near women like that. It's a *life* sentence." He groaned, then crouched down, next to this woman who, presumably, was *less* goddesslike.

He waved at them. He did deep knee-bends and told a couple of jokes, but the exquisite creatures ignored the skinny boy. Besides, Mike was back.

"There—push the hair off your face. Let the sun get at you," he said, dropping to Alice's side. He removed a lick of sandy, oil-soaked hair and sprinkled water on her forehead. "Or do I sound like your mother?" he asked, laughing. Yes, she thought; but, of course, she felt like *his* mother. There was a horrible tightness in her limbs. The brightness was blinding, her head throbbed. For the hundredth time she ran her tongue across her salty lips.

"The outdoor life suits you," said Mike, brushing more sand from her eyebrows. "You just need to toughen up. I have big plans for next year. We're going to go hiking, canoeing, then skiing." And when there was no reply from the lump on the sand, he said, "You think I'm not serious?"

"About what?"

"About wanting to take you *away?* To stop you feeling old and insecure."

"Are you saying I'm insecure because I have no desire to be sporty? An interesting argument. The *old* we can talk about later."

"You're angry?"

"Not at all." But she was, although she knew she had no good reason to be.

He refused to acknowledge her grumpy mood. He chatted on as though his humor were enough for both of them. Finally he knelt down, his mouth close to her hot ear. "Do you know what Benchley's traveling advice was?" he whispered, laughing. "Always keep a thin native girl between yourself and the ground."

Alice's anger melted. She held on to his neck and went to kiss him, but he stiffened and pulled away, glancing back awkwardly at the boys. The opposite of Oscar, she thought, when it came to sex. Though a born exhibitionist in the bedroom, Mike was all decorum in the street. If she made a lewd grab at him in the car, he slammed on the brakes as though a small animal were suddenly gnawing at his pants. He had been raised to hold women's hands, to carry their coats just as her father had obediently (though reluctantly) cradled her mother's fur wraps. Never did he criticize what Alice wore. In fact, unlike Oscar, he never seemed to notice her clothes. But why, she wondered, was she making the comparison? And *what* comparison? That Mike didn't work without Oscar to back him up? All Mike wanted was to cherish her. Was she not cherishable?

An hour later, Alice felt herself drifting down, relaxing into the depths of the sand. Everything washed over her: the drowsy voices, the gentle roar of the waves. With her fourth beer the irritability had slipped away. It was late. The sun had dissolved a bank of clouds into a strip of fiery orange; the sea was no longer a cool green but a shadowy gray. Sunbathers, arms laden with possessions, were starting to trudge slowly up the beach toward the parking lots.

"Let's go," said Mike.

"Oh, God, yes, please," she murmured.

"You wanted to leave before?"

"Yes."

"Why didn't you say something. Not everything's a fight to the death, you know."

He smiled down at her. He was right of course. And before she dared admit that the bottom of her feet were burnt, he had hoisted her up like a sack of Idaho reds and carried her across the sand to the car.

That evening, he cooked dinner for her in his tiny apartment off Pico. The living room boasted a threadbare sofa, a few art posters hung haphazardly across the yellowing walls, and a dozen cartons of unpacked books. In these spartan surroundings, his charming hospitality was all the more impressive. Full of admiration, Alice sat on a wooden stool and watched as he spun around the five square feet of kitchen, from the refrigerator to the stove to the sink, juggling the ingredients for his chicken Sonya. A recipe, he explained, he had lifted from an old girlfriend. Because the ceramic knobs on the stove had disappeared—"around 1953," he remarked proudly—he used a hefty pair of pliers to adjust the flame on the gas burners.

Later, lying on his cool sheets, he massaged soothing lotion into her skin. The large creaky bed took up most of the small bedroom. Law books were stacked in uneven piles against the walls, and to block the noise of the traffic below, he had taped ragged-edged squares of insulating foam across the windows. As soon as the sun set, her sunburn had turned several shades darker. And except for the startling white center of her torso—the precise shape of her bathing suit—every inch of her naked body shone a raw crimson. Carefully, with slow strokes, Mike smoothed the oil across her stomach. Then he slipped his head down between her legs. He lifted her buttocks and pulled her toward him to lick the sand from between the pink folds of her skin. Sand was everywhere. In her dry matted hair, grinding between her shoulder blades as her body rose and sank with his rhythmic pushing. Then he turned her over and with a certain brutality fucked her from behind while, silently, she egged him on. It excited her to be taken amidst this semisqualor. She suddenly wanted to be pinned to the wall, beaten senseless, suffocated, drowned—anything to lay siege to the endless wanderings of her mind. Arched like a predatory bird, he went at her, head back, veins popping on his thick neck until, finally, she was saved.

During her blissful sleep, one burnt leg out of bed resting on his set of *Witkin's Summary of Californian Law,* she had a vague memory of the telephone ringing. It seemed to ring a long time, stop, then start again. She remembered Mike crawling over her, the salty smell of his arm brushing her cheek as he lifted the receiver. He spoke only a few words, something about "sleeping" and "tomorrow," then hung up.

Because he had been away almost three weeks and because normally her adept mind was very conscious of the flow of time, she might have computed the possibility that Oscar would call. But when she heard his voice on the phone, for a moment she was rendered speechless.

"Alice?"

There was static on the line and a peculiar hum.

"*Alice*? Are you there?"

"Yes, I'm here."

"I just wanted to say hello. How *are you*?"

He sounded giddy and overexcited. It was only ten-thirty and she wondered if he could already have had a drink.

"Well, I'm fine," she said lightly.

"God, you sound *wonderful*."

The hum had suddenly turned into an ear-splitting roar. It was as if he were trying to shout and keep his voice down at the same time. "Look, I'm leaning against some goddamn *toilet door*," he boomed.

Alice heard a woman's voice in the background. Oscar apologized to her rather effusively, then came back to Alice. "I've *missed* you so much."

"Where are you?" Alice asked.

But the woman's voice was there again, polite, concerned. She called him Mr. Lombardi and said he was allowed to take the phone back to his seat. Laughing, he told her he was fine; he *liked* it there. Alice realized, of course, that he was on a plane. That he was talking to—no, actually *flirting* with—a stewardess and that he couldn't make the call from his first-class seat because Mrs. Lombardi would be sitting right next to him.

"Alice, are you *there?*"

"Why are you calling?" she asked. A cool solemnity had seized her.

"I told you. Because I *miss* you." It was announced childishly, and he sounded quite pleased with himself. "OK, so right now I've had a drink or two. The truth is, I can't stand flying. But every day in Chicago—*every day*, I thought about you."

"I hate you for doing this." And she did. She felt herself hovering on the edge of something awful.

"Well, if I'd known it was going to upset you, I wouldn't have called."

"You knew and you called anyway."

"No, no, no, no," he said, laughing again. "Didn't you think of me once?"

"No."

"I don't believe you."

"Why? Because you are so wonderful and memorable?"

There was silence, then a crackle on the line. Finally he spoke, his voice incredulous. "What's happened? Why are you so angry?"

But she refused to tell him. The fact that his wife was sitting there, the fact that he was drunk, that he presumed he could just call her and that she, the discarded mistress, would be charmed. No doubt in the last few weeks, Oscar had asked for and received divine benediction, forgiveness, and renewed trust from his wife. That, combined with a couple of glasses of wine, apparently allowed him to simply pick up where he'd left off.

"I'm miserable," he said. "I have to see you. Just one more time. To say good-bye properly."

"Why would you want to start something again that we can't finish?" she asked.

Though determined to remain cool, she felt hostile, on the brink of tears.

"To torture myself," he shouted. "I'm not happy unless I'm anxious or miserable. It's a condition all directors live with. Couldn't you indulge me this one *last* time?"

"Why? So that you can find out if I still love you? *For God's sake, stop playing games, Oscar.*"

Had she screamed out loud? She couldn't tell. But when she hung up on him, she found herself pressing hard on the receiver, as though to prevent any more of him from seeping back into her life.

10

After his drunken phone call from the plane Oscar called every day, sometimes six or seven times, insisting that they both deserved a civilized farewell. Refusing to see him, she forced herself to listen to his voice on the machine instead, as if by not answering it, by staring at it across the living room, she would maintain some strength. But if she managed to get through the day, she would thrash around in bed at night, reasoning, vacillating, reprimanding herself for her weakness. Telling herself *No*. Until one morning she awoke to realize that, far from ridding herself of Oscar, he was there more than ever, dominating her life.

And so with trepidation she agreed to meet him for a drink at the Coronet Bar, an appropriately dusty hole in West Hollywood. He arrived looking his usual stooped but authoritative self, only more haggard, which pleased her because she was determined to stay removed. At first, both of them behaved civilly. Like family members skirting the issues of past treacheries, the conversation was light and breezy until the first margaritas were thrown back. Then Oscar bore down with his engaging if somewhat delinquent smile. Grasping her hand, he told her that giving her up was out of the question; he had forgotten how beautiful she was.

"I'm not beautiful. You just like to think that. It makes your case stronger." Though she had replied quite coolly, she could feel herself softening. When, she wondered, could she not be had for a flattering remark?

"What case?"

"That you need me."

"*Want* you."

"Oscar . . ."

"*Love* you."

"Please don't say that."

"No listen . . ." And by this time the margaritas were coming fast and furious. "I've been looking for a woman like you all my life. Why can't we go on? Just a few more weeks. *Admit* you love me. That's why you're here."

"I don't know why I'm here," she replied, panicked. She jumped up, then tried to maneuver through the crowd to the exit. But Oscar barred her way at the door. All his exhilaration was now replaced by jealousy and remorse.

"Where are you *going?*" he demanded to know.

"I'm meeting someone."

"Who, Mike?" he asked, eyes swimming.

"No."

"You're lying. I drove past your house last night and saw his car."

"You drove past my house? What are you? A director by day, and a detective by night?" she said triumphantly and swept past him out into the street.

And triumphant she was for a day or two, until he called. Then came flowers, notes, and a telegram containing cryptic words of love. One minute she was resolved, implacable, the next she was driving like a madman to meet him, only to stop herself halfway there. But however hard she tried, she still could not end it. And when they did meet, in the Coronet or the old Roosevelt Bar, or for a tepid cappuccino in some beachfront café, all they did was argue. Not at first about the real issue, the *situation,* but about topics they had previously, in their former bliss, positively agreed on. "What do you mean, you *hate* Truffaut? You loved him. He inspired you. You told me you stole his style of editing, his fantastic—what was it?—moments of intensity." "*Please*—nothing but a series of vignettes held together with flat, rather sad pieces of narration. Episodic. All too remote. And too autobiographical. Frankly, after *The Four Hundred Blows* he completely fell apart." "What about *Jules and Jim?* Our favorite?" "Hopelessly maudlin," he told her, dismissing it with a caustic laugh.

Then, as if the weight of his anguish were too much to bear, Oscar would open up the old wound as a kind of relief.

"Look. This is stupid. It can't go on."

"No."

"I mean, who are we kidding? How long would it last anyway?"

"What?"

"*This.* I mean talking, talking. What happens when real life comes in? What happens when we start annoying each other over breakfast?"

"It's never going to get to that."

"No. Because I can't leave."

"Please. I *know* why you can't leave."

"I can't just toss away twelve years of marriage."

"God, I don't *want* you to. You don't have to explain."

"Because it's not clean."

"I hate that expression. As if anything in life is clean or *uncomplicated.*"

And even if he should leave, she doggedly told herself, it would never work because she knew all his rotten little secrets—all the things he preferred not to know about himself—things he would hate her for later. But deep down she was beginning to wonder. What exactly was this morbid plot the two of them shared? Tragedy or pure farce?

"Christ, I really shouldn't be here," Oscar would inevitably groan, and the whole ghastly thing would start up again.

"Then why did you call me?"

"Why did you come? You could have refused."

"Don't make *me* the bad guy here so that you can feel *less* guilty about Ruth."

"I *do* feel guilty about Ruth. Should I lie about that?"

"Perhaps just once. Out of *politeness*."

Afterward there would be the morose farewell. Not the impassioned parting of two people never to see each other again but the weariness of a couple expecting more rounds to come. "You love all this *owning* up," Alice would toss over a shoulder, striding to her car. "But I refuse to be your sounding board. You want someone to reprimand you and I *won't* do that." And though occasionally they would steal a soulful kiss in the parking lot, it was a far cry from their previously hilarious and lustful days, wallowing in the bliss of their little game. There *was* no more game. In fact, since Oscar had returned from Chicago, sex, like the subject of their future, lay submerged, like a beast beneath them, groaning now and again but ignored. A feat requiring extraordinary skill. Apparently, each had decided that abstinence was the only hope if they wished to remain sane.

Which was probably why Alice's nights were so insufferable. Unable to sink into her pillow without Oscar's face rising up to meet her, she wondered if her suffering were synonymous with breathing, that if in some perverse way it gave her an identity. She was drawn to it—back and forth, thrust and parry. The giddy martyr. Because whatever this was with Oscar, it could *not go on!* But short of being held down and having the living daylights beat out of her, she had no idea how to end it.

Work was the key, she told herself. "The great salvation, the great *usurper* of life's tragedies," her father used to say. And just as Alice's teenage preoccupation with Colette,

Céline, and all the rest had served as a secret escape, as an adult Alice found refuge in her own writing. At her desk, in the safety of the converted laundry room (where the dry acid smell of Clorox and laundry detergents still lingered), she could fashion order out of chaos. One morning she wrote a sizzling column about the dearth of upstanding female characters in current film. Then in a roar of energy, she roughed out a lengthy scene where Tania, intergalactic slave and gutsy heroine of the masses, confronted Panic in a mine shaft. Too late she realized that the love goddess was sounding less like a twentieth-century gladiator and more like some acid-tongued *lumineuse* from the forties, but she kept on writing anyway. Alice forged ahead, as if she might stumble on an answer to the unanswerable question: *What was this hold Oscar had on her?*

By late morning, however, she would find herself staring idly out the window, the same susceptibilities creeping in. Sometimes she tried working in her car. Apparently Albert Brooks, parked outside his local Lucky's supermarket, was able in this manner to steam through an entire screenplay in three weeks. Henry Miller, incorrigible bon vivant though he was, had written: "Like a sloth, the writer clings to his limb while beneath him life surges by, steady, persistent, tumultuous." But Alice was incapable of letting anything surge by without her. Though exhausted by her emotions as they rose and sank like the tide, the need to simply *talk* to Oscar became overwhelming. His anger, his openness, his directness—the very things she told herself she despised—were exactly what drew her to him. "The trouble with you is that you're afraid of opening yourself up," he had told her, albeit affectionately. "Afraid that people like you for your wit and that there's nothing underneath. That you are not *lovable*. So you use your flippant behavior to keep people at arm's length."

"Well, I'm not doing such a good job with you, am I?" she had replied smartly.

"There. You see. That's *exactly* what I mean. But I admit I love it. I love that you keep it all inside like that. Where I grew up, the day started with everyone screaming at each other. A discussion about the toast sent family members flying from the table, doors slamming. But you don't show anything. I have to pry it out of you."

"Well, please *don't*."

"I can't help it," he said. "I love you. I just want to know if you love me."

"I'm trying *not* to," she would hurl back on the brink of tears.

And so it went. They wallowed in each other's misery, not sure if they were loving it or not, blaming each other, trying to find the culprit where there appeared to be none. They stacked up the days, conscious that each hour spent together, each drink, each argument, each gesture of forgiveness made it more impossible.

In this state of exhaustion, they drove aimlessly around the city. A tape of *La Traviata* playing, they solemnly held hands, like a couple who had their affairs in order, children and dogs at home, washing machines picked out for the basement. They were accomplices locked in some strange rhythm, unable to go backward or forward.

One afternoon—the last day of October—they were on the freeway. The first of the winter rains had come, falling in wide sheets across the cars. There was a theatrical quality to the light. Strips of bright pink and gray lay on the western horizon as black thunder clouds rolled overhead. It was appropriately dramatic, the sky and the panorama of drivers' faces eerily lit up as they clung to their steering wheels. Oscar weaved impatiently in and out of cars while Alice sat silently beside him, willing herself to be calm. Except she didn't want to be calm. Better to stay angry, she thought, better to do something. *To fight.* She still had a column to finish. Billy Hawkins's secretary had called two days ago and she hadn't had the strength to call back. There was too much on her mind; too much, but clearly nothing specific enough to solve her problem.

"I guess it's not that complicated. In a clinical way it's like anxiety or anger," Oscar was saying. Shoulders thrust forward, hair falling over his face, he moved through the traffic in furious bursts, accelerating, honking, swearing left and right. "The phenomenon of falling in love. I was reading about it last night."

"Where were you reading? At home? In bed?" Alice was practicing distancing herself. The words came out smoothly.

"In the den. Ruth goes to bed early," replied Oscar. "So you see," he went on, "even though love promotes euphoria and is highly addictive, basically it's just the *same* as any highly charged emotional state."

They lurched forward, zigzagging between two cars, gaining a few precious feet.

"Like driving?"

"You're not listening."

"I am. Why does Ruth go to bed early?"

"She exercises. She goes to a dance class first thing in the morning."

The vision of Ruth doing leg lifts, knee bends, and possibly a jazzy buck-and-wing across some polished floor at dawn sent a wave of despair through Alice. His wife of twelve years, light on her toes, a fabulous sense of rhythm, fit, sane, *and* with a forgiving heart. She stared morosely at the sleek dashboard—the burled wood beneath heaven knows how many coats of varnish—and thought, *God save me from this.*

"Let's say it's a hormone produced by the body. Some natural amphetamine. When does it wear off? How long? If it's a chemical and has no true *emotional* life, isn't that some kind of ugly joke?"

And as though frustrated by the thought, Oscar jerked the car into the fast lane again, only to slam on the brakes a second later when the rear lights of a truck flashed red in their faces. "Christ!" he shouted, then almost as an afterthought, "To be honest, I don't trust my emotions. That's how I got married. Guilt, I suppose."

"Guilt?"

She looked at him, daring him to go on, which to her amazement, he did.

"Ruth was my assistant editor. We would sit in the car every night—*her* car, of course—talking about movies. Kurosawa, Godard, Renoir. After three years, I thought, well, I should do the right thing. I thought I must be happy because I felt so *relaxed*. Everything was easy. And when we got married, people told me, 'Oscar, this is a great woman to go through a tragedy with.' And it's true. She's a rock. She's always there. I can barely have a headache because she's rubbing my neck *before* it happens. If the dog barks next door, she writes letters. She can cook dinner for twenty at the drop of a hat. She's kind, smart, intuitive . . ."

"You left out 'saintly' and 'immortal,' " said Alice. It was all she could do not to open the door and run screaming out into the traffic.

"And do you know what I do? I go home and shout at her."

"Soon you'll be shouting at me. That's how it works."

The light had gone. The horizon was sealed in a dull

uniform gray. Rain, suddenly heavier, washed over the freeway like a babbling brook, and water that moments ago had streamed aerodynamically from the tops of cars now poured steadily off rear bumpers as the traffic slowed.

"You?" said Oscar with a laugh. "You are perfect. If they welded you both together, the result would be a woman so extraordinary, she'd go right in the *time capsule!*"

"You're saying you want us both?" Alice asked, incredulous.

She took a good look at him hunched over the wheel. A sweater too big for him hung down in folds over his lap. Perhaps Ruth had knitted it. It was in a shade of green that cast a sickly hue across his face. And the chin! He hadn't shaved in days! He had all the dash of the enslaved and ragged husband. Even the way he pushed out his jaw to punctuate his explosions was beginning to aggravate her. Less than a week earlier, sitting together at the Coronet Bar, a mere glance at his pale butter-colored socks and his brown suede brogues had sent her into a near swoon. One of these days she would wake up, and everything he did, the way he walked, ate, talked, breathed, would irritate her. A year down the road, she would watch him spit in the sink as he brushed his teeth and she would want to strangle him.

"It's over," said Alice. She was surprised at how easily the words escaped. A reflection, she hoped, of her implacable inner strength.

It was stifling in the car. She rolled down the window and leaned her head outside. The air was cool and sweet-smelling. She could hear the high-pitched, whooshing sound of tires rolling through water. "Oscar," she shouted, "I don't want to *see you* anymore!"

But apparently her words had floated out the window. Either that or Oscar refused to pay attention. "My problem," he moaned, still caught in his own dilemma, "is that I'm living with the horror of constantly disappointing two women."

Alice brought in her head. Just then the rain began pounding heavily on the roof of the car. They could barely hear one another speak. "Stop the car!" she yelled. "*Stop the goddamn car, Oscar!*"

"Alice . . ."

"I hate this. It's *finished*. It's over! *Stop the car.*"

"What the . . . ?"

"I want to GET OUT!"

Fortunately the traffic was moving at no more than five miles an hour. Alice ran like a basketball player, light-footed, weaving and dodging in front of the car headlights, moving swiftly toward the off-ramp. Drivers honked, and yelled at her, unsure if she were a suicide or a madwoman. Within seconds she was soaked. The rain had a soothing effect. She felt liberated—delirious, all the while ignoring Oscar's pleading voice: "Alice, Alice, for God's *sake!*"

Chest pounding, her feet skidding on the slick grass, she ran down the side of the off-ramp. Like an escaped convict luxuriating in a dreamt-of breath of fresh air, she strode across Van Nuys Boulevard, then down toward a Texaco gas station and a small motel. Here she stood frozen, soaked to the skin, fascinated by the motel's tiny leaded windows and the quaint fretwork balconies, the dovecote, all built in the style of a Swiss chalet. Suddenly, Oscar grabbed her from behind.

"What are you *doing?*" he yelled, gripping her arm. He was panting, eyes streaming, his shirt plastered to his chest. "Where the hell are you *going?*"

Furiously, he dragged her up onto the curb. There was an insane look on his face. Rabid dogs might have been close on his heels. "Do you know what happened back there?" he asked thickly. "I'll tell you. The traffic has stopped. I'm leaning out of the car window screaming your name when I see my *mother* pull up in the next lane. My mother!"

"Who *cares* about your mother!" she shouted defiantly.

". . . Not screaming my wife's name but *yours.* So I duck down and pretend I'm not in the car. Pretending that this car—a car, believe me, whose license number is etched for eternity on her memory—actually has *no driver.*" He gasped for air, his chest heaving. Alice tried to pry loose Oscar's fingers, but he held her tighter. He was not finished. "She's in the car with her friend Mrs. Giler from the book club. They are both frantically shouting my name as I am shouting *yours* . . . Do you understand this INSANITY?"

Water poured down from her hair, into her mouth, down the neck of her T-shirt. Drowning, furious, she longed to take a swing at him. All she could think of was *too many women*—Ruth, his mother, herself. "How dare you, how dare *you!*" she yelled, repeatedly. "How *dare* you use me to get out of your marriage!"

From the sheer force of wrestling back and forth, by this time they had worked their way into the motel parking lot.

"Use *you?* It would be simpler just to kill myself," Oscar roared back, incredulous. "And who knows, it'll probably be any minute, judging from the pains in my chest." He was bellowing now, hands flapping above his head. "This is all so goddamned *stupid.*"

Alice suddenly understood why people resort to violence. Frustrated, crazed, she thrust her elbow hard into his ribs. She was about to follow it with a punch in the nose, but just then someone else cried out. In front of the motel entranceway an overweight man and woman stood by a parked Ford Impala. They had identical faces. Identical bodies were squeezed into Disneyland T-shirts, and four chubby hands held blue anoraks over their heads against the rain. They stared openmouthed at the battling couple, as if watching the shenanigans of a game show. "Give it to him, honey!" shouted the man heartily, waving a fist. "Go for it!"

Alice, still seething, turned her back on them. "Look, I hate the absolute *predictability* of it," she screamed at Oscar. "Don't you understand? I'm mobilizing my defenses against danger. It's called preservation of the species. Fight or flight. Well, I'm not fighting anymore, I'm *fleeing* . . . ," she said, her voice almost hoarse. But before she could finish, Oscar had grabbed her around the waist. Half-dragging, half-carrying, he hustled her into the motel.

Within minutes they were in a room. After thirty seconds, they were out of their sopping clothes. While Alice grappled with his pants, Oscar yanked her soaked, leaden blue jeans over her knees. He tore off her T-shirt and made an athletic dive for her breasts, then flung her down on the floor and wedged his body between her legs. Alice pushed him off and crawled on top of him. Straddling him, she pinned his arms against his sides and dug her fists into his shoulders. Her head flung back, pumping up and down, she wanted to beat the life out of him, annihilate him for good, fuck him into oblivion. "I heard that most Jewish men have their first real sexual experience *after* they're married!" she roared. "Don't you believe it," he screamed back, "I've been fucking actresses since film school." "Including Niki?" she asked, a surge of hatred rising in her. But he refused to answer. Instead, he grabbed her arms and flipped her over. Squeezing her waist, he held her sprawled forward, her face buried in an armchair, and went at her from behind. Had they held weapons instead of pieces of flesh in their hands, they might have killed one another. Like a tumbling act in a circus, back and forth, they rolled across the room, sideswiping furniture, dragging themselves in and out of the bathroom, over the bed, each one daring the other to give in first. As if by this maniacal screwing they could end it once and for all, the last bout before they were dragged off to the loony bin.

Finally, and with an excruciating effort, Oscar lifted her up, yanked her legs around his waist, and flattened her against the wall. Gasping for air, drowning, moaning, choking, deep rivers flowing over their heads, both surrendered and slid exhausted to the floor.

After that, they lay there silently, chests heaving. Two weary opponents staring at each other, panting like animals. The truth was, nothing had ended. They were in it up to their necks.

11

Alice had never underestimated the power of love and now she surrendered without reservation. She realized that Oscar had captured her soul and carried it away. It was a shocking feeling. The lines were blurred. He had become her, she him. *I am Heathcliff*, she told herself rather poignantly, and they renewed their afternoon rendezvous with as much fervor as before. She was positively floating on a sea of love, aching, longing, dizzy. Would she ever be the same? Jessica feared not. But when she warned Alice that she was living a life of diminishing returns, "feeding on a neurosis that had nothing to do with love," Alice explained that the affair was out of her control. High-wire famine or flood, it was taking place all by itself. Frankly, she told Jessica, the whole thing came as a relief. With the burden of being a modern, responsible woman gone, she felt suddenly blessed by a luxurious freedom.

"I wake up saying to myself, I am doomed. Perfectly happy, like a madwoman."

"Yes," said her friend, positively appalled. "A madwoman."

But Alice was determined to defend her position. "I don't know what's going on. I think he's penetrated some inner level that was safe for years, untouchable. Now a kind of trust has been established. I feel terrible when I don't tell him the truth," she admitted. "Imagine—a man you can't lie to."

"There's no such thing," replied Jessica firmly. "Anyway, what about his wife?"

"He's leaving her."

It was a breezy afternoon. They were sitting in a café in Santa Monica. One of Alice and Oscar's old haunts. With the self-possession of recent triumph, Alice repeated the words that had escaped Oscar's mouth as they left the Swiss motel a few days before: "I've decided to leave Ruth." It was said stooped over, as if the burden of the admission were literally too much for him to bear. And before Alice had had time to think, she asked, "When?" not exactly sure if she wanted him to leave or not. In fact, secretly terrified by the idea, she had never allowed herself to properly entertain the thought.

"Is this separation going to take place soon?" inquired Jessica skeptically as she rigorously stirred a café au lait.

"Right after Thanksgiving," said Alice. If she was feeling at all dubious, the sensation was augmented by Jessica's sage reply.

"Remember, where men are concerned, all major decisions are made by the reptile part of the brain."

But in truth, Alice saw her love as poetic, as courage rather than capitulation. She embraced all of the old clichés, growing misty-eyed at popular songs, seeing an imaginary Oscar in unfamiliar cars, on sidewalks, in restaurants. The ordinary adulterous lovers had become Tristram and Isolde.

"More likely Dodgson and Alice in Wonderland," remarked Jessica. She tried to convince Alice of the obvious. It would never work. Men are weak. "Women have always had a larger bridge across both sides of their brain, blending reason and emotion."

"Is this public knowledge?" replied Alice skeptically.

"Of course not, imagine the uproar. But the trouble is, women suffer from inherent shame. So they are always looking for men's approval or forgiveness. That's why they willingly surrender under pressure."

Jessica spoke as if she'd been born a full-blown woman

with all the horror of experience piled on her doorstep, her destiny being to wade through it unscathed. No weepy lovesick scenarios in her life. To Jessica, romance was a meal served preferably piping hot and often. A loss was nothing more than a challenge to start again. Right now she was feeling particularly buoyant since she had rid herself of Adam, the executive she had picked up at the AA meeting. It had only taken a week for their steamy nights to slide into decline. Exhausted from the studio, instead of applying his last gasp of energy to the desirable woman lying next to him, Adam apparently had buried himself in a pile of scripts, reading until dawn. Jessica, enraged beyond reason—so she said—had finally accused him of "saving his tongue for pitch meetings." And with that he was gone. Now she was seeing a young landscaper, a man of twenty-nine. Shy, overflowing with generosity, he was apparently blessed with a perfectly proportioned body. A physique that, after a day of planting sago palms in her backyard, he had, on his knees, humbly offered to Jessica. Who was she to refuse?

"And what about Mike?" Jessica asked.

Alice wasn't exactly sure why she had postponed telling Mike the truth. Perhaps, selfishly, she was loath to give up one man until she secured the second. Or was she waiting for Mike to guess—which, judging from her recent behavior, should be any minute now. Lightheaded, almost delirious after one of her lascivious afternoons with Oscar, she could be found at dusk barefoot, a drink in hand, dancing wildly across the kitchen floor, heavy metal music turned up loud enough to shake the walls. This was Mike's kind of music. Music Alice had previously dismissed, actually complained about, but now, her spirits soaring, something that she threw herself into with girlish abandon. Mike was entranced. It was as though her sudden elation was a direct reflection of his youthful presence. He idolized her more. Inevitably, this devotion began to weigh heavily. Struck by the horror of her promiscuity and her steadily mounting guilt, she decided to tell him the truth. But each time she was on the verge of a confession, Mike would invariably do something so sweet, so winning—washing the dishes, running out to buy more wine—that it took the wind out of her. After that she grew resentful. Because he refused to see, to even *try* to discover the true reason behind her great tidal wave of emotion, she drank too much and baited him for being so innocent and so good.

"You never refuse me anything. Are you like this with all women?" she asked coolly one day. "Some people, you know, would read this as weakness on your part."

"I'm eager to keep you happy," he said. "I admit it, I'm your slave. I am shamelessly at your feet. So I'm weak."

"Saintlike behavior has a limited appeal," she replied. "Goodness makes people feel inadequate. It becomes a burden for everyone else."

"I can't help it. Someone has to take care of you. It's as if I've adopted a Cambodian waif. Look at you. You're worn out lately. You work too hard. And you drink too much for your age."

"But not for *your* age?" she inquired. "That's what happens as you get older. Life becomes more complicated. You drink to get *away* from your feelings, whereas you used to drink to get a closer look." And to prove her point, she opened another bottle of wine.

His sense of righteousness ground on her. And though she hated herself for attacking him, his refusal to acknowledge her hostility made the accusations irresistible. "What I mean is, I feel like I'm running for the local Miss Perfect competition. This *ideal* you have of me is exhausting."

"Why, if it's *my* ideal?"

"Because it might be wrong. *Is, in fact, wrong.* I am not who I appear to be."

"Nobody is. What's really bothering you? You think that every relationship should be a constant power struggle?" he said calmly, on the move. He was in the living room, busy straightening furniture. "You think it can't work if one person is doomed to be the subservient one?"

"Yes. Doomed. That is the correct term."

"Surrender is just as powerful a position. It's the old master-slave theory. It's the slave who is in fact free. He has no responsibility but to serve."

By that time, he was laughing. Grabbing her round the waist, he bent her over his knee. And then, after pretending to give her a sound thrashing, he carried her off to the bedroom where, like some drunken hooker, she spoiled him terribly to make up for what she didn't feel.

To discourage him from coming over, she made excuses about her work. But he became more insistent, often showing up uninvited. One evening in November as she pulled into the driveway, she saw the light on in her kitchen. There at her sink, as cheery as ever, an apron tied round his waist, was Mike, busy creating his version of domestic harmony.

"I let him in."

It was Julio crouched half in shadow next to what she realized was the open hood of Mike's GTO. "About an hour ago," he said. Dressed in a short green kimono and holding a grease-sodden roll of tools in his hand, he resembled some mad surgeon.

Yet in a way she and Julio had become friends. Awash in her passion for Oscar and temporarily released from the mundane problems of the normal world, Alice had begun extending a giddy courtesy to the public at large, some of this joie de vivre spilling over onto her landlord. Instead of avoiding him as he loitered outside her front door or maniacally clipped the geraniums under her bedroom window, she found herself commenting favorably on his clothes. "Interesting shorts," she would say pleasantly. "Hand-painted? Fabulous!" Or on another occasion: "Really? An undershirt that Robbie Robertson actually wore at Woodstock? It looks hardly used!" Flattering him to such an extent that it appeared he began to dress expressly for her, changing outfits sometimes three times a day and going so far as to dye his hair.

"I found some old Clairol bottles in a box my mother left in the garage. I was experimenting," he announced one morning, his face smiling beneath what had become a frighteningly orange fur-ball. "Titian Red. What do you think?"

Repeatedly, he had asked her out to dinner. After the fourth time in one week, she confided in him. "As you know I already have two boyfriends. To take on a third might seem at the very least greedy, if not immoral." Somehow, this strange logic struck a chord, because the subject never came up again. Nevertheless, by discussing her liaisons with him, a certain intimacy had been established. Each time they spoke, he made a point of standing alarmingly close. So close that she could see red dye stains on his forehead, and on his body smell what she could only guess was a mixture of Old Spice and turpentine.

"Why did you let Mike in?" Alice now asked, stepping back a foot, glancing toward the street. She was thinking about Oscar, praying that he wouldn't drive past as he sometimes did on his way home.

"He said he was doing some chicken thing for dinner," replied Julio, adjusting the neck of the kimono and exposing a healthy coating of chest hair. "He also wants me to take a look at his car. You can see the back end's all adrift. Twenty to one it's the rear axle."

Alice stood silently in the kitchen doorway. Bent over a pile of raw vegetables, Mike was frantically peeling, chopping, dicing. Every few seconds he swiveled to adjust the gas flame under a pan of simmering chicken or to slather more drumsticks in batter. Steady and relentless, he pushed through the tasks at hand like a bulldozer moving through a building. Only when he finally took a breather to open a bottle of wine did he notice Alice who, suddenly at a loss for words, turned and headed down the corridor.

"What, no kiss?" he shouted, and followed her, wiping his hands on the apron. "Bad day at the office?"

"Yes, as a matter of fact," she shouted back. "Apparently some people are unhappy about my column."

Which was true. Her somber mood had been triggered that day at the paper. Naturally, her complicated life had so affected her work that rarely did she get her column in on time. Even when she did, Cameron Fischer never wasted an opportunity to gripe. "I noticed you forgot that convention required you leave *yourself* out of the picture," he had sneered, referring to that week's piece regarding female writers and directors and their lamentable struggle for the top-paying jobs in the movie industry. "A little indulgent? Or are we paving the way for a new career?" Even Leonard Lativsky, once her admiring and fervent supporter, had not been able to hide his distress.

"My editor mentioned the words sloppy *and* morose," said Alice, still walking away. "So I'm not in great shape."

Eager to postpone the inevitable confrontation, she went through the back of the house to her office. Diligently, Mike had straightened the papers on her desk, just enough so that the mess, still sufficiently intact, would insure her continued creativity. Unlike previous boyfriends, he respected her work. He would tiptoe past her doorway and occasionally interrupt, head appearing briefly round the door, to inquire if she'd like something to eat. A veritable saint. So why couldn't she have fallen in love with him? She was thinking about this when she noticed a card from Oscar propped against her desk lamp. Why was it suddenly there? Originally the love note had been attached to flowers Oscar had sent the previous week. They had arrived while she was out, and Julio, with a good deal of fanfare, had presented them to her as she drove up in her car. Had Mike read it? And if he had, would he say anything? Had he in fact known all along that she was seeing Oscar again, and was he now torturing her? Perhaps his saintliness was some kind of bizarre revenge. Whatever it was, she could no longer postpone telling him the truth. But what truth? That Oscar had promised—no, had simply *said*—that he was leaving his wife at Thanksgiving. Mike would give her the old speech about being a silly girl. "You are *so* gullible, so easily taken in . . ." Or he might ask her with one of his knowing looks, striding across her kitchen with a plate of chicken Sonya, "Honestly, which Thanksgiving will that be, Ally? This year or *next* year?"

"Well, I'm sorry you're depressed," he said.

Bristling with vigor, he was now setting the table. Salt and pepper shakers were laid out, two paper napkins, two wineglasses, and then, just as symmetrically, two pairs of knives and forks. "But we're going to fix that," he announced cheerfully, handing her a glass of wine. "Have a drink. Dinner's almost ready."

And just as Alice was trying to form some appropriate words, Mike bent over and kissed the nape of her neck. "Ah—the silkiest, most swanlike neck in the Western Hemisphere," he murmured playfully. "I love this neck."

"Please, I'm a little tired," she said testily. She pulled

away, then added apologetically, "And I'm sorry, but I'm not really hungry. In fact I think we need to have a serious talk." She turned so that he wouldn't see the awful look on her face. But he was back at the stove, sliding chicken pieces around in a pan.

"Aren't you going to ask me why *I'm* in such a good mood?" he asked, and as if to illustrate his lightheartedness, he started whistling softly.

"Why? Did they find a cure for cancer? World peace? Or was it simply that the sun came out today?" she shot back.

Having said the words, she felt terrible. He stopped stirring and threw her a reprimanding look over his shoulder.

"Sorry," she said morosely. "Listen, what I want to say is . . ." She stopped and stared up at the ceiling. All too selfishly she realized that her eagerness to confess was actually an overwhelming desire to *share* her feelings with Mike. Good, understanding, affable Mike. "Do you believe in true love? I mean the possibility of true *happiness*," she asked, unable to suppress a guilty smile. "That sometimes you find a soulmate, a person who incorporates all the senses—sex, of course, the comfort of friendship, *and* the feeling of being *safe?* Does that sound corny? Well, maybe it is. But all day on the radio I listen to women who swear they'd be happy if they could just find a man who was *kind* to them, who made them *laugh.* Imagine, if women get more than that, they're delirious, running wild in the streets."

Due to this small confession, her spirits suddenly lifted. The relief was enormous. Without spilling a drop of wine, she hoisted herself up onto the countertop. "You see," she went on, "sometimes what happens with a man is that you start out pretending you're someone else. Then you spend most of the relationship trying to get *back* to the point of who the hell you were in the *first place.* So if you come across a man who doesn't regard you as simply a reflection of himself or what *his* ideal is, but who returns your own life to you, well, it's almost terrifying. It throws a woman completely. Am I making sense?"

During most of the speech, Mike had been bent over the sink. Once Alice thought she had detected a stiffening of his shoulders, portraying, she imagined, a slight ripple of aggravation; but when he turned, a steaming pot of carrots in his hand, he was holding back a grin. "Two cannibals," he said. "One says to the other, 'I really hate my mother-in-law.' The other says, 'Well then, just eat the *vegetables!*' "

"Could you be serious, *please?*" she said soberly, swallowing a mouthful of wine.

"Christ, this is a tough room to work." He grimaced but continued spooning out carrots into a bowl. He spilled a few on the linoleum and crouched down to retrieve them. "You know, after I do a joke, most women say I'm great," he shouted from under the table. "It's after sex that they say, 'Oh, *you're so funny!*' "

But he knew it wasn't working. Alice had heard the line before. And it occurred to her that, as little as she understood him, he hadn't the faintest notion what made *her* tick.

Mike stood up. "Let's see," he said, serious now, chin down, eyes locked on the floor. "Tolstoy said, 'There is no such thing as true happiness or true despair.' Meaning, I think, that the *delirium* that comes with extreme emotion is not based on truth. It's always influenced by memory, nostalgia, need, self-delusion, and often the threat of loss. So it would be naïve to think either could be a *perpetual* state."

"What does that mean? That you don't believe true love exists for anyone?"

"I'm not sure. Maybe it's like sex. Everyone else has a better story."

He was composed, confident again, and none of this had sidetracked him from the preparation of dinner. He flipped the chicken pieces with a spatula, then drained the potatoes in the sink, each move wondrously smooth and coordinated.

"Do you believe it could happen to me?" she asked. "Have you noticed anything different?"

"Thinner?"

"No. Pay attention. What do you see?" Alice slipped off the countertop. She stood with her hands on her hips, her face thrust forward, urging him to take a closer look.

"You? Truthfully?" he asked, with a zesty smile. "A gorgeous but insecure woman who needs to be separated, almost immediately, from her clothes."

"God, Mike, what is the matter with you?" she said. "What would you say if I said I was *confused.* That I couldn't see you anymore. That I need a break. That I want to see *other people?*"

"I'd say it should wait until after dinner."

"Are you kidding?"

"No. I am *serious,*" he shouted suddenly. And, as though shocked by his own angry voice, he flushed scarlet. "We should eat first, *then* discuss it." He had been arranging lemon slices around the edge of a serving dish. Now he scooped up a couple of plates from the draining rack. "The reason I was in a good mood," he said, banging them down hard on the table, "is because I've been asked to do an opening monologue for the Comedy Club next week. So I thought you could listen to it and give me your *opinion.* Is that too much to ask?" He wiped the plates, then threw the towel across the room. "Do you think you could do this one thing for me, Alice?"

Alice couldn't have felt more humbled. She realized

that it had never occurred to her, even out of good manners, to simply ask what was going on in his life. How selfish. Obediently and like the reasonable adult she aspired to be, she would wait until after dinner, after his monologue, to sensibly and honestly discuss the demise of their relationship.

To create a small platform for his performance, Mike lay two telephone directories side by side on the living room floor. Alice dimmed the lights. A warm saucer-shaped glow from a corner lamp illuminated his face. "Ladies and gentlemen, I grew up in Connecticut," Mike began quietly. Gone was the sprightly chef of an hour ago. Standing in the half-light, a shadow falling across his perfectly pink cheek, he looked angelic and vulnerable. He let out a small chuckle and the words came rushing out. "Let me tell you. When I was born, I was so ugly, the doctor slapped my mother! No, *seriously*. . . . I had a totally normal childhood, but privileged, you might say. During my formative years, my father stayed in his study all day. Then, at six o'clock, he would come out and shout 'Gin tonic' to my mother. At three years old I thought that was my mother's nickname. 'Gin tonic, easy on the ice.' As a young boy, I addressed my father as 'sir.' Naturally, I was scared of him. Even though I was an only child, I knew I wasn't his *favorite!* So there were no names in our house. He was 'sir.' I was 'Look here, young man,' and later on my mother was called 'For Christ's sake, where *are* you?' I'm not saying there was a lack of intimacy in my family, but my father's love was measured by the firmness of his handshake in the morning."

Alice was completely taken aback. Then it dawned on her that this was the truth. These maudlin recollections of his youth were in fact an accurate if rather funny portrayal of the *other* Mike. The inert, suspended Mike. The baffled boy who existed alongside the flawless man but who, for the sake of decency and decorum, had been kept in line by commandeering parents. "My father would cut out *Esquire* cartoons and leave them on my plate at dinner," he went on. "He instructed me to study the raunchy ones for good men's club conversation. I was *six!*" Although Mike was laughing heartily, his hands, clasped in front of him, were busy wringing each other to death. "My father was also very clear about sex," he continued. " 'Women are in love,' he said, 'but men are in *business!*' "

Mike kept on in this vein, joking about the bickering that had belied his parents' polished demeanor. The amusing spectacle of a boy hiding under his bed while his mother threw ashtrays down the cavernous hallway. "She said she always planned to divorce my father. But she could never find a way of doing it without making him happy!"

Why, Alice wondered, had she never bothered to delve deeper? Brought up in such confines, it was obvious that Mike's only chance for survival had been in his own metamorphosis: the irrepressible optimist, the prankster, a man exploding with bluster and bravado.

Mike's adrenaline dimmed for a moment. "Isn't it funny?" he asked Alice. "You're looking at me as if it isn't funny."

"No, it's wonderful. Go on." Then fearing her expression had given her away, she asked casually, "This couldn't possibly be you, could it?"

"You think my life was like that? No, God no," he assured her. "I'm simply highlighting the dull parts."

"Ah," she said smiling, the perfect straight man to his own deception.

After applause and congratulations they went to bed and nothing more was discussed. Later, however, lying awake, her preoccupation grew into a giant cloud, the kind that exists only in the dead of night. She wondered if she was destined to go on: raucous afternoons with Oscar only to collapse every night after Mike's home-cooked dinners as he massaged her feet or buried his head between her thighs for hours, uncomplaining. Even though Mike's overwhelming affection seemed odd to her, something she couldn't quite put her finger on, the truth was, Alice had enormous feeling for him. She knew that had she discussed ending it, Mike would have tried to talk her out of it, with tears no doubt on both sides. Either that or he would have called Oscar and given him a severe talking-to. Perhaps her decision to do nothing was a positive move. As if instead of running away, for once she had given herself permission to live it out. Whatever *it* might be.

12

Oscar invited Alice to come to Pasadena where he was shooting the final scenes for the beauty pageant in *Body and Soul.* Because this was their first opportunity to spend one entire night together, simply to exist side by side, oblivious to all else, they anticipated the evening with tremendous excitement, like lovesick teenagers whose parents were out of town.

Dinner and sex were foremost on the agenda. But before that there had been Marvin to contend with. All afternoon, Alice lay hidden in the hotel room to avoid detection from the producer, who would no doubt use the discovery of the director's philandering to humiliate him further. Patiently she listened to Oscar's fiery complaints against the man he now called "the stone around my neck." Racing up to their room in between shots to let off steam, Oscar howled: "Listen to this! I just tried to explain to Marvin that Niki's story is a sensual journey, in some way borrowed from *Lolita.* I said, 'Did you ever read the book?' and he replied, 'What for? I saw the movie—and it was a *stinker!*' " More pacing, then Oscar started up again. "You know what it's like having to face this every day? It's like a combat course. Worse—a fucking war zone." And sucking up a few lengthy breaths, he raced back into the hallway where, waiting for the elevator, he hurled back, "I'm a director who is *supposed* to have some integrity—even with his *failures,* for Christ's sake!" Then he was gone, back to the set for more punishment.

Around six Oscar returned. Alice first heard his voice in the courtyard below, then Marvin's voice close behind, barking like a madman. "For Chrissakes," he screamed, "you're turning this into some godawful documentary. Where's your fucking audience?"

Alice, her head now out of the window, watched while Marvin prowled back and forth between the potted palms like a caged panther, sweat staining his Hawaiian shirt.

Though in private the mere mention of Marvin made Oscar's blood boil, face to face with the enemy he wore the detached expression of a hired killer—charming, lethal. "Sorry I can't give you one of your schlock action pieces," Oscar informed him calmly. "And to be honest, Marvin, I don't care about being embraced by the *mainstream*."

"Well, I care. I *care!* I don't want *realism*," Marvin wailed, his chest heaving from the exertion. "Of course, I want to do *quality* work. But if I've said it once, I've said it a thousand times: I am not in the quirky art-film business. Wim Wenders need *not* apply . . ."

But by this time, Oscar was headed up the hotel steps. A few minutes later, Alice heard the elevator doors open, then the diatribe continue in the corridor outside. Marvin had followed Oscar upstairs.

"Money and Art often brush shoulders as they pass in different directions," Oscar shouted breezily.

"Oh, no. Don't give me *that* shit." The voices were now right outside the room. ". . . that old Commerce-has-overwhelmed-Art speech. *Spare* me!"

Suddenly the door gave way. Oscar burst in. And in order to prevent the advance of the raging lunatic behind him, he wedged himself across the opening while Alice flattened herself against the wall. "All I'm trying to say is that movies are made up of small truthful moments. My characters experience pain. Because that's what life is, Marvin. Pain, pain, and more pain," Oscar announced sorrowfully, one hand moving to caress Alice's ass. But Marvin had to have the last word. Just as Oscar closed the door on him, he screamed, "You want pain, Oscar? I'll give you pain. Wait for the fucking public *agony* when this turkey comes out. Because, in case you forgot, failure in Hollywood is punishable by *death!*"

Alice and Oscar locked the door and ordered dinner. With unbridled passion and in full view of the imperious waiter, they necked furiously while the man uncovered two club sandwiches and opened a bottle of champagne. A little later, they took a bath. Dizzy with anticipation, they slid into the soothing warm water. Oscar slowly soaped Alice's breasts. At the same time he slipped his toe between her legs until, so excited, she spilled her champagne, finally dropping the glass entirely. Then Alice tried to arouse Oscar. She started with her hands, then worked on him with her mouth, underwater for so long that she nearly drowned. "Perhaps the water's too hot," she said, laughing, hair plastered to her head.

"No," he said, a little sheepishly. "I think it's because I've surrendered completely. I've lost my fear since I decided to break away from Ruth. Since I've given myself totally to you."

"Have you?"

"Yes."

There was barely any room to move. When he squeezed his long legs round her waist, she glided forward in the water, knees bent, and rubbed against his soapy chest. "I feel like I've been propelled into the unknown," he said. "I'm possessed, engulfed. It's like being a child again; I'm happy being an utter fool. I keep asking myself, Why do I love this woman? And then I think, Maybe we really are a perfect pair.

We're in a business that requires not only that we survive our disasters but that we live them out in order to be creative."

"Art before pleasure. Sounds a little grim."

"Or maybe a better appreciation of both? Love, tragedy, hysteria—this is our métier. But why do you love *me?*"

"Because you're intelligent, you're witty, you're a fabulous lover. *And* you think I'm beautiful."

"You're not always beautiful, but I love you anyway."

"Ahhh," she murmured, sinking back.

Drying off after the bath, they squeezed past one another shyly. After months of voraciously exploring each other's bodies, now faced with temporary domesticity, they found they were confused as to how to behave. "Look, do we or don't we pee with the door open?" asked Alice.

"Closed. It's the only place I ever got any privacy in my life."

And then, as they arranged their wash kits on the fake marble sink-top: "OK, let's get this over with. You show me yours, and I'll show you mine," Oscar announced.

While he tried out her face lotions, Alice discovered a pouch full of prescription drugs. "What are all these for? Are you ill?"

"I can't afford to be ill, I've got six weeks of shooting left," he replied. "No, this is simply life after forty. Something you have to look forward to."

And then, presumably to allay her fears, he picked her up and carried her into the bedroom. After ten minutes of rolling around, Alice took him in her mouth again to try to excite him. She worked on him for ten minutes until, red in the face and exhausted, she collapsed, panting beside him. "Maybe not such a good lover," he said, a little morosely.

"You know what the French say?" whispered Alice. "You must treat sex like a meal in a high-class restaurant. You don't complain if *occasionally* it's only average. Ambiance counts for a lot, too."

Later, they slept, Alice with her head on his shoulder, Oscar's arm around her waist. When she felt him roll away from her, she panicked. Was she supposed to be here? Was *he* meant to be somewhere else? Then with relief she sank back luxuriously. But five minutes later, Oscar was awake. He rolled over, coughed, sighed several times. He turned his body in every direction until finally he threw back the covers and sat up.

"What's wrong?" asked Alice.

"Nothing."

"There's something wrong. You're panting."

And watching him run his hands through his hair—a gesture she knew so well—she waited for the bombshell.

"The truth is . . . I'm lying here, and I keep thinking about Ruth." He gazed soulfully out the window. Almost comically on cue, Alice heard thunder rumbling in the distance. Great black clouds rose against the dark sky and a chilling breeze wafted into the room. "I can't help it," he went on. "It sounds ridiculous, but she has this hold over me."

And instead of Alice saying calmly, "Of course she does, but that has nothing to do with us. She will always be in your life, and we will make a place for her," words that would have no doubt rolled off a shrewder woman's tongue, she sank back silently.

"I'm happy—and it makes me nervous."

"My kind of man," she said dryly, forcing a laugh. But he was perfectly serious and it made her feel stupid. The tiresome comedienne. Dorothy Parker. Soon, no doubt, to be weeping on the inside.

"Look, I'm just not very good at this. I didn't do drugs in the seventies because feeling *good* for more than five minutes bothered me," he said, shaking his head. Then realizing how absurd this sounded, he offered a weak smile. "What I'm trying to say is, How can I be so happy when she's so miserable?"

"How do you *know* she's so miserable?"

"I don't. But she asked me if I would leave after Christmas instead of Thanksgiving."

Alice lay there, eyes on the ceiling, feigning inner peace.

"You should have seen the way she looked at me. No reprimands, no shouting, nothing . . . just *asked.* She loves Christmas. I keep thinking—what will happen to her? How will she find another man like me to make her happy?"

Despite the arrogance of the remark, it was said with such sincere hopelessness, actually on the brink of tears, that Alice thought, Oh God, if he's going to cry, *I*'m going to cry. Even though she had consumed enough champagne to sound reasonable, apparently it was not sufficient to stop the ghastly feeling rising up inside her. "The problem, Oscar," she eventually managed to say, "is that you're telling me this as though you're sitting here with one of the guys. I'm not your confidante or your buddy. I'm in this. I'm *right here.*"

"If we're going to live together, this is what you'll get," he said. "Someone who feels terribly bad. Do you know why people hang on to marriages? Because as they get older, they're afraid that after all the horror it will be the same with someone else. And sometimes it seems a big price to pay for happiness." He turned toward her. "I'm sorry if I'm spoiling things, but I'm being honest. Have I ever lied to you?"

"Sometimes I wish you would."

If he noticed her air of desperation, he ignored it. He continued nobly, eyes closed, addressing himself to the great wound within: his conscience. "I can't pretend that I don't worry about the potential bloodbath. My father is ill in the hospital. Naturally, Ruth goes to see him all the time, while I, the errant son, am far too busy. And what should I tell him? Or should I *not* tell him? Just wait for him to die?" He had picked up a pillow and was squeezing the life out of it. "And what about my mother?"

"You're a grown man. Why are you worrying about your mother?"

"Because she's a hostage taker. She can cry on cue. I used to say to her, 'I'll never call you again if that tear reaches the corner of your mouth.' And you know what? She could actually make it *go backwards.*" He shook his head, laughing. "When I was young, she told me that no woman would love me as much as she did but that I shouldn't let it ruin my life."

"Could there be a certain self-obsession here?"

"I'm as self-obsessed as the next person. I just express it more. *And* I try to be amusing. OK, so I'm not Milton Berle. I don't run around in a dress, but at least I try and keep it *light.*" Smiling foolishly, he released the pillow and pulled Alice toward him. "Look, I plan on changing my whole life because I love you so much. Just let me complain about it first," he said, gently kissing her.

And he was right, of course. A sophisticated, self-assured woman loved by this man would be able to wait until Christmas.

Another groan of thunder rumbled in the distance. large drops of rain flattened against the window pane, and miraculously the feeling of despair vanished as quickly as it had come. They made love, softly, slowly, then afterwards lay in the dark. Questions and answers until dawn. First Oscar told her of his strained relations with his father, who had wanted his only son to be a restaurateur, like himself. And like *his* father before that, a man who "*despite the incredible odds*" had opened the best Italian chophouse in Chicago after World War I. Now of a ripe old age himself, Frank Lombardi had been literally dumbfounded that after he and his wife had done everything to insure their son an idyllic childhood, Oscar's movies were stories of such violent domestic unhappiness. Tentatively then, as the soothing sound of rain enveloped them in the dark, Oscar asked Alice what she really thought of him as a director. So she told him. She said that regardless of his pursuit of artistic integrity, obviously, more than anything, he wanted to be a success. And there lay the confusion. Though not prepared to give up the money, he couldn't help feeling he'd sold out. That he was losing his goal. "Like a lot of artists," she said finally, "you're terrified you're not as clever as you used to be. That one day you'll wake up and people will shout '*Fraud.*' "

For a moment he didn't move. He was sitting up in bed now, his silhouette black against the sodden night sky. Eventually, looking somewhat stunned, he murmured, "You're absolutely right, of course."

And because of his honesty, it was suddenly easier for Alice to talk about herself: her mother's hysteria, her father's inaccessibility, the loss of her grandfather. All the old neuroses came pouring out: the child who wanted to please; the woman afraid she was not talented, convinced she had no depth. And finally (the hardest for this self-proclaimed romantic to admit), Alice confessed that she had often found herself susceptible to men who *said* they loved her.

"What does that mean? That you love *me* out of insecurity?" he asked.

"No," she said, and for the first time realized it was true. "Not *you.*"

He smiled. The storm had passed. The last rumble of thunder was breaking in the distance. Nothing was left but the cool, sweet smell of rain. Exhausted, exhilarated, she lay beside him. Unable to sleep, she studied his face in peaceful repose. She had revealed everything, dredged up the worst. Was it possible? she wondered. She had given a man the dire secrets of her life and he still loved her?

Even though most of her days and nights revolved around Oscar, she had managed nevertheless to work on Tania, the unyielding contender for the legendary Panic. It was like nothing she had ever written before and she was quite pleased with the work. A racy fight scene, biting dialogue, sophisticated weaponry (for her a Merrimax Interfacer, for him a Helix Laser-5). Slick, sophisticated Tania, the militant superhuman help-mate who confounds Panic. Snappy one-liners and an abundance of sexual steam.

The meeting with Billy took place the morning after her stay in Pasadena with Oscar. She had driven back at dawn. There had been no time for breakfast and she was exhausted from lack of sleep. Once again Billy was upstairs when she arrived and he called for her to join him. This time she found him standing in a wide walk-in closet off the bedroom. Beyond the closet was a newly built twelve-foot-square room, roughly laid out in plywood sheets. "*How* many phone lines?" Billy was shouting.

A man in overalls was down on his hands and knees, carefully winding tape around the ends of bare electrical wires. "Just the one, sir," he said smartly, straightening up in order to offer the attention this major star required.

"No," said Billy. "*Two* phone lines and a cable outlet. And what about the *alert button?*"

Shoulders thrown back, Billy's darkly tanned chest bulged from his bulky green toweling robe. Apparently he had nothing else on underneath. Perhaps, she thought, like a lot of people who exercised strenuously, he never felt completely comfortable in normal clothes. Or was this display merely for her benefit? His nails were manicured; his hair shone with some kind of pomade. On his oddly small feet, he wore black velvet slippers, gold initials woven on the toe in elaborate swirls.

"No one mentioned an alert button, sir."

"*I*'m mentioning it."

He explained to Alice that he was designing a human safe. If anyone broke into the house, he could lock himself in for the night. All modern conveniences were to be installed. Cable TV, refrigerator, fax, and a direct line to the police. "What do you think?" he asked, delighted with himself.

Of course he was not really interested in her opinion. But life revolved around the star, and his talents must be applauded no matter how superficial. Alice managed a smile, a sunny glaze to imply interest and hide her exhaustion.

"Should we talk about Tania?" she inquired. Emboldened by lack of sleep and somewhat distracted, she walked back into the bedroom. What actually dominated her thoughts just then was whether or not she was capable of waiting until Christmas for Oscar. Eventually Billy followed her, strolling to the bay window. "I was wondering what you thought about the pages?" she asked pleasantly.

To survey his rolling acreage he rocked back on his slippered heels, hands clasped in front, large blue veins bubbling over the knuckles. "Perhaps I should explain what *I'm* trying to do as a director before we try to find out who Tania is," he announced. And with his familiar stagey saunter, he began to pace the smooth expanse of carpet. "I'm not afraid to say I need help. I've been reading about the great directors. First I started with the film noir stuff. You know, *Written on the*

Wind, On Dangerous Ground. Douglas Sirk, Nicholas Ray—those guys."

Nodding politely, Alice wondered how these subversive themes of unrequited love and blind madness could have any connection to the netherworld of Panic. Well, maybe the "blind madness" part . . .

"Then I found this book on Martin Scorsese. In *Taxi Driver* he says Travis Bickle goes right to the edge and explodes. He says that when you live in a city you have a constant sense society is in a state of decay. And Travis just wants to tidy up a bit. *This* is Panic—not so dark, of course, but that same sense that he wants to clean up life, clean up the *soul.* Scorsese talks about the atmosphere of a city. A seeping virus, he called it, like you can smell it in the air, taste it in your mouth. God, Scorsese is amazing when he talks about New York. I grew up there like him, so I know we have a *thing* here. And that's what I want to capture in this movie, in *Panic*'s city, the city of the future, the great metropolis. Because what I think Scorsese meant was, What is civilization in a place like that? It's *nonexistent.*"

He went on in this vein. Flamboyant, deadly earnest. Perhaps it was the fatigue but Alice was beginning to find his zealousness a little less appealing now. He was of course every inch the star. And like most stars, he was smart about one thing: himself. His ambition, how to play it out. But there seemed to be nothing here in the larger sense. The subtext of Billy was simply more Billy. By now Alice could barely keep her eyes open. A dull pain throbbed over her left eye, and her legs hurt. No one had so much as offered her a cup of coffee. Obviously, Billy was never going to ask her to sit down—manners clearly not uppermost on the busy agenda of a world hero.

"So imagine a combination of that and a modern John Wayne," he continued excitedly, waving one of his big hands in the air. "Did you ever see *The Searchers?*"

"Yes. John Ford," she replied and slid quietly onto the edge of a wing chair.

"Wayne had one great line in it: 'That'll be the day.' Just like I have the line 'Tough it out, pal.' 'That'll *be the day,*' he said, savoring the words, slipping into a slow cowboy drawl. "Buddy Holly took that line for his song, you know. Anyway, like John Wayne, Panic gets carried away in his search for the girl. He kills a few too many people, just like *Wayne* killed a whole bunch more buffalos than he needed to. That's Panic. Tough, but with a spiritual thing. An avenging angel floating through the city."

There was a silence. Had he finished? He was humming to himself, a few chords of Buddy's song. Finally he looked over at Alice and shook his head. And then it struck her. Her heart sank. He hadn't liked her pages. Not just a little bit but a whole lot he hadn't.

"So, what you're saying is that Tania is completely wrong," she managed feebly.

"Look, maybe I don't understand women," he said. "But then most of the great unwashed who watch my movies—my hard-core action fans—don't either. But what they definitely don't want is to see Panic pussy-whipped by some big girl."

"Not even in a city of the future?" she asked, attempting a touch of humor. But deep down all she felt was humiliation. The unmistakable sensation of *failure.* That and the sneaking feeling that Billy was right. All of a sudden she saw Tania as too slick, too abrasive, much too fantastic. In fact as soon as he had dismissed her work, instead of rejecting him as an illiterate or a buffoon, her estimation of him actually *soared.* Imagine! Her miserable self-doubt actually allowed her to respect his rejection!

The night before, in Pasadena, she had admitted to Oscar doubts she was having about her writing, a problem augmented by the current criticism from the paper. "The trouble is you're too influenced by what people say," Oscar had told her. And she had demurred: "You're right, you're right." Whereupon he had chastised her again. "You see—you're doing it! No, *I am not necessarily right . . .*"

"I never really saw her as aggressive," she offered more positively now. "If the scene is done correctly, with subtlety, it should be a tease—"

"Yeah—maybe," Billy interrupted. "But I'm not subtle. I'm *not* that kind of actor. I don't think and think and analyze. I just feel it in my *gut.*" He was standing in front of her. The smile was back, along with a raised eyebrow, letting her know that his self-deprecation was part of the overall charm. "I've never been one for that head stuff. If I have a problem, I go hit a bag." He sighed and leaned over her, supporting himself on the back of her chair. He was smiling down at her now—flirting with her, Alice realized—*while* he dismissed her work.

"But you wanted the woman to be hip. You said you wanted her to have sharp lines like a guy," she said, trying to sound normal. "A woman like a man. A woman of the *future.*"

"Yeah, I know," said Billy wistfully. With a slippered toe he was coyly tracing his own initials in the carpet, no doubt trying to recall these exact words. "But we don't want it to be Meryl, do we? We don't want some thinking man's sex symbol."

Alice was trying to imagine Meryl Streep in a studded leather bodice kicking Billy sharply in the crotch when, mercifully, there was a small tap on the door. Jim poked his head in. "Ovitz on line one. Says it's important," he announced cheerily, nodding to Alice by way of hello.

"Look," said Billy, straightening up. "Don't worry. You'll get it. You know what I say to career women? Leave your balls at the office. I mean, *I* respect it, but the audience won't." He lifted her out of the chair. Throwing his massive arms round her, he pulled her sharply against his chest, almost squeezing the breath out of her. She could smell rubbing lotion on his skin, or was it the pomade on his smooth velvety hair? Ex-fighter, bodybuilder, suave heartthrob; a short Beau Brummell. Just as she was about to protest, he released her, padding off nimbly toward the door. "Just give me more of this stuff," he said, one fist inside his robe, banging on his rosy pecs. Alice looked at him nonplussed. He pounded again. "Give me *heart*, Alice."

13

One morning a terror-stricken Oscar called Alice. He had received an anonymous letter. Typed on airmail stationery, obviously with an old portable (some of the letters almost comically cockeyed), it read: STAY WITH YOUR WIFE—OR ELSE. Who would have written it? Had Alice, he wondered nervously, sent it as a kind of joke?

She assured him truthfully that she had nothing to do with it. How could he even imagine such a thing? For a moment, she feared it might have been Mike. But any letter, even an anonymous one (presuming he knew about Oscar), seemed too overt a move, too alien to his nature. With dexterity, she calmed Oscar down. "Simply ignore it," she said. "It"s nothing. Merely a malicious joke. The penalty for being a controversial director."

"*Failed* and controversial," he replied gloomily. But he agreed he was probably overreacting and returned to what he considered the primary source of his woe: "It's the stress of the movie. Everything will be fine once I've finished this damn thing."

Immersed in his daily torture at the studio, Oscar's behavior was becoming more introspective and reserved. Alice questioned him repeatedly until finally he admitted to a recent preoccupation with death. He had visions of himself lying in the gutter, weakly bleating out a message for help as the traffic thundered an inch from his head. Alice coolly suggested that in the past his sense of mortality had been wrapped up in the safe, if somewhat dull, predictability of his marriage. Now that circumstances had changed, he obviously felt adrift. Oscar nodded silently, distracted as ever, but happy to accept her wisdom.

Then a week later, Oscar received another anonymous letter. Underneath the banner headline BEWARE, ADULTERER were admonitions against sleazy behavior in smaller type, and below that, a detailed critique of his previous films. The remarks were scathing, with particular attention to missed opportunities in character development and plot, not to mention his total disregard for the modern woman. As for *Sacred Cow,* Oscar's second movie, the anonymous writer had this to say: ". . . an abundance of flashy camera moves that did nothing to alleviate the stench of amateur and derivative storytelling—material blatantly lifted, *ad absurdum,* from Fellini, Godard, Bresson, Truffaut."

"Ruth sent it," announced Jessica. "It's obviously from someone who knows how to get him where it hurts. And it's clever. I mean, let's face it, she's pretending to be civilized about the whole thing while she's scaring him on the sly."

What really disturbed Jessica, however, was having to watch Alice hover in no-man's-land, meekly guarding Oscar's sacred flame. No longer was it the dire consequences that alarmed Jessica but rather Alice's sudden passivity. Signs had been clearly posted, she pointed out; Oscar's attentions were dwindling. She warned that even with the best intentions Christmas could easily drift into January or more likely spring. And why would Oscar bother to get rid of his wife anyway when it looked like he could have them *both?* "Happiness is often the perpetual state of being well deceived," she remarked quite convincingly. "Frontiers are always open. It's important to manipulate a change."

Just that week, Jessica told Alice, she had quite happily severed relations with the landscaper. Though she admitted that as a lover he soared above the rest, she balked at his suggestion that they include his ex-wife in their torrid all-night lovemaking. This dilemma was brought on not by moral considerations, she explained, but by the fact that the woman was simply not attractive enough. Jessica's sense of aesthetics had been offended.

However, it was not only Alice's complacency that concerned her; Jessica was worried about the way she looked. Since Oscar had told Alice he found her more "adorable" without makeup, she had stopped wearing it.

"You see what he's doing?" said Jessica, seizing upon this immediately. "He's turning you into his second wife. It's the Jewish man's dilemma, not to mention that old seventies mentality. That rock-and-roll shit. The tired philosophy of the placid good woman. Make her into a scrubbed-down waif, she's more malleable," she explained, thoroughly enjoying herself. "Soon he'll try to convince you he fell in love with your pot roast. The worst tragedy for a woman is to be admired for something she's not. I mean, just look at you. You're like some nurse ready to roll bandages at the front line. You're probably not even jealous of Ruth anymore."

Admittedly in the last few weeks, Alice's emotional state had been sliding downhill. Was Oscar being honest? She had endowed him with this virtue, even though last week, consumed with doubt, she had found herself parked after dark across the street from his Brentwood house, obsessed by the idea of seeing Ruth in the flesh. Short or tall? Slender or zaftig? Would they be arguing, or would Mrs. Lombardi be happily ministering to her husband right up to the eleventh hour (with as much consideration as the woman afforded her refugees)? But after two hours, all Alice had seen was Oscar, not Ruth, sitting in the living room watching TV. He looked so relaxed in the roomy chintz armchair, so blissfully *at home* with his mug of beer that she couldn't imagine him ever leaving his cozy lair for the great uncertainty of unmarried life.

And then there had been the episode with Mike. Alice was beginning to wonder if she were gullible to the point of idiocy.

Mike had taken her to a cocktail party in a colleague's apartment. In advance he had warned that he would not be holding her hand or showing any untoward affection because one of the partners of the law firm he was planning to join would be there. Such decorum. Quite contentedly, Alice sat perched on a granite slab next to the roaring log fire while these prospective kingpins tippled hot cider. As they talked, the young career women listened. Nervously they adjusted their suit lapels as their heels sank into the tobacco brown, wall-to-wall carpet.

Watching Mike, Alice still saw the sad boy who had received nothing more than a cool handshake from his father and, God knows, little else from his mother. Like some devoted aunt, she proudly followed him with her eyes as he sauntered from one group to another, heralding them with a little joke or some hilarious law-school tidbit. During the drive over, feeling guilty again, she had begged to be taken back home, pointing out that he would make a better impression on his law buddies if he arrived at the party alone. But, as usual, he had felled her with his terrifying patience. "Listen to you, how did you get so insecure?" he had said, then squeezing her arm as they stepped into the elevator: "You'll be the most gorgeous woman in the room."

Around nine o'clock, she excused herself from a man named Max Shellman who was intent on drilling her with the finer points of California divorce law and went in search of

Mike. Rounding the kitchen door she saw, in the shadows of a laundry room beyond, Mike pressed against a tall dark woman whose hand just happened to be lingering on the fly of his wrinkled chinos. It lay there peacefully, as if calming a favorite but errant pet. Returning to the passageway, she cheerily shouted Mike's name, then came in again. By that time, Mike was leaning casually against the kitchen refrigerator (he still had that classic prep-school talent for scrambling at the last moment); he introduced her to the woman, who was now busy opening a can of mixed nuts. She was a cool number: olive skin, a healthy cleavage, and astonishingly about five years older than Alice.

"This is Sonya James," he said, as if the coincidence of Alice's arrival couldn't be more delightful. "Sonya, this is my friend, Alice Wilder."

A bold stare passed between the two women, the unmistakable look of two old hands who know what's up. Not missing a beat, Mike went on talking. First he said something about Sonya's work in the firm, about her extraordinary ability to tackle tricky civil cases; then he gave Alice a turn, expounding on her growing reputation as a journalist and screenwriter. And all Alice could think of was chicken Sonya. She had a vision of this woman showing Mike how to baste drumsticks, one hand holding the frying pan, the other gently cupping his balls.

Content between these two mature women, Mike went on smiling. Smiling and lying. His cardinal values, his smooth servility. What a laugh! thought Alice. What an incredible foil! And yet, what a relief. Surely now, the guilt of having two men in her life could be ceremoniously exorcised. She should feel liberated. But no, quite the opposite. What she felt was *enormous jealousy!* And for this moral ambiguity, this envy, spite, and revenge that ran through her addled brain, she was convinced God would strike her down. She would go straight to hell.

The rains were over. In fact, the last few days had been a balmy seventy-five degrees. In the backyard, Julio's rectangle of marijuana plants had shot up above their bamboo enclosure, the large spiky leaves poking through the green netting. Alice and Jessica lay on squeaky metal chaises. Jessica wore Capri pants, a halter top, white pineapple-shaped ivory earrings, and a wide-brimmed straw hat. Throughout the Mike story, she had been laughing wildly. Now, head thrown back, cigarette in hand, she reminded Alice of a photograph she had seen in *Life*: Barbara Hutton in the fifties, poised just as luxuriously on the stern of her yacht.

"Mike used to call her. She used to call *him* in the middle of the night," said Alice, remembering the ringing phone, the whispering voices that had floated through her dreams. "I was too stupid to put it together."

"Of *course*," howled Jessica, slapping her muscular thigh. She was making so much noise that Julio stepped out of his house to have a look. He peered at her for a moment, then confused by the gaudiness of the display, stepped back inside. "For Mike, one woman isn't enough. He wants to give back rubs to the whole world so that he can feel needed and *loved!*"

In the car on the way home from the party, Mike, overexcited and slightly drunk, had reached affectionately for Alice's hand. More inclined to murder just then, she had turned to stare out the window. But in typical fashion, he lavished her with comforting words. "Poor Ally, I left you alone with those dreary, boorish lawyers," he said, one hand on the wheel, the other swimming across the icy divide between them. "Can you ever forgive me? Tell me, how can I make you happy . . . ?" So much adoration that, despite her mood, by the time they got home the absurdity of the situation was beginning to amuse her. No wonder he stayed so calm, she thought. No wonder he was unaffected by her moods. He took what he needed, left the rest. Was there some secret nastiness here? Or had he, in all innocence, appointed himself the patron saint of the older, confused woman? She almost admired his passionate self-absorption, his self-generated ebullience. She decided never to bring up Sonya. Never would she give him the satisfaction of letting him know that *she* knew. A small victory at a time when she felt her life slipping away. Of course, her insidious conduct was no better than Mike's—perhaps worse. Why then did she still feel so horribly betrayed?

"Because you were under the impression that he loved you," explained Jessica, dipping the straw hat lower to cover her nose. "You relied on it. You needed it to balance your confusion about Oscar. You *reveled* in it, as most women would if they could get away with it. Then you were insulted because you found out you were wrong."

"Maybe," said Alice, knowing Jessica was right. In her selfish desire not to be alone, she had told herself that Mike needed her, whereas, of course, the opposite was true.

"Why do I do it?" she asked, miserably. "Why do I live like this? I used to tell myself it was for the writing. That you had to experience life like a madwoman if you wanted to get something interesting down on the page. But it's a lie. I never got that great *reservoir of experience* down anywhere. No time for introspection. Always too busy forging ahead."

"Escaping more and more into drama, for its own sake," remarked Jessica. "Which gives you the opportunity to chastise yourself once again for your bad behavior."

And because she sounded just like the austere and worldly Dr. Hansrud, Alice nodded silently—doing just that: chastising herself, then hating herself further.

"Now you have to decide whether you really want Oscar," said Jessica. To sun her breasts, she rolled down the straps on her halter top, then lay back flat on the chaise, her legs stretched on either side on the patchy lawn.

"What do you mean?"

Alice noticed Julio's window blinds move.

"Do you want to declare war?"

"War?"

As an idealist, she had never felt combative action to be part of her style. In fact she had always been amazed at the devious lengths to which some women went to entrap a man. But in the last few weeks, something depressing had occurred to her: No longer was she the master of her own destiny. While earnestly balancing the attentions of two men, Alice, the bold individual, had completely ceased to exist. What had happened to the woman Oscar had fallen in love with? And what *was* this great love, anyway, if she didn't have the courage to fight?

"Yes."

"Then it's time to play tough. If you really want Oscar, you have to play to win." Jessica sat forward, fired up by the idea. "The truth is we're all deceived by the *availability* of things. You saw Sonya and you got jealous. Why? Because no one can make any decision in life anymore unless there is the threat of something being *taken away.*" She sighed from the exertion of imparting such wisdom. "Do you remember what Woody Allen said about a relationship in *Annie Hall?*"

"No."

"It's like a shark in water. If it doesn't keep moving, it dies. This thing with Oscar is dying in front of your eyes."

14

Though it was only the weekend before Thanksgiving, a vaguely hysterical holiday spirit had swept through the guests. "*Hello*," people shouted loudly, "*great* to see you," as the herd spilled from the hallway to join the crush of bodies laughing and yelling in the living room. There was a definite East Coast feel here. Pumpkins and gourds overflowed from straw baskets, and flames reflected from an enormous roaring fire lit up the guests' faces, giving everyone an unusually cheery, polished glow. Everything radiated luxury, money spent, and spent frequently. Mounds of silver gleamed on the buffet, and over at the piano, a robust black man gaily hammered out "South of the Border"—accompanied by a small group of the musically inclined, already a little drunk, their rear ends swaying back and forth in unison.

Jessica and Mike cut a path through the crowd. Alice lagged behind. Even though her heart was pounding, she must have been grinning foolishly because people grinned back; in fact, smiles bombarded her on all sides. A waiter, nattily attired in a white jacket and gloves, stopped to offer champagne, but she declined, afraid she was already too drunk. The first vodka at home had calmed her nerves; it was the second that had been the mistake. She was now way past that pleasant level where conversation with total strangers was tolerable, sometimes even enjoyable.

"Remember," said Jessica, leaning back and whispering in her ear. "You simply have to make up his mind for him. Just tell him—'The buffet is *closing.*'" The plan was traditional, though possibly overdramatic: Oscar's jealousy on seeing Alice with Mike would jolt him into action. Of course, the risk of acute embarrassment to Alice, not to mention the possibility of a nasty scene with Mike tagging innocently along, appealed enormously to Jessica. She was on a mission and nothing excited her more; her face glowed, her short dress shimmered. Made of some kind of greenish taffeta, covered with bobbing, translucent fish scales, it barely scraped the tops of her muscular thighs. "Be honest with yourself," she went on. One hand was braced on Alice's shoulder while the other performed a flurry of complicated sign language to someone across the room. "Coming *over*!" she shouted, then bent down to whisper the last rites in Alice's ear. "Ask yourself: When have you *not* been totally available for the great Mr. Lombardi?" And with that, nostrils flared, lips parted, she floated away, absorbed by the fatuous attention, the shrill hellos, and the general rumpus of the party.

"Ahhhh, you must be Mike," said a throaty voice, and a woman swooped down to latch on to Mike's elbow. She had a strong jaw and a voice to match with just a hint of Brooklynese. "I'm Nancy Sears," she gurgled into his shoulder. "Jessica told me you were coming." Their hostess was a dark-haired woman. In an attempt to ward off her fifties, she wore a hefty layer of makeup, black leggings, a too-tight red sweater, and gold amulets spiraling to her elbows.

"Great deal!" an eager young man shouted, pushing past Alice to grab Nancy's arm. Then, a touch insincerely, he added, "Honestly—I can smell it. Success and *more* success."

"Thanks, Bill," drawled Nancy, her heavy-lidded eyes rolling skyward. "From your lips to God's ears."

The party was given in celebration of Nancy's deal at

Paramount. Although the incident directly responsible for this lucrative contract was supposed to be a secret, everyone knew the shocking truth. Six months previously, Nancy had been a newcomer. Without much success, she had been trying to get Mark Rothburg, a production head at one of the studios, to finance a low-budget film. Rothburg had little interest and, as it happened, had been planning to retire because of a severe kidney complaint. Then out of the blue, Nancy's husband, a big drinker, collapsed of heart failure while jogging. Within hours, bypassing the long list of legitimate patients—desperate people who had been waiting for many years—Sam's kidney was successfully transplanted into Mark's body. A few months later, Nancy signed a five-year deal with the studio.

"Did I meet you in Aspen?" she now cooed, fascinated by the sturdy pile of Mike's tweed jacket.

"Unfortunately not," Mike grinned back, ever gracious.

"Well, go over there and get a drink, and then come *straight* back and talk to me," she ordered coquettishly. Then, waving a manicured finger at Alice, she said by way of dismissal, "Aren't you writing movies now?" her voice laced with condolence, as if writing screenplays were a fate that awaited only the lowliest. Alice was about to defend herself when there was a squeal.

"Mother!" cried the desperate voice. And careening across the parquet floor, dodging the crowd, came Nancy's overweight thirteen-year-old daughter, Beverly, dressed in jeans and T-shirt, her short legs encased in giant new riding boots. "The bartender says he needs more *champagne*—now!" she shouted petulantly, dragging Nancy away past several extended hands eager to congratulate the woman on her astonishing success.

Robert Redford was rumored to drop by, and although

it was already after ten, each time a welcoming cry went up, people's heads swiveled expectantly toward the hallway. Mike and Alice pushed on, gaining a few feet before they were temporarily halted in the crush at the bar. Three young executives—the Ivy League alumni—were in front of them, heads locked in a huddle, laughing uproariously. "Listen," one shouted, "I said to Jeff, 'This is a great script. It's a Henry *James* story.' And you know what he said? He said, 'Fabulous, I love it. My father used to listen to his band on the *radio!*' " "Come *on,*" yelled another, rocking back on his heels. "No—scout's honor. I *swear* on my Christmas bonus . . ."

Alice had come to an abrupt halt. She thought there was a possibility she was smiling but apparently not. "Are you all right?" asked Mike, one hand protectively on her shoulder.

The sight of Oscar across the room had taken her by surprise. Wearing a soft black sweater and corduroy pants, a warm halo of light behind his head, he suddenly appeared mysterious and exotically bohemian. It was like seeing him for the first time. Talking, gesticulating wildly, hair flopping over his face—no doubt instructing the granite-faced man opposite him on the pitfalls of working in such a ghastly medium—he was behaving with his usual demonic excitement, and, she realized, existing quite nicely *without* her.

And Ruth? There was a knot of actresses huddled by the fireplace. Dressed in black, with various hues of streaked blond hair, they turned now and then to flash toothy smiles to the throng. Not one of them, however, looked like she had discussed Godard or Renoir with the naïve but blossoming Oscar way back when.

Overcome by a wave of alcoholic nausea and a tremendous rush of affection (if not agonizing love), Alice's first impulse was sheer panic and a desire to run away. Earlier she had felt horribly dishonest—the reason, of course, why she had got drunk in the first place. "What have women ever gained in life by being honest?" Jessica had wanted to know, as she pulled Alice into the skin-tight black cocktail number (the battle dress, she called it). She had insisted on the sultry makeup, the scarlet lipstick, the catastrophically high heels. Precisely the reason Alice's journey across the room was now proving such a perilous experience. "What in life *isn't* a game?" Jessica had said. But wasn't that exactly what Alice had told herself she *didn't* have to do with Oscar: play games? If only she were sober, she might have a clue. God, she told herself, eat something before you go mad.

As it happened, with much ceremony, the lids were being removed from the silver serving dishes on the buffet, revealing mountains of steaming fried chicken and ribs, plus all the trimmings. But they were too far away. Guests were jostling each other impatiently, the line snaking back as far as the piano. "Food—give me food!" someone shouted down the line, the chorus taken up by the throng.

"Come on, Alice," Mike insisted, hand around her waist, "I need a drink. It's boiling in here." And he pulled her past a bulbous-faced man who was shouting, "Look, I don't bullshit. You know I never bullshit. But this is the greatest movie I've seen in my *entire life*, so help me!"

Since the evening with Sonya, Alice had been treating Mike with an almost indiscernible flippancy. Quite ashamed by her wave of jealousy, she was relieved when it disappeared as quickly as it had come. After that, however, her casualness toward him had grown so apparent, her voice on the phone so matter-of-fact that in his confusion he had professed undying love for her, an outpouring of affection that appeared for the first time to be completely genuine, a touch desperate, and almost against his will. He still wanted to give her everything. (Everything, thought Alice, except himself!) And when he asked, actually *begged* her, to go back East to see his parents at Thanksgiving and then on to ski, naturally she had declined, mysteriously citing other plans.

It was six deep at the bar: a crush of bodies, arms aloft, empty glasses raised, while a harassed bartender frantically mixed batches of margaritas. Alice pulled at Mike's sleeve, steering him a few feet nearer to Oscar. "I want you to meet someone," she said.

"Who?" he asked.

Masochism had replaced all lucid behavior. Rather than live in limbo, she was prepared to exchange it for total loss. "Just a friend," she replied, not daring to look him in the eye.

At precisely that moment Oscar turned their way. He looked at Alice horrified, stopping dead in the middle of a sentence. Then, flushing scarlet, he swiveled back and with accelerated words tried to finish what he had been explaining noisily to the young man whom Alice now recognized as Tom Emery, Oscar's agent.

"The trouble is," bellowed Oscar, one finger marking time on the man's shirt, "this is an industry based on laziness, stupidity, and fear. And Marvin happens to be the proud possessor of all *three* qualifications. He's a major waste of electricity—a wacko." Tom listened stoically. While trying to hide his alarm at his client's vitriol, he busily jotted something in a black notebook. "One wacko among *many*, of course," Oscar thundered on. "Because if it weren't for the movie business, God knows, the lunatic asylums would be *overflowing!*"

Having exhausted himself, Oscar was now laughing at his own tirade. Then, drink in one hand, the other outstretched, he turned toward them. "Oh, Alice, how *are* you?" he asked vaguely, wearing a rather facetiously broad smile.

"Hello," she said, shaking his hand.

Across the room she could hear a cheer go up as the piano player thumped out the first few chords of "Only the Lonely."

"This is Mike."

"Mike, this is Oscar Lombardi."

"Mike with the GTO?"

"We've met?"

"No, but Alice has spoken about you, haven't you, Alice?"

The scene had all the banality of a family gathering when someone drops by to introduce the new boyfriend. Both men were looking at Alice. Oscar, in particular, studied her tight dress, her overabundance of fiery lipstick. The Scarlet Woman, thought Alice, here, right out in the open. And though her heart pounded and the blood rose to her cheeks, she kept on grinning.

"And do you know Tom Emery?" said Oscar. He turned to Mike, his face locked in a frozen smile.

"Hello," offered Tom cheerily, pushing a hand into the circle and pumping hands. Apparently he had no memory of Alice at the Beverly Hills Hotel, or he did and was simply putting on a good show.

"Anyone got a light?" asked Oscar. He screwed a cigarette into his mouth, then made a big display of searching through his pockets.

"Sorry," Tom replied.

Mike was patting down his jacket. "Maybe I do."

"But you don't *smoke*," said Alice, touching Mike's arm and laughing girlishly. All of a sudden she felt horribly sober and in desperate need of a drink.

"No, I don't," Mike admitted with a short laugh, giving up the search. Then, directing his words at Oscar: "I'd just like to say, I admire your films enormously," he announced sincerely, glancing reverently at the carpet for extra emphasis.

Oscar knocked back the remainder of his drink and, save for an inquiring tilt of the head at Alice, said nothing. Could it be that Mike was a genuine fan? Alice had no idea. As usual, Mike's manners were impeccable. He would rather be shot than give himself away by a look or a gesture.

"Why don't *I* go for a light?" she suggested affably. "And perhaps a couple of drinks." Then touching Oscar's sleeve, "What about you, can I fill you up?"

Oscar shook his head. His face, already strained with joviality, had suddenly turned pale. As Alice backed up, he reached out as if to warn her, but she had landed on someone's foot. "Gangway," said a rather melodious but commanding voice, reminiscent of a young recruit in the armed forces. Alice was aware of a woman behind her cradling plates loaded with fried chicken and corn bread. "Food," the woman announced, "and it looks *fantastic!*"

"This is Ruth," a voice said. Then the same voice—Oscar's—"And this is Alice Wilder." *Ruth and Alice. Alice and Ruth.* Alice found herself momentarily struck dumb.

"Sorry," Alice said, moving out of the way. And when her eyes focused correctly, there, beaming back at her, was a plump woman with an equally rotund face and loose shoulder-length brown hair. Only then did Alice realize that this warm earth mother offering to share her deep-fried chicken legs was Oscar's wife.

"Hungry?" Ruth inquired. Then nodding at Alice, "Of course, you're so thin and pretty, you probably don't eat any of this." She laughed musically again and handed a plate to Oscar. The remark had not been made maliciously, Alice realized. There was no snarling on the word *thin,* no raised eyebrow at the end of the sentence. This jovial woman who had lived with Oscar for twelve years now pulled a wad of napkins from the sleeve of her flowing dress and carefully tucked one into the top of her husband's black cashmere sweater.

"I'll be right back with the drinks," said Alice.

With some relief, Alice felt the crowd close around her at the bar. She ordered a vodka, a double on the rocks. A wide-faced kid with glassy eyes stood next to her. A writer. Waving a glass of beer, he was drilling a small entourage with the story of his meteoric rise, his fantastic conquest of this barren land.

"Drink?" a voice asked. It was Barry Glazer, a producer she had interviewed once for the paper. A tall beak-nosed man with liver-spotted hands, one of which was now resting on her bare shoulder.

"Thanks," she said politely, holding up her glass. "Got it."

"Still working at the paper?"

"Yes."

The red-faced man Barry had been talking to tugged impatiently at his elbow. "So what *about* going to Columbia?"

"Please," said Barry, finger jabbing upward, scotch flying everywhere. "All we've got is a hundred pages and two Jews who want to make a movie. We've got *nothing!*"

Alice slid away. She was in no mood to renew the acquaintance, nor did she wish to turn around lest the tightness she felt in her chest, her sheer panic and nervous exhilaration project themselves right back across the room to Oscar. Apparently, she had not been prepared to meet this earth goddess. Skin that glowed like pale chestnuts and breasts like firm melons; Ruth was so thoroughly *natural.* Oscar was right: This was a woman who stood like a rock in a crisis, the solid defender of his adulthood. Someone Alice herself might have been happy to have as a friend—no, as a *mother!* A domesticated angel.

More than likely she could run up an evening dress from the dining room drapes, and then, no doubt—yes, hadn't Oscar mentioned her culinary expertise?—rustle up a meal for twenty from an old ham bone. In an emergency she probably had two hundred jars of her own preserved fruit in the cellar. Oh God, the horror. No longer could Alice allow herself the satisfaction of hating someone this wholesome, this *womanly*. Contemplating her own white, painfully thin arms, boyish breasts, and glaring red mouth, she suddenly felt like Edie Sedgwick risen from the dead. She wiped off the lipstick with a paper napkin and drank down the vodka.

Immediately, she felt coolheaded. Her fingers were numb from holding the icy glass, but so were her legs. In fact from her waist down, it was some other person she now propelled across the room. With enormous relief, she spotted Jessica.

It was quite a picture. Neck arched, Jessica lay sprawled across a sofa, one arm draped ceremoniously round a man's neck. Alice knew him: Walter Koloffski, the Czech director, a man to reckon with. Once in Robin Perry's office at Fox, a Black and Decker table saw in hand, he had threatened to cut off his own little finger if a "green light" was not immediately given to his picture. Suffering from what looked like several decades of alcohol, he now barked, "Actors are like galley slaves. You don't tell them where they're going, you just tell them when to *row!*"

"I couldn't agree more," purred Jessica, arching her neck farther. She whispered something in his ear, what Alice could only guess was a stream of racy proposals because the director's face broke into a craggy but salacious smile. "Unfortunately, Hollywood doesn't know *what* to do with actresses over forty," Jessica announced suddenly.

"No one knows what to do with *any woman* over forty,"

said the gravelly voice, his hand smoothing the scales on her fishy skirt.

"Except you?"

"Except me."

Alice stationed herself alluringly on the arm of the sofa. "Olé, olé!" came a jubilant shout from across the room, accompanied by a rousing cheer. An older man, leather jacket flapping around his elbows, ass out, hips twisting, shoes tapping, was doing an exaggerated dance. While, as best he could, the piano player tore along with him, improvising an upbeat version of "Lover, Come Back to Me," a pretty young Asian girl flew in and out, a touch unsteady on her thin legs.

Against the piano, corralled by Mrs. Lombardi, were Mike and Oscar. While Mike seemed pleasantly engrossed with Ruth, Oscar stared ahead, a desperate look on his face. His jaw hung down, as if fate could not have dealt him a more cunning blow. Alice had imagined the evening might be embarrassing—perhaps, by now, even tragic—but spurred on by Jessica's breezy composure, lulled by the voices, the music, and the four vodkas pumping through her, the idea of playing the *game* seemed nothing less now than an extremely sophisticated idea. And despite the fact that she had to close one eye to stop the room from spinning, she told herself she was only doing what poor Oscar lacked the courage to do himself. For twelve years, he had stared into those moist velvety eyes, held onto those gigantic hips, been drowned in sympathy and warmth. Now Alice was going to save him.

A hand squeezed her arm. "He's coming over," Jessica murmured with a knowing smile. And sure enough, ice cubes clinking in his drink, Oscar was headed her way.

Seconds later, he pulled her off the sofa and out into the corridor to join the traffic flowing to and from the bathroom. For a moment, wild-eyed, he stared at her, saying nothing. Alice steadied herself against a wall, an area crammed with twenty or thirty photographs testifying to Nancy Sears's full and rewarding life. And just then, apparently worn out with hospitality, Nancy herself swung around the corner, daughter Beverly in tow. "Mother says you *must* eat the stone crabs," the child shouted, obviously echoing her mother's instructions. "They were flown in from *Florida*," she pleaded, her tired feet clunking louder than ever as, arm in arm, the hostesses hurtled onwards. For some reason, Alice remembered seeing an item in the *Recorder* a few months ago. Apparently, for Beverly's bat mitzvah, Nancy had hired a musician who, clad to her specifications in rags, had been ordered to the roof to fiddle away for the entire evening's celebration.

"What are you *doing*?" shouted Oscar furiously, sounding already hoarse.

"Doing?"

"Yes, what the *hell*— " He stopped when a small knot of people turned to stare, then lowered his voice. "Why did you *come* to this party?"

"I didn't know you'd be here." Alice felt her cheeks go hot, but inside she was amazingly cool. "Then when I saw you, I thought it would be better if I came over," she went on, letting out a small laugh. "You know—to keep it aboveboard."

"Aboveboard?" repeated Oscar, incensed. "What about Mike? What are you doing with *him?*"

"He's going out with someone else. It's nothing. We're friends," she said, aware that she sounded aloof and slightly weary. Just then a waiter, balancing a gigantic silver platter stacked with the famous stone-crab claws, skidded alongside. Alice maneuvered two into the palm of her hand. "Are you jealous?" she asked cavalierly, offering one to Oscar.

He waved the food away. "No," he said tersely. Then,

"Yes, *of course* I'm jealous!" he shouted, incredulous at the glee with which she appeared to be torturing him. "Christ, he looks about eighteen. The man has shoulders you could land a plane on. Obviously he loves older women. You know what he's doing now? He's head to head with Ruth discussing the merits of *nationwide homeless shelters!* Am I losing my fucking mind?" And throwing his head back, he drained the remainder of his drink. "Christ," he murmured under his breath, the glass still against his lips, "don't look now . . ."

Storming down the corridor toward them was Harvey Fine, the CEO at the studio responsible for Oscar's movie. Though of a perfectly respectable height with a sturdy frame, his ashen face gave the impression of one rising from the depths. And so smooth were the few remaining strands of his sandy hair plastered over his scalp, they might have been painted on. "Oscar, I need to *talk* to you," he announced sternly, on the move. He walked with small, rather effeminate steps, his pigeon chest thrust to the fore. For years his sexual persuasion had been a subject of discussion, although he had been married to his wife—the diminutive woman now trotting behind him—for twenty-five years. He was part of the old guard, the upward mobility of his career based on cronyism.

"Oscar," he said, chest rising, "are you aware that we have major *overages?*"

"Well, Harvey," Oscar began, chin up, presenting an icy smile. "No one ever says, 'Let's go and see this movie, I hear they brought it in under schedule.' I'm simply trying to make it *good.*"

"Marvin doesn't think so."

"Marvin's a whore."

A hush fell in the corridor. A few yards away, someone barked, "Instinct first, dear—*then brains!*" rather rudely to an attractive but aging actress who, a moment later, was hurtling toward them. Angry, slightly drunk, a purse thrust up against her cleavage, the woman squeezed past Harvey Fine in order to yank open the bathroom door. Gracelessly, she slid inside.

"And you know what they say," Oscar roared on. "If you get into bed with whores, you're bound to get screwed." And though he was having difficulty maintaining control, the last phrase came out as wistful sigh. "And I'm *screwed*, Harvey."

Harvey's sickly white cheeks rose a notch in color. By now muffled sounds of sobbing could be heard from the bathroom. "This is not the correct place," he remarked coolly, glancing at Alice, then forcing a more diplomatic tone: "Look, every movie has its setbacks. In the best of circumstances, it's a monumental task . . ."

"Not really," said Oscar, butting in, another chilly laugh escaping his lips. "I always say"—and now he was looking past Harvey, smiling cheekily at the man's wife—"it's like kissing an ugly girl. At first there's the fear of the unknown, but once you get started it's not so bad."

Mrs. Fine colored, but by that time the swollen-eyed actress had emerged from the bathroom. No sooner was she gone than Oscar grabbed the door. He pulled Alice inside, slamming it behind them.

"Jesus," said Alice, leaning over the washbasin. She took a close look in the mirror: eyes a little glassy, lipstick smeared, but the overall effect was definitely alluring—more Ava Gardner now than Edie Sedgwick, the tight black dress riding up her thighs. "I can't believe—"

But Oscar was already talking. "He's something, isn't he? An original. A very special combination of coldness and stupidity. All the belligerence of a man with a tiny dick!" He was shouting now, revealing his current state of drunkenness.

"Harvey and the little fair-haired wife. The blond leading the blonde—HA HA!" And clapping his hands, he fell back against the bathtub. Then with a surge of affection and possessiveness, as if suddenly noticing Alice, he grabbed the bottom of her skirt and pulled her to the floor. He kissed the top of her breasts, her neck, and finally sunk his mouth into hers, sliding her head under the porcelain toilet bowl. Red-faced, moaning, perspiration popping on his forehead, he ran his hand up her thigh and inside her black underwear.

The ceiling spun. Drowning in alcohol, suffocating under Oscar's full weight, Alice struggled to keep in mind what this reinvention of herself had been designed to achieve.

"Ruth is out there," she managed to say. Quite a feat considering the trouble she was having breathing.

"Thank you. I know," he said, pushing her head back down. He kissed her again, eyes open, careful to watch her reaction.

And when she murmured coolly, "This is not a good idea," he looked crestfallen, jealous all over again because she appeared so contained.

"Look," he said, furious. "What *is* the matter?"

"Nothing."

"Listen . . ." He sat up and leaned against the bathtub. His head fell onto his chest as he let out a heartbreaking sigh. "I realize I've been a bit . . ." He broke off, sunk for a moment in resolute silence. It was obvious to Alice what he was thinking. Like an actor poised, she waited for the next line.

"Thanksgiving," he said finally, as if announcing his own funeral. "OK, I'll move out then. That's it. A few more days. It's *settled*."

The gravity of Oscar's words hung in the air. Alice ran a hand over his head, a soothing gesture—respectful and in accordance with this monumental declaration.

"Maybe that's too soon," suggested Alice, now more than sufficiently confident to go on with the game.

"No, I've decided."

"What about Ruth? What about Christmas?"

"Look," said Oscar, his voice growing edgy again, "I'll *deal* with that. What about you? Do you think you could possibly get rid of *Mike* by then?"

By this time Alice was gazing pensively at the ceiling. With her long legs propped seductively against the white-tiled wall, she imagined for a brief moment she might actually have *become* Jessica. Terribly nobly she said, "I can't replace her, you know."

"Who?"

"Ruth. Writers make dreadful housewives. Old coffee cups and papers strewn all over the floor. No dinner waiting in the oven."

"What are you trying to say?"

"She's so nice."

"Actually, she's *not* so nice, if you want to know."

"She *seems* to love you so much."

"For Christ's sake, whose side are you on? Don't you want me to leave?" he said, practically pleading. Eyes swimming, he leant over and carefully stroked her legs. "God, you look incredible tonight," he murmured. "I really do love you."

And though, once again, she felt her cool reserve begin to slip away, she offered him a soulful smile, the smile of a mature woman weighed down by the responsibility of a man's love.

"Do you know that it almost *killed me* when I saw you walk in with another man?" The very thought of this made Oscar start shouting again; angry red splotches spread across his cheeks. "The fact that you slept with him, that he's been touching you . . . it drives me *crazy*, it makes me *so* . . ."

Suddenly there was a frantic pounding on the door.

"Hello . . . hello," a muffled voice was heard inquiring. Then louder, in a singsong warble, like that of a concerned parent, the voice asked, "Are you in there, Oscar?" Unmistakably, it was Ruth. Oscar leapt to his feet. During his roll on the bathmat a heavy sprinkling of white lint had stuck to his sweater. Hands flying, spinning wildly, he furiously attempted to pick himself clean. He patted down his hair, his trousers, his back, and when he finally came to a halt he looked utterly disoriented, like a beaten dog.

"You go, I'll stay," whispered Alice. He stared at her as if she had lost her mind. As if to say, Stay? Stay *where, for God's sake?* Alice pointed to the bathtub. As she climbed in and drew the shower curtain, she heard Oscar clear his throat. "What is it, dear?" he asked stiffly. Then a second later, the door was thrown open and all the hubbub of the party flooded in. Incredibly, the piano player was pounding out "The Other Woman."

"People are looking for you. Someone said you might be in here," Ruth said, not a hint of suspicion in her voice. Then, girlish and confidential, "Wait for me, I won't be a minute."

There was a click as the bathroom door closed, another click at the turn of the lock. A moment later, Alice heard the swish of rustling skirts, then the thud of flesh hitting porcelain, accompanied by a long sigh. Crouched down, hanging for dear life onto the faucets, Alice's view between the wall and the plastic curtain was a mere slither of bathroom—tile, mirror, a rectangle of floor, and half a washbasin. Ruth had removed her sensible patent flats with the grosgrain bow and was luxuriously wiggling her unpainted toes in the soft carpet. Another sigh and she was on her feet, layers of skirt flying as she organized her underwear. A flash of sturdy thigh and then she was on to adjusting her bra strap, the shoulder of her flowered dress pulled down to the elbow. Ruth smiled at herself in the mirror, pleased with what she saw. The brown freckled skin, the miracle of white cotton machinery holding up the mountains of flesh. Then the flare of a match and she lit a cigarette. No—*not* a cigarette, but a minuscule joint! Amazing. Who over thirty-five in these blasé eighties, wondered Alice, smoked dope anymore? Except Ruth, who sucked in loudly, then whistled blissfully as she exhaled. Presumably she had been comfortable this way for decades—loaded, robed, and sandaled since the seventies. A champion of sit-ins, bake-ins, love-ins. Soothing the troops as, in unison, they hummed their favorite Leonard Cohen song. Could this be the woman who recently had been informed by her husband that he was leaving her? Such serenity, such unwavering confidence. And a zestiness that hardly belonged to the embittered author of Oscar's poisonous notes.

Alice's knees were killing her; her feet, pushed painfully into the tips of the crippling pointed shoes, were swollen; her neck was stiff. Water from the shower head dripped torturously onto her forehead. She was just about to give in, to cry out, to *demand* that Ruth pay attention to what was going on under her nose when, with a passing flash of glossy chestnut hair, then the snap of the door handle, the bathroom was suddenly empty.

When she emerged, Oscar and Ruth were nowhere to be seen. Neither was Jessica. The party had thinned out and the guests, once regaling each other with show-business conquests, now lolled on the arms of chairs, sat drunkenly entrenched in sofas, or stood propped against the wall.

"That's how they see us, mothers or whores," the limpid-eyed actress from the bathroom complained, gasping for air between sips of champagne. "If you're tough and mean as an actor, it means you're *talented.* But if you're like that as an actress, it means you're *difficult and dumb!*"

The man across from her nodded. His eyes drifted over to Tom Emery. The piano player had gone home and Tom, nose to the ivories, was slowly and repetitively picking out "Chopsticks."

"Christ," the actress went on wearily, "I need to find someone outside this goddamned business."

"This was a good place to start," the man replied dryly.

Alice walked out onto the patio. The butler had opened the French doors to let out the smoke, and a chilly but welcome breeze wafted into the room. A dark-haired woman, hands clasped rather desperately, was pleading softly for director Tony de Palmo's attention. Stony-eyed, arms folded protectively across his bush jacket, he nodded and remained silent. "It's about a scientist who takes over a young boy's body, set in the fifties," she said breathlessly. "Call it a sort of cross between *Frankenstein* and *Rebel without a Cause.* It's about innocence. It's the child within *all* of us."

Behind them, in the near dark, sitting side by side in two rattan armchairs, were Mike and Nancy Sears. While Nancy's right arm imprisoned her bored teenage daughter round the waist, her left hand rested none too casually on Mike's shoulder. "Beverly wants to be an actress, don't you, sweetie?" she cooed, jerking the child's body even closer.

"Really," said Mike. He winked at the girl, but she turned her head.

"So I said, 'Fine, sweetheart, knock yourself out.' Then she wanted to know if it would mean she'd have to *sleep* with directors to get the job. 'Jesus,' I said, 'if that still worked, we'd all be up there in Panavision. The trouble is, most of them don't fuck *anything* anymore, except us poor producers.' "

Mike and Nancy both laughed, and so did the couple now leaning over to tell Nancy good-night. "Lovely," murmured the woman, a little giddy-eyed, "just *lovely!*"

"Redford didn't come," said her husband morosely; obviously he had been waiting around for just that.

"No," replied Nancy, unabashed. Outside there were the sounds of car doors slamming, people shouting.

"Lunch?" someone called. "Tuesday, I've got you down." Then as car wheels crunched over gravel, the faint cries of "Have a good Thanksgiving . . ."

Alice kicked off her shoes and balanced on the arm of Mike's chair. Rather obviously, he coughed, and Nancy's arm bounced back into her own lap. Five minutes before, Alice had felt triumphant—as though dashing offstage after a nerve-racking performance. But now she was weary and strangely disappointed that the whole thing could have been pulled off with such incredible ease. Love regained, power newly possessed . . . and feeling more like a whore finishing up with the last customer, she leaned back against Mike, eyes half-closed, exuding what she hoped would be taken as genuine late-night fatigue.

"Should we go?" she asked dreamily.

"Where have you *been?*" he whispered.

Suppressing a yawn, she replied, "In the bathroom."

In the car on the way home, Mike asked her how long she had known Oscar Lombardi. Characteristically, Mike's suspicions manifested themselves almost indiscernibly—perhaps a slight tightening of his hands on the steering wheel and a sudden recklessness while taking corners. Lately Alice felt that she and Mike had both begun to detest each other a little. "Oh, God," she replied, hesitating, as if to apply serious thought to the question. "I don't know, it seems like *forever* . . ."

15

Had it been any other Thanksgiving, Alice might have welcomed her parents' arrival, but on the eve of her permanent liaison with Oscar, this was no time to be crawling back into the womb.

Something in her voice must have tipped them off because when she called to tell them that she wouldn't be home, that screenwriters weren't supposed to take vacations, there was confusion and disbelief on the other end. "But dear, what will you *do,* where will you *go?*" asked her mother. "You're spending the holiday all alone?" Meaning, of course, that *they* would be spending the holiday all alone in New York. As a married woman, Alice had entered the sanctity of the male-dominated world with their blessing. The decision of whether or not to fly East for the holidays had been left, naturally, to the wisdom of her husband. Now a free woman, a *childless* woman of thirty-five, what possible reason could there be not to resume her premarital status of the loving daughter?

"Well, that's settled then," her father announced, yanking the phone from his wife's hand. "We'll come *there.*"

They arrived on the Tuesday, her father struggling with the suitcases, her mother dressed as if she were spending five days with Jackie Kennedy rather than her daughter in West Hollywood with the tawdry fashion of Gay America raging on her doorstep. Luggage was opened immediately. Out came the duck terrine, the pâté de campagne, the quenelles—

some of these delicacies prepared by her mother, some acquired from a French charcuterie off Madison Avenue. Kitchen cupboards were thrown open. "Where are your dishes, dear?" inquired her mother, as layers of rubber bands, plastic, and tin foil were removed.

When Alice opened the refrigerator door her father howled. Rows of vitamin bottles lined up where the milk and eggs were supposed to be. "Look at this!" he exclaimed. "Doesn't she know she's got to *eat* once in a while? What happened to the balanced American diet?" And with professional concern, hands placed firmly on his thickening waist, the doctor stepped back to take a look at her. "You're too thin," he announced, exactly as he had done countless times in the past twenty years.

"Tell her to push her hair off her face!" shouted her mother, now a distant voice from the bedroom. "She has a nice face, but no one ever gets to see it." And to prove that the fight was not altogether lost, she came running into the kitchen—high heels replaced by satin mules—carrying two immense jars of Elizabeth Arden heavy moisturizing cream.

"*Nice?*" said her father, waving her away. "What do you mean, *nice?* Don't tease her. My baby's *beautiful* . . ."

The next day the promised excursion to see the town took place. Her mother pleaded to be taken to the Brown Derby. "The Brown Derby," scoffed her father. "They tore it down years ago." So they went to Mann's Chinese Theater, then to lunch at the Ivy because the last time they had eaten there—out for Alice's wedding—Charlton Heston had sat at the next table and graciously passed her mother an ashtray. But it was empty of celebrities, so they moved on to Rodeo Drive. "Christ, it looks like Tokyo," remarked her father, pushing past the swell of Asians loaded down with camera equipment and shopping bags. They sped onward to the West Side

Shopping Mall where Alice's mother announced proudly that she wouldn't dream of buying any of their junk. "Not if you gave me a million dollars." Although shrunken and more bird-like compared to her glory days, she had not lost any of her fire. And in a way, Alice was still in awe of her. Not only because of her rocklike strength but for her ability to cling to life as she saw it—as it *should* be. To go out that morning, she had dressed in one of her sharp little numbers, just as she had done every day for years in New York, regardless of whether or not she was going anywhere. She had brought close to a dozen more *ensembles* with her, some squeezed into Alice's tiny closets or hanging behind doors. Her favorite, a Chanel suit from the seventies, was carefully laid out on an armchair, encased in so much tissue paper it might have contained the Shroud of Turin.

At the end of the day they sat and had drinks in the back garden. As soon as the sun went down, Alice's father sent her inside to get a sweater in case she caught cold. The grown woman who had happily rolled naked with a married man, legs thrown over her head, on the floor of some of the seedier hotels of Los Angeles, was apparently now incapable of taking care of herself. She did exactly as she was told. Overnight she had become the sullen twelve-year-old, swept back into the great ravine of her childhood.

"That's how you get sick in this place. The temperature drops thirty-five degrees at night, and the body goes into shock," her father said knowledgeably, polishing off another glass of the Chilean white wine he had found on sale for $3.99 a bottle at the corner liquor store. As a chaser he swallowed down one of his beta-blockers, pills for the lingering heart condition, which he kept along with the loose change in his pants pocket. His days of skirt-chasing behind him, Dr. Wilder's focus had narrowed. The gleam in his eye was now more likely to appear when with schoolboy delight he managed to save a few dollars on wine or some rare second-hand camera. "Listen," he would say in defense, lapsing into one of his familiar platitudes, "people just don't learn to spend money *overnight*, you know."

Eventually, the subject Alice had been avoiding came up.

"What about your love life?" he inquired, eyes closed, face pointing toward the last rays of sun dipping behind the palm trees. "Your mother said something about a film director."

It was true. A few weeks earlier, Alice had mentioned that she was "going out" with Oscar. However, still apprehensive after all these years, she had lied and told her mother that Oscar was separated from his wife. Then in a vain attempt to impress her, she had dropped a few of his credits. Her mother remembered *Deception* from a showing on TV but frankly hadn't thought much of it.

"I was seeing this guy, Mike Pearce, but now I'm seeing Oscar Lombardi."

"Is it *going* anywhere?" asked her father. In the space of minutes Alice had advanced from the twelve-year-old to the loose-moralled teenager.

"And when are we going to meet this Oscar person?" her mother wanted to know, intrigued despite her dismissal of his talent.

"Possibly tomorrow. Mike is dropping by tonight before he goes back East for the holiday."

"Mike? I thought that was *over*," barked her father, the third glass of wine settling in.

"He's the lawyer," her mother said.

"I *know* he's the lawyer," her father remarked impatiently. "But if it's *over* . . ."

"Perhaps he just wants to pay his respects."

"*Respects?* Listen to you. This is the eighties."

Despite the fact that the doctor still managed to make his wife's eyes close in aggravation, by now their bickering had become part of their daily life. And though this was not a blissful arrangement, Mrs. Wilder wore her placid acceptance graciously, as though it were one of her better coats.

"It *is* over," explained Alice. "He just wants to meet you."

Alice had been hoping that Mike would slip off to Connecticut for Thanksgiving and that by the time he returned her new life would be *there*, with no need for further explanations. But with his frustration and growing suspicion at her evasiveness, he had insisted that the least she could do was introduce him properly to her parents. *Properly.* Good God. Despite all the backstage shenanigans with the sturdy Sonya, there it was, the ever-present convention, the exemplary decorum. How could they not love him?

"Let me do that," Mike said obligingly one minute after his arrival as her mother trotted in with a plate of duck pâté and a chilled bottle of wine. Having relieved her of the appetizers, he helped pour the drinks while he pumped her father's hand. "Delighted to meet you," he announced, in his best speaking voice. Naturally, they had been smitten the moment he walked in. He was every inch the debutante's delight: bristling with energy, rosy cheeked, hair glistening from the shower, wearing his sensible tweed jacket and corduroy pants in anticipation of the great trek eastward.

Alice's father took the lead, running through a barrage of questions—Mike's work, his schooling, his hobbies—as if he were interviewing a son-in-law for a top position in the family firm. Where exactly in Connecticut did his parents live?

Westport? Yes, a beautiful spot. As a boy he used to go fishing up there himself. "The Aspetuck River, I believe."

"Amazing! I still go there with *my* father," said Mike. "It's great for trout."

No one seemed the tiniest bit embarrassed that this was the man supposedly on his way *out*. Her mother had on a new outfit, something inspired by *Breakfast at Tiffany's:* a girlish pink slip of a dress, a short matching jacket, and Audrey Hepburn pumps with Louis heels. As she bobbed up and down offering more pâté, Mike inquired, "Did you make this?" Then a look of astonishment on his face when the chef nodded coyly and the compliments came flying. "I can't believe it," he exclaimed, devouring the stuff. "You've been holding out on me, Ally. Your mother's a gourmet cook." More wine was poured, there was a request for the pâté recipe, then Mike steamed ahead with a flattering remark about the cut of her mother's dress. "Or is that a suit, Mrs. Wilder?" he inquired.

"Just a little *ensemble*," chirruped her mother.

Whatever it was, he wasn't able to resist adding, "Well, you look particularly lovely in that shade of pink." Leslie Howard couldn't have tossed it off better. The room was practically glowing.

And where was the prodigal daughter? Transformed into the mature, if slightly insane older woman, she stood frozen in the kitchen doorway. Initially relieved that no major faux pas had taken place, she was busy suppressing an overwhelming desire to scream. She heard her father, now well in his cups, telling Mike the old story about meeting the young Mrs. Wilder at La Guardia, right after they were married. She was due to arrive from Paris where she had been visiting relatives. He was at the gate, when a stream of passengers walked past him. "I saw this woman. She was in a huge hat—what was it, felt?"

"Navy straw," said her mother.

"Anyway, this big thing over her face, dark glasses, and a tight black dress with slits."

"Slate gray."

"Hey, who's telling this?" he said, shushing her. "She walks right past me. I say to the guy standing next to me. Who is *that?*" Her father was mimicking the look of abject wonder his own face had expressed upon seeing this apparition. "The guy says, 'I don't know, probably some movie star.' Who was it? It was my *own wife*. She looked so glamorous, I didn't *recognize her!*" Grinning, he collapsed back into the sofa. Mike laughed uproariously; then Mrs. Wilder slid down next to the doctor, hands fluttering, waving away the ancient, silly story.

"Can I talk to you?" Alice heard herself say as she leaned over the back of Mike's chair. Crisp, no-nonsense words that might have come from a head nurse's mouth.

She pulled him into the kitchen. As soon as she closed the door, everything came rushing out. "Look, you have to leave. It's over. I'm in love with someone else," she said, trying to keep it down to a frantic whisper. And then, as if to cosset the blow, she added rather wistfully, "I'm sorry. I should have told you sooner."

"It's Oscar Lombardi, isn't it?"

Alice nodded.

"I knew the moment I saw him," said Mike, not flinching.

"Really." She was genuinely surprised. "Why didn't you say something?"

Mike leaned against the countertop. "I've known for a long time you were seeing *someone*."

"But you never asked, did you?" Alice hurled back, feeling unreasonably angry. Mike stood motionless, his face turned away. "Were you hoping it would eventually just *go away?*" she asked, eager now to force some kind of reaction out of him.

"I suppose so."

"It won't. I'm in love."

"It'll never work," he said quickly. "Never. I feel bad for both of you."

"It *is working*, for Christ's sake. Don't be so goddamn considerate." All her past anger suddenly swam to the surface. His niceness, his coddling, and in particular his recent deception made her want to strangle him. "Don't play that game with me. Waiting for it all to collapse so that you can rush in and save me. I can't stand your endless pitying of people as a way of feeling *superior* to them. It's over."

"Shut up!" he said, raising his voice. Color flooded into his face. "Just be *quiet!*" Back in the living room, the talking stopped. Except for Mike's feet shifting on the linoleum floor, there was an eerie silence. Alice felt the kitchen slide away from her; she felt removed, as though viewing Mike in miniature. Now that the truth was out, selfishly she longed for it to be over quickly.

"Look, I was seeing someone too, but it's finished now," he said, as if the admission were enough to get them back on track.

"I know. Sonya."

"Yes," he said, startled; then he carried on defiantly, "You can't do this, Alice. *Please.* This is not the correct choice."

"What do you mean, the 'correct choice'? I'm not picking a college, I'm trying to choose a life."

"I want to marry you. Are you *listening?*" He was shouting now. The manners were gone, but the audacity was still there. He banged his fist on the countertop. Dishes drying from breakfast—cups, plates, silverware—clattered into the sink. "I want to get married. I want to have children. *I want a life, too.* What about me?"

"Now?" Alice asked incredulously, trying to raise her voice above the din. "Now, suddenly because it's over with Sonya and I'm leaving, you want to get *married?*"

It occurred to her just then that Sonya too might have turned him down for the skiing trip. Alice heard the phone ring in the living room, then her mother's voice.

"Not only for me," Mike said, rather desperately. "For *you* too. You should have children, Ally, before it's too late."

And as Alice shouted back defiantly, "Did it ever occur to you that I may not *want* children?" she saw her mother's face peering through three inches of open kitchen door. The woman looked petrified. Even as the main contender for the Queen of Drama award, the last screeching line had cut her to the quick. "It's for you, dear," she whispered, eyes trained on the kitchen floor. "Should I say you're busy?"

While Alice was on the phone with Oscar (as far away from her parents as the phone cord would allow), she was aware of her mother talking politely to Mike in the background. Only when she heard the words "Well, good-bye, have a good trip" and the sound of the front door slamming did a sense of relief flood through her. Her father switched on the TV. Alice whispered to Oscar that no, she couldn't really talk now, but she would see him tomorrow—and that yes, he *just had to* come, they were dying to meet him, adding, "I love you and I miss you" as quietly as possible before she hung up. But not quietly enough. Her mother, shaking her head, sank lifelessly in a chair. Her father, eyes fastened on a ball game, refused to look at her. The silence, the disgrace, the unspoken horror . . . of what? Men? Yes, always problems with their little girl and men. Nothing had changed.

Except that this was worse. Here she was sleeping with

two men when she should have been at home with one. A new husband, preferably, since she had seen fit to get rid of the first. And what about the noisy brood, at her age? Where, for God's sake, were those promised grandchildren? Earlier that evening, uninvited, Alice's mother had come into the bathroom and sat on the edge of the tub where her daughter had retreated in an attempt to realign her sanity. "What I wanted to say, dear," she had whispered covertly, pushing a few wet strands from Alice's forehead, "is that your father and I have talked it over. We've decided that it would be all right if you went ahead and had children *without* being married."

Meaning, Alice supposed, that they might have accepted the ghastly vision of their daughter in flagrante delicto with every Tom, Dick, and Harry as they awaited their solitary graves—but all that and no *issue?* No heir to carry on the family name?

As far as her parents were concerned, in comparison to Mike, Quasimodo might have been standing at the front door the next day instead of Oscar Lombardi, celebrated director. He was unshaven, there were dark circles under his eyes, the sleeve of his jacket was torn. Alice, flushed and a little skittish herself, presumed that in his rush to leave his house—with the confusion and lingering guilt, Ruth finally realizing what was afoot—there had perhaps been some sort of scuffle in the hallway and Oscar had been forced, literally, to wrench himself away.

It was the second shock of the day for her mother. In the middle of preparing Thanksgiving lunch, her hands covered with turkey fat, hair dusted with flour, she had answered the doorbell. Standing there in all his splendor was Julio: leather motorcycle pants, a fringed snakeskin bolero barely concealing an otherwise naked chest, a bandana round his head, and grease-stained hands cradling a homemade pumpkin pie. Her mother had cried out. In an attempt to calm her down, Julio, eyes on fire, had stepped into the living room, whereupon she had let out a genuine scream. Alice had then run in from the bedroom to explain that he was her landlord, Julio, a good friend. Friend? Or simply another *man*, her father wanted to know. Because just when the doctor came in to find out what all the commotion was about, Julio was busy engaging Alice in a giant bearlike squeeze.

In the surprise and confusion, her mother ended up inviting him to stay for the Thanksgiving meal. Quite delirious with happiness—food, wine, and a captive audience—Julio started a challenging discussion about old movies versus the new and the shocking dearth, these days, of any "real stars."

Her mother, surprisingly coolheaded after the initial shock, listened spellbound as Julio recounted an afternoon spent with Marilyn Monroe. "Not many people know that she predicted her own death," he said solemnly. "She told me about a dream she had one night where a giant eagle landed on her and smothered her. She never realized what that eagle represented—her country, her own *government*, who, in fact, *did* murder her." Of course, Alice's parents hadn't realized this either. And for her father, the tale produced some giddy memories of his own. The day Marilyn died he had retired to his study and consumed an entire bottle of brandy. "Lonely?" he said. "How could this gorgeous creature be lonely? *I* would have taken her out." After which there ensued a respectful silence from the bereft male fans.

Alice was barely paying attention. "Sit down," her father said every time she went to the window to see if Oscar's car had arrived. "Sit down. And for God's sake, *eat* something."

Reticent as he was about meeting her parents, Alice

had persuaded Oscar to come by on his way to the apartment he had rented a few blocks up the street. The place he planned to live in semibachelorhood for the next few months. "They think you were separated years ago. I didn't really know what to say," Alice had told him. "Tell them I'm like Woody Allen, without the fame or the money," he had replied morbidly.

But his moods no longer depressed her. Not only was she buoyed by her recent party performance as the late night femme fatale, but as an out-and-out sinner she felt she had found, if not redemption, then some justification for her behavior. It was an incident she could never have predicted, something that, on reflection, filled her with such venal satisfaction, she was barely able to contain herself.

A few days before, standing in the checkout line of the Beverly Glen market, she had recognized a large woman standing by the deli counter. The wide hips, the sandals, her tanned fleshy arms waving as she ordered a pint of this and two scoops of that: It was Ruth. Standing beside her was a wiry young man. He had a forlorn baby face and a wispy goatee beard. There was something about their closeness, the proximity of their shoulders that caused Alice to wait, then follow them discreetly out into the parking lot. Crouched behind a row of shopping carts, immobile, her heart beating like a lowlife criminal, Alice watched as Ruth slid into the driver's seat of a Volvo station wagon. Two seconds later, after checking furtively behind him, the young man leaned in the open car door and slipped a hand up inside Ruth's blouse. The gesture was acknowledged by a lazy smile—a smile of such familiarity that as Oscar's wife tilted back her head, her face glowing like a beacon, the man unhesitatingly bent down and kissed her on the mouth.

Could Oscar know about this? Alice wondered. No, definitely not. A man who spent his waking hours embracing the *truth,* defining it, pursuing it, living it out so painfully, would be incapable of hiding even the slightest suspicion of his wife's infidelities. What it did explain, however, was Ruth's serenity, the chilling self-assuredness that Alice had witnessed at the party.

Naturally Jessica had strongly advised her to tell Oscar. Alice's deal-closer, she called it. But Alice had decided to remain silent until Oscar extricated himself of his own accord, thereby for once in her life retaining some dignity.

Fortunately, Julio left minutes before Oscar drove up. But despite her parents' gay mood (her mother had gone so far as to comment favorably on his forearm tattoo—a naked girl being eaten feet first by a cobra), upon Oscar's arrival, the holiday spirit sank like a stone.

"I had the window seat on the way out and I hate that because of the draft" was her mother's reply to Oscar's somewhat forced inquiry about the plane ride from New York. They were sitting in the living room, Oscar in the same armchair that Mike had occupied the night before. Unlike Mike, however, Oscar was collapsed wearily against the pillows, eyes searching the room as if, in his confusion, he were unable to find any point of reference. "The *draft?* On an airplane? Listen to her," her father chipped in, good-naturedly. Slyly, however, he stared at the stubble on Oscar's chin and the torn jacket until finally his gaze rested on Oscar's feet. Alice immediately read her father's thoughts. *Tennis shoes* for Thanksgiving—my God! And not very clean ones at that.

An awkward silence followed. Julio's pumpkin pie was offered around but everyone refused, Oscar requesting a scotch on the rocks instead. Dutifully Alice rushed off to the kitchen to fetch it, and by that time her father, blindly trying to keep things afloat, had launched into an account of his glorious years as an ear, nose, and throat specialist. The early days, the struggle to build up a practice. Not a glamorous business like Hollywood of course but, in the beginning, extremely rewarding. Now things had changed, he said. No one trusted the doctor, everyone knew everything about his own body. "A man is suing me because I gave him antibiotics for an ear infection. He got a rash across his chest. He got headaches, got depressed. Then he argued with his wife, so she left him. And *I*'m to blame," he said, incredulous, helping himself to another glass of the Chilean wine.

"The real problem with Western medicine is that it only operates on an emergency level," announced Oscar, pulling himself forward in the armchair. He was suddenly alert, as if someone had challenged him with the subject on *The $64,000 Question*. "It's completely shortsighted," he went on stridently. "It's like good old American politics. We *always* know best. And hell and damnation to anyone who comes up with an unorthodox approach. Alternative medicine? Good grief say our stern protectors. Homeopathy, herbal therapy, acupuncture . . . What is this? Voodoo? Astrology? The great boondoggle of the seventies and eighties? Squelch creativity, say our doctors, busy pushing their murderous pills and potions. Stay in the mainstream. And now, God forbid, these know-nothings, the *patients*, in their arrogance are *also* trying to debunk traditional medicine. With notions that have *no scientific data to back them up . . .*"

Her father was dumbfounded, not so much that his sacred medical profession was being challenged but with such hostility from a man who, by all traditions, should be on his best behavior. Alice's mother, also startled, was now surreptitiously checking out Oscar's profile—the large nose, the unruly dark hair—as if to say, *this* is the man she loves? The one she misses so much on the telephone? Mr. Aggressive and Impolite, instead of that clean-looking dreamboat she threw out yesterday. "Look, I realize there are two schools of thought . . . ," her father started to say, but Oscar forged ahead, moaning about doctors prescribing the latest fashionable drug willy-nilly, all of us being hapless guinea pigs for the so-called advancement of modern medicine.

"This is California, Dad," Alice suddenly broke in. She was beginning to feel like a stranger in her own living room. Taking refuge behind Oscar's chair, she leaned over him in an effort to transmit some good manners through his shoulder blades. "You know how it is," she said heartily, "*everyone* in California is into preventive medicine." Oscar could really be so funny, so charming and *gracious*, she wanted to tell them, but he's under this immense stress, his wife, the movie . . . "He's in the middle of directing a film," she went on a little desperately. "It's been such strenuous work. And a lot of pressure from the studio."

Her mother, panicked and prepared to lie if necessary to save the day, piped up. "I saw your film *Deception*. Wonderful. Very sad at the end when he's ruined his life and shoots himself." Then, seeing she had gained a few yards, she plunged headlong into romantic memories of Paris in the fifties, her salad days when she and Yves Montand had a brief affair, or *partially* did or just *missed out* because of her decampment to the United States. The story changed periodically, depending on the audience. "He introduced me to left-wing politics and gin rummy. He drank like a sailor but you could never tell. Once in the lobby of the Plaza-Athénée, he assaulted a man for simply trying to—," until Alice's father, noticing Oscar's eyes drift to the window, cut in.

"You know, I've always been confused as to who does what," he said, more subdued now, but still ticking over. "What *is* the difference between the director and the producer?"

There was a pause. Then a confused look from Oscar.

"The director *directs* the actors," her mother explained impatiently.

"So what does the *producer* do then?" asked her father, heating up.

"God knows, not much," Oscar groaned wearily. "Frankly the whole process is too difficult to explain."

"What he means is—," said Alice.

"I mean, to people who aren't in the business, it would never make sense," replied Oscar. And the two people sitting there, those obviously *not* in the business, fell silent again. "Even my mother doesn't understand what *I* do, for God's sake," Oscar added, as if this final admission would perhaps shut them up.

"Well," said her father, willing to go for one last try, "all I know is, it's very competitive. Alice tells us that people should be congratulated for just getting a job, *any* job out here. I guess show business has always been like that," he laughed dryly. "Many are called but few are chosen."

"He said 'the chosen.' "

"No, he said 'chosen.' 'Few are *chosen.*' "

"Well, he meant *The Chosen.* You could tell the way he was looking at me. It was clearly an anti-Semitic remark."

"A lot of my father's patients are Jewish. Jewish *and* Italian. You're paranoid. And you could have been more polite. You could have laughed at his jokes."

"What jokes? He wasn't funny."

"You could have indulged him, pandered to him a little instead of being so hostile."

"I'm forty-two. I don't have time to pander."

They were driving down Melrose Avenue to a destination unknown. A few minutes earlier, back at the house, Oscar had suddenly leaped to his feet pleading a frantic need for fresh air, indicating clearly that he wished Alice to go with him.

Now, as if to explain the outburst *and* his paranoia, he handed Alice a buff-colored envelope, his name and address typed across the front in red. Inside was a sheet of the now-familiar cream-colored foolscap, featuring a single line of capitals: THOU SHALT NOT SCREW AROUND.

"What can we do?"

"Nothing," Oscar replied.

"There must be something," she said, realizing that the chance of Ruth having written these letters was now close to zero. "Maybe you should tell the police."

"No," said Oscar flatly.

Obviously under enormous strain, he drove on. She should never have asked him to meet her parents, thought Alice. It was too soon, too overbearing. Brand new in-laws when he had an original set at home. More obligations when he was being driven mad by work and vicious hate mail.

"I can't do it," he announced suddenly. "I was up all night, and frankly I just can't do it."

"What?"

"I can't leave Ruth." Hands gripping the steering wheel, the words suddenly exploded. "Listen, maybe we'll be together some day. Maybe in a couple of years. Say—eighteen months. If I'm still crazy about you, who knows. I'll come and get you. Because last night I decided one thing—" He was panting, trying to keep up with himself. "—I've decided I don't want to be happy anymore. I just want to be *calm*."

She felt a kind of inward collapse. Noises from the traffic filtered in. On the street, people walked normally, carefree. Was she losing her mind? Perhaps he hadn't spoken. If she had heard the words correctly, they seemed fantastic, incomprehensible.

"Maybe you'll have married someone in between," he

went on, less frantic now but still unable to look at her. "And that might be what I need. The remorse at *losing* you. Maybe you'll be taken—gone forever. Well, that would be my bad luck. But if you *are* taken then ultimately I would have made the right choice."

"Right choice?" What exactly was he *saying?* Was this an attempt to explain some perverse fantasy? "Why?" she asked, stupefied. "Because I couldn't wait for you? So that would make me what—*unreliable?*"

"Look, if it's ever possible for us to be together, I have to try and make my marriage work first *without* you. Then if it's no good, I can leave and I'll have a clean conscience." In order to give the conversation its due, he had pulled into the parking lot of a minimart. "The thing is," he was saying, sounding almost sanctimonious now, "I want to do the right thing, the *sensible* thing. Perhaps it's time to bring the curtain down on the melodrama."

She sat staring ahead. The composure of a sphinx. A fat Mexican boy, holding a soda and wearing oversized spongy earphones, was crouched on a milk crate in front of the store. He held a cardboard box in his lap, and just visible over the flaps were the heads of four brown puppies who squealed and wriggled pitifully each time he dribbled diet Coke into their pink mouths. It occurred to Alice that this angelic, yet somehow appalling tableau would be locked forever in her memory. She heard Oscar go on about truth and guilt. His honesty, his shame, his sinfulness. He was making a clean breast of it, determined to go the whole hog. Except that his owning up had a nasty way of belittling things, making everything ordinary and of course so conveniently *solvable.*

"Can't you *stop!*" she finally said. The voice seemed to come from someone else, a hysterical woman shouting miles away. "Just *stop!*"

And for a moment he did. Then taking her hand, he

went on steadily. "What I'm trying to say is that my loyalty to Ruth has nothing to do with the way I feel about you. It doesn't mean I don't love *you,*" he said, gently pleading to get her full attention. "I do. I *love you.*"

"Great."

"Don't be angry."

"I'm not angry!" she yelled, furious. "Goddammit, I'm *sad.*" She tried to hold back, but the tears were cascading down her face. "I just can't believe you're *doing this.*"

But she had known. She had guessed it when he was reluctant to meet her parents. She had guessed it when she got in the car and there was no luggage. No overnight bag, no mementos from the house, *nothing.* But still she had gone on pretending, smiling. When in life had her sunny smile not got her through? And what now? As a parting blow, should she inform him of his wife's infidelity? The thought only depressed her further.

"I can't help it," he said. He was staring at her morosely, as if the utter simplicity of the finale scared him. "It's the guilt, I've got enough to fill the Vatican, let alone the whole of Israel."

"Then go back. You're doing the right thing," she found the courage to say.

Sorrow hung in the air, suffocating both of them. "Do you really understand?" he asked.

"Yes, I understand," she said, wondering if similar words would be carved on her tombstone: IT DOESN'T MATTER. IT'S FINE. I UNDERSTAND.

In the fading light, she stood on the sidewalk outside her house, unable to go inside. How could she explain it to her parents? That this man who had introduced her to tenderness as well as a host of sexual depravities, this lewd lover, her soulmate, whom she had trusted implicitly and perhaps foolishly, would not be in the lineup to rescue their unmarried daughter from her lingering adolescence, if not further degradation. Because that's how they would see it. The blow would be directed at them. The grief caused by her gullibility would hurt them more than it hurt her. Once again, she had let them down, she was disallowing them a normal life, one without *any hope whatsoever.* On top of Alice's bewilderment and grief, this was almost too much to bear. Through all the shouting matches, the slammed doors, the whining about boyfriends, the escape to points West—despite everything she had done to dissociate herself from her parents—she still desperately wanted their approval.

She walked around the back of the house. She hoped to creep noiselessly into bed, but there, sitting outside the kitchen door, one hand still cradling a glass of Chilean wine, was her father. He saw her silhouetted against the garage wall and waved.

"Your mother's down for the count," he said. "There must have been something in that pumpkin pie. No one else ate it. She got all silly and giggly like a teenager, then felt nauseous. So I put her to bed."

And while she was thinking (quite dispassionately) of Julio lacing the pie with his homegrown weed, her father asked: "So, did you have fun?" Whereupon she burst into tears. Gazing foolishly at the ground, she started sobbing and couldn't stop. Without hesitating, her father leaped up and took her in his arms. Her chest heaving, he led her to one of the rusting chaise longues where he pulled her onto his lap and cradled her in his arms. She tried to speak but he shushed her. There was no need to explain. It was not important and anyway he could guess. She was safe now. And while the grown woman sat collapsed in pain and confusion, the aging father—his face a road map of broken veins, and most of his hair gone—stroked her head as if she were an eight-year-old. Right then she wanted nothing more than to be young and stupid and stay in his arms forever.

Her parents left the next day. Her mother had recovered. In fact, she had never slept better and proclaimed her sinuses miraculously cleared up. No one mentioned the drugs in the pumpkin pie in case the sinuses, the backache, the pleurisy, and her periodic "nightmare," the arthritis, all struck back in revenge.

And in the family tradition of moving on, no mention was made of Alice's breakdown the day before. Only at the last minute—her father waiting while her mother rewrapped every item of clothing in tissue paper—did he whisper tenderly to Alice, "It's going to be just fine, baby." Then laughing as though he couldn't help himself, he added, "Anyway, couldn't you have fallen for the *handsome* one?"

16

It was unbearable. Not only had she lost him, but gone, it seemed, was her entire personality, so much of herself had she invested in Oscar. Time slowed to a snail's pace. For the next few days she moved stupidly from room to room or sat for hours in the same chair. Breakfast was merciless in its emptiness; and with nothing for her to look forward to, the smallest errand became an impossible task. The sight of laundry or dishes in the sink sent her reeling back to bed where the terrible need to mourn swept over her once again. Pain was the only reality—that and the fact that she was finally alone. Because despite her fanciful escapades as adulterer, seducer, mother figure, and femme fatale, the truth was (and this was hardly a revelation) that rarely in her adult life had she operated without a man at her side. And not one man to make her a liberated woman; with her talent for exaggeration, she needed two! Caprice and melodrama overlapping until, inevitably, the entire thing exploded. And how far back, she wondered, did the falsification go? Perhaps her childhood misery was also a distortion. Could her father only *now* take the grown woman in his arms because the brooding teenager had been too busy fighting him off to be loved? Had the young writer's ill-conceived notion of pain been nothing more than *self-pity?* "Our own journey is entirely imaginary. Therein lies its strength," Céline wrote, and it had been duly noted by the fifteen-year-old in her journal. But what about now? If this feeling for

Oscar was not actually love but self-delusion, why then was she holding on to it for dear life?

"You've got to push through the sadness," Jessica insisted, choosing to ignore the fact that her master plan had backfired. Undaunted, she informed Alice that melancholia gave her a tragic glow, a somewhat haunting beauty that, frankly, at her age could not be wasted. "The truth is, if Oscar had left Ruth now, she would have become his goddess lost for life. You would have had to listen to the guilt and horror forever. Move on," she said enthusiastically. "Get angry. I want to see hatred. I want to see revenge."

Revenge? Anger, perhaps. Because Alice knew that her self-absorption with sadness, like everything else, was also a perversion of what *was.* Time to consider the hard facts. Where there had been insinuations and fantasies (and more often Oscar's ever-present hard-on) masquerading as true love, what now remained was a rather unoriginal case of a mistress scorned. What Alice needed was something to put the whole sordid affair into perspective. As befitting this age-old tragedy, she decided to send Oscar a letter. After several abortive attempts, she wrote:

> Dear Oscar,
>
> Please do not regard this letter as anything more than an attempt to clarify my thoughts. This is *not* an invitation for you to reply. It is simply easier now to voice my opinion on paper than it was when we said good-bye. You always did have that annoying habit of either not listening to me or silencing me with your stream of consciousness, your own *engrossment,* which you allowed to spew forth uncensored, like a five-year-old burdening everyone in his path with his colossal drama. Because that's

what your life is all about, isn't it—theatrics and sensationalism? And it now occurs to me that that is precisely what's lacking in you as a fully formed adult. You have never really "lived" off camera. Your entire life has been your movies. And so what happens when your movies no longer give *you* a life? You must find a different kind of plot. So you start an affair, a new masterpiece, starring, this time, yourself. No doubt to relive old passions that drove you so hard as a boy and, who knows, perhaps to find *new ones*. Nothing comes from nothing, huh? Then at some point, as in every good story, the melodrama goes on a little too long, you have seen it all, experienced it thoroughly, and it is time to wind it up. Though the last act is all tears and remorse, in a way it's a giant sigh of relief. After all, this is *not* real life, it's a movie—and better than that, you don't even have to see how it plays out. You can simply go *home!*

While basking in this heady feeling of escape—the "calm" that you led me to believe was, in the end, preferable to your happiness—you might consider the fidelities of your wife. Or should I say *infidelities?* Yes, Ruth too, it seems, has been rewarding herself with a little extra passion on the side. Or didn't you know?

I say all this, believe it or not, with great affection.

Alice

Well, the revenge was there in the end. She had told him about Ruth. Only after she'd addressed the envelope to Oscar at the studio did the irony strike her: She had informed him that Truth is not an adventure, that Drama eventually plays itself out. Precepts that she herself had ignored for most of her life. In view of this, she decided to wait a few days before mailing it. She left the letter propped on the hall table. A moment later she heard a knock at the door.

It was Julio. In the spirit of the season and aided no doubt by the ever-modulating effects of his homegrown weed, he was perched on a ladder, happily stringing Christmas lights over her front door. And this was merely the finishing touch to the masterpiece he had built on the front lawn, something Alice must have missed during her recent reclusive days. Life-sized papier-mâché figures of Mary and Joseph with glittering wire halos were flanked by two beasts of burden, all bent forward in adoration of an empty cardboard manger. Empty because Julio had not, as yet, taken the baby Jesus from his cellophane-wrapped box.

"Last Christmas someone *stole* him. Imagine that. So this year I bought a half dozen. For only fifty bucks. Made in China, wouldn't you know?" And sure enough, as Julio pulled the infant from his box, Alice saw that the alabaster face had slanted eyes and a thatch of jet black hair.

"What do you think?"

"Very festive."

"What about the Nativity? It was my father's. Do you know how we made it?" Julio asked, adjusting a mere centimeter the cardboard crook in Joseph's hand. "You have to dip hundreds and hundreds of strips of paper in glue, then mold them one by one round the wire. I was only ten," he said, his moon face looking as serene now as no doubt it had been then, "but I got to paint all the silver parts."

Alice nodded her head, thinking that what her letter needed was less accusation and more eloquence. A little poetry. Some sturdy Byronic image for him to remember her by.

"So, how is everything?" he asked. He was back at her

front door, peering into the hallway. What was he looking for? wondered Alice. Signs of destruction? Empty gin bottles, old pizza boxes, slashed drapes? The catastrophic manifestations of a woman who'd gone over the edge? In the last week, sensing that all was not well, he had interrupted what had become his daily routine of harvesting his marijuana crop to knock on her door and shout, "I'm here if you need me!" only to be met with stony silence from his grieving tenant.

"Everything's fine," she said. And affecting a look of studious distraction, she stepped back into the hallway. "I've been busy working."

"I didn't see your column this week."

"No," she said, quickly closing the door. "I'm on sabbatical."

This was not strictly true. The trouble had started the week before Thanksgiving. In her obsession with Oscar and her sympathy for his arduous grind at the studio, she had written—with somewhat flowery exuberance—a piece that defended the great métier of the director, the auteur so continuously exploited and, in her opinion, misunderstood by Hollywood. She pointed out that the top executives were making such fortunes that not only were they not interested in movies with any artistic merit, but they were no longer interested in making movies *at all.* Their luxurious days, she speculated, were spent assessing stock options or organizing dinners with the Kissingers. It was a departure from her usual innocuous pieces, and, worse than that, irate phone calls had been made to Henry Worth.

On the Friday after the column had appeared, Alice stopped briefly at the drinking fountain on her way out of the Weekend section. She felt a light tap on her elbow. It was Henry Worth. He spoke softly, a foxy glint in his eyes—evidence that he had put away his lunchtime quota of martinis at the Jonathan Club.

"Could it be, as a small bird told me, that you are trying to achieve too many things at once?" he asked, a look of forced benevolence swimming across his puffy face. "And none of them much to do with journalism?" Alice imagined Cameron Fischer, Henry's faithful foot soldier, being the humble but very honest bearer of the information—that Alice had been slavishly devoting the paper's time not only to Oscar Lombardi but to a screenwriting job for Billy Hawkins.

Then the following Friday, her column had not run. Written during the height of her misery, it was an abrasive piece about Hollywood's misogynistic writers and producers who, she proclaimed, saw the female only in the traditional male-inspired form. Women characters who actually liked sex were depicted on screen as either dangerous or psychotic.

Alice called Leonard Lativsky, who feigned surprise and confusion. Could the piece have been lost? He would ask around. Naturally, no one was fessing up. A day later, Alice was called into his office by Leonard. A man constantly at the mercy of his nervous system, and saddled that day to deliver the bad news, his gaze penetrated the ceiling while his hands tapped out a disjointed ditty on his desk. In rapid spurts, he informed Alice that it was not his decision to discontinue her column. It had been the consensus at management level for some time. What was needed was a more serious look at the business of Los Angeles, its effect on the times we live in. "L.A. has a tremendous influence on American culture. Film, TV, music, it's all funneled out of here," he said, sighing, as though obliged to state the obvious. "Let me just say, this is not your fault, Alice. Quite simply, we're going in a different direction." And eyeing her dolefully through a forelock of his moplike hair, he threw his hands in the air, as if to say that while he had fought valiantly for her talent, he could do nothing about her apparent sexual confusion—the fate of which *might* have lain in his hands, had she only had the good sense to allow it.

She was fired. Compared to the horror she felt grieving for Oscar, the disappointment was minor—no, *expected.* It fulfilled her dismal view of life in the aftermath. Life after love. Life alone. Bad news had become her daily serenade. The "different direction," Alice discovered (revealed to her by one of the junior reporters), was Cameron Fischer who, on top of doing movie reviews, would be writing a column called "The Deal."

17

"The tragedy with Panic is his intelligence. He reflects too much. Things weigh him down. His admirable qualities are the very things that plague his everyday life."

"Uh-huh."

"So I decided to create a sidekick. I thought first about giving him a dog."

"A dog, yes."

"No. *Not* a dog. I thought, better a robot. Or, better still, a half-cyborg, half-human, *like* a little dog. Something that befriends Panic and gives him its undivided attention—someone he can *talk to.* A pet, a comrade. A mindless go-getter who's not afraid of violence."

"Oh, I see."

At the center of Paramount's cavernous Stage 22 sat a midget, legs dangling in midair, fleshy fingers gripping the pages resting on his tiny pressed pants. Pitched forward on his stool, blinking rapidly in the glaring spotlight, he was trying to determine exactly where Billy Hawkins stood. Not an easy task since the star kept jumping around in the darkness. Today Billy sported black, skin-hugging workout tights, a black T-shirt, and elaborately tooled cowboy boots to go with the Victor Mature hair. He boasted all the showmanship of a professional ringmaster, minus the whip. Richard Fenn, his casting director, sat several respectful feet behind him. Then farther back, perched on director's chairs were Jim Lynch and

Sam, Billy's trainer, both silently bent forward in order to demonstrate their loyal attention.

"Uh, in these pages," said the midget, again peering timidly into the gloom, "your character, Mr. Hawkins, seems to be even *more* violent than in the previous movies."

"It's a sequel, it *has* to be more violent," said Billy. "But Panic shows his hatred for it. More violence but more *conscience*. Get it?"

The midget nodded, reflecting for a moment.

"Shall I read?"

"Sure. Fire away," said Billy.

Alice stood watching from the wings. Pages in hand, she was once again waiting for Billy's undivided attention.

Getting back to the script had been easier than she'd thought. There were moments, of course, between the escape of writing and the grim reality of her life when old obsessions crept back in. But after a week, she found she could draw on her passionate afternoons with Oscar to create Panic and Tania's required steamy romp without her stomach churning in despair. In fact, so successfully did she manage to channel her own resentment into the violence of the script that by the time she wrote the final escape—Panic and Tania chased through the underground tunnels by the hydra-headed alien force—she felt purged, almost light-headed with optimism.

The midget had run through the dialogue given him. Now, voice straining, arms flailing, he launched into an off-the-cuff recitation from *The Tempest*, presumably to dispel any notion that he might be less than a professional or, indeed, a full-blown man.

Confused at the outburst, Billy interrupted the actor in midroar. "Whoa—what was *that?!*" he shouted. He was still hopping around like Jack Dempsey when he saw Alice standing in the gloom. "Alice, hey, come over *here*. Sit down. Always so *timid*," he said, cracking his princely smile. The grin and the mild put-down were not for her, she understood, but for the edification of his captive audience. Nevertheless, she sat obediently in an empty director's chair. And by this time, Billy was crouched down, eye to eye with the startled midget.

"Let me give you a tip. Acting is like boxing," he instructed in a fatherly tone. "It's subtle. You gotta know when to let it fly, when to pull back. When to conceal, when to reveal." He performed a deft flurry of fist work as he spoke. "Of course, everything will be minimalized inside the cyborg suit. Your voice will be distorted mechanically, so nuances might end right there. Also it will be as hot as all hell. How do you feel about that?"

Half an hour later, Billy, followed by Alice and Jim Lynch, walked the twenty yards to the star's trailer, parked around the corner from Stage 22. The inside was sumptuous, fantastically gaudy, like the boudoir of some aging hooker whose passion for blue velvet has run amok. It was everywhere: blue walls, ceiling, even the dainty curtains over the porthole-shaped windows.

Jim poured coffee from a machine percolating in the small kitchen and Billy slid into the breakfast nook, the seats also covered in a blue furry material. When Jim arrived with three steaming mugs, Alice shifted along the banquette. She felt claustrophobic trapped behind the table, squeezed tightly between Jim and the wall. Opposite her, however, rising above the booth like a building, Billy looked perfectly comfortable.

Silently and with great concentration, he read through her work. But when he reached the love scene in Tania's subterranean apartment, he started to shake his head. His lips moved as he scanned the words, his brow wrinkled, and a stern annoyance began to tug at the corners of his mouth, which Alice found reduced his good looks considerably.

"Wait a minute," he said suddenly. "I don't get it. Panic's coming toward her, and Tania says, 'I admit you don't look like you'd *kill* me anymore. But I'm a notoriously bad judge of character. Especially of men.' Then she pauses and says, 'Are you married?' And Panic says, 'No.' And she says, 'Are you *lying?*' "

Billy looked inquiringly over the top of the pages. "He's married?"

"Well, she's not sure," said Alice. The proximity of the two men in the booth was beginning to make her feel mentally as well as physically diminished. "She's attracted to him. She's a little insecure."

Billy went back to the pages. But after a minute he sighed again and shook his head. "And then, here, Panic says, 'Relax, this will be painless.' And Tania says, 'Since when is a relationship with the opposite sex *painless?*' And he replies, 'Honey, let's bring the curtain down on the melodrama, shall we?' What does that mean?"

"They're warming up," said Alice, shrinking further. "He's joking. He sort of throws it away, to calm her down."

"Throws what away? *'Let's bring the curtain down on the melodrama, shall we?'* Sweetheart, *no one* talks like that. Marlon at his peak couldn't say that line."

Alice said nothing. Jim, doing some serious thinking, sipped noisily at his coffee.

"And this whole bit. What is Tania going *on* about? She says, 'Don't tell me I'm smart again, because if I'm so smart, how come I'm so *miserable* all the time? So far my life has been one horrible mistake after another.' " Billy closed his eyes for a moment, then continued dumbfounded. " 'And don't tell me you're being *honest.* Men are incapable of telling the truth. They say they're going to do something, but what they mean is if nothing more important *comes up*—' Jesus, Alice, isn't this supposed to be a *sex* scene?"

"I was trying to give her more depth. Make her more—well, more modern and sympathetic," Alice heard herself say, thinking, more docile, more pliable—more *what you asked for!* But by then the familiar wave of anxiety had washed over her. She took a sip of coffee, swallowing hard to try to settle her insides. Billy read on, his enormous jaw tightening every second. It occurred to Alice that never had she disliked anyone quite so much.

"'Do you still hate me?' Panic says. 'Less,' says Tania. Well, I guess that's not bad," Billy sighed, "Because *now* he's kissing her. But basically that's four pages too late. Too many lines, too many words. Too *talky*." He dropped the script, then leaned back. To calm himself he ran his hands over the curves of his pecs. "Look," he said, still absorbed in thought, "I know that maybe the best films are the ones dealing with people's *inner lives*, but when *I* make movies, I can't gamble on shit like that. This," he said, slapping the pages, "is beginning to sound like some goddamn *Neil Simon thing!*"

"And what kind of a *farchadat* movie is that?" yelled Jim, hands exploding in the air.

Alice's mortification turned to tears. Like a silent river, out of control, it rose on its own tide, overflowing the banks of all reasonable behavior. She felt impossibly feeble. A sissy. Why was she crying? Because, once again, he had criticized her writing? When had writers—celebrated ones at that—*not* been made to rewrite scenes ten, sometimes twenty times? Was that so terrible? No. Evidently, despite her recent bravado, any small rebuff was all that was required to send her reeling. It was as though she purposely sought out more pain, more *misery*, in order to remain part of the mourning process and therefore connected to Oscar.

Her shoulders heaved and she covered her face with her hands. A moment later, she was aware of the booth moving as Jim slipped silently away. She heard the trailer door click, then felt Billy's leg touch hers as he sat beside her.

"Hey, hey, c'mon," he whispered. "It's not that bad."

He slipped his arm around her shoulder; his hard muscles rolled across the nape of her neck. "Do you know what's funny?"

"No." The word escaped so softly she had to shake her head for emphasis.

"*This* is what you need to give Tania. Not words, but *tears.* So we can *see* how vulnerable she is. This is what makes her attractive and sexy. When she finally *gives up* the fight. Use it."

Of course. Sex and tears. A natural aphrodisiac. And by that time his hand was stroking her right breast—an action performed so awkwardly he might have been idly strumming a guitar. He was staring down at her, intent, wide open. Then he smiled. That close it was horribly wide, almost menacing. "You're a great broad," he said. "By the way, I mean that as a compliment."

It was the kind of remark she had come to expect. She let it go. Besides, she was not functioning too well. She felt curiously removed from her body. His hand slipped down to her thigh and she thought, Go ahead, I am numb. Too many demands have been made, I am a woman who can no longer distinguish between solace, pleasure, or a good opportunity. Make yourself at home. He bent his head and whispered something barely audible; it was the soothing, cooing sound of a man comforting a two-year-old. Of course, in his all-consuming vanity, Billy suddenly saw her as someone to be protected, coddled, and then, later, with his great benevolence, *deservedly fucked!* But whose fault was that? As an attractive woman, she had made herself compliant so that he would hire her. The old quid pro quo. Flattery, submission. The downward spiral. Where did it end? Then to her surprise, in place of apathy came a flicker of outrage.

"Take your hand away, please," she said. "I'm leaving." Though trapped between his hulking body and the velvety blue wall, she managed to uncoil herself.

"Ah, Alice," he sighed, sounding, she thought, vaguely amused. But he moved sideways to let her out.

Saying nothing more, she slid by him and headed for the door. Except that this continued politeness out of sheer fear was too draining. Spineless. "The trouble with you, Billy," she heard herself say. "Like most successful actors, you are cosseted and spoiled." Though she spoke quite coolly, her eyes remained pinned to the trailer's blue furry walls. "For your information, sex is supposed to be a reciprocated *emotion.* Give and take. Otherwise it's merely repetitive. Boring. Instinct without desire. Of course, in your case that's ideal. One more thing you can easily control . . ." She drew in a short breath, then, daring to look at him, she said, "Listen. To be honest I find your movies stupid, violent, and meaningless." And when Billy looked back at her—rather, blinked back at her—she added quite calmly, "So I think it would be better if you found a new writer."

Despite the cool exit, Alice's heart was racing as she drove home. In the car she continued to compose pithy epithets to Billy. Contempt and loathing overwhelmed her. However, fifteen minutes later, as she maneuvered past the clots of traffic lining up for a concert at the Hollywood Bowl, the fury was gone, unbuckled. She had exorcised her rage. Not only for Billy but apparently for Oscar too. Could it be that her outcry in the trailer had actually been a proclamation for *self*? If so, revenge now hardly seemed a noble pursuit for one so enlightened. And she therefore decided it was no longer necessary to send Oscar her malicious letter, which had been languishing on the hall table for close to a week.

As she pulled into her driveway, she was surprised to see Julio kneeling across the threshold of her open front door. The Nativity scene on the front lawn had been enlarged to include two rubbery-looking sheep and a cardboard shepherd, his head draped in what looked like an old checked tablecloth. In his rapid-fire voice, Julio explained that with the flashing lights above the crib and two extra spots to illuminate Mary and Joseph, there had been an overload. The fuse had blown in the garage, and with her permission he was using an outlet in her living room. Inexplicably jolly, he wore a red Santa hat with a soiled pom-pom, shorts (or were they *under*shorts?) decorated with leaping reindeer, and green Wellington boots. Alice said nothing. As she went to squeeze past him, he looked up, head cocked saucily to one side. "By the way, I mailed that letter for you. The one sitting on the table."

Christmas in California. A season sadly lacking in hot pretzels or fat Santas roaming the streets, ringing their tinkly bells. There was, of course, no swirling snow, although the occasional flurry of a fur coat could be seen on Rodeo Drive where, in the cool of a sixty-degree afternoon, tarnished reindeer swayed aloft, and rich housewives' faces glowed with the urge to buy. Alice could have flown back East. There was nothing stopping her, nothing except a nagging feeling about the letter to Oscar. Her remorse and her insistence that she did not want a reply plagued her. Now she *did* want a reply. She very much wanted the damn thing acknowledged, if only, somehow, to assuage her guilt. To distract herself she went shopping. But for whom did she have to buy presents? She had no work, no men in her life, and the rituals of joy and excess served only to exasperate her more. Women who would otherwise be languishing by turquoise pools now roared through Saks or Neiman-Marcus grabbing sweaters, socks, and cashmere dressing gowns for loved ones as though the stores were on fire. On vacant lots, flocked Christmas trees from Oregon stood tied and waiting. Every commercial on TV boasted squealing children or loving couples, glasses raised in anticipation, or entwined before a roaring log fire while a cacophony of carols blasted away in the background: food, family, and forgiveness as the panacea to the other eleven months of hell. As Jessica would say, Christmas was at their throats.

One day Alice came home to find a message from Mike. From the tone of his voice, the skiing trip seemed to have subdued rather than invigorated him. When he asked her to call him back, however, so that they could meet for a yuletide drink (he actually said yuletide), Alice heard a familiar sigh. Hope springing eternal, she thought, reminding herself that it was Mike's implacable optimism that she had always found so endearing. What's more, at this distance, unpleasant memories faded fast. Suddenly Mike represented all the myth of male potency: strength, integrity, and that other delusory quality—trust.

She considered calling him back but decided to postpone the decision. Safely cocooned in her bedroom, feeling virtuous and desirable once more, she lay down to watch TV. It was the usual horror on the news. Mayhem and madness. Locally a jealous husband had killed his pregnant wife's lover. He had hacked off the man's head, then delivered it (transported in a bowling bag, announced the commentator with a milky reverence in his voice, the kind usually reserved for golf commentary) to the hospital. Placing it on his wife's bed just after she had given birth, he had greeted her with the words: "Now you can sleep with him *every* night!"

Alice was thinking about the brutal lengths to which people went in order to get a person's attention when she heard a sharp tapping noise at her bedroom window. It was Julio. He was holding up the front page of *Variety*. While his open mouth made steamy rings against the glass, his bulbous eyes jerked sideways, indicating a headline in the top right-hand corner. Even at that distance, Alice could read it quite clearly: OSCAR LOMBARDI HEART ATTACK.

Locked in the bathroom, with trembling hands she read:

> Director Oscar Lombardi was rushed to UCLA Medical Center yesterday after he collapsed on location. He was 12 weeks into "Body and Soul." Rumors run rampant that this controversial director suffered considerable stress during the problematic shoot. Producer Marvin Shapiro cites "creative differences." "Lombardi is the German shepherd of directors. You never know when he's going to turn," says Shapiro. "But talented."
>
> From the beginning, there has been a considerable backlash from the feminist movement, which argues that the sex scenes in particular are demeaning. "The sex is graphic but only by puritanical American standards," Lombardi was reported as saying a few weeks ago (V. 10/28), complaining of interference by the studio. "It's a movie about a young woman who uses her beauty and cunning as a basketball player might use his talent to get out of the ghetto. A modern-day Becky Sharp,

> if you will. Typically, the studio wanted to make it about urban terrorism and murder."

And Alice could not keep from imagining Oscar collapsed on the street, one hand over his heart, the other clutching her vitriolic letter. After an exhausting day of fighting with Marvin on the set, he had been informed not only that he was a liar and a fraud, but that what remained of his life—the tranquility of his hearth and home—did *not* exist because his wife was out *shtupping* some guy on the side. This hostility in his darkest hour from a woman who had claimed to love him.

The worst of it, thought Alice, was that she had trivialized his talent. She had mocked the artistry of a man who, that very morning, had been lauded by Charles Champlin in the *Los Angeles Times* as "a visceral but aesthetic genius." A piece she had missed due to her recent refusal to read newspapers, but which, naturally, had been saved for her by Julio. It was more somber than the *Variety* piece, almost a eulogy, as though the poor man were already in his grave.

> He believed in the power of movies to shape our dreams, aspirations, and fears. He could never bridge the gap between individualism and Hollywood's approval, but in his unique way he exploded many of America's myths.

As the perpetrator of this tragedy, Alice wondered if she would go down in motion-picture history as the Jezebel responsible for the great director's death.

18

The hospital was so hugely ominous, so extensively spread out, it hardly seemed a place anyone entered willingly, let alone came out of alive. Nevertheless, by the time Alice found the correct building, then the correct elevator for the fourteenth floor—the coronary care unit—she was bursting with anxiety, and ready to check in herself. Driving there she had gone over the letter a hundred times in her mind. Of course, she blamed Julio, her maniac in residence, but mainly she blamed herself, and was beginning to wonder if she might be *legally* responsible.

At the nurse's station, a lone Asian nurse was listening to an elderly couple who spoke in whispers. Here a mood of terrifying sobriety pervaded, possibly to remind the visitor of not only the patients' tenuous hold on life but also the fact that several of them would soon be leaving this joyous planet for good. Even the décor was funereal. Compared to the riot of Christmas decorations elsewhere in the hospital, only one small wreath adorned the wall. And the walls themselves, painted a dismal gray, seemed to have been designed, if not to absorb human suffering, then to swallow up all human sound. The faint buzz of the low-hanging strip lights over the desk, the occasional clank of a gurney, or the squeak of a door opening somewhere down the corridor was all that could be heard.

"Relative?" inquired the nurse when Alice asked if she could see Oscar Lombardi.

"Sister," replied Alice, her heart racing.

"Only ten minutes." The nurse pointed to the smoky glass doors at the end of the corridor.

"How is he?" Alice asked, enough trepidation in her voice for three siblings.

"He's dysrhythmic. There's still the possibility of an MI."

Alice nodded silently. But the relief was enormous; at least he was still alive.

He lay on a narrow bed, head thrown back, eyes closed. Like the other patients in the glassed-in cubicles or in beds half-visible between the sections of floating curtains, he was hooked by a cluster of wires to a monitor displaying his vital signs. He looked terrible. His skin was gray and papery. There were tubes in and out of his nose, tubes disappearing under the covers. His right arm was plugged into an IV, the left thrown awkwardly across the thin blanket. Only one hand retained a faint suggestion of life: a clenched fist, in whose fingers Alice half-expected to see the protruding ends of her dreaded letter.

Afraid to go in, Alice leaned her face against the cubicle glass. She felt like an interloper. This, she thought, was the flip side of their clandestine afternoons, of drinking and cavorting until all hours. In fact, lying there, Oscar barely looked like the same man who had pressed her countless times to hotel floors while she begged to be fucked into kingdom come. She now felt ashamed. This was the truth. This was life and death. What was their fleeting romance compared to the horror of his condition?

Alice must have stood there for five minutes before Oscar suddenly lifted his head off the pillow. Huge childlike eyes, ringed in dark circles, stared at her through the glass. The constant flickering of the monitors gave his face an eerie glow.

He opened his mouth a fraction, as though in preparation to speak. If he did, she wondered, what should she reply? *Sorry, I didn't mean to . . .* She was just about to enter the cubicle when a voice behind her said, "Sir, *please* . . . he's only allowed *one* visitor at a time."

It was a nurse. With a notable amount of impatience she was pleading with Marvin Shapiro, who brushed her away from his sleeve, then held up a pudgy hand as though to halt any further physical contact. "Swear to God, we'll be in and out," he said. He was flanked by another man holding a miniature Christmas tree festooned with colored balls and a string of lights. "This is *business,* dear," Marvin went on, a touch more pleasantly. Then to accommodate her further, he dropped his voice to a whisper. "The studio wants to pay its *respects.*"

Unimpressed, the nurse stood blocking the doorway. "One of you will have to wait outside."

The person accompanying Marvin was a tall, angular man wearing a tweed jacket, gray worsted slacks, tennis shoes, and a paisley silk ascot, tied perfectly around his slender neck. Standing erect, smiling awkwardly, he appeared as if he had just stepped out of the road-show company of *Private Lives.*

"I'll wait," he said with obvious relief.

"It's OK. This person is a *doctor,*" Marvin explained to the nurse who, now worn out and obviously with better things to do, stepped aside. "And can I get an extension cord for this?" he called after her, pointing to the tiny tree. "It lights up."

Marvin hesitated for a moment when he saw Alice. There was a faint sign of recognition, but obviously he was in no mood for social niceties. Pulling the other man after him, he stepped into the dimly lit cubicle where, cautiously, he inclined his body over the bed as though the area were contaminated. "It's not my fault," he whispered, breathing into Oscar's face. It was an impassioned plea and he repeated it. "It's *not* my fault, I swear. I said to the studio, I told them, 'How can you do this to this great man? Lock him out of his office? Fire him with a goddamned *memo* for Christ's sake? He's an *artist* . . .'" Marvin was wringing his hands, as if trying to squeeze every last drop of emotion from his soul.

Oscar, whose eyes had remained open during Marvin's appeal, sank back tight-lidded against the pillow.

The man in the tweed jacket holding the Christmas tree hovered at the door. "Perhaps you two should discuss this alone," he suggested nervously.

"No, no," said Marvin. Then, impatiently, "Over *there*," he barked, instructing the man to place the tree on top of the monitor. "Oscar," he said, lightly tapping the top sheet. "This is John Coleman. He's a professor from Columbia. I'm paying him a fucking fortune to teach me some things for a couple of weeks. You know, interesting facts about the *universe*. He knows incredible stuff." At this crude summation, the professor winced, a lifetime's work reduced to "stuff." "And I thought he might have an opinion on *your* condition," Marvin added brightly. He made a closer examination of the tubes worming in and out of Oscar's body, then whispered over his shoulder to the professor, "Christ, will you look at this mess?"

"I'm not *that* kind of doctor, I'm an astrophysicist," the professor whispered back. Clearly, this was not the first time he had been obliged to remind the producer.

But Marvin was not listening. "Oscar, I *fought* for you," he continued, still desperately trying to get the director's attention. "I want you to know that. Your assistant fought for you. When they came in to pack up your office, she actually lay across the doorway until *security* was called to drag her away." Excited at the memory, the words bounced rapidly from his mouth. "Judy. What a feisty little thing. I offered her a job."

Oscar opened his eyes. "You took my assistant?" With some amount of difficulty, he pulled himself up and grabbed a corner of Marvin's jacket.

"The movie has to go on," Marvin responded defensively, trying to pry open Oscar's hand. The professor, whose demure bedside manner contrasted so sharply to Marvin's, gasped when the producer yanked the jacket out of Oscar's clutches, causing the patient to collapse like a bundle of rags against the bed.

"Mr. Shapiro, I *really* think we should . . ."

But Marvin flapped a hand impatiently behind his back, "Look," he said firmly to Oscar, "the studio wants *me* to go ahead—to finish shooting the movie." And in reaction to Oscar's horrified look, he flung out both arms, relinquishing all responsibility. "After all," he said, "*somebody*'s got to make the fucking release date for next June."

"I don't know how big your dick is, but your balls must be the size of grapefruit," Oscar managed in a strained whisper.

"Hey, hey," said Marvin. He was offended by the remark in the presence of the professor. "I didn't *have* to come here, you know. You were fired, not me. Let's face it, Oscar, with or without this *problem*"—he jerked a finger distastefully at Oscar's chest—"you were getting too *close* to the movie."

"Too close?" queried Oscar, wheezing a little under the strain.

"Yes. Not objective enough."

"Too close!" With one fist, Oscar feebly beat out his frustration on the top sheet. "Try saying that to Nicholson. Try saying, 'Oh listen, the grip here is going to step in for this scene because you're *too close* to it, Jack!' It's like me saying, 'I'm going to fuck *your wife* tonight, Marvin, if you *had* a wife, because you're *just too close to her!'* I'll kill you if you touch a foot of my film."

A nurse rushed in. She was a pretty blonde, quite young and not at all sure how to deal with these unruly men. "Look, you're disturbing the other patients!" she bleated, quite red in the face. "And Mr. Lombardi is a *sick man.*"

"We're leaving," barked Marvin, and waved her out of the room.

"Mr. Shapiro," insisted the professor, pointing nervously at the monitor where Oscar's heartbeat had dramatically changed levels. "He *is* very sick. His P-waves are lengthening. He's in a state of persistent arrhythmia."

"I thought you didn't *know,*" replied Marvin, dismissing him. Like a live wire, he now lunged back and forth across the tiny room. "There's talk of you being laid up for two months or more, for God's sake!" he shouted at Oscar.

"Mainly from you and the studio."

"You think I can't direct the last ten days of this lousy movie? Are you kidding?" He was still pacing, his head nodding like a gigantic doll. "Could it be that you really don't understand the game or that you just *pretend* not to? I'll explain it again. See—it's like you're an architect building your own house. Right? You can build it any goddamn way you like. But if you want to get paid, Oscar—*PAID*—we get to say, 'Well, we'd like an extension here, maybe a bigger kitchen there.' Because it's our money—get it? OUR MONEY!" Impressed with himself, panting, he leaned on the end of the bed. "You see, my strength is that I understand the business and the *show part* of show business. I'm a *creative* producer."

"That's an oxymoron," croaked Oscar, one of his hands clutched at his throat as if to squeeze out the words. "Ask the professor what *that* means."

By now, the pretty blonde was back with two hefty, no-nonsense senior nurses. Marvin was finished anyway. And without another look or word to Oscar, he allowed the women to escort the professor and himself out of the cubicle and down the corridor.

With enormous relief, Alice realized she had not been directly responsible for Oscar's collapse. Although in a vague sense she felt slightly cheated, which in turn alarmed her all over again. Of course, it was possible that the letter had actually augmented the shock of being fired. It was also possible that the letter was completely insignificant. Was the fact that she was *standing there* also insignificant? No longer a murderer or a mistress, what was she? An intruder. Humbled, she realized only one task remained. She must tell Oscar she had lied about his wife. After all, what had she seen? A casual embrace, nothing more than a mild flirtation.

But before she could walk the short distance necessary to reach Oscar's cubicle door, she saw someone striding toward her. It was Ruth. Two choices were open to Alice: Either she could walk out, head straight past her down the corridor without a word; or she could duck behind the curtain belonging to the adjacent cubicle. Uncharacteristically, she chose to stand still, then stuck out her hand. "Hello," she said rather stiffly—Bette Davis offering a dry branch to Miriam Hopkins. Except the courtesy was returned with a tight-lipped, icy stare. Though Ruth's ample body was draped in a rose-colored shift, far from typifying the adorable mother figure, today she exuded all the charm of a sergeant major. She moved briskly past Alice and pressed her face against the window of Oscar's cubicle. Not to be outdone, Alice also stepped up to the glass. At that very moment, the patient opened his eyes. Oscar's surprise at this vision—the two women side by side—was registered first with a look of anxiety, then outright panic. Like a stone, his head fell back against the pillow. Why, she wondered, were they tormenting him?

As if in answer to her question, Ruth turned to face Alice, leveling her with her terrifyingly placid brown eyes. There were no catastrophes in this woman's life, thought Alice, simply things to be done, obstacles to hurdle. Alice was debating what to say as an opening shot when Ruth unsnapped the clasp of her shoulder bag. With the deliberation of a master thief, she removed an envelope then waved it in the air, temporarily causing Alice's knees to buckle. It was her letter to Oscar. She considered snatching it out of Ruth's hand; instead she stared up at it innocently, noting that the top had been hastily ripped open. No doubt more care had been applied in digesting its contents.

"That was addressed to Oscar."

"The studio sent it on to me after he collapsed," said Ruth matter-of-factly.

Alice tried to grasp her meaning. *After he collapsed.* "But it was private."

"So I found out," Ruth commented dryly.

"Well," said Alice, "to be honest, I'm relieved."

And she was. The fact that Oscar had never seen the letter gave her strength—enough anyway to face the rancor of the icy matron who, in a rather menacing way, had taken hold of Alice's arm. However, just then a voice inquired: "Mrs. Lombardi, is that you?"

A doctor with thinning red hair and bushy eyebrows stood a few feet behind Ruth. In a well-trained gesture, obviously meant to facilitate the tricky doctor-patient relationship, he approached her head-on, hands clasped behind his back for ballast. "Well," he said cheerfully, chin to the fore, "the scare's over. His enzymes are normal. As far as we can see the irregular heartbeat was due quite simply to pericarditis. In other words, *hypertension.*"

Ruth dropped Alice's arm, her face devoid of emotion. The rock, thought Alice, whose own relief flooded through her so strongly she felt her neck burn.

"What about his chest pains?" asked Ruth.

"Ah, that old barbarian," said the doctor. He sighed loudly, a person frequently wearied by his own superior knowledge. "Stress, and more *stress!* We'll keep him in another day or two in case of fluctuation. Basically he needs rest and time away from his work. Although I realize how impossible *that* is." He winked and gave a low chortle as if to say, "I know the pressure of the movie business. They wheel 'em in from the studios every day and we patch 'em up. What a town!"

"This is such a relief," said Ruth in her detached but oddly syrupy voice, a hand now lying reassuringly on the doctor's arm.

But he had no intention of ending the conversation there. "Would you please tell your husband *Deception* is one of my favorites? Terrific," he went on. Then, blushing, he pulled a thin manuscript from inside his coat. There was a brown spot on the worn blue cover. Dried blood? Alice wondered, or merely the coffee required to get the juices flowing? He presented it to Ruth as a priest might offer Communion, a sacred gift, to one of his flock. "I know he must be busy as all hell, but if he could just take a look at this treatment. Tell me if I'm on the right track. It's about a doctor who turns into a mass murderer."

Alice heard the good doctor elaborate on his tale of horror, but she was already on her way to the elevators.

Outside, a heavy drizzle was falling, the sky full of ominous rolling clouds. Streetlights glowed mistily and the cars, several with Christmas trees lashed to their roofs, maneuvered slowly over the street's slick surface.

At first she was a little suspicious of her own high spirits—and, yes, a little guilty, not at all sure why she was experiencing such a marvelous release. She felt out of the loop, cleansed, lucid, as a sick person does emerging from the horror of a near-fatal disease. There was a certain wisdom here. Finally, she could step down and relinquish her post as mourner to a mightier woman: Ruth the Treacherous.

It was dark by the time Alice arrived home. To her surprise, there was no familiar glow on the front lawn. The Nativity scene was unlit, as were the colored lights that trimmed her front door. Another fuse gone, she thought. But inside her bungalow all the electrical switches were dead, too. Holding a newspaper above her head against what was now a steady downpour, cursing Julio under her breath, she ran across the lawn to find him. His back door was open. She called out his name and when there was no answer tiptoed inside. A small metal lamp burned with an orange glow in the living room—or what might have been called a living room, but which looked more like a Middle Eastern bazaar. Barely an inch of wall space was visible. Hung in random fashion were cowboy hats, Indian masks, lassos, hubcaps, odd limbs from store mannequins, a collection of Nazi paraphernalia, medical equipment, license plates, and near the fireplace, lined up on shelves, wrinkled brown objects in glass jars that did not bear closer examination. The collection was as diverse as it was insane, yet somehow not so surprising. Again she called out Julio's name. No response. It was on her way out that she saw something on his desk. Visible beneath the piles of magazines, newspapers, and clipped supermarket coupons was an old Remington typewriter, a sheet of cream-colored paper rolled in the top. In the dim light she managed to see an unfinished sentence typed in red capitals, a line taken from popular philosophy: HE WHO DOES NOT LEARN FROM . . .

It seemed incredible, yet so obvious. Shocked, she realized that it was Julio who had been sending the anonymous letters. Forced to watch the lewd sexual drama played out right there in his own backyard; it had all been too much for him. But why such moralizing? And to what end? To uphold decency? To champion the sanctity of marriage? Or so that, eventually, he might get a go at her himself?

She would have to move out. Perhaps a fitting end to a spectacularly draining year. She was standing in the dark driveway debating this when she heard someone whisper her name. It sounded like a child's voice. But when she turned, she saw it belonged to a very slender woman, almost painfully thin, with a ton of black hair cascading past her waist. She was practically drowning in hair. It was the only thing that gave her any bulk, as though without it she would have blown away. "I live next door in the apartments," the woman said by way of introduction. Two brown furry eyes came up to meet Alice's. "I knew Julio," she said somberly. The past tense. Was he dead? thought Alice. Worse than that, judging from the woman's quivering mouth. "He's been arrested," she said tearfully. Not only for growing marijuana, but also, the woman told her, for harboring stolen property—articles from studio prop departments that had disappeared consistently over the years. Alice was about to mention the anonymous letters but was not sure what kind of relationship, if any, existed between Lady Godiva and the incarcerated Julio. "The terrible thing is," the whispery voice was saying, "there's no one to post bail."

Once more the imploring eyes unfurled in her direction. Taking this as her cue, trying hard not to smile, Alice walked the few paces to her pitch black bungalow where she let herself in and slammed the door.

19

The holidays were welcomed with a long sigh of relief—Hawaii, Aspen, and the East Coast being the favored places of retreat. However, for those in the industry who thrived on a maximum of daily anxiety, there was much trembling at the thought of two weeks' enforced isolation from their habitual torture.

The weekend before the great exodus, Jessica took Alice to a party on the Fox lot. It was the classic boomtown celebration, incorporating the studio's annual Christmas affair and the premiere of their big holiday release, a fifty-million-dollar epic about a wily New York detective who unwittingly takes on the Chinese Mafia.

The parking lot had been flooded, then frozen to resemble the skating rink at Rockefeller Plaza. It was flanked by mock-ups of great Manhattan landmarks—the El, the Public Library, and the Metropolitan Museum, the buildings dramatically reduced in scale for the desired effect. Near the production offices, a plasterboard facsimile of Main Street Chinatown had been put up, each booth decorated with red and white lanterns and painted dragons. Here the crowd surged thickly, anxious to heap their plates with sweet-and-sour pork, chili dogs, chop suey, and turkey burgers, all to be washed down with vats of mulled wine. Dotted among the crush were groups of Dickensian-costumed singers who labored harmoniously through "Silent Night" and "Away in a Manger," struggling to be heard over the roar of excited voices and the continuing wail of "New York, New York" blasting across the skating rink.

Jessica, flaunting her usual party spirit, sailed aggressively into the throng. Despite her swagger, however, and the outward show of festivity—red platform heels, an exquisitely molded silk dress, platinum hair glowing phosphorescent under the arc lights—Alice thought she detected a touch of fatigue, an unexpected solemnity in Jessica's eyes, as though she were already exhausted by the forced gaiety. Or possibly it was because a few days earlier she had broken off with the Czech director. She had mentioned the split casually to Alice, only a hint of anger glinting in her pale green eyes. Then as the familiar throaty laugh erupted from the depths, she had dismissed the entire affair. "Like all foreigners, he continually missed the *nuance*," she said knowledgeably, choosing not to elaborate further.

Now as they pushed through the hordes of merrymakers toward the skating rink, Alice was relieved to see Jessica break into a genuine smile. Despite the fact that both women were older than the melon-breasted actresses who sashayed through the crowd, Alice noticed young men throwing admiring glances their way. And the sight of these eager faces, hell-bent on having a good time, suddenly reminded Alice of Mike.

He had called again the day before, insisting she meet him for lunch, pleading an urgent need to see her even for ten minutes. It was tempting, but she refused. And though she congratulated herself on her restraint, in the back of her mind was a lingering curiosity. Though a partner was no longer needed for that cumbersome task of renewing faith in herself (she was almost sure of this), it was still hard to ignore Mike's dogged enthusiasm. And with the old restrictions gone, she wondered what his appeal might be.

But when she mentioned Mike's phone call to Jessica,

her friend seemed disproportionately shocked. They were standing at the edge of the ice rink, where Bing Crosby's velvety "White Christmas" filled the chilly air. Here, in an amusing turnaround, a group of studio executives, momentarily at peace with their inferiors, now labored in their servitude. Wearing jaunty elves' costumes with pointy hats and displaying an overload of jovial etiquette, the executives helped secretaries and lesser mortals navigate a safe path across the treacherous surface. Alice noticed one bright-eyed man holding onto her agent, Carol Gottleib. Though beaming ecstatically, Carol refused to let go of the outside rail while she gingerly sidestepped the perimeter of the ice.

"When did he call?" asked Jessica.

"Yesterday."

"But you wouldn't really want to see him again." One of Jessica's eyebrows rose in what Alice thought could only be mock concern.

"No, absolutely not," replied Alice. "But I can't help admiring him. Always forging ahead, regardless of obstacles in his path."

Jessica directed her voice upward with the music. "A woman can *never* go back," she said with some finality.

"No," agreed Alice, hoping it was true. But by then Carol was furiously waving a gloved hand.

After taking laborious pigeon-steps across the ice, the short, well-stacked woman arrived panting, one hand across her chest. Alice introduced her to Jessica. Taking in the tight dress, the ice blond hair, Carol's professional interest was sparked, until her mental arithmetic calculated the age of this statuesque creature. Realizing the actress was over forty, Carol's beaconlike smile dimmed, only to be regenerated when a more interesting thought came to mind.

"Oh, yes. Aren't you seeing Walter Koloffski?"

"No," replied Jessica.

"Really, I thought . . ."

"Not anymore."

Carol nodded, once again pausing for a discerning look. "Well, you're gorgeous, honey," she announced, dismissing the problem with a gurgling laugh. "No doubt you'll survive."

"Right," said Jessica dryly. "Pretty women aren't allowed to be unhappy." Carol laughed again but glanced at Alice, unsure of the humor in the remark. Then Jessica leaned over toward Carol, not uncoincidentally showing a fair amount of cleavage. "I have no right to ask for *more,* do I?"

Carol was silent. For a moment the three of them stood transfixed, as though this might be a fine opportunity to appreciate the music echoing across the rink. Carol even hummed a few bars of "I Saw Mommy Kissing Santa Claus" along with the Ronettes. "You know," she said finally, shoulders still swaying, "Fox spent half a million for this little bash, and the movie's a real turkey." Then she leaned in to Alice, a satisfied smile on her lips. "Guess who called this morning? Billy Hawkins. He thought you did a pretty good job. He *liked* you. Said he'd definitely want to work with you again."

Alice was taken aback. She had been too humiliated to explain to Carol what had happened. But before she could say anything now, the excited woman was on to the next thing. "And listen. I think I've got you another rewrite. James Hill is doing some gangland thing. South Central L.A. Only they're women."

"Gangs, I don't know if I—"

"Predictable, I know, but who cares? You've got a reputation for the tough stuff now. You're *hot,*" she said with an exaggerated wink. "We'll set up a meeting after the first."

And with that, she tottered back onto the ice, shouting cheery holiday greetings to the crowd.

≈

Soon after that Jessica wanted to leave. Her spirits had sagged even further, resulting in an unprecedented silence as they walked to the parking lot. Even in the car, her moodiness persisted. Instead of dropping Alice off, Jessica persuaded her to come home with her.

The house was moderate-sized, a rambling Spanish hacienda in the Hollywood hills. Some interior walls had been knocked down so that the living area was a vast unadorned room. Painted white and sparsely furnished (one remarkably large television set and two deep sofas), the simplicity of the surroundings seemed in direct contrast to Jessica's own flamboyance, as though she had decided to save further embellishment for herself.

For ten minutes, Alice sat waiting for her. Eventually she came out of the bedroom, transformed, dressed in ivory silk pajamas with delicately woven Chinese sandals on her feet. She lived in a magical world, thought Alice. Each metamorphosis bore no resemblance to the last or those to come. What was real for Jessica was happening right *now*.

Before disappearing into the bedroom, Jessica had poured herself a tumbler of vodka. When Alice asked if, in fact, she was going to drink it, Jessica had replied airily that it was her policy during the holidays to test herself to see if she could handle the rush. Apparently, having easily handled the first vodka, with a certain swiftness, she poured herself another.

Though alarmed, Alice suspected she might have been brought there specifically to witness some shocking revelation. Whatever it was, nothing Alice could say would stop her. Besides, merely by changing her clothes, Jessica suddenly appeared rejuvenated, newly impervious, and, surprisingly, far from drunk. Glass in hand, she sat down on the sofa facing Alice.

"So you might have a job in the new year?" she asked, flashing a smile.

"Maybe."

On the drive over, Alice had been wondering if things could be that simple. A clean slate, a word of validation, the mere suggestion of work, and lo and behold a brand new life.

"Me too. CBS is doing a miniseries," Jessica announced. "A comedy-Western. Shoots in February—Utah and Mexico."

"Terrific," replied Alice, surprised. "Why didn't you tell me?"

But Jessica was up, on her way back to the kitchen, murmuring something about more ice. "*Not* terrific," she shouted. Alice heard the unmistakable sound of a bottle top being unscrewed. "I can't do it."

"Why not?"

"Because I can't *stand* it anymore." She was still shouting, although by now her voice had lost some of its vivacity. The refrigerator door slammed. "Do you know what it's like on location? Two months in some god-awful Holiday Inn waiting to go to work. Suddenly the grip with the tattoo cracks a joke and you think, Well, *this* might be inviting. It might be better than watching TV every night in your cell. Of course, the old gag is still true: They don't travel well. But you pretend. You tell yourself he'll look very fetching back home, cleaned up, in a Ralph Lauren suit. And *he* pretends he doesn't have a wife—whom he loathes—living in the Valley with his two lousy kids." Her glass full, slopping a few drops on the carpet, Jessica walked back stiffly and lowered herself lengthwise on the sofa. "But if you don't have *someone*," she went on, carefully balancing the glass between her small breasts, "how the hell do you keep enough adrenaline pumping every day to get out there and say the dumb lines? So, you deceive yourself brilliantly. And for *years!* Then one morning you wake up and you feel like Diane Keaton in *Looking for Mr. Goodbar.* You're flushing barbiturates down the toilet and trying to remember your own *fucking name.*"

Vodka had spilled on her silk pajamas. She licked her finger to rub the spot, then gave a to-hell-with-it gesture and drank some more. "Do you know the first thing they asked me in rehab?" she said, liquid gurgling in the back of her throat. " 'What is your drug of choice?' 'Sodium Pentothal,' I replied. Then I said—extremely amused by myself, 'Failing that, scotch, vodka, gin, brandy. You name it, sister.' " She raised herself up a few inches. "Listen, you want to know the great thing about drinking? *Feeling absolutely nothing!* Bliss! Sheer bliss. Without it, every day sits there like some giant fucking bird of prey—"

She broke off and tears started to roll down her face. Alice said nothing for a moment. "Why didn't you mention this before?" she asked quietly.

But Jessica shrugged impatiently between sobs as though she could hardly bear the thought herself. "Hell," she managed to say, catching her breath, "is other people *and* their misery." She sat up. With one finger, she furiously stirred her drink, but her shoulders were still jerking and the ice cubes bounced and fell onto the carpet.

"You're an actress, you thrive on instability," said Alice softly. She took hold of Jessica's hand and tried to remove the glass of vodka, but Jessica swung it away.

"Let me tell you," she went on fiercely, eyes filling up again. "This is not a place where you can grow old with any dignity. People keep reminding you that everything pleasant happened twenty years ago when you weighed ten pounds *less.* God, I hate it. I hate the forced dedication, the responsibility of being someone to reckon with. I hate having to be cool, beautiful. *I hate it all*—"

She drew in a deep breath and the last giant sob subsided. Then, as if suddenly bored by her outburst, she lay back on the sofa, eyes closed. Once again, she was the lithe and plausible femme fatale, no less charming after the explosive confession.

"Why do you think so many people break up at this time of the year?" she said, sighing. "It's Christmas and the whole world is mourning because of love. You go into a supermarket and half the women are holding Kleenex to their noses because some boyfriend has decided *not* to be with them for the holidays."

"Perhaps people can't bear the idea of starting a new year with the same problems," Alice suggested. "The same old doubts, the same obsessions." Then, without thinking, she asked, "Were you in love with the Czech?"

Jessica's eyes fluttered to the ceiling.

"You said you didn't care," said Alice, pushing a little.

"But I *do* care. I care about every *fucking one* of them." She was on the verge of crying again but managed to swallow it.

"You once told me that as long as you *need* someone you can't really love them," said Alice. "Fear of losing him won't allow you to see love for what it is. And so you can't be happy."

"I don't believe it."

"But *I* do!"

"Look, a woman of my age is too used to drawing her strength from men," Jessica said morosely. "Despite what everyone writes about, moans about, the reason for the moaning in the first place is *because* of the dreadful dependability. If I am not attractive to men, who *am* I attractive to?"

"But what about all the advice you've given me? All that rousing stuff about self-esteem?"

"Oh yes, I'm very good at *giving* advice."

"Are you saying you're attracted to the humiliation?"

"No," Jessica replied, and Alice could see a little of the old brio creeping back. "What I'm attracted to doesn't exist anymore. *That's* the tragedy. The romance, the gamesmanship, the longing, the intrigue—practically nonexistent. What happened to the mystery? Even eroticism is gone."

"Perhaps you expect too much," said Alice.

"*Of course* I expect too much. But unlike other women, I don't blame men. I don't feel I'm constantly held *hostage* by them. Christ, nobody knows how to behave anymore. Everyone's fighting for control. Exactly the one thing I don't want, by the way. I *want* to suspend belief. Isn't one of the joys of being in love about *not* being in control?" She was gazing up at the ceiling again, one arm floating languorously above her head. "Of course," she added wistfully, "it's important not to suffer *banally*."

Alice anticipated more drunken wisdom, but none was forthcoming. It appeared Jessica had something else on her mind. She pulled herself up off the sofa and walked gracelessly over to the window and opened it. When she lifted one foot onto the ledge, she lost her balance for a split second. But she hung on, draping herself dramatically against the curtains, chin tilted back, luminous face framed against the dark sky. After a moment's silence she turned and smiled. The anguish was over; she was not about to throw herself out into the chilly December night. "I hope you're not upset, but I've been seeing quite a lot of Mike. On and off. I may even join him for Christmas," she said, managing a girlish grimace as if to add, *Christ, Alice, don't be angry*. "You don't *mind*, do you?"

For a moment Alice was too surprised to speak. She realized that this information must have been weighing heavily on Jessica for some time, hence her moodiness at the party, not to mention her shocked reaction to Mike's call. And what about Mike's call? His burning desire to see her was, of course, only a need to confess. Admittedly, Alice felt stupid; why then didn't she feel remotely angry? The truth was, it had taken no more than a few seconds to forgive Jessica—if forgiving were in order. After all, hadn't Alice relinquished her claim on Mike? Well, if not, the self-deception stopped here. Moreover, unlike any relationship with a man—so fragile, so easily disrupted—there was no real competition between the two of them. No rounds to be won. Whatever Jessica revealed herself to be, whatever selfishness, mania, or duplicity lay at the heart of her, it was acceptable. And not because Alice particularly condoned her behavior but because it was all so terribly familiar. Alice looked at Jessica as though she *were* herself.

"Remember, he wants everyone to love him," Alice offered with a smile.

"I want everyone to love *me*," Jessica replied humbly. "We're a perfect pair."

With great difficulty, Alice managed to book a seat to fly back East for Christmas. On arrival, she continued the ritual of former years. She went through her closets and rediscovered old clothes, threadbare toys, books—a spiritual digging to see what vestiges of the child remained. And there ensued the usual arguments. How could her mother have thrown away her porcelain doll collection? her first editions of Virginia Woolf?

"What first editions? The walls were bulging with books," her mother replied. "And the dolls were falling to pieces. I gave them to your cousin Leslie's twins *years ago!* Besides, I needed the closet space to hang your father's good suits," she said, dismissing the problem, waving a hand as if to say, "What would a grown woman want with dolls *anyway!*"

Alice exchanged gifts with strangers (people who at least seemed like strangers, such distant family members they were), an assortment of people who arrived at the apartment at all hours during the four-day Christmas hysteria. She marveled at their new children, their new hairdos, and at her mother's prompting wove elaborate stories about her success in Hollywood, all in the pleasant, semihypnotic daze of a woman without responsibility or expectations outside the family apartment. In fact, everything that had so annoyed her on previous visits—the heavy swagged drapes in the living room, the overstuffed, overgilded furniture, her cramped yellow bedroom (predictably, even smaller than she remembered it)—she now found surprisingly charming, even comforting in its familiarity. No longer was it all a ghastly reminder of her claustrophobic childhood. It was hard to tell, however, if this calmness emanated from herself or from the two aging people who had lived there for nearly forty years.

On her last evening, after the doctor had retired, she and her mother sat at the kitchen table. Alice was expecting a few follow-up questions about Oscar or Mike or some customary queries about men in general. But too tired, her mother wanted only to talk about the old days. The St. Teresa days, the trips to Elizabeth Arden, the facials, pedicures, leg waxing, tea at the Plaza days. There were the Sunday excursions to Uncle Toby on Long Island, Alice carrying on about Simone de Beauvoir or showing off in front of the relatives with some morsel from Descartes while her mother quoted, "A woman who isn't loved is lost," courtesy of the great Coco Chanel. These memories now shared by two girls wearing flimsy nightgowns, faces covered in crème de cacao, heads bent over their *verveine* tea; stories repeated over and over with frothy laughter and a tenderness that a couple of years earlier would have been impossible. How had this happened? Had they both, without realizing it, let *go*, given up the fight? Or was there simply nothing more for either to win?

Under the harsh overhead light, her mother's fading eyes and the uncertain, unmade-up mouth seemed suddenly so fragile. Barely was anything left of the young woman famous for her fabulous éclat and élan. What remained, however, was something more subtle. The stubbornness was there but with it a kind of quiet charm, a gentleness that Alice now felt a need to protect. Could it be that her mother's vulnerability was something Alice had for years overlooked? Or was that exactly the thing she had been afraid of inheriting, so badly did the daughter want to be something unique and *apart?* Except that no longer did she have to fight for approval from her mother or her father—stoic, kindly, immersed as ever in his own pleasures. There was no need for them to see her as different. She *was* different. Finally the child was able to forgive her parents merely for being human.

Back in Los Angeles she found two phone messages from Oscar. The first was to wish her a Merry Christmas; the second was more elaborate, his voice betraying a touch of desperation.

"In the spirit of the season I've decided to celebrate the coming year with a suite at the Château Marmont Hotel. I'll be living here, alone, until further notice. What's incredible is that we never passed this way on our travels. The beds are huge and the bathrooms old-fashioned, if not downright romantic. You might like to know that I feel relatively sane and healthy. My doctor has advised no physical stress, so I guess hookers are out of the question for a week or so. Ha, ha! Or would you like to save me from this fate worse than death? Keep this under your hat, but I have in my possession—actually, locked in the trunk of my car—the first reel of *Body and Soul.* The studio is going crazy. They're threatening legal action—or worse, excommunication from Hollywood! Am I a maniac or just an artist in despair? Perhaps we could discuss this, then progress to more racy topics over a quiet lunch . . ."

The machine clicked off; the tape had run out. Listening to his voice, she was aware that her heart had not so much as missed a beat. Truth or self-deception? No, to her relief, she felt exonerated, almost spiritually blessed. Stripped bare, she had, it seemed, survived intact. No longer was she torn between feeling guilty and being the great adventurer. She could wrap it up. Move on. She decided to wait a few days, then call Oscar to let him know that she would have little extra time, as she planned to be busy with her next screenplay. Because if there *was* any extra time, she was determined to use it for better things. The novel, for instance. And no more did this seem like some inflated schoolgirl's dream. She remembered a line from Gide she had feverishly copied down in her journal some decades before: "The most beautiful things are those that madness prompts and reason writes." Well, she would get *that* down on paper—the madness. Finally, the real honest-to-God truth.

With renewed faith she lay down on her bed. In the backyard the lawn was strewn with fallen palm fronds, dried out, crackling in the breeze. Julio's marijuana patch, now nothing more than a mess of bamboo spikes and tangled string, appeared faintly exotic, like a ruined estate in the tropics. Only the geraniums, unwatered outside her window, miraculously lived on. Red bands of color reflected from the setting sun illuminated her bedroom. A sense of peace, pleasantly unfamiliar, washed over her. Peace here, in these four walls? Incredible!

And in light of this wisdom (the rosy heat in the room had a kind of opiate effect on her), she wondered to what end she was testing herself by not calling Oscar. What difference was there between talking to him now, or in a few days, or even a few weeks? Rationalizing further, she told herself that the meeting with James Hill probably wouldn't be for another week, perhaps two, and that apart from her mornings spent working on the novel, she had virtually nothing to fill the rest of her days. She would suggest that she and Oscar become friends. A little clichéd perhaps, but might they not, after all, go for a simple lunch? Some quiet conversation, unencumbered by their obsession and mania from the previous year . . .

Curiously, the number for the Château Marmont was one she had memorized in the first few weeks after arriving in Los Angeles.